I0592070

Ernest Alfred W. Budge

The Nile

Notes for travellers in Egypt. Sixth Edition

Ernest Alfred W. Budge

The Nile
Notes for travellers in Egypt. Sixth Edition

ISBN/EAN: 9783337330286

Printed in Europe, USA, Canada, Australia, Japan

Cover: Foto ©Andreas Hilbeck / pixelio.de

THE NILE.

Notes for Travellers in Egypt.

BY

E. A. WALLIS BUDGE, M.A., LITT.D., D.LIT., F.S.A.,

FORMERLY TYRWHITT HEBREW SCHOLAR, AND SCHOLAR OF CHRIST'S COLLEGE, CAMBRIDGE, KEEPER OF THE EGYPTIAN AND ASSYRIAN ANTIQUITIES, BRITISH MUSEUM.

SIXTH EDITION.

WITH A MAP, PLANS, &c.

LONDON:
THOS. COOK & SON (EGYPT), LTD.
LUDGATE CIRCUS.

CAIRO:
THOS. COOK & SON (EGYPT), LTD.

1898.

HARRISON AND SONS,
PRINTERS IN ORDINARY TO HER MAJESTY,
ST. MARTIN'S LANE, LONDON.

INTRODUCTION.

Having for some years felt the insufficiency of the information given by Dragomans to travellers on the Nile, and finding with one or two striking exceptions how limited is their knowledge of facts relating to the history of the antiquities in Upper Egypt, Messrs. Thos. Cook and Son have arranged with Dr. E. A. Wallis Budge to compile the following pages, which they have much pleasure in presenting to every passenger under their Nile arrangements on their Tourist Steamers and Dhahabiyyehs. In this way passengers will no longer be liable to be misled (unintentionally) by Dragomans, but will be able at their leisure to prepare themselves for what they have to see, and thus by an agreeable study add to the interest with which their visits to the various places are made.

WORKS

BY

E. A. WALLIS BUDGE, M.A., LITT.D.,

KEEPER OF THE EGYPTIAN AND ASSYRIAN ANTIQUITIES IN THE BRITISH MUSEUM.

NEW EDITION OF THE BOOK OF THE DEAD.

(Limited to 750 copies.)

The Book of the Dead. In three Volumes. Vol. I. The Egyptian Texts printed in hieroglyphics; Vol. II. Vocabulary; Vol. III. Translation. Illustrated by three large facsimiles of sections of papyri, and eighteen plates in black and white. Demy 8vo. Price of the complete work £2 10*s.* Vols. I. and II. (not sold separately) £1 10*s.*; Vol. III. (may be sold separately) £1 5*s.* net.

The Book of the Dead. The papyrus of Ani, in the British Museum. With translation and transliteration. 4to. Half-morocco, £1 10*s.*

First Steps in Egyptian. Demy 8vo. 9*s.* net.

An Egyptian Reading Book for Beginners. With a Vocabulary. Demy 8vo. 15*s.* net.

The Dwellers on the Nile. 8vo. 3*s.*

The Sarcophagus of Ankhnesneferabra. On texts from the sarcophagus of this Queen, with translations, vocabulary, etc. 4to. 7*s.* 6*d.*

The Mummy, or Chapters on Egyptian Archæology. 8vo. 12*s.* 6*d.* Many illustrations.

Catalogue of the Egyptian Antiquities in the Harrow School Museum. 8vo. 3*s.*

Catalogue of the Egyptian Antiquities in the Fitzwilliam Museum. Cambridge. 8vo. 10*s.* 6*d.*

The Martyrdom and Miracles of St. George of Cappadocia. Coptic texts with English translation. £1 1*s.*

St. Michael the Archangel. Three Encomiums in the Coptic texts, with a translation. Imperial 8vo. 15*s.* net.

The Earliest-known Coptic Psalter. The text in the dialect of Upper Egypt, edited from the Unique Papyrus Codex Oriental 5000 in the British Museum. Imperial 8vo.

The Edition is strictly limited to 350 copies.

LONDON: KEGAN PAUL, TRENCH, TRÜBNER & Co., LTD., Paternoster House, Charing Cross Road.

PREFACE TO THE SIXTH EDITION.

The short descriptions of the principal Egyptian monuments on each side of the Nile between Cairo and the Second Cataract (Wâdi Ḥalfah), printed in the following pages, are not in any way intended to form a "Guide to Egypt": they are drawn up for the use of those travellers who have a very few weeks to spend in Egypt, and who wish to carry in their memories some of the more important facts connected with the fast-perishing remains of one of the most interesting and ancient civilizations that has been developed on the face of the earth. The existing guide books are generally too voluminous and diffuse for such travellers; and are, moreover, in many respects inaccurate. Experience has shown that the greater number of travellers in that country are more interested in history and matters connected with Egyptian civilization from B.C. 4400 to B.C. 450, than with Egypt under the rule of the Assyrians and Persians, Greeks and Romans, Arabs and Turks. It is for this reason that no attempt has been made to describe, otherwise than in the briefest possible manner, its history under these foreign rulers, and only such facts connected with them as are absolutely necessary for a right understanding of its monuments have been inserted. In addition to such descriptions, a few chapters have been added on the history of the country during the rule of the Pharaohs, its people, the religion and method of writing. At the end of the book a fairly full list of the most important Egyptian kings is appended, and in order to make this list as useful as possible, a transliteration of each name is printed beneath it, together with the ordinary form of the name. The list of three hundred hieroglyphic characters and their phonetic values, printed on pp. 62–68, will, it is hoped, be useful to those who may like to spell out the royal names on tombs and temples and the commoner words which occur in the inscriptions. For those who wish to study independently the various branches of Egyptology, a list of the more readily obtained books is given in the "Programme" issued yearly by Thos. Cook and Son (Egypt), Ltd.

In transcribing Arabic names of places the most authoritative forms have been followed, but such well-known names as "Luxor," in Arabic *El-Uḳṣûr* or *El-ḳuṣûr*, and "Cairo," in Arabic *Ḳâhira*, have not been altered. Similarly, the ordinary well-known forms of the Egyptian proper names "Rameses," "Thothmes," "Amenophis," "Amāsis," "Psammetichus," "Hophra" or "Apries," etc., etc., have been used in preference to the more correct transcriptions "Rā-messu," "Teḥuti-mes," "Ȧmen-ḥetep," "Ȧāḥ-mes," "Psemthek," "Uaḥ-ȧb-Rā."

The transliteration of Egyptian and Arabic words is that in common use throughout Europe.

The dates assigned to the Egyptian kings are those of Dr. H. Brugsch, who based his calculations on the assumption that the average duration of a generation was thirty-three years. Hence it will be readily understood that the date assigned to Rameses II. (B.C. 1333), for instance, is only approximately correct.

During recent years Prof. Sir J. Norman Lockyer, K.C.B., F.R.S., has been engaged in making careful investigations into the subject of the orientation of Egyptian temples, from which we may one day hope to obtain data for finding within a few years the age of each. Mr. Cecil Torr (*Memphis and Mycenæ*, p. ix.), however, takes the view that many of our dates want bringing down lower, and he places the beginning of the XIIth dynasty at about B.C. 1500, instead of about B.C. 2500. Although these researches already enable us to rectify many important points in the chronology of Egypt, it has been thought best to retain for the present the system of the late Dr. H. Brugsch.

In this edition descriptions of the principal monuments in the Gîzeh Museum have been added; a description of the tomb of Nekht has been inserted; the chapter on the Egyptian religion has been enlarged; and several new illustrations have been given. A brief notice of the splendid results obtained from the excavations carried out by M. de Morgan and others has also been inserted on pp. 395 ff.

E. A. WALLIS BUDGE.

August 20, 1898.

CONTENTS.

NOTES FOR TRAVELLERS IN EGYPT.

EGYPTIAN HISTORY.

THE history of Egypt is the oldest history known to us. It is true that the earliest of the Babylonian kings whose names are known lived very little later than the earliest kings of Egypt, nevertheless our knowledge of the early Egyptian is greater than of the early Babylonian kings. A large portion of Egyptian history can be constructed from the native records of the Egyptians, and it is now possible to correct and modify many of the statements upon this subject made by Herodotus, Diodorus Siculus and other classical authors. The native and other documents from which Egyptian history is obtained are:—

I. **Lists of Kings** found in the **Turin Papyrus**, the **Tablet of Abydos**, the **Tablet of Saḳḳârah**, and the **Tablet of Karnak.** The Turin papyrus contained a complete list of kings, beginning with the god-kings and continuing down to the end of the rule of the Hyksos, about B.C. 1700. The name of each king during this period, together with the length of his reign in years, months and days, was given, and it would have been, beyond all doubt, the most valuable of all documents for the chronology of the oldest period of Egyptian history, if scholars had been able to make use of it in the perfect condition in which it was discovered. When it arrived in Turin, however, it was found to be broken into more than one hundred and fifty fragments. So far back as 1824, Champollion recognized the true value of the fragments, and placed some of them in their chronological order. Its evidence is of the greatest importance for the history of the XIIIth and XIVth dynasties, because in this section the papyrus is tolerably perfect; for the earlier dynasties it is of very little use.

On the monuments each Egyptian king has usually two names, the prenomen and the nomen; each of these is contained in a cartouche.* Thus the prenomen of Thothmes III. is  Rā-men-cheper, and his nomen is  Teḥuti-mes. Rā-men-cheper means something like "Rā (the Sun-god) establishes becoming or existence;" Teḥuti-mes means "born of Thoth," or "Thoth's son." These names are quite distinct from his titles. Before the prenomen comes the title  *suten net*,† "King of the North and South," and after it comes  *se Rā*, "son of the Sun," preceding the nomen. Each prenomen has a meaning, but it is at times difficult to render it exactly in English. Every king styled himself king of "the North and South," and "son of the Sun." The first title is sometimes varied by "Beautiful

* Cartouche is the name which is usually given to the oval , in which the name of a royal person is enclosed.

† The ordinary word for "king" is 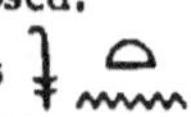 *suten*. The word Pharaoh, פַּרְעֹה, which the Hebrews called the kings of Egypt, is derived from the Egyptian  *er āa*, otherwise written  or 

god, lord of the two earths."* In the earliest times the kings were named after some attribute possessed by them; thus Menȧ, the first king of Egypt, is the "firm" or "established." In the Turin papyrus only the prenomens of the kings are given, but its statements are confirmed and amplified by the other lists.

The **Tablet of Abydos**† was discovered by Dümichen in the temple of Osiris at Abydos, during M. Mariette's excavations there in 1864. This list gives us the names of seventy-five kings, beginning with Menȧ or Menes, and ending with Seti I., the father of Rameses II.; it is not a complete list, and it would seem as if the scribe who drew up the list only inserted such names as he considered worthy of living for ever. The **Tablet of Saḳḳârah**‡ was discovered at Saḳḳârah by Mariette, in the grave of a dignitary who lived during the reign of Rameses II. In spite of a break in it, and some orthographical errors, it is a valuable list; it gives the names of forty-seven kings, and it agrees very closely with the Abydos list. It is a curious fact that it begins with the name of Mer-ba-pen, the sixth king of the Ist dynasty. The **Tablet of Karnak** was discovered at Karnak by Burton, and was taken to Paris by Prisse. It

* Some kings had a large number of titles. Thus Thothmes III. is

styled "Horus, mighty bull, diademed with law, the lord, maker of things, Rā-men-cheper," etc., etc. He is also called: , "King of the North and South, mighty of terror in all lands"; , "Horus, exalted one of the white crown, beloved of Rā"; 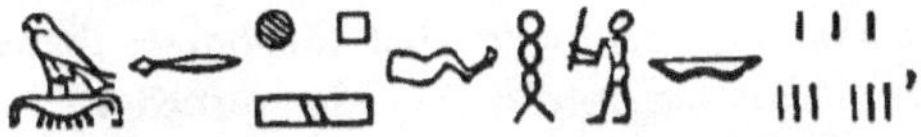, "Golden Horus, mighty of valour, smiter of the Nine Bows," etc.

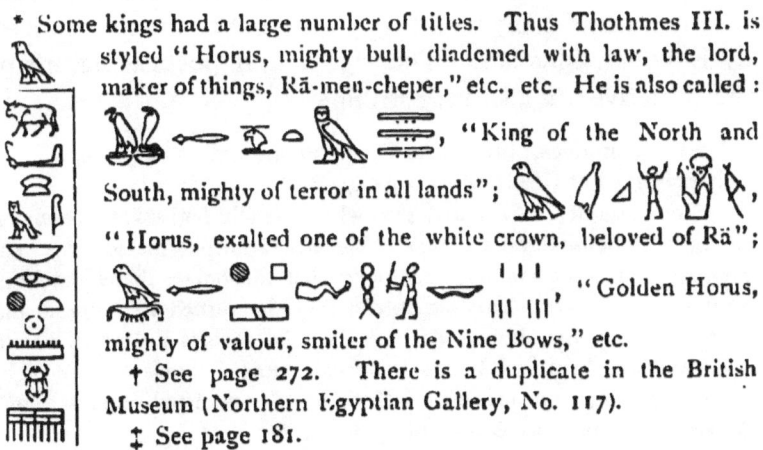

† See page 272. There is a duplicate in the British Museum (Northern Egyptian Gallery, No. 117).

‡ See page 181.

was drawn up in the time of Thothmes III., and contains the names of sixty-one of his ancestors. They are not arranged in any chronological order, but the tablet is of the highest historical importance, for it records the names of some of the rulers from the XIIIth to the XVIIth dynasties, and gives the names of those of the XIth dynasty more completely than any other list.

II. Annals of Egyptian Kings inscribed upon the walls of temples, obelisks, and buildings. The narrative of such inscriptions is very simple, and practically these records merely represent itineraries in which the names of conquered and tributary lands and people are given ; incidentally facts of interest are noted down. As the day and month and regnal years of the king by whom these expeditions were undertaken are generally given, these inscriptions throw much light on history. The lists of tribute are also useful. for they show what the products of the various countries were. The poetical version* of the history of the famous battle of Rameses II. against the Cheta by the poet Pen-ta-urt is a pleasant variety of historical narrative. The inscription on the stele† of Piānchi, the Ethiopian conqueror of Egypt, is decidedly remarkable for the minute details of his fights, the speeches made by himself and his conquered foes, and the mention of many facts‡ which are not commonly noticed by Egyptian annalists. The vigour and poetical nature of the narrative are also very striking.

* See the notice of the official Egyptian account on page 354 f.

† Preserved at Gizeh. See page 177.

‡ For example, it is stated that when Piānchi had taken possession of the storehouses and treasury of Nemart (Nimrod) his foe, he went afterwards into the stables, and found that the horses there had been kept short of food. Bursting into a rage, he turned to Nimrod and said, "By my life, by my darling Rā, who revives my nostrils with life, to have kept my horses hungry is more heinous in my sight than any other offence which thou hast committed against me." Mariette, *Monuments Divers*, pl. 3, ll. 65, 66.

III. Historical Stelæ and Papyri, which briefly relate in chronological order the various expeditions undertaken by the king for whom they were made. Egyptian kings occasionally caused summaries of their principal conquests and of the chief events of their reign to be drawn up; examples of these are (*a*) the stele of Thothmes III.,* and (*b*) the last section of the great **Harris Papyrus**, in which Rameses III. reviews all the good works which he has brought to a successful issue to the glory of the gods of Egypt and for the benefit of her inhabitants. This wonderful papyrus measures 135 feet by 17 inches, and was found in a box in the temple at Medînet Habû, built by Rameses III.; it is now in the British Museum.

IV. Decrees, Scarabs, Statues of Kings and Private Persons are fruitful sources of information about historical, religious, and chronological subjects.

V. Biblical notices about Egypt and allusions to events of Egyptian history.

VI. The Cuneiform Inscriptions. In 1887 a number of tablets† inscribed in cuneiform were found at Tell el-Amarna. The inscriptions relate to a period of Egyptian history which falls in the fifteenth century B.C., and they are letters from the kings of Babylon, and cities of Mesopotamia and Phœnicia relating to marriages, offensive and defensive alliances, military matters, etc., etc., and reports on the rebellions and wars which took place at that time, addressed to Amenophis III. and to his son Chut-en-âten or Amenophis IV. The Babylonian king who writes is called Kurigalzu. Thothmes III. had carried his victorious arms into Mesopotamia, and one of his successors, Amenophis III., delighted to go there and shoot the lions with which the country abounded. During one of these hunting expeditions he fell in love with the lady 

* Preserved at Gîzeh; see page 181.

† See the description of the Gizeh Museum, pp. 186–189.

Thi (in cuneiform 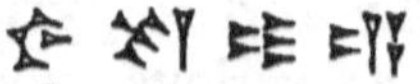 Ti-i-e), the daughter of Iuáa  and Thuáa , and married her, and he brought her to Egypt, with another wife named  Kilḳipa (in cuneiform   Gi-lu-khi-pa), accompanied by 317 of her attendants. It will be some time before these inscriptions are fully made out, but the examination of them has already been carried sufficiently far to show that they will throw most valuable light upon the social condition of Egypt and of the countries which were subject to her at that time. One of the tablets is written in the language of Mitani, and others are inscribed with cuneiform characters in a language which is at present unknown; and some of them have dockets in hieratic which state from what country they were brought. The discovery of these tablets shows that there must have been people at the court of Amenophis III. who understood the cuneiform characters, and that the officers in command over towns in Phœnicia subject to the rule of Egypt could, when occasion required, write their despatches in cuneiform. The greater part of these tablets are now in the Museums of London and Berlin, some are at the Gîzeh Museum, and some are in private hands.

The Assyrian kings Sennacherib, Esarhaddon, and Assurbanipal marched against Egypt; Tirhakah defeated Sennacherib at Eltekeh, but was defeated by Esarhaddon, the son of Sennacherib, who drove him back into Ethiopia. Esarhaddon's son, Assurbanipal, also attacked Tirhakah and defeated him. Thebes was captured, and Egypt was divided into twenty-two provinces, over some of which Assyrian viceroys were placed. A fragment of a Babylonian tablet states that Nebuchadnezzar II. marched into Egypt.

VII. The Greek and Roman writers upon Egypt are many; and of these the best known are Herodotus,

Manetho, and Diodorus Siculus. **Herodotus** devotes the whole of the second and the beginning of the third book of his work to a history of Egypt and the Egyptians, and his is the oldest Greek treatise on the subject known to us. In spite of the attacks made upon his work during the last few years, the evidence of the hieroglyphic inscriptions which are being deciphered year after year shows that on the whole his work is trustworthy. A work more valuable than that of Herodotus is the Egyptian history of **Manetho** (still living in B.C. 271) of Sebennytus, who is said by Plutarch to have been a contemporary of Ptolemy I.; his work, however, was written during the reign of Ptolemy II. Philadelphus (B.C. 286–247). According to words put into his mouth, he was chief priest and scribe in one of the temples of Egypt, and he appears to have been perfectly acquainted with the ancient Egyptian language and literature. He had also had the benefit of a Greek education, and was therefore peculiarly fitted to draw up in Greek for Ptolemy Philadelphus a history of Egypt and her religion. The remains of the great Egyptian history of Manetho are preserved in the polemical treatise of Josephus against Apion, in which a series of passages of Egyptian history from the XVth to the XIXth dynasties is given, and in the list of the dynasties, together with the number of years of the reign of each king, given by Africanus and Eusebius on his authority. At the beginning of his work Manetho gives a list of gods and demi-gods who ruled over Egypt before Menes, the first human king of Egypt; the thirty dynasties known to us he divides into three sections:—I–XI, XII–XIX, and XX–XXX. **Diodorus Siculus,** who visited Egypt about B.C. 57, wrote a history of the country, its people and its religion, based chiefly upon the works of Herodotus and Hekatæus. He was not so able a writer nor so accurate an observer as Herodotus, and his work contains many blunders. Other important ancient writers on Egypt are Strabo,* Chaeremon,† Josephus,‡ Plutarch§ and Horapollo.||

According to Manetho, there reigned over Egypt before Menȧ, or Menes, the first mortal king of that country, a number of beings who may be identified with the Shesu Ḥeru, or "followers of Horus"; of their deeds and history nothing is known. Some have believed that during their rule Egypt was divided into two parts, each ruled by its own king; and others have thought that the whole of Upper and Lower Egypt was divided into a large series of small, independent principalities, which were united under one head in the person of Menes. There is, however, no support to be obtained from the inscriptions for either of these theories. The kings of Egypt following after the mythical period are divided into thirty dynasties. For the sake of convenience, Egyptian history is divided into three periods:—I, the **Ancient Empire**, which includes the first eleven dynasties; II, the **Middle Empire**, which includes the next nine dynasties (XIIth–XXth); and, III, the **New Empire**, which includes the remaining ten dynasties, one of which was of Persian kings. The rule of the Saïte kings was followed by that of the **Persians, Macedonians, Ptolemies** and **Romans**. The rule of the Arabs which began A.D. 641, ended A.D. 1517, when the country was conquered by the Turks; since this time Egypt has been nominally a pashalik of Turkey.

The date assigned to the first dynasty is variously given by different scholars: by Champollion-Figeac it is B.C. 5867, by Böckh 5702, by Bunsen 3623, by Lepsius 3892, by Lieblein 3893, by Mariette 5004, and by Brugsch 4400. As far as can be seen, there is much to be said in favour of that given by Brugsch, and his dates are adopted throughout in this book.

* About A.D. 15. † About A.D. 50. ‡ About A.D. 75.
§ About A.D. 100. || About A.D. 400.

HISTORICAL SUMMARY.

ANCIENT EMPIRE.

Dynasty I, from This.

B.C.

4400. Menà, the first human king of Egypt, founded Memphis, having turned aside the course of the Nile, and established a temple service there.

4366. Tetà, wrote a book on anatomy, and continued buildings at Memphis.

4266. Ḥesep-ti. Some papyri state that the 64th Chapter of the Book of the Dead was written in his time.

Dynasty II, from This.

4133. Neter-baiu,* in whose reign an earthquake swallowed up many people at Bubastis.

4100. Kakau, in whose days the worship of Apis at Memphis, and that of Mnevis at Heliopolis, was continued.

4066. Ba-en-neter, in whose reign, according to John of Antioch, the Nile flowed with honey for eleven days. During the reign of this king the succession of females to the throne of Egypt was declared valid.

4000. Senṭ. Sepulchral stelæ of this king's priests are preserved at Oxford and at Gizeh; see page 143.

—— Nefer-ka-Seker, in whose reign an eclipse appears to be mentioned.

Dynasty III, from Memphis.

* Or 

Dynasty IV, from Memphis.

B.C.

3766. Seneferu. Important contemporaneous monuments of this king exist. During his reign the copper mines of Wâdi Ma'arah were worked.

3733. Chufu (Cheops), who fought with the people of Sinai; he built the first pyramid of Gîzeh.

3666. Chā-f-Rā (Chephren), the builder of the second pyramid at Gîzeh.

3633. Men-kau-Rā (Mycerinus), the builder of the third pyramid at Gîzeh. The fragments of his coffin are in the British Museum. Some copies of the Book of the Dead say that the 64th chapter of that work was compiled during the reign of this king.

Dynasty V, from Elephantine.

3366. Ṭeṭ-ka-Rā. The Precepts of Ptaḥ-ḥetep were written during the reign of this king.

3333. Unȧs, whose pyramid at Saḳḳârah was explored in 1881.

Dynasty VI, from Memphis.

3266. Tetȧ, the builder of a pyramid at Saḳḳârah.

3233. Pepi-meri-Rā, the builder of a pyramid at Saḳḳârah.

3200. Mer-en-Rā.

3166. Nefer-ka-Rā.

3133 (?). Nit-ȧqert (Nitocris), "the beautiful woman with rosy cheeks."

3100. { *Dynasties VII and VIII, from Memphis.*
Dynasties IX and X, from Heracleopolis. }

Nefer-ka.

Nefer-Seḥ . . . .

Ȧb.

Nefer-kau-Rā.

Charthi.

B.C.

3033. Nefer-ka-Rā.
3000. Nefer-ka-Rā-Nebi.
2966. Ṭeṭ-ka-Rā-. . . . .
2933. Nefer-ka-Rā-Chenṭu
2900. Mer-en-Ḥeru.
2866. Se-nefer-ka-Rā.
2833. Ka-en-Rā.
2800. Nefer-ka-Rā-Tererl.
2766. Nefer-ka-Rā-Ḥeru.
2733. Nefer-ka-Rā Pepi Seneb.
2700. Nefer-ka-Rā-Ānnu.
2633. Nefer-kau-Rā.
2600. Nefer-kau-Ḥeru.
2533. Nefer-àri-ka-Rā.*

Dynasty XI, from Diospolis, or Thebes.

From the time of Nitocris to Åmenemḥāt I. Egyptian history is nearly a blank. The names of a large number of kings who ruled during this period are known, but they cannot, at present, be arranged in exact chronological order.

2500. Se-ānch-ka-Rā. This king is known to us through an inscription at Ḥamâmât, which states that he sent an expedition to the land of Punt; this shows that at that early date an active trade must have been carried on across the Arabian desert between Egypt and Arabia. The other kings of the XIth dynasty bore the names of Åntef-āa, Ån-àntef, Åmentuf, Ån-āa, and Mentu-ḥetep. Se-ānch-ka-Rā appears to have been the immediate predecessor of the XIIth dynasty.

* These names are obtained from the TABLET OF ABYDOS; see pages 3, 272.

MIDDLE EMPIRE.

Dynasty XII, from Diospolis, or Thebes.

B.C.

2466. Åmenemḥāt I. ascended the throne of Egypt after hard fighting; he conquered the Uaua, a Libyan tribe that lived near Korosko in Nubia, and wrote a series of instructions for his son Usertsen I. The story of Senehet was written during this reign.

2433. Usertsen I. made war against the tribes of Ethiopia; he erected granite obelisks and built largely at Heliopolis.

2400. Åmenemḥāt II. Chnemu-ḥetep, son of Neḥerȧ, whose tomb is at Beni-hasân, lived during the reign of this king.

2366. Usertsen II.

2333. Usertsen III.

2300. Åmenemḥāt III. During this king's reign special attention was paid to the rise of the Nile, and canals were dug and sluices made for irrigating the country; in this reign the famous Lake Moeris, in the district called by the Arabs El-Fayyûm,* was built. The rise of the Nile was marked on the rocks at Semneh, about thirty-five miles above the second cataract, and the inscriptions are visible to this day.

2266. Åmenemḥāt IV.

2233. *Dynasties XIII–XVII. The so-called Hyksos Period.*

According to Manetho these dynasties were as follows:—

Dynasty	XIII,	from Thebes,	60 kings	in 453	years.
,,	XIV,	,, Choïs,†	76 ,,	,, 484	,,
,,	XV,	Hyksos,	6 ,,	,, 260	,,
,,	XVI,	,,	10 ,,	,, 251	,,
,,	XVII,	from Thebes,	10 ,,	,, 10	,,

* In Arabic ٱلْفَيُّوم, from the Coptic ⲪⲒⲞⲘ, "the lake."

† A town in the Delta.

Unfortunately there are no monuments whereby we can correct or modify these figures. The Hyksos appear to have made their way from the countries in and to the west of Mesopotamia into Egypt. They joined with their countrymen, who had already settled in the Delta, and were able to defeat the native kings; it is thought that their rule lasted 500 years, and that Joseph arrived in Egypt towards the end of this period. The principal Hyksos kings of the XVIth dynasty are Åpepå I. and Åpepå II.; Nubti and the native Egyptian princes ruled under them. Under Se-qenen-Rā, a Theban ruler of the XVIIth dynasty, a war broke out between the Egyptians and the Hyksos, which continued for many years, and resulted in the expulsion of the foreign rulers.

Dynasty XVIII, from Thebes.

B.C.

1700. Åāḥmes, who re-established the independence of Egypt.

1666. Åmen-ḥetep (Amenophis) I.

1633. Teḥuti-mes (Thothmes) I.

1600. " " II.

1600. Ḥāt-shepset, sister of Thothmes II. She sent an expedition to Punt.
Teḥuti-mes (Thothmes) III. made victorious expeditions into Mesopotamia. He was one of the greatest kings that ever ruled over Egypt.

1566. Åmen-ḥetep II.

1533. Teḥuti-mes IV.

1500. Amen-ḥetep III. warred successfully in the lands to the south of Egypt and in Asia. He made it a custom to go into Mesopotamia to shoot lions, and, while there he married a sister and daughter of Tushratta, the king of Mitani, and a sister and a daughter of Kallimma-Sin, king of Karaduniyash; he afterwards made proposals of marriage for another daughter of this latter king called Sukharti.

The correspondence and despatches from kings of Babylon, Mesopotamia, and Phœnicia were found in 1887 at Tell el-Amarna, and large portions of them are now preserved in the Museums of London, Berlin, and Gîzeh.

Àmen-ḥetep IV. or Chu-en-Àten ("brilliance, or glory of the solar disk"), the founder of the city Chu-àten, the ruins of which are called Tell el-Amarna, and of the heresy of the disk-worshippers. He was succeeded by a few kings who held the same religious opinions as himself.

B.C. *Dynasty XIX, from Thebes.*

1400. Rameses I.

1366 Seti I. conquered the rebellious tribes in Western Asia, and built the Memnonium at Abydos. He was famous as a builder, and attended with great care to the material welfare of his kingdom. He is said to have built a canal from the Nile to the Red Sea.

1333. Rameses II. undertook many warlike expeditions, and brought Nubia, Abyssinia, and Mesopotamia under the rule of Egypt. He was a great builder, and a liberal patron of the arts and sciences; learned men like Pentaurt were attached to his court. He is famous as one of the oppressors of the Israelites.

1300. Seti Meneptaḥ II. is thought to have been the Pharaoh of the Exodus.

NEW EMPIRE.

Dynasty XX, from Thebes.

1200. Rameses III. was famous for his buildings, and for the splendid gifts which he made to the temples of Thebes, Abydos and Heliopolis. His reign represented an era of great commercial prosperity.

1166–1133. Rameses IV.–XII.

Dynasty XXI, from Tanis and Thebes.

B.C.	I. Tanis.	II. Thebes.
1100–1000.	Se-Mentu.	Ḥer-Ḥeru.
	Pasebchānu I.	Pi-ānchi.
	Åmen-em-åpt.	Pai-net'em I–III.
	Pasebchānu II.	

Dynasty XXII, from Bubastis (Tell-Basṭa).

966. Shashanq (Shishak) I. (see 1 Kings, xiv. 25–28; 2 Chron., xii. 2–13) besieged Jerusalem.

933. Uasarken I.
900. Takeleth I.
866. Uasarken II.
833. Shashanq II.
Takeleth II.
Shashanq III.
800. Pamai
Shashanq IV.

These kings appear to have been of Semitic origin; their names are Semitic, as, for example, Uasarken = Babylonian *Sar ginu* (Sargon); Takeleth = *Tukulti* (Tiglath).

Dynasty XXIII, from Tanis.

766. Peṭā-Bast.
Uasarken III.

Dynasty XXIV, from Saïs (Sâ el-Ḥager)

733. Bak-en-ren-f (Bocchoris).

Dynasty XXV, from Ethiopia.

700. Shabaka (Sabaco).
Shabataka.

693. Taharqa (Tirhakah, 2 Kings, xix. 9) is famous for having conquered Sennacherib and delivered Hezekiah; he was, however, defeated by Esarhaddon and Assurbanipal, the son and grandson respectively of Sennacherib. Tirhakah's son-in-law, Urdamanah, was also defeated by the Assyrians.

Dynasty XXVI, from Saïs.

B.C.

666. Psemthek I. (Psammetichus) allowed Greeks to settle in the Delta, and employed Greek soldiers to fight for him.

612. Nekau II. (Necho) defeated Josiah, king of Judah, and was defeated by Nebuchadnezzar II. son of Nabopolassar, king of Babylon.

596. Psammetichus II.

591. Uaḫ-àb-Rā (Hophra of the Bible, Gr. Apries) marched to the help of Zedekiah, king of Judah, who was defeated by Nebuchadnezzar II. His army rebelled against him, and he was dethroned; Amāsis, a general in his army, then succeeded to the throne.

572. Ååḫmes II. favoured the Greeks, and granted them many privileges; in his reign Naucratis became a great city.

528. Psammetichus III. was defeated at Pelusium by Cambyses the Persian, and taken prisoner; he was afterwards slain for rebelling against the Persians.

Dynasty XXVII, from Persia.

527. Cambyses marched against the Ethiopians and the inhabitants of the Oases.

521. Darius Hystaspes endeavoured to open up the ancient routes of commerce; he established a coinage, and adopted a conciliatory and tolerant system of government, and favoured all attempts to promote the welfare of Egypt.

486. Xerxes I.

465. Artaxerxes I., during whose reign the Egyptians revolted, headed by Amyrtæus.

B.C.

425. Darius Nothus, during whose reign the Egyptians revolted successfully, and a second Amyrtæus became king of Egypt.

405. Artaxerxes II.

Dynasty XXVIII, from Saïs.

Åmen-ruṭ (Amyrtæus), reigned six years.

Dynasty XXIX, from Mendes.

399. Naifāauruṭ I.

393. Haḳar.

380. P-se-mut.

379. Naifāauruṭ II.

Dynasty XXX, from Sebennytus.

378. Necht-Ḥeru-ḥeb (Nectanebus I.) defeated the Persians at Mendes.

360. T'e-ḥer surrendered to the Persians.

358. Necht-neb-f (Nectanebus II.) devoted himself to the pursuit of magic, and neglected his empire; when Artaxerxes III. (Ochus) marched against him, he fled from his kingdom, and the Persians again ruled Egypt.

PERSIANS.

340. Artaxerxes III. (Ochus).

338. Arses.

336. Darius III. (Codomannus) conquered by Alexander the Great at Issus.

MACEDONIANS.

332. Alexander the Great founded Alexandria. He showed his toleration of the Egyptian religion by sacrificing to the god Åmen of Libya.

PTOLEMIES.*

B.C.

305. Ptolemy I. Soter, son of Lagus, became king of Egypt after Alexander's death. He founded the famous Alexandrian Library, and encouraged learned Greeks to make Alexandria their home; he died B.C. 284.

285. Ptolemy II. Philadelphus built the Pharos, founded Berenice and Arsinoë, caused Manetho's Egyptian history to be compiled, and the Greek version of the Old Testament (Septuagint) to be made.

247. Ptolemy III. Euergetes I. The stele of Canopus † was set up in the ninth year of his reign; he obtained possession of all Syria, and was a patron of the arts and sciences.

222. Ptolemy IV. Philopator defeated Antiochus, and founded the temple at Edfû.

205. Ptolemy V. Epiphanes. During his reign the help of the Romans against Antiochus was asked for by the Egyptians. Coelesyria and Palestine were lost to Egypt. He was poisoned B.C. 182, and his son Ptolemy VI. Eupator, died in that same year. The Rosetta Stone was set up in the eighth year of the reign of this king.

* For the chronology of the Ptolemies, see Lepsius, *Königsbuch*, Synoptische Tafeln 9.

† This important stele, preserved at Gîzeh, see page 284, is inscribed in hieroglyphics, Greek and demotic with a decree made at Canopus by the priesthood, assembled there from all parts of Egypt, in honour of Ptolemy III. It mentions the great benefits which he had conferred upon Egypt, and states what festivals are to be celebrated in his honour and in that of Berenice, etc., and concludes with a resolution ordering that a copy of this inscription in hieroglyphics, Greek and demotic shall be placed in every large temple of Egypt. Two other copies of this work are known.

B.C.

—— Ptolemy VI. did not reign a full year.

181. Ptolemy VII. Philometor was taken prisoner at Pelusium by Antiochus IV., B.C. 171, and died B.C. 146. He reigned alone at first, then conjointly (B.C. 170—165) with Ptolemy IX. Euergetes II. (also called Physcon), and finally having gone to Rome on account of his quarrel with Physcon, he reigned as sole monarch of Egypt (B.C. 165). Physcon was overthrown B.C. 132, reigned again B.C. 125, and died B.C. 117.

170. Ptolemy VIII. is murdered by Physcon.

146. Ptolemy IX. Euergetes II.

117. Ptolemy X. Soter II. Philometor II. (Lathyrus), reigns jointly with Cleopatra III. Ptolemy X. is banished (B.C. 106), his brother Ptolemy XI. Alexander I. is made co-regent, but afterwards banished (B.C. 89) and slain (B.C. 87); Ptolemy X. is recalled, and dies B.C. 81.

81. Ptolemy XII. Alexander II. is slain.

81. Ptolemy XIII. Neos Dionysos (Auletes), ascends the throne; dies B.C. 52.

52. Ptolemy XIV. Dionysos II. and Cleopatra VII. are, according to the will of Ptolemy XIII. to marry each other; the Roman senate to be their guardian. Ptolemy XIV. banishes Cleopatra, and is a party to the murder of Pompey, their guardian, who visits Egypt after his defeat at Pharsalia. Cæsar arrives in Egypt to support Cleopatra (B.C. 48); Ptolemy XIV., is drowned; Ptolemy XV., brother of Cleopatra VII., is appointed her co-regent by Cæsar (B.C. 47); he is murdered at her wish, and her son by Cæsar, Ptolemy XVI., Cæsarion is named co-regent (B.C. 45).

B.C.

42. Antony orders Cleopatra to appear before him, and is seduced by her charms; he kills himself, and Cleopatra dies by the bite of an asp. Egypt becomes a Roman province B.C. 30.

ROMANS.

Cæsar Augustus becomes master of the Roman Empire. Cornelius Gallus is the first prefect of Egypt. Under the third prefect, Aelius Gallus, Candace, queen of the Ethiopians, invades Egypt, but is defeated.

A.D.

14. Tiberius. In his reign Germanicus visited Egypt.

37. Caligula. In his reign a persecution of the Jews took place.

41. Claudius.

55. Nero. In his reign Christianity was first preached in Egypt by Saint Mark. The Blemmyes made raids upon the southern frontier of Egypt.

69. Vespasian. Jerusalem destroyed A.D. 70.

82. Domitian causes temples to Isis and Serapis to be built at Rome.

98. Trajan. The Nile and Red Sea Canal (Amnis Trajânus) re-opened.

117. Hadrian. Visited Egypt twice.

161. Marcus Aurelius caused the famous *Itinerary* to be made.

180. Commodus.

193. Septimius Severus.

211. Caracalla visited Egypt, and caused a large number of young men to be massacred at Alexandria.

217. Macrinus.

218. Elagabalus.

A.D.

249. Decius. Christians persecuted.

253. Valerianus. Christians persecuted.

260. Gallienus. Persecution of Christians stayed. Zenobia, Queen of Palmyra, invades Egypt A.D. 268.

270. Aurelian. Zenobia becomes Queen of Egypt for a short time, but is dethroned A.D. 273.

276. Probus.

284. Diocletian. "**Pompey's Pillar**" erected A.D. 302, persecution of Christians A.D. 304. The Copts date the era of the Martyrs from the day of Diocletian's accession to the throne (August 29).

324. Constantine the Great, the Christian Emperor, in whose reign, A.D. 325, the Council of Nicæa was held. At this council it was decided that Christ and His Father were of one and the *same* nature, as taught by Athanasius; and the doctrine of **Arius**,* that Christ and God were only *similar* in nature, was decreed heretical.

337. Constantius. George of Cappadocia, an Arian, is made Bishop of Alexandria.

379. Theodosius I., the Great, proclaims Christianity the religion of his empire. The Arians and followers of the ancient Egyptian religion were persecuted.

* "He was a most expert logician, but perverted his talents to evil purposes, and had the audacity to preach what no one before him had ever suggested, namely, that the Son of God was made out of that which had no prior existence; that there was a period of time in which He existed not; that, as possessing free will, He was capable of virtue, or of vice; and that He was created and made."—Sozomen, *Eccles. Hist.*, Bk. I., ch. 15. For the statement of the views of Arius by his opponent Alexander, Bishop of Alexandria, see his letter addressed to the Catholic Church generally, in Socrates, *Eccles. Hist.*, Bk. I., chap. vi.

THE BYZANTINES.

A.D.

395. Arcadius, Emperor of the East. The Anthropomorphites,* who affirmed that God was of human form, destroyed the greater number of their opponents.

408. Theodosius II. In his reign the doctrines of Nestorius were condemned by Cyril of Alexandria. Nestorius, from the two natures of Christ, inferred also two persons, a human and a divine. "In the Syrian school, Nestorius had been taught (A.D. 429–431) to abhor the confusion of the two natures, and nicely to discriminate the humanity of his *master* Christ from the Divinity of the *Lord* Jesus. The Blessed Virgin he revered as the mother of Christ, but his ears were offended with the rash and recent title of mother of God, which had been insensibly adopted since the origin of the Arian controversy. From the pulpit of Constantinople, a friend of the patriarch,† and afterwards the patriarch himself, repeatedly preached against the use, or the abuse, of a word unknown to the apostles, unauthorized by the church, and which could only tend to alarm the timorous, to mislead the simple, to amuse the profane, and to justify, by a seeming resemblance, the old genealogy of Olympus. In his calmer moments Nestorius confessed, that it might be tolerated or excused by the union of the two natures, and the communication of their *idioms* (*i.e.*, a transfer of properties of each

* The leader of this persecution was Theophilus, Bishop of Alexandria, who, before he discovered that the majority of the Egyptian monks were Anthropomorphites, was himself opposed to this body.

† Anastasius of Antioch, who said, "Let no one call Mary *Theotokos;* for Mary was but a woman; and it is impossible that God should be born of a woman."—Socrates, *Eccles. Hist.*, Bk. VII., chap. xxxii.

A.D.

nature to the other—of infinity to man, passibility to God, etc.): but he was exasperated, by contradiction, to disclaim the worship of a newborn, an infant Deity, to draw his inadequate similes from the conjugal or civil partnerships of life, and to describe the manhood of Christ, as the robe, the instrument, the tabernacle of his Godhead."—Gibbon, *Decline and Fall*, chap. 47.

450. Marcianus. The Monophysite doctrine of Eutyches was condemned at the Council of Chalcedon, A.D. 451. Eutyches, from the one person of Christ, inferred also one nature, viz., the Divine—the human having been absorbed into it. Silco invaded Egypt with his Nubian followers.

474. Zeno. He issued the *Henoticon*, an edict which, while affirming the Incarnation, made no attempt to decide the difficult question whether Christ possessed a single or a double nature.

481. Anastasius.

527. Justinian. The Monophysites separated from the Melchites and chose their own patriarch; they were afterwards called Copts, القِبْط.*

610. Heraclius. The Persians under Chosroes held Egypt for ten years; they were expelled by Heraclius A.D. 629.

MUḤAMMADANS.

638. 'Amr ibn el-'Âṣi conquers Egypt.

644. 'Othmân.

750. Merwân II., the last of the 'Omayyade dynasty, was put to death in Egypt.

* The name given to the native Christians of Egypt by the Arabs, from ΚΥΠΤΑΙΟϹ for Αἰγύπτιος.

A.D.

750–870. The 'Abbasides rule over Egypt.

786. Harûn er-Rashîd.

813. Mâmûn visited Egypt, and opened the Great Pyramid.

870. Aḥmed ibn-Ṭulûn governs Egypt.

884. Khamarûyeh enlarges Fosṭât.

969–1171. The Fâṭimites govern Egypt, with Maṣr el-Ḳâhira * (Cairo) as their residence.

975. Azîz, son of Mu'izz, great grandson of 'Obêdallâh.

996. Ḥâkim, son of 'Azîz, founder of the Druses. This remarkable prince wished to be considered as God incarnate.

1020. Ẓâhir, son of Ḥâkim.

1036. Abu Tamîm el-Mustanṣir.

1094. Musta'li, son of el-Mustanṣir, captured Jerusalem (A.D. 1096), but was defeated by the Crusaders under Godfrey de Bouillon.

1160. 'Aḍîd Ledînallâh, the last of the Fâṭimites.

1171. Ṣalâḥeddîn (Saladin) defeated the Crusaders at Ḥittîn, and recaptured Jerusalem.

1193. Melik el-'Adîl.

1218. Melik el-Kâmil, the builder of Manṣûrah.

1240. Melik eṣ-Ṣâleḥ, the usurper, captured Jerusalem, Damascus, and Ascalon. Louis IX. of France, attacked and captured Damietta, but was made prisoner at Manṣûrah, with all his army.

1250–1380. The Baḥrite Mamelukes.

1260. Bêbars.

1277. Ḳalaûn.

1291. El-Ashraf Khalîl captured Acre.

1346. Ḥasan.

1382–1517. Burgite or Circassian Mamelukes.

1382. Barḳûḳ.

* القاهرة.

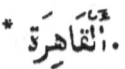

A.D.

1422. Bursbey.

1468. Ḳait Bey.

1501. El-Ghûri.

1517. Ṭûmân Bey is deposed by Selim I. of Constantinople, and Egypt becomes a Turkish Pashalik.

1771. 'Ali Bey sulṭân of Egypt.

1798. Napoleon Bonaparte stormed Alexandria; battle of the Pyramids; and French fleet destroyed off Abuḳîr by the English.

1801. French compelled by the English to evacuate Egypt.

1805. Muḥammad 'Ali appointed Pasha of Egypt.

1811. Assassination of the Mamelukes by him.

1831. Declares his independence.

1848. Ibrâhîm Pasha.

1849. Death of Muḥammad 'Ali. 'Abbâs Pasha was strangled at Benha.

1854. Sa'îd Pasha. The railway from Alexandria was completed, and the Suez Canal begun in his reign. He founded the Bûlâḳ Museum, and encouraged excavations on the sites of the ancient cities of Egypt.

1863. Isma'îl, son of Ibrâhîm Pasha, and grandson of Muḥammad 'Ali, was born in 1830. He was made Khedive in 1867. He caused railways, docks, and canals to be made, systems of telegraphs and postage to be established; he built sugar factories, and endeavoured to advance the material welfare of Egypt. The Suez Canal was opened during his reign (1869). He greatly extended the boundaries of Egypt, and obtained possession of Suakin (Sauâkin), Masowa (Masau'a), and two ports in the Gulf of Aden, a part of the Somâli coast, a large part of the frontier of Abys-

sinia, and the Province of Dârfûr. The tribute paid by him to the Porte amounted to nearly £700,000. During his reign the national debt of Egypt became so great, that a European Commission was appointed to enquire what steps should be taken in the matter. In 1879, as a result of
A.D. pressure put upon the Porte, Isma'îl was dethroned,
1880. and Tewfik, his eldest son, was appointed to
1881. succeed him.

1882. Massacre of Europeans in June; bombardment of Alexandria by the English fleet in July; occupation of Egypt by English troops; defeat of 'Arabi Pasha.

1885. Murder of Gordon, and the abandonment of the Sudân.

1886–1892. English troops continue to occupy Egypt, but the number of soldiers is being gradually reduced. Great financial and administrative reforms effected under the advice of English officials. Corvée abolished, a system of irrigation works established and perfected under the direction of Sir Colin Scott Moncrieff, taxes and interest on the Debt reduced, railways extended, and army re-modelled, etc.

1892. Death of Tewfik Pasha; accession of Abbâs Pasha his son.

1896. Expedition to the Sudân and utter defeat of the forces of the Khalîfa at Ferket; the victorious Egyptian troops, led by Sir Herbert Kitchener, K.C.B., Sirdar of the Egyptian Army, entered Dongola on September 23.

1898. Utter defeat of the forces of the Khalîfa under Mahmûd on the Atbara by Sir Herbert Kitchener, K.C.B., on Good Friday, April 8th, 1898.

Dates assigned to the Egyptian Dynasties by Egyptologists.

Dynasty.	Champollion-Figeac.	Lepsius (in 1858).	Brugsch (in 1877).	Mariette.
I.	B.C. 5,867	3,892	4,400	5,004
II.	5,615	3,639	4,133	4,751
III.	5,318	3,338	3,966	4,449
IV.	5,121	3,124	3,733	4,235
V.	4,673	2,840	3,566	3,951
VI.	4,425	2,744	3,300	3,703
VII.	4,222	2,592	3,100	3,500
VIII.	4,147	2,522	——	3.500
IX.	4,047	2,674	——	3,358
X.	3,947	2,565	——	3,249
XI.	3,762	2,423	——	3,064
XII.	3,703	2,380	2,466	2,851
XIII	3,417	2,136	2,235	——
XIV.	3,004	2,167	——	2,398
XV.	2,520	2,101	——	2,214
XVI.	2,270	1,842	——	——
XVII.	2,082	1,684	——	——
XVIII.	1,822	1,591	1,700	1,703
XIX.	1,473	1,443	1,400	1,462
XX.	1,279	1,269	1,200	1,288
XXI.	1,101	1,091	1,100	1,110
XXII.	971	961	966	980
XXIII.	851	787	766	810
XXIV.	762	729	733	721
XXV.	718	716	700	715
XXVI.	674	685	666	665
XXVII.	524	525	527	527
XXVIII.	404	525	——	406
XXIX.	398	399	399	399
XXX.	377	378	378	378
XXXI.	339	340	340	340

THE COUNTRY OF EGYPT.

The Ancient Egyptians called Egypt *Baq* or *Baqet;* *Ta-merà;* and *Kamt.* Baq seems to refer to Egypt as the olive-producing country, and Ta-merà as the land of the inundation; the name by which it is most commonly called in the inscriptions is Kam, *i.e.*, "Black," from the darkness of its soil. It was also called the "land of the sycamore," and the "land of the eye of Horus" (*i.e.*, the Sun). It was divided by the Egyptians into two parts: I. Upper Egypt *Ta-res* or *Ta-qemā*, "the southern land;" and II. Lower Egypt *Ta-meḥ*, "the northern land." The kings of Egypt styled themselves *suten net*, "king of the North and South," and *neb taui*, "lord of two earths."* The country was divided into nomes, the number of which is variously given; the list given by some of the classical authorities contains thirty-six, but judging by the monuments the number was nearer forty. The nome (*ḥesp*) was divided into four parts; 1, the capital town (*nut*); 2, the cultivated land; 3, the marshes, which could only at times be used for purposes of cultivation; and 4, the canals, which had to be kept clear and provided with sluices, etc.,

* As ruler of the two countries, each king wore the crown, which was made up of, the *teśer*, or red crown, representing the northern part of Egypt, and, the *ḥet'*, or white crown, representing the southern part of Egypt.

for irrigation purposes. During the rule of the Greeks Egypt was divided into three parts: Upper, Central, and Lower Egypt; Central Egypt consisted of seven nomes, and was called **Heptanomis.**

LIST OF NOMES OF EGYPT—UPPER EGYPT.

	Nome.	Capital.	Divinity.
1.	Ta-Kens.	Ābu (Elephantine), in later times Nubt (Ombos).	Chnemu.
2.	Tes-Ḥeru.	Ṭeb (Apollinopolis magna, Arab. Uṭfu or Edfû).	Ḥeru - Beḥu tet.
3.	Ten.	Necheb (Eileithyia), in later times Sene (Latopolis), Esneh.	Necheb.
4.	Uast.	Uast (Thebes), in later times Hermonthis.	Ȧmen-Rā.
5.	Ḥerui.	Kebti (Coptos).	Ȧmsu.
6.	Āa-ti.	Taenterer (Denderah).	Hathor (Ḥet Ḥert).
7.	Sechem.	Ḥa (Diospolis parva).	Hathor.
8.	Ȧbṭ.	Ȧbṭu (Abydos), in earlier times Teni (This).	Anḥur.
9.	Ȧmsu.	Ȧpu (Panopolis).	Ȧmsu.
10.	Uat'et.	Ṭebu (Aphroditopolis).	Hathor.
11.	Set.	Shasḥetep (Hypsele).	Chnemu.
12.	Ṭuf.	Nen-ent-bak (Antaeopolis).	Horus.
13.	Atefchent.	Saiut (Lycopolis, Arab. Sîûṭ).	Ȧp-uat.
14.	Atef-peḥ.	Kesi (Cusae).	Hathor.
15.	Un.	Chemennu (Hermopolis).	Thoth.
16.	Meḥ-maḥet.	Ḥebennu (Hipponon).	Horus.
17.	....	Kasa (Cynonpolis).	Anubis.
18.	Sapet.	Ḥa-suten (Alabastronpolis).	Anubis.
19.	Uab.	Pa-mat'et (Oxyrhynchos).	Set.

	Nome.	Capital.	Divinity.
20.	Am-chent.	Chenensu (Heracleopolis magna).	Ḥeru-shefi.
21.	Am-peḥ.	Se-men Ḥeru.	Chnemu.
22.	Maten.	Ṭep-âḥet (Aphroditopolis).	Hathor.

LOWER EGYPT.

1.	Aneb-ḥet'.	Men-nefer (Memphis).	Ptaḥ.
2.	Aā.	Sechem (Letopolis).	Ḥeru-ur.
3.	Åment.	Nenten-Ḥapi (Apis).	Ḥathor-nub
4.	Sepi-res.	T'eka (Canopus).	Åmen-Rā.
5.	Sepi-emḥet.	Sa (Sais).	Neit.
6.	Kaset	Chesun (Choïs).	Åmen-Rā.
7.	. . . Åment.	Sent-Nefer (Metelis).	Ḥu.
8.	. . . Åbṭet.	T'ukot (Sethroë).	Atmu.
9.	At'i.	Pa-Åusår (Busiris).	Osiris.
10.	Kakem.	Ḥataḥeråb (Athribis).	Ḥeru-chenti chati.
11.	Kaḥebes.	Kaḥebes (Kabasos).	Isis.
12.	Kat'eb.	T'eb-neter (Sebennythos).	Anḥur.
13.	Ḥakaṭ.	Ånnu (Heliopolis).	Rā.
14.	Chent-åbeṭ.	T'an (Tanis).	Horus.
15.	Teḥuti.	Pa-Teḥuti (Hermopolis).	Thoth.
16.	Char.	Pabaneb-ṭeṭ (Mendes).	Ba-neb-ṭeṭ
17.	Sam-beḥutet.	Pa-chen-en-Åmen (Diospolis).	Åmen-Rā.
18.	Amchent.	Pa-Bast (Bubastis).	Bast.
19.	Am-peḥ.	Pa-Uat' (Buto).	Uat'.
20.	Sept.	Kesem (Phakussa).	Sept.

Egypt proper terminates at Aswân (Syene); the territory south of that town for a certain distance on each side of the river Nile is called Nubia. The races who lived there in very early times caused the Egyptians much trouble, and we know from the tomb-inscriptions at Aswân that expeditions were sent against these peoples by the

Egyptians as far back as the XIIth dynasty. The area of the land in Egypt proper available for cultivation is about 11,500 square miles; the Delta contains about 6,500 miles, and the Nile Valley with the Fayyûm 5,000 miles. The Oases of the Libyan Desert and the Peninsula of Sinai are considered as parts of Egypt. Lower and Upper Egypt are each divided into seven Provinces, the names of which are as follows:—

Lower Egypt.	Upper Egypt.
Beḥêreh (capital, Damanhur).	Gîzeh.
Ḳalyûb (capital, Benha).	Beni-Suêf (capital, Beni-suêf)
Sherḳîyeh (capital, Zaḳâzîḳ).	Minyeh (capital, Minyeh).
Daḳhalîyeh (capital, Manṣûrah.	Sîût (capital, Asyûṭ).
Menûf.	Girgeh (capital, Ṣuhag).
Gharbîyeh (capital Ṭanṭa).	Ḳeneh (capital, Ḳeneh).
	Fayyûm (capital, Wasṭa).

Large towns like Alexandria, Port Sa'id, Suez, Cairo, Damietta, and El'arîsh are governed by native rulers.

In ancient days the population of Egypt proper is said to have been from seven and a half to nine millions; at the present time (1898) it is probably well over ten millions. The population of the provinces south of Egypt, which originally belonged to her, has never been accurately ascertained. The country on each side of the Baḥr el-Abyaḍ is very thickly peopled; it is generally thought that the population of this and the other provinces which belonged to Egypt in the time of Isma'îl amounts to about ten millions.

THE ANCIENT EGYPTIANS.

The Egyptians, whom the sculptures and monuments made known to us as being among the most ancient inhabitants of the country, belong, beyond all doubt, to the Caucasian race, and they seem to have migrated thither from the East. The original home of the invaders was, apparently, Asia, and they made their way across Mesopotamia and Arabia, and across the Isthmus of Suez into Egypt. It has been suggested that they sailed across the Indian Ocean and up the Red Sea, on the western shore of which they landed. It is, however, very doubtful if a people who lived in the middle of a huge land like central Asia, would have enough experience to make and handle ships sufficiently large to cross such seas. No period can be fixed for the arrival of the new-comers from the East into Egypt; we are, however, justified in assuming that it took place before B.C. 5000.

When the people from the East had made their way into Egypt, they found there an aboriginal race with a dark skin and complexion. The Egyptians generally called their land 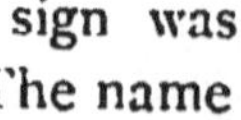 Kamt, *i.e.*, "black"; and if the dark, rich colour of the cultivated land of Egypt be considered, the appropriateness of the term will be at once evident. The hieroglyphic which is read *Kam*, is the skin of a crocodile, and we know from Horapollo (ed. Cory, p. 87), that this sign was used to express anything of a dark colour.* The name "Ham" is given to Egypt by the

* "To denote *darkness*, they represent the TAIL OF A CROCODILE, for by no other means does the crocodile inflict death and destruction on any animal which it may have caught than by first striking it with its tail, and rendering it incapable of motion."

Bible; this word may be compared with the Coptic ⲔⲎⲘⲈ, ⲔⲎⲘⲒ or ϪⲎⲘⲒ. The children of Ham are said to be Cush, Mizraim, Put, and Canaan. The second of these, Miṣraim, is the name given to Egypt by the Hebrews. The dual form of the word, which means "the double Miṣor," probably has reference to the "two lands" (in Egypt. ), over which the Egyptian kings, in their inscriptions, proclaimed their rule. The descendants of Cush are represented on the monuments by the inhabitants of Nubia and the negro tribes which live to the south of that country. In the earliest times the descendants of Cush appear to have had the same religion as the Egyptians. The Put of the Bible is thought by some to be represented by the land of Punt, or spice-land, of the monuments. The people of Punt appear to have dwelt on both sides of the Red Sea to the south of Egypt and on the Somâli coast, and as far back as B.C. 2500 a large trade was carried on between them and the Egyptians; it is thought that the Egyptians regarded them as kinsmen. The aboriginal inhabitants of Phœnicia were probably the kinsfolk of the descendants of Miṣraim, called by the Bible Canaanites. Diodorus and some other classical authorities tell us that Egypt was colonized from Ethiopia; for this view, however, there is no support. The civilization, religion, art of building, etc., of the Ethiopians are all of Egyptian origin, and in this, as in so many other points relating to the history of Egypt, the Greeks were either misinformed, or they misunderstood what they were told.

An examination of the painted representations of the Egyptians by native artists shows us that the pure Egyptian was of slender make, with broad shoulders, long hands and feet, and sinewy legs and arms. His forehead was high, his chin square, his eyes large, his cheeks full, his mouth wide, his lips full, and his nose short and rounded. His jaws protruded slightly, and his hair was smooth and fine. The evidence of the pictures on the tombs is supported and confirmed by the skulls and bones of mummies which anthropologists have examined and measured during the last few years; hence all attempts to prove that the Egyptian is of negro origin are overthrown at the outset by facts which cannot be controverted. In cases where the Egyptians intermarried with people of Semitic origin, we find aquiline noses.* One of the most remarkable things connected with the Egyptians of to-day is the fact that a very large number of them have reproduced, without the slightest alteration, many of the personal features of their ancestors who lived seven thousand years ago. The traveller is often accompanied on a visit to a tomb of the Ancient Empire by a modern Egyptian who, in his attitudes, form, and face, is a veritable reproduction of the hereditary nobleman who built the tomb which he is examining. It may be that no invading race has ever found itself physically able to reproduce persistently its own characteristics for any important length of time, or it may be that the absorption of such races by intermarriage with the natives, together with the influence

* A very good example of this is seen in the black granite head of the statue of Osorkon II., presented to the British Museum (No. 1063) by the Committee of the Egypt Exploration Fund. The lower part of the nose is broken away, but enough of the upper part remains to show what was its original angle. It was confidently asserted that this head belonged to a statue of one of the so-called Hyksos kings, but the assertion was not supported by any trustworthy evidence. The face and features are those of a man whose ancestors were Semites and Egyptians, and men with similar countenances are to be seen in the desert to the south-east of Palestine to this day. A clinching proof that the statue is not that of a Hyksos king was brought forward by Prof. Lanzone of Turin, who, in 1890, had in his possession a small statue of Osorkon II., having precisely the same face and features. The XXIInd dynasty, to which this king belonged, were Semites, as their names show, and they were always regarded by the Egyptians as foreigners, and , the determinative of a man from a foreign country, was placed after each of their names

of the climate, has made such characteristics disappear; the fact, however, remains, that the physical type of the Egyptian fellâḥ is exactly what it was in the earliest dynasties. The invasions of the Babylonians, Hyksos, Ethiopians (including negro races), Assyrians, Persians, Greeks, Romans, Arabs, and Turks, have had no permanent effect either on their physical or mental characteristics. The Egyptian has seen the civilizations of all these nations rise up, progress, flourish, decay, and pass away; he has been influenced from time to time by their religious views and learning; he has been the servant of each of them in turn, and has paid tribute to them all; he has, nevertheless, survived all of them save one. It will, of course, be understood that the inhabitants of the towns form a class quite distinct from the Egyptians of the country; the townsfolk represent a mixture of many nationalities, and their character and features change according to the exigencies of the time and circumstances in which they live, and the influence of the ruling power.

THE MODERN EGYPTIANS.

The total population of Egypt proper was on June 1, 1897, 9,734,405, of whom 112,526 were foreigners.

In a country where an increase in population always means an increase in taxation, it is quite impossible to obtain an accurate census. As far back as the time of David* the idea of "numbering the people" has been unpopular in the East.

It is exceedingly difficult to obtain an exact idea of what the population of Egypt actually was in Pharaonic times, for the inscriptions tell us nothing. Herodotus gives us no information on this matter, but Diodorus tells us that it amounted to 7,000,000 in ancient times. The priests at Thebes informed Germanicus, A.D. 19, that in the times of Rameses II. the country contained 700,000† fighting men; it will also be remembered that the Bible states that the "children of Israel journeyed from Rameses to Succoth, about six hundred thousand on foot that were men, beside children. And a mixed multitude went up also with them." Exodus xii. 37, 38. In the time of Vespasian 7,500,000 persons paid poll-tax; we may assume that about 500,000 were exempt, and therefore there must have been at least 8,000,000 of people in Egypt, without reckoning slaves. (Mommsen, *Provinces of Rome*, Vol. II., p. 258.) It is probable, however, that the population of Egypt under the rule of the Pharaohs has been greatly exaggerated, chiefly because no accurate data were at hand whereby errors might be corrected. During the occupation of the country by the French in 1798–1801 it was said to be 2,460,200; Sir

* "And Satan stood up against Israel, and moved David to number Israel." 1 Chronicles xxi. 1.

† "Septigenta milia aetate militari." Tacitus, *Annals*, Bk. ii., 60.

Gardner Wilkinson, however, set it down at as low a figure as 1,500,000. In 1821 the population numbered 2,536,400, and in 1846 it had risen to 4,476,440. The last census was ordered by Khedivial decree on December 2, 1881, and it was completed on May 3, 1882. According to the official statement published in the *Recensement Général de l'Égypte*, at Cairo, in 1884, it amounted in 1882 to 6,806,381 persons, of whom 3,216,847 were men, and 3,252,869 were women. Of the 6,806,381 persons, 6,708,185 were inhabitants of the country, and 98 196 were nomads. It showed that there were in the total 245,779 Bedâwin and 90,886 foreigners.

According to the census of 1897 the population in Lower Egypt was 5,676,109, and in Upper Egypt, 4,058,296. The distribution of the population in the cities having governors and in the provinces is as follows :—

Cairo, 570,062; Alexandria, 319,766; Port Sa'îd and Canal, 50,179; Suez, 24,970; Damietta, 43,751; El-Arîsh, 16,991; Beḥêreh, 631,225; Sherḳîyeh, 749,130; Daḳhaliyeh, 736,708; Gharbîyeh, 1,297,656; Ḳalyûb, 371,465; Menûf, 864,206; Asyûṭ, 782,720; Beni-Suêf, 314,454; Fayyûm, 371,006; Gîzeh, 401,634; Minyeh, 548,632; Girgeh, 688,011; Ḳeneh, 711,457; Nubia, 240,382. In the Oasis* of Sîwa, 5,000; Donḳola, 56,426; Sawâkin, 15,713. The males numbered 4,947,850, and the females, 4,786,555. The number of houses occupied was 1,422,302. The increase in the population since 1882 is 43 per cent. The Muslims number 8,978,775; Jews, 25,200; Christians (of all sects), 730,162. Males and females able to read and write were 467,886; and 9,266,519 were illiterate.

* The Egyptian Oases are five: Wâḥ el-Khârgeh, or Oasis Major, 90 miles from Thebes; Wâḥ ed-Daḳhaliyeh, or Oasis Minor with warm springs, to the west of the city of Oxyrhynchos; Farâfra, about 80 miles north of Oasis Minor; Siwa, where there was a temple to Jupiter Ammon, to the south-west of Alexandria; and Wâḥ el-Baḥriyeh, to the north of Wâḥ el-Khârgeh.

The population of Egypt to-day comprises the Fellâḥîn, Copts, Bedâwin, Jews, Turks, Negroes, Nubians and people from Abyssinia, Armenians and Europeans.

The **Fellâḥîn** amount to about four-fifths of the entire population of Egypt, and are chiefly employed in agricultural pursuits. In physical type they greatly resemble the ancient Egyptians as depicted on the monuments. Their complexion is dark; they have straight eyebrows, high cheek bones, flat noses with low bridges, slightly protruding jaws, broad shoulders, large mouths and full lips. The colour of their skin becomes darker as the south is approached. The whole of the cultivation of Egypt is in the hands of the fellâḥîn.

The **Copts** are also direct descendants from the ancient Egyptians, and inhabit chiefly the cities of Upper Egypt, such as Asyûṭ and Aḥmîm. The name Copt is derived from قبط *Ḳubṭ*, the Arabic form of the Coptic form of the Greek name for Egyptian, Αἰγύπτιος; it may be mentioned, in passing, that Αἴγυπτος, Egypt, is thought by some to be derived from an ancient Egyptian name for Memphis, Ḥet-ka-Ptaḥ, "The house of the genius of Ptaḥ." The number of Copts in Egypt to-day is estimated at about 350,000, and the greater number of them are engaged in the trades of goldsmiths, clothworkers, etc.; a respectable body of clerks and accountants in the postal, telegraph and government offices in Egypt, is drawn from their community. They are clever with their fingers, and are capable of rapid education up to a certain point; beyond this they rarely go. Physically, they are of a finer type than the fellâḥîn; their heads are longer and their features are more European.

The Copts are famous in ecclesiastical history for having embraced with extraordinary zeal and rapidity the doctrines of Christianity as preached by St. Mark at Alexandria. Before the end of the third century A.D. Egypt was filled with hundreds of thousands of ascetics, monks recluses, and solitaries who had thrown over their own weird and confused religious beliefs and embraced Christianity; they then retired to the mountains and deserts of their country to dedicate their lives to the service of the Christians' God. The Egyptians, their ancestors, who lived sixteen hundred years before Christ, had already arrived at the conception of a god who was one in his person, but who manifested himself in the world under many forms and many names. The Greeks and the Romans, who successively held Egypt, caused many changes to come over the native religion of the country which they governed; and since the conflicting myths and theories taught to the people of Egypt under their rule had bewildered their minds and confused their beliefs, they gladly accepted the simple teaching of Christ's Apostle as a veritable gift of God. Their religious belief took the form of that of Eutyches (died after 451), who sacrificed the "distinction of the two natures in Christ to the unity of the person to such an extent as to make the incarnation an absorption of the human nature by the divine, or a deification of human nature, even of the body." In other words, they believed that Christ had but one composite nature, and for this reason they were called Monophysites; in their liturgies they stated that God had been crucified. They formed a part of the Alexandrian Church until the Council of Chalcedon, A.D. 451, when it was laid down that Christ had a *double* nature—human and divine—but after this date they separated themselves from it, and were accounted heretics by it, because they obstinately refused to give up their belief in the *one* divine nature of Christ which embraced and included the human. To the sect of Monophysites or Eutychians the Copts still belong. The orthodox church of Alexandria and its heretical offshoot continued to discuss with anger and tumult the subtle points of their different opinions, until the fifth Œcumenical Council held at Constantinople A.D. 553, made some concessions to the Monophysite party. Shortly after, however, new dissensions arose which so weakened the orthodox church that the Monophysite party hailed with gladness the arrival of the arms of Muḥammad the Prophet, and joined its forces with his that they might destroy the power of their theological opponents. After 'Amr had made himself master of Egypt (A.D. 640), he appointed the Copts to positions of dignity and wealth; finding, however, that they were unworthy of his confidence, they were degraded, and finally persecuted with vigour. From the time of Cyril, Patriarch of Alexandria, A.D. 1235 and onwards, but little is known of the history of the Coptic Church. The Copt of to-day usually troubles himself little about theological matters; in certain cases, however, he affirms with considerable firmness the doctrine of the "one nature."

The knowledge of the Coptic language is, generally speaking, extinct; it is exceedingly doubtful if three Coptic scholars, in the Western sense of the word, exist even among the priests. The language spoken by them is Arabic, and though copies of parts of the Bible are found in churches and private houses, they are usually accompanied by an Arabic version of the Coptic text, which is more usually read than the Coptic. The Bible, in all or part, was translated from Greek into Coptic in the third century of our era; some, however, think that the translation was not made until the eighth century. The versions of the principal books of the Old and the whole of the New Testament, together with lives of saints, monks and martyrs, form the greater part of Coptic literature. The Coptic language is, at base, a dialect of ancient Egyptian; many of the nouns and verbs found in the hieroglyphic texts remain unchanged in Coptic, and a large number of others can, by making proper allowance for phonetic decay and dialectic differences, be identified without difficulty. The Copts used the Greek alphabet to write down their language, but found it necessary to borrow six* signs from the demotic forms of ancient Egyptian characters to express the sounds which they found unrepresented in Greek. The dialect of Upper Egypt is called "Sahidic"† or Theban, and that of Lower Egypt "Memphitic."‡ During the last few years the study of Coptic has revived among European scholars, but this is partly owing to the fact that the importance of a knowledge of the language, as a preliminary to the study of hieroglyphics, has been at length recognized. The Roman Propagandist Tuki§ published during the last century some valuable works; in spite, however, of the activity of scholars and the enterprise of publishers, it still costs nearly £5 to purchase a copy of as much of the Memphitic Coptic version of the Bible as has come down to us.

The **Bedâwin** are represented by the various Arabic-speaking and Muḥammadan tribes, who live in the deserts which lie on each side of the Nile; they amount in number to about 250,000. The Bisharîn, Hadendoa, and Ababdeh tribes, who speak a language (called 'to bedhawîyyeh') which is like ancient Egyptian in some respects, and who live in

* These signs are:

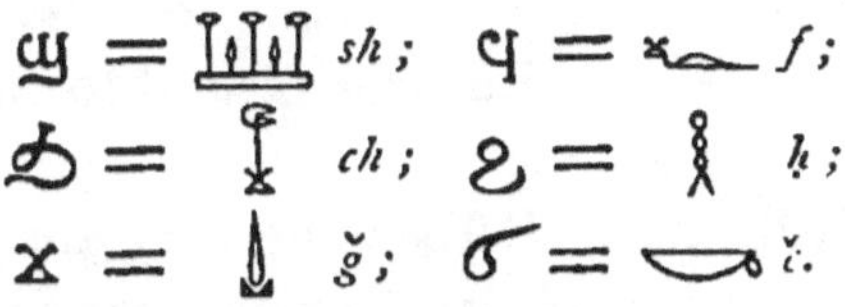

† This is the older and richer dialect of Coptic, which was spoken from Minyeh to Aswân.

‡ More correctly called Boheiric, from the province of Boheirâ in the Delta; the name Bashmuric has been wrongly applied to this dialect, but as it appears to have been exclusively the language of Memphis, it may be styled "Middle Egyptian." The dialect of Bushmûr on the Lake of Menzaleh appears to have become extinct about A.D. 900, and to have left no traces of itself behind. See Stern, *Kopt. Gram.*, p. 1.

§ Among more recent scholars may be named Wilkins, Zoega, Tattam, Ideler, Schwartze, Revillout, Hyvernat, Amélineau, Stern, Guidi, Lagarde, Schmidt, Horner, etc the most southern part of Upper Egypt, Nubia, and Abyssinia, are included among this number. Among these three tribes the institutions of Muḥammad are not observed with any great strictness. When the Bedâwin settle down to village or town life, they appear to lose all the bravery and fine qualities of independent manhood which characterize them when they live in their home, the desert.

The inhabitants of Cairo, Alexandria, and other large towns form a class of people quite distinct from the other inhabitants of Egypt; in Alexandria there is a very large Greek element, and in Cairo the number of Turks is very great. In the bazaars of Cairo one may see the offspring of marriages between members of nearly every European nation and Egyptian or Nubian women, the colour of their skins varying from a dark brick-red to nearly white. The shopkeepers are fully alive to their opportunities of making money, and would, beyond doubt, become rich but for their natural indolence and belief in fate. Whatever they appear or however much they may mask their belief in the Muḥammadan religion, it must never be forgotten that they have the greatest dislike to every religion but their own. The love of gain alone causes them to submit to the remarks made upon them by Europeans, and to suffer their entrance and sojourning among them.

The **Nubians** or Berbers, as they are sometimes called, inhabit the tract of land which extends from Aswân or Syene to the fourth cataract. The word Nubia appears to be derived from *nub*, 'gold,' because Nubia was a gold-producing country. The word Berber is considered to mean 'barbarian' by some, and to be also of Egyptian origin They speak a language which is allied to some of the North African tongues, and rarely speak Arabic well. The Nubians found in Egypt are generally doorkeepers and domestic servants, who can usually be depended upon for their honesty and obedience.

The **Negroes** form a large part of the non-native population of Egypt, and are employed by natives to perform hard work, or are held by them as slaves. They are Muḥammadans by religion, and come from the countries known by the name of Sûdân. Negro women make good and faithful servants.

The Syrian Christians who have settled down in Egypt are generally known by the name of **Levantines.** They are shrewd business men, and the facility and rapidity with which they learn European languages place them in positions of trust and emolument.

The **Turks** form a comparatively small portion of the population of Egypt, but many civil and military appointments are, or were, in their hands. Many of them are the children of Circassian slaves. The merchants are famous for their civility to foreigners and their keen eye to business.

The **Armenians** and **Jews** form a small but important part of the inhabitants in the large towns of Egypt. The former are famous for their linguistic attainments and wealth; the latter have blue eyes, fair hair and skin, and busy themselves in mercantile pursuits and the business of bankers and money-changing.

The European population in Egypt consists of Greeks, 38,175; Italians, 24,467; English, 19,557; French, 14,155; Austrians, 7,117; Russians, 3,193; Germans, 1,277; Spaniards, 765; Swiss, 472; Americans, 291; Belgians, 256; Dutch, 247; Portuguese, 151; Swedes, 107; Danes, 72; Persians, 1,301; Miscellaneous, 923. The greater part of the business of Alexandria is in the hands of the Greek merchants, many of whom are famous for their wealth. It is said that the Greek community contributes most largely to the crime in the country, but if the size of that community be taken into account, it will be found that this statement is not strictly true. The enterprise and good business habits of the Greeks in Alexandria have made it the great city that it is. The French, Austrian, German, and English nations are likewise represented there, and in Cairo, by several first-rate business houses. The destructive fanaticism peculiar to the Muḥammadan mind, so common in the far east parts of Mesopotamia, seems to be non-existent in Egypt; such fanaticism as exists is, no doubt, kept in check by the presence of Europeans, and all the different peoples live side by side in a most peaceable manner. The great benefit derived by Egypt from the immigration of Europeans during the last few years is evident from the increased material prosperity of the country, and the administration of equitable laws which has obtained.

THE NILE.

The river Nile is one of the longest rivers in the world; its Egyptian name was Ḥāpi, 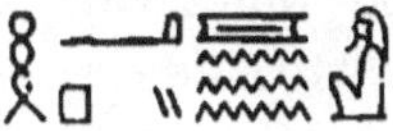, and the Arabs call it *baḥr*, or 'sea.' It is formed by the junction, at 15° 34′ N. lat., and 30° 30′ 58″ E. long., of two great arms, the *Baḥr el-Azraḳ*, *i.e.*, the 'turbid,' or Blue Nile, from the S.E., and the *Baḥr el-Abyaḍ*, *i.e.*, the 'clear,' or White Nile, from the S.W.* The eastern branch rises in Goyam, in Abyssinia, at an elevation of about 10,000 feet above the level of the sea. Flowing through the lake of Dembea it passes round the eastern frontier of Goyam, till, when nearing the 10th degree N. lat., it takes a north west direction, which it preserves until it reaches Kharṭûm; here it unites with the Baḥr el-Abyaḍ, the other great arm, which flows from the S.W. The Baḥr el-Abyaḍ, or White Nile, is called because of the fine whitish clay which colours its waters. It is broader and deeper than the eastern arm, and it brings down a much larger volume of water; the ancients appear to have regarded it as the true Nile. There can, however, be no doubt that the Baḥr el-Azraḳ has the best right to be considered the true Nile, for during the violent and rapid course which it takes from the Abyssinian mountains, it carries down with it all the rich mud which, during the lapse of ages, has been spread

* The White Nile rises in the mountainous districts a few degrees north of the Equator, and the principal streams which flow into it are those of the Sobât, Giraffe, and Gazelle rivers. It is not navigable, and its banks are so low that its whitish slimy deposit often extends to a distance of two miles from the stream. For about a hundred miles south of Kharṭûm the river is little more than a marsh.

over the land on each side of its course and formed the land of Egypt. In truth, then, Egypt is the gift of the Baḥr el-Azraḳ. The course of the Baḥr el-Abyaḍ was traced by Linant in 1827 for about 160 miles from its confluence with the Baḥr el-Azraḳ. At the point of confluence it measures about 600 yards across, a little farther up it is from three to four miles wide, and during the inundation the distance from side to side is twenty-one miles. In an ordinary season it is about 24 feet deep.

The source of the Nile was not discovered by Bruce, but by Captains Grant and Speke and Sir Samuel Baker. Its parents are the Albert Nyanza and Victoria Nyanza Lakes. The fountain-head of the Nile, Victoria Nyanza, is a huge basin, far below the level of the country round about, into which several streams empty themselves. About 200 miles below Kharṭûm the united river receives, on the east side, the waters of the Atbara, which rises in the mountains of Abyssinia, and from this point onwards to its embouchure, a distance of about 1,750 miles, the Nile receives no affluent whatever. From Kharṭûm to Cairo the Nile falls about 400 yards; its width is about 1,100 yards in its widest part. The course of the Nile has been explored to a length of about 3,500 miles. At Abu Ḥammed the river turns suddenly to the south-west, and flows in this direction until it reaches Donḳola, where it again curves to the north. The river enters Nubia, flowing over a ledge of granite rocks which form the third cataract. Under the 22nd parallel N. lat. is the second cataract, which ends a few miles above Wâdi Ḥalfah, and about 180 miles lower down is the first cataract, which ends at Aswân, or Syene, a little above the island of Elephantine. After entering Egypt, the Nile flows in a steady stream, always to the north, and deposits the mud which is the life of Egypt. The breadth of the Nile valley varies from four to ten miles in Nubia, and from fifteen to thirty in Egypt. The width of the strips of cultivated land on each bank of the river in Egypt together is never more than eight or nine miles.

In ancient days the Nile poured its waters into the sea by seven mouths; those of Damietta and Rosetta* are now, however, the only two which remain. The Delta is, in its widest part, about ninety miles across from east to west, and the distance of the apex from the sea is also about ninety miles. Many attempts have been made to ascertain the age of Egypt by estimating the annual alluvial deposit; the results, however, cannot be implicitly relied on.

The **inundation** is caused by the descent of the rain which falls on the Abyssinian mountains. The indications of the rise of the river may be seen at the cataracts as early as the beginning of June, and a steady increase goes on until the middle of July, when the increase of water becomes very great. The Nile continues to rise until the middle of September, when it remains stationary for a period of about three weeks, sometimes a little less. In October it rises again, and attains its highest level. From this period it begins to subside, and, though it rises yet once more, and reaches occasionally its former highest point, it sinks steadily until the month of June, when it is again at its lowest level.

The modern ceremony of 'Cutting the Dam' of the river takes place generally in the second or third week of August at Fum el-Khalig, at Cairo. In ancient days the ceremony of cutting the canals was accompanied with great festivities, and great attention was paid to the height of the river in various parts of Egypt, that the cutting might take place at the most favourable time. We learn, on the authority of Seneca, that offerings of gold and other gifts were thrown

* The seven mouths were called the Pelusiac, Tanitic, Mendesian, Phatnitic, Sebennytic, Bolbitic, and the Canopic.

into the Nile at Philæ by the priests to propitiate the divinity of the river.

If the height of the inundation is about forty-five feet the best results from agricultural labour are obtained; a couple of feet of water, more or less, is always attended with disastrous results either in the Delta or Upper Egypt. The dykes, or embankments, which kept the waters of the Nile in check, and regulated their distribution over the lands, were, in Pharaonic days, maintained in a state of efficiency by public funds, and, in the time of the Romans, any person found destroying a dyke was either condemned to hard labour in the public works or mines, or to be branded and sent to one of the Oases. If we accept the statements of Strabo, we may believe that the ancient system of irrigation was so perfect that the varying height of the inundation caused but little inconvenience to the inhabitants of Egypt, as far as the results of agricultural labours were concerned, though an unusually high Nile would, of course, wash away whole villages and drown much cattle. If the statements made by ancient writers be compared, it will be seen that the actual height of the inundation is the same now as it always was, and that it maintains the same proportion with the land it irrigates. According to Sir Gardner Wilkinson (*Ancient Egypt*, II., 431), the cubit measures of the Nilometers ought, after certain periods, to be raised proportionately if we wish to arrive at great accuracy in the measurement of the waters. The level of the land, which always keeps pace with that of the river, increases at the rate of six inches in a hundred years in some places, and in others less. The proof of this is that the highest scale in the Nilometer at the island of Elephantine, which served to measure the inundation in the reigns of the early Roman emperors, is now far below the level of the ordinary high Nile; and the obelisk of Heliopolis, the colossi at Thebes, and other similarly situated monuments, are now washed by the waters of the inundation and imbedded to a certain height in a stratum of alluvial soil which has been deposited around their base. The land about Elephantine and at Thebes has been raised about nine feet in 1,700 years. The usual rise of the river at Cairo is twenty-five feet, at Thebes thirty-eight feet, and at Aswân forty-five feet. The average rate of the current is about three miles per hour. As the river bed rises higher and higher the amount of land covered by the waters of the inundation grows more and more. It is estimated that, if all the land thus watered were thoroughly cultivated, Egypt would, for its size, be one of the richest countries in the world.* The ancient Egyptians fully recognized how very much they owed to the Nile, and, in their hymns, they thank the Nile-god in appropriate and grateful terms. Statues of the god are painted green and red, which colours are supposed to represent 1. the colour of the river in June, when it is a bright green, before the inundation; and 2. the ruddy hue which its waters have when charged with the red mud brought down from the Abyssinian mountains.

* Those who are interested in the work of the Irrigation Department in Egypt will find a great deal of useful information on the subject in Major R. H. Brown's *History of the Barrage*, where the story of this famous work is told concisely but clearly. The more curious reader may consult Mr. Willcock's *Egyptian Irrigation*.

EGYPTIAN WRITING.

The system of writing employed by the earliest inhabitants of the Valley of the Nile known to us was entirely pictorial, and had much in common with the pictorial writing of the Chinese and the ancient people who migrated into Babylonia from the East. There appears to be no inscription in which pictorial characters are used entirely, for the earliest inscriptions now known to us contain alphabetic characters. Inscriptions upon statues, coffins, tombs, temples, etc., in which figures or representations of objects are employed, are usually termed 'Hieroglyphic' (from the Greek *ἱερογλυφικός*); for writing on papyri a cursive form of hieroglyphic called 'Hieratic' (from the Greek *ἱερατικός*), was employed by the priests, who, at times, also used hieroglyphic; a third kind of writing, consisting of purely conventional modifications of hieratic characters, which preserve little of the original form, was employed for social and business purposes; it is called demotic (from the Greek *δημοτικός*). The following will show the different forms of the characters in the three styles of writing—

I. Hieratic.

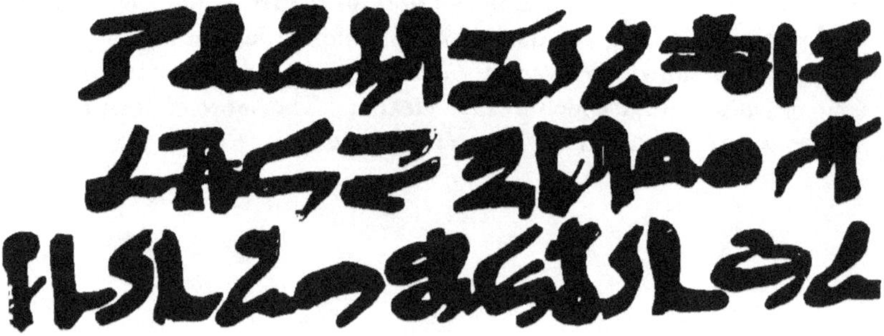

II. Hieroglyphic Transcript of No. I.

III. Demotic.

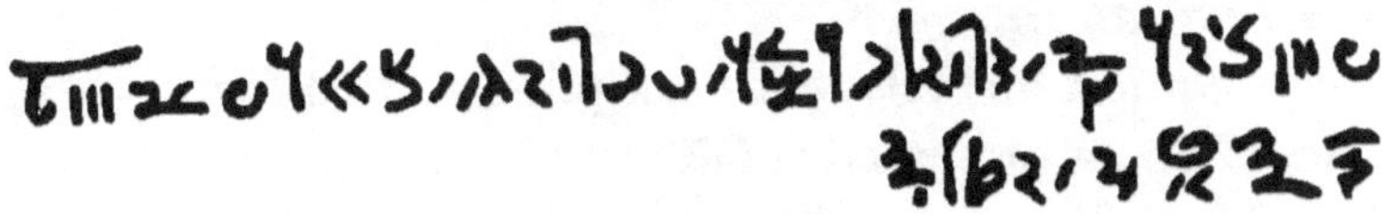

IV. Hieroglyphic Transcript of No. III.

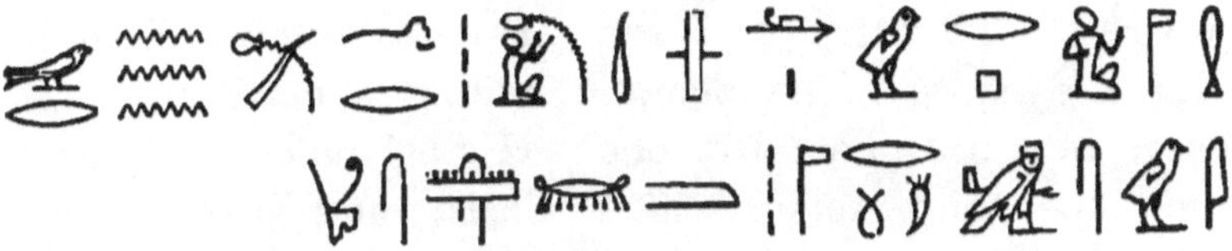

No. I is copied from the Prisse* papyrus (Maxims of Ptaḥ-ḥetep, p. V, l. 1), and is transcribed and translated as follows :—

àb *temu* *àn* *seχa - nef* *sef*
. . . . the heart fails, not remembers he yesterday.
qes *men-f* *en* *āuu* *bu nefer χeper em-*
The body suffers it in [its] entirety, happiness becomes
bu [*bàn*]
wretchedness.†

No. III is copied from the demotic version inscribed on the stele of Canopus (see p. 18), and No. IV. is the corresponding passage in the hieroglyphic version of the

* This papyrus is the oldest in the world, and was written about B.C. 2500 ; it was presented to the Bibliothèque Nationale by Prisse. who acquired it at Thebes.

† Ptaḥ-ḥetep is lamenting the troubles of old age, and the complete passage runs : "The understanding perisheth, an old man remembers not yesterday. The body becometh altogether pain ; happiness turneth into wretchedness ; and taste vanisheth away."

Decree. The transliteration of the Demotic, according to Hess (*Roman von Stne Ha-m-us*, p. 80), is:—*p-ḥon nuter . . . . . ua n-n-uêb' ent sâtp er-p-ma uêb er-ube p-gi-n-er mnḫ n-n-nuter'*, "a prophet, or one of the priests who are selected for the sanctuary to perform the dressing of the gods." The transliteration of the hieroglyphic text is: *ḥen neter erpu uā àmθ ābu setep er āb-ur àu smā er māret neteru em sati-sen.*

The earliest hieroglyphic inscription is that found on the stelæ of Sherà preserved at Gîzeh and Oxford; it dates from the second dynasty. The oldest hieratic inscription is that contained in the famous Prisse papyrus which records the advice of Ptaḥ-ḥetep to his son. It dates from the XIth or XIIth dynasty. The demotic writing appears to have come into use about B.C. 900. Hieroglyphics were used until the third century after Christ, and hieratic and demotic for at least a century later. The inscriptions on the Rosetta and Canopus stelæ are written in hieroglyphic, demotic, and Greek characters. The Egyptians inscribed, wrote, or painted inscriptions upon almost every kind of substance, but the material most used by them for their histories, and religious and other works was papyrus. Sections from the stem of the papyrus plant were carefully cut, and the layers were taken off, pressed flat, and several of them gummed one over the other transversely; thus almost any length of papyrus for writing upon could be made. The longest known is the great Harris papyrus, No. 1; it measures 135 feet by 17 inches. The scribe wrote upon the papyrus with reeds, and the inks were principally made of vegetable colours. Black and red are the commonest colours used, but some papyri are painted with as many as eleven or thirteen. The scribe's palette was a rectangular piece of wood varying from six to thirteen inches long by two, or two and a half, inches wide. In the middle was a hollow for holding the reeds, and at one end were the circular or oval cavities in which the colours were placed.

At the beginning of the Greek rule over Egypt, the knowledge of the use of the ancient Egyptian language began to decline, and the language of Greece began to modify and eventually to supersede that of Egypt. When we consider that Ptolemy I. Soter, succeeded in attracting to Alexandria a large number of the greatest Greek scholars of the day, such as Euclid the mathematician, Stilpo of Megara, Theodorus of Cyrene and Diodorus Cronus, the philosophers, Zenodotus the grammarian, Philetas the poet from Cos, and many others, this is not to be wondered at. The founding of the great Alexandrian Library and Museum, and the endowment of these institutions for the support of a number of the most eminent Greek philosophers and scholars, was an act of far-sighted policy on the part of Ptolemy I., whose aim was to make the learning and language of the Greeks to become dominant in Egypt. Little by little the principal posts in the Government were monopolised by the Greeks, and little by little the Egyptians became servants and slaves to their intellectually superior masters. In respect to their language, "the Egyptians were not prohibited from making use, so far as it seemed requisite according to ritual or otherwise appropriate, of the native language and of its time-hallowed written signs; in this old home, moreover, of the use of writing in ordinary intercourse the native language, alone familiar to the great public, and the usual writing must necessarily have been allowed not merely in the case of private contracts, but even as regards tax-receipts and similar documents. But this was a concession, and the ruling Hellenism strove to enlarge its domain." Mommsen, *The Provinces of the Roman Empire*, Vol. II., p. 243. It is true that Ptolemy II. Philadelphus, employed the famous Manetho (*i.e.*, , Mer-en-Teḥuti, 'beloved of Thoth') to draw up a history of Egypt, and an account of the ancient Egyptian religion from the papyri and other native records; but it is also true that during the reigns of these two Ptolemies the Egyptians were firmly kept in obscurity, and that the ancient priest-college of Heliopolis was suppressed. A century or two after the Christian era, Greek had obtained such a hold upon the inhabitants of Egypt that the Egyptian Christians, the followers and disciples of St. Mark, were obliged to use the Greek alphabet to write down the Egyptian, that is to say Coptic translation of the books of the Old and New Testaments. The letters ϣ, *sh*, ϥ, *f*, ϧ, χ, ϩ, *ḥ*, ϭ, *č*, ϫ, *ǵ*, were added from the demotic forms of hieratic characters to represent sounds which were unknown in the Greek language. During the Greek rule over Egypt many of the hieroglyphic characters had new phonetic values given to them; by this time the knowledge of hieroglyphic writing had practically died out.

The history of the decipherment of hieroglyphics is of great interest, but no thorough account of it can be given here; only the most important facts connected with it can be mentioned. During the XVIth–XVIIIth centuries many attempts were made by scholars to interpret the hieroglyphic inscriptions then known to the world, but they resulted in nothing useful. The fact is that they did not understand the nature of the problem to be solved, and they failed to perceive the use of the same hieroglyphic character as a phonetic or determinative in the same inscription. In 1799, a French officer discovered at Bolbitane or Rosetta a basalt slab inscribed in the hieroglyphic, demotic, and Greek characters; it was shortly after captured by the English army, and taken to London, where it was carefully examined by Dr. Thomas Young.*

* Thomas Young was born at Milverton, in Somersetshire, on the 13th of June, 1773; both his parents were Quakers. At the age of fourteen he is said to have been versed in Greek, Latin, French,

The Society of Antiquaries published a fac-simile of the inscription, which was distributed among scholars, and Silvestre de Sacy and Akerblad made some useful discoveries about certain parts of the demotic version of the inscription. Dr. Young was enabled, ten years after, to make translations of the three inscriptions, and the results of his studies were published in 1821. In 1822 M. Champollion * (Le Jeune) published a translation of the same inscriptions, and was enabled to make out something like an alphabet. There appears to be no doubt that he was greatly helped by the publications and labours of Young, who had succeeded in grouping certain words in demotic, and in assigning accurate values to some of the hieroglyphic characters used in writing the names of the Greek rulers of Egypt. Young made many mistakes, but some of his work was of value, Champollion, to whom the credit of definitely settling the phonetic values of several signs really belongs, had been carefully grounded in the Coptic language, and was therefore enabled with little difficulty to recognize the hieroglyphic forms of the words which were familiar to him in Coptic; Young had no such advantage. Champollion's system was subjected to many attacks, but little by little it gained ground, and the labours of other scholars have

Italian, Hebrew, Persian and Arabic. He took his degree of M.D. in July, 1796, in 1802 he was appointed professor of natural philosophy at the Royal Institution, and in 1810 he was elected physician to St. George's Hospital. He was not, however, a popular physician. He died on the 10th of May, 1829.

* Jean François Champollion le Jeune was born at Figeac, department du Lot, in 1796. He was educated at Grenoble, and afterwards at Paris, where he devoted himself to the study of Coptic. In the year 1824 he was ordered by Charles X. to visit all the important collections of Egyptian antiquities in Europe. On his return he was appointed Director of the Louvre. In 1828 he was sent on a scientific mission to Egypt, and was afterwards made professor of Egyptian antiquities at the Collège de France. He died in 1831.

proved that he was right. The other early workers in the field of hieroglyphics were Dr. Samuel Birch in England; Dr. Lepsius in Germany, and MM. Rosellini and Salvolini in Italy. The study of hieroglyphics has become comparatively general, and each year sees books of texts published, learned papers on Egyptian grammar written, and translations made into the various European languages.

In hieroglyphic inscriptions the signs are used in two ways: I, Ideographic, II, Phonetic. In the ideographic system a word is expressed by a picture or *ideograph* thus: *māu*, 'water'; in the phonetic system the same word is written *m* + *ā* + *u*, no regard being paid to the fact that represents an owl, a hand and fore-arm, and a rope. Similarly *emsuḥ* is a 'crocodile' in the ideographic system, but phonetically it is written *m* + *s* + *u* + *ḥ*. The ideographic system is probably older than the phonetic.

Phonetic signs are: I, Alphabetic, as *m*, *s*, *u*; or II, Syllabic, as *mer*, *χeper*, *ḥetep*. The sign *χeper* can be written 1, ; 2, ; 3, ; 4, ; the sign *nefer* can be written 1, ; 2, ; 3, ; 4, ; 5, . The scribes took pains to represent the exact value of these syllabic signs in order that no mistake might be made.

The ideographic signs are also used as determinatives, and are placed after words written phonetically to determine their meaning. For example, *nem* means 'to sleep' 'to walk,' 'to go back,' 'to become infirm,' 'tongue' and 'again'; without a determinative the meaning of this word in a sentence would be easily mistaken. DETERMINATIVES are of two kinds: I, *ideographic*, and II, *generic*. Thus after ⦅⦆ *màu*, 'cat,' a cat, 🐾, was written; this is an *ideographic* determinative. After △ 𝄞 *ḳerḥ*, 'darkness,' the night sky with a star in it, ▭, was written; this is a *generic* determinative. A word has frequently more than one determinative; for example, in the word ⦆ *bāḥ*, ' to overflow,' 🦅 is a determinative of the sound *bāḥ*; 〰 is a determinative of water, ▭ of a lake or collection of water, and ▷ of ground. The list of hieroglyphic signs with their phonetic values given on pp. 62-69 will be of use in reading kings' names, etc.; for convenience however the hieroglyphic alphabet is added here. The system of transliteration of Egyptian characters used in this book is that most generally adopted.

🦅	*a*	▭, 🦅	*m*
⦅	*à*	𝄞, 〰	*n*
▬	*ā*	▭, 🐝	*r* or
⦅⦆, \\	*i*	⊓	*h*
🦆, ℮	*u*	𝄞	*ḥ*
⦆	*b*	●	χ *(kh)*
▤	*p*	▬, ∩	*s*
🐍	*f*	▭	*sh*

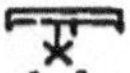

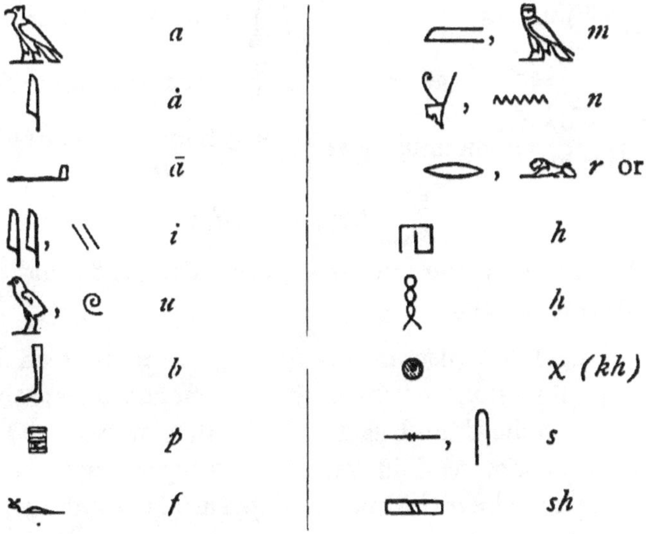

k	*t*
q	*ṭ*
ḳ	*θ* (*th*)

t' (like *ch* in child)

The number of hieroglyphic characters is about two thousand.

NUMBERS.

uā, *one*	paut *or* psṭ, *nine*
sen, *two*	met', *ten*
chemet, *three*	t'et, *twenty*
fṭu, *four*	māb, *thirty*
ṭua, *five*	śaā, *a hundred*
sas (?), *six*	cha, *a thousand*
sechef, *seven*	t'ebā, *ten thousand*
chemennu, *eight*	ḥefnu, *a hundred thousand*

ḥeḥ, *a million*

The forms of the numbers 40, 50, 60, 70, 80 and 90 are not known exactly.

Hieroglyphic inscriptions are usually to be read in the opposite direction to which the characters face; there is however no hard and fast rule in this matter. On the papyri they are read in various directions, and there are instances in which the ancient copyist mistook the end of a chapter for its beginning, and copied the whole of it in the reverse order. Some inscriptions are to be read in perpendicular lines.

The following transliterated and translated extract from the first page of the "Tale of the Two Brothers" will explain the foregoing statements.

1. 

ȧr ementuf χertu sen sen

There were once on a time brothers two [the children]

en uā muθet en uā ȧtf

of one mother and of one father;

Ȧnpu ren pa āa ȧu Batau

Anubis was the name of the elder, was Bata

ren pa śerȧu χer ȧr

the name of the younger. Now as regards

Ȧnpu su χeri pa χeri ḥemt

Anpu, he possessed a house and had a wife,

2. 

ȧu paif sen śerȧu emmā-f

and was his brother younger [living] with him

mȧ seχeru en śerȧu ȧu ementuf
after the manner of a servant, for it was he

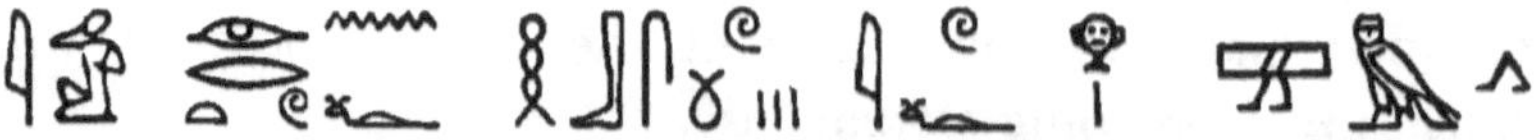

ȧ ȧritu-nef ḥebsu ȧuf ḥer seśem
who made the clothes, it was he who followed

em-sa nai-f ȧaut er seχet
after his [Anpu's] cattle in the fields,

3. 

ȧu ementuf ȧ ȧritu seka
he it was who did the ploughing,

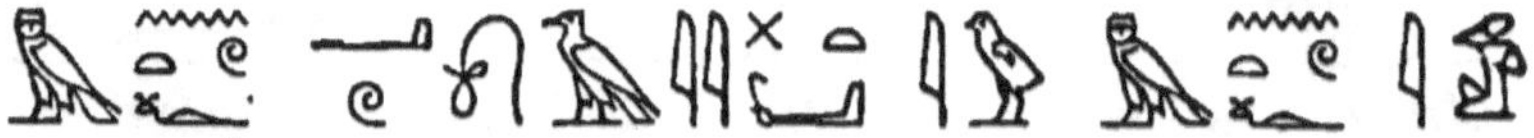

ementuf āuuait ȧu ementuf ȧ
he it was who laboured, he it was who

ȧritu-nef ȧput neb enti em
performed the duties all which were [connected] with

seχet ȧs-tu ȧu pa śerȧu
the fields; and behold was the young man

4. 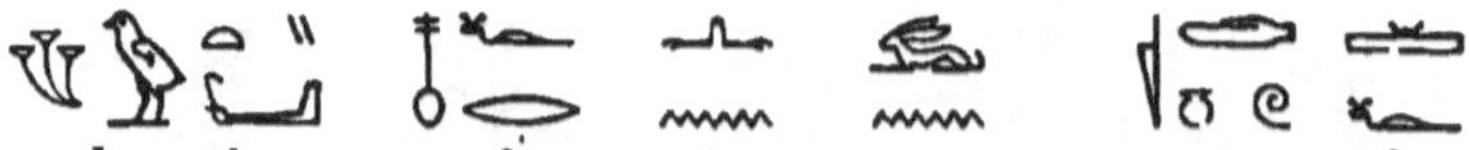

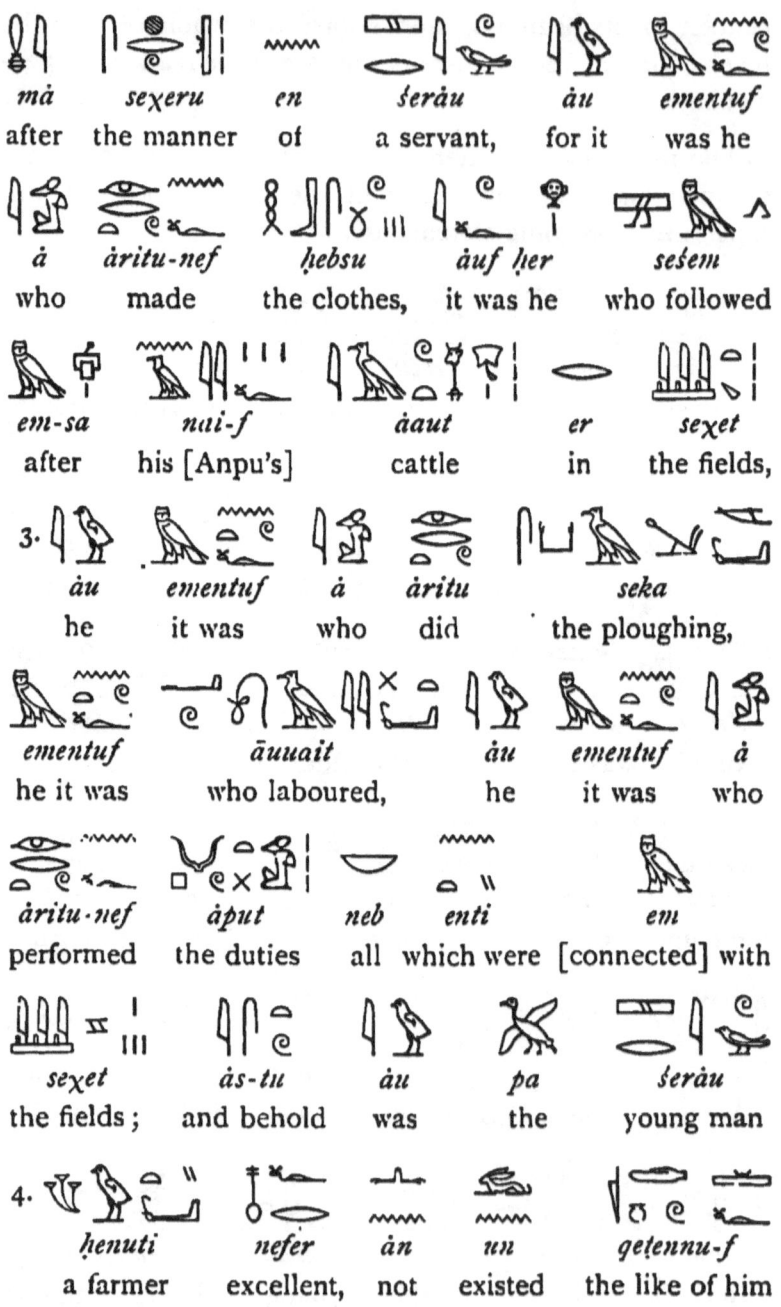

ḥenuti nefer ȧn un geṭennu-f
a farmer excellent, not existed the like of him

em *ta* *ṭer-f* . . . *χer* *ȧr* *emχet*

in the land the whole of it . . . Now thus it was during

hru *qennu* *ḥer-sa* *enen* *ȧu*

days many upon those [days] that

paif *sen* *šerȧu* 5. *emsa* *naif*

was his brother younger following after his

ȧaut *em* *paif* *seχeru* *enti*

cattle according to his wont of

hru *neb* *ementuf* *ḥer* *uāu* (or *beḥāu*) *er*

every day, and he returned to

pai-f *pa* *er* *tennu* *ruha*

his house every evening, and

ȧuf *ȧtep* 6. *em* *simu* *neb*

he was laden with vegetables of all kinds

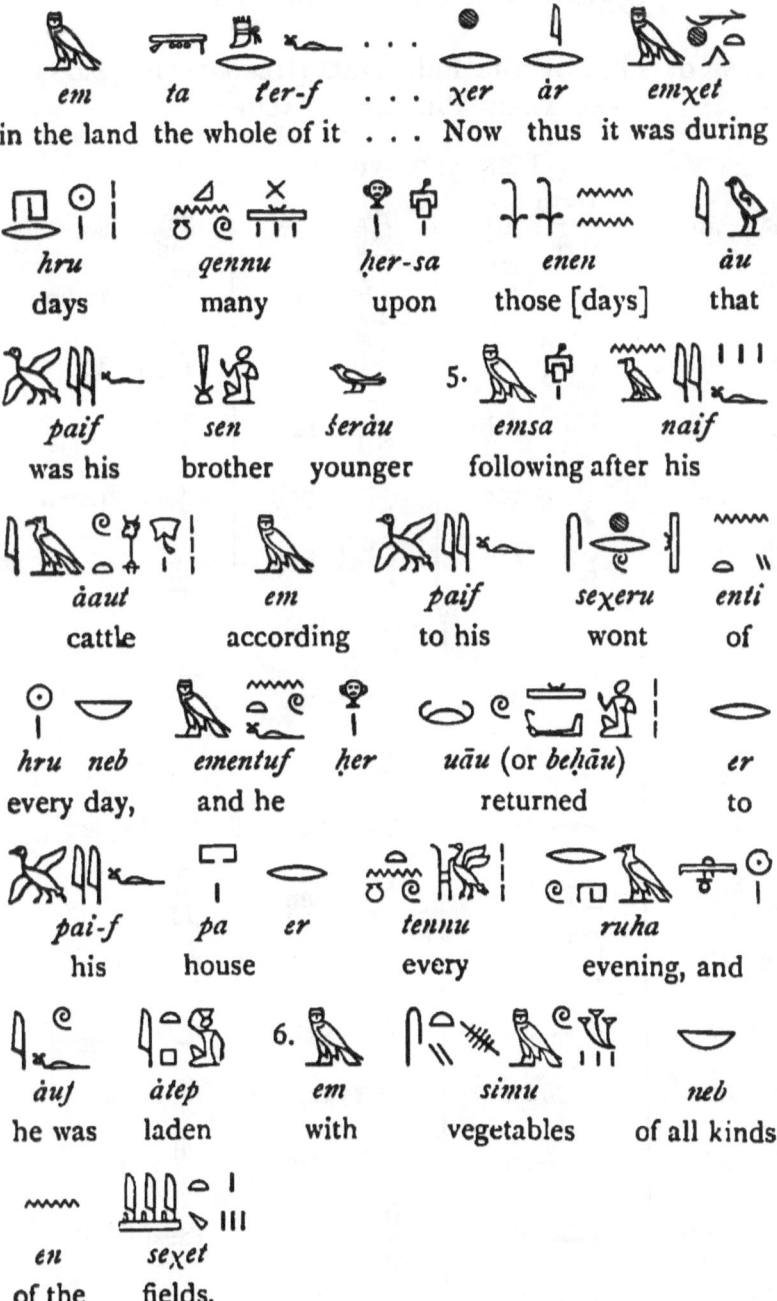

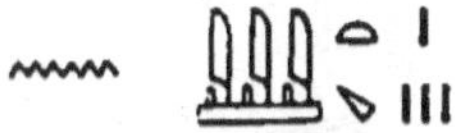

en *seχet*

of the fields.

A List of some of the Principal Hieroglyphic Signs and their Phonetic Values.

Men and Women.

ȧn	āχ	ȧm	śeps
ḥa	qa	ȧr	ȧmen
ur	qeṭ	sa	āb
ser	seḥer	fa	χer
ȧθi	tut	ḥeḥ	ḥenen
ȧau	ȧ	ḥeḥ	maāt

beq

Limbs, &c., of Men.

ṭep, t'at'a	ḥu	χu	sem
ḥrȧ	sept	t'eser	seśem
ȧnem	ka	χen	ȧn
ut'a	χen	ṭ	śes
tȧa	ȧn, ȧt	t'ebā	tet *or* θeθ.
ȧn	ā	ka, met	reṭ
ȧri	mā	sem	b
ȧr, sa	neχt	i	āā, āu
r or l	ṭā	seb	

ANIMALS.

l, r	āb	nefer	ȧb
neḅ	sāb	ka	ba
ser	set	āu	mȧu

LIMBS, &c., OF ANIMALS.

peḥ	śef	χent, fenṭ	āb
ḥā	us	setem	χepes
at	bȧ	ȧp	peḥ
śes	χen	ȧau	nem or uḥem

BIRDS.

Ḥeru, bak	ur	m	u
ba	ba	neḥ	pa
χu	mut	qem	ten
āq	sa	ti	reχ
śerȧ	mẹr	a	t'a
			senṭ

PARTS OF BIRDS.

meḥ	maāt, śu	sa

FISH.

ȧn	χa	betu

REPTILES.

sebek	t'	f
ḥefen	āf, net, χeb seχet	χeper
serq	qam	

TREES AND PLANTS.

åm	net'em	su	i
χet	uat'	resu	mes
ḥen	χa	qemā	ḥet'
un	meḥ	renp	sen
uaḥ	ḥa	śa	ḥen
sek	neχeb	seχet	ås
bener	enen	å	t'er

CELESTIAL OBJECTS.

pet, ḥer	rā	χā	seb, ṭua
θeḥen	χu	åāḥ	

OBJECTS OF EARTH.

ta	ṭu	set	åner

WATER.

mu	n	ś	mer	āb

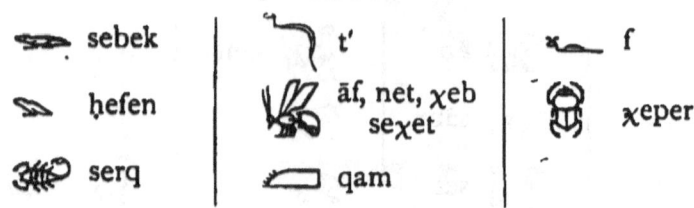

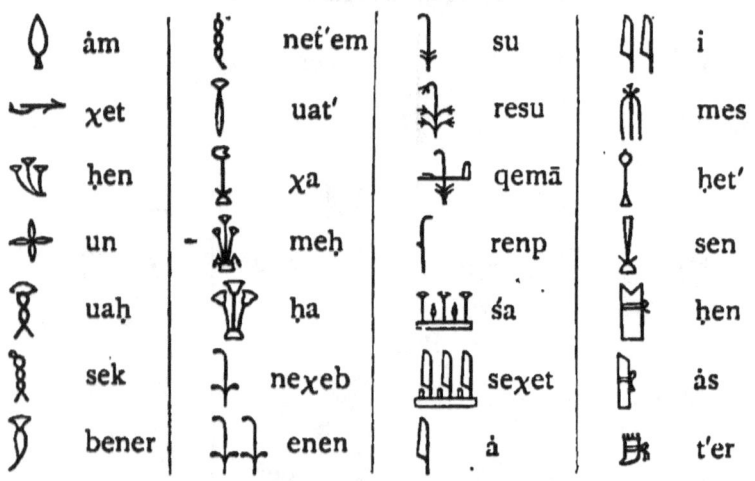

BUILDING.

nu	seḥ	ā	ṭeṭ
per	ḥeb	s	àuset
ḥet	àneb	àn	

ARMS, ETC.

neter	ma	s	net'
ṭes, ṭem	meḥ	ām, t'ā, qem	āb or ḥem
sem	śeṭ	set'eb	menχ
nemmat	χu	χen	χa
seq	ṭem	ut	sa
ṭep	ḥeq	meṭ	sam
āa	āu	θ	setp
uā	us	t'a	ut'ā
peṭ	seχem	men	θ
śemer	χerp	θes, res	mer
àba or aḥā	men	āb, qes, ḳen	
qeṭ	āb	seḥ	

Musical Instruments.

nefer	seχem	maāt
ḥes	men	sa

Crowns.

ḥet'	meḥ	seχet
net	śu	atf

Cords.

qes, śes	ut, ḥeseb	nes	ṭeb
śen	u	āṭ	nub
reṭ	set	θes	χaker
śen	ua	net	śen
ḥ	net, seχet	sa	sāḥ
menχ	mer	āper	ānχ

Mathematical Figures.

χ	ḥu	h	ḥer
sep	sept	mer	t'eṭ
paut	ṭā	rer	qen, t'at'a
t	p	ṭeben	ȧmsu
χemt	ḥap	ren	ȧp
q	uu, ur, śes	tenȧ, peχ	

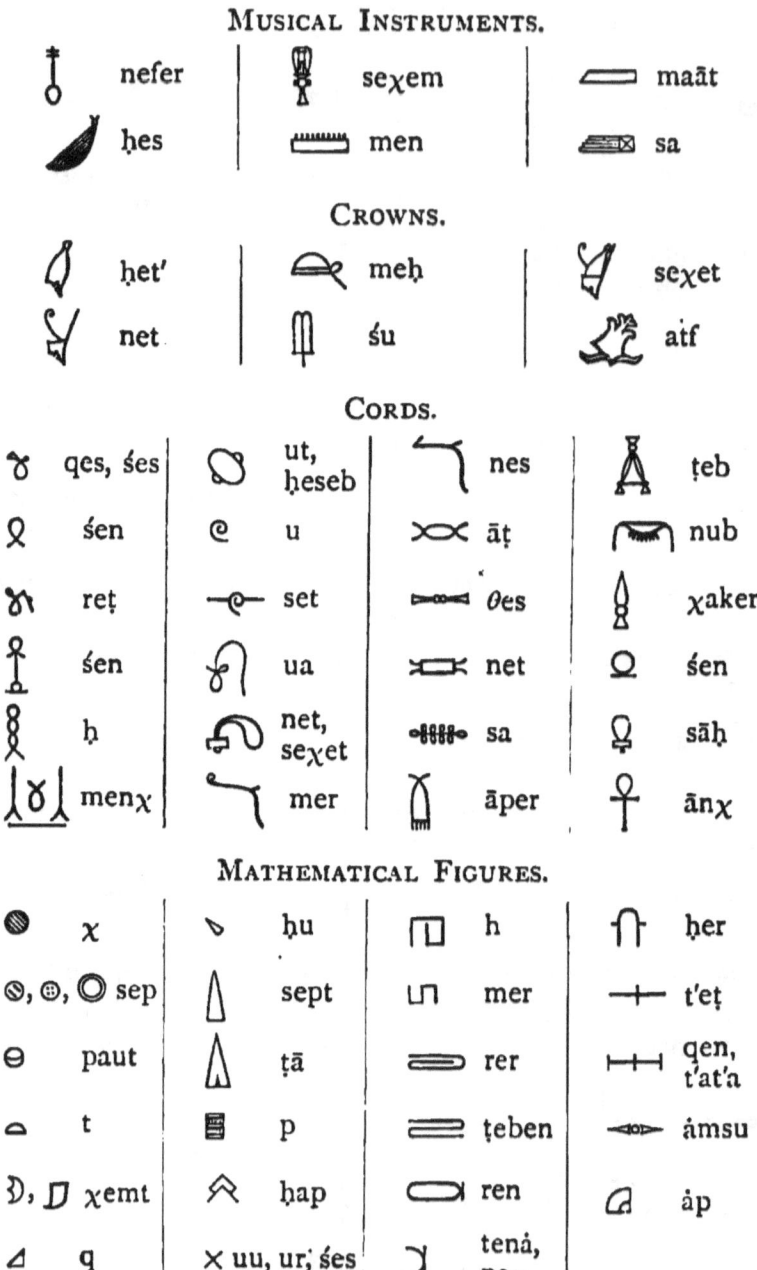

Vases, etc.

	nu		qebḥ		ta		χer
	χnem		ḥen		ta		k
	ȧb		mȧ		ḥetep		neb
	ḥes		āu, āb		ȧa		ḥeb
	χent		ba		ḳ		nā, ān

Ships, etc.

	χent		ḥem		seśep		ȧmaχ
	ȧm		nef		āu		ȧm
	uā, beḥā		āḥā		ḥer, māten		χesef
	χer, ḥep		χent		tem		seχt

Determinatives.

	to call		of women		of birds
	to pray		of birth		of goddesses
	to rejoice		to see		of trees
	to dance		of strength		of grain
	to plough		to give		of heaven
	foes		to walk, stand		of light
	of men		of flesh		of country
	of gods		to breathe, smell		of towns

DETERMINATIVES—*continued.*

	of iron		of metals		of festival
	of water		writing, computation, knowledge, and abstract ideas		of unguents
	of houses				of roads
	of writing				of ships
	of ground		of fire		of winds

THE ARABIC ALPHABET.

Elif	ا	*a*	Zäd	ض	*ḍ* aspirated
Bâ	ب	*b*	Tâ	ط	*ṭ* palatal
Tâ	ت	*t*	Zâ	ظ	*z* palatal
Thâ	ث	*th* = *θ*	‘Ain	† ع	
Gîm	ج	*g* (like *g* in *gin*)*	Ghain	غ	*g* guttural ‡
Hâ	ح	*ḥ* (a smooth guttural aspirate)	Fâ	ف	*f*
Khâ	خ	*ch* (like *ch* in *loch*)	Ḳâf	ق	*ḳ* guttural
Dâl	د	*d*	Kâf	ك	*k*
Zâl	ذ	*th* (like *th* in *that*)	Lâm	ل	*l*
Râ	ر	*r*	Mîm	م	*m*
Zây	ز	*z*	Nûn	ن	*n*
Sîn	س	*s*	Hâ	ه	*h*
Shîn	ش	*sh* (like *sh* in *shut*)	Wâw	و	*w*
Ṣad	ص	*ṣ* (like *ss* in *hiss*)	Yâ	ى	*y*

* Pronounced hard in Egypt.
† Usually unpronounceable by Europeans.
‡ Accompanied by a rattling sound.

The Coptic Alphabet (31 letters).

ⲁ	*a*	ⲙ	*m*	ⲯ	*ps*
ⲃ	*b*	ⲛ	*n*	ⲱ	*ô*
ⲅ	*g*	ⲝ	*x* or *ks*	ϣ	*sh*
ⲇ	*d*	ⲟ	*o*	ϥ	*f*
ⲉ	*e*	ⲡ	*p*	ϧ	χ or *ch*
ⲍ	*z*	ⲣ	*r*	ϩ	*ḥ*
ⲏ	*ê*	ⲥ	*s*	ϫ	*ǵ*
ⲑ	*th*	ⲧ	*t*	ϭ	*c*
ⲓ	*i*	ⲩ	*y*	ϯ	*ti*
ⲕ	*k*	ⲫ	*ph*		
ⲗ	*l*	ⲭ	*ch*		

* In the Boheiric dialect there are thirty-two.

† Six letters of the Coptic alphabet are modifications of the forms o Egyptian characters in demotic. *See* p. 41. The names of the letters in Coptic are ⲁⲗⲫⲁ, ⲃⲓⲇⲁ, ⲅⲁⲙⲙⲁ, ⲇⲁⲗⲇⲁ, ⲉⲓ, ⲍⲓⲧⲁ, ⲏⲧⲁ, ⲑⲓⲧⲁ, ⲓⲁⲩⲧⲁ, ⲕⲁⲡⲡⲁ, ⲗⲁⲩⲗⲁ, ⲙⲓ, ⲛⲓ, ⲝⲓ, ⲟ, ⲡⲓ, ⲣⲟ, ⲥⲓⲙⲁ, ⲧⲁⲩ, ⲩⲉ (ϩⲉ), ⲫⲓ, ⲭⲓ, ⲯⲓ, ⲁⲩ, ϣⲉⲓ, ϥⲉⲓ, ϧⲉⲓ, ϩⲟⲣⲓ, ϫⲁⲛϫⲓⲁ, ϭⲓⲙⲁ, ⲧⲓ.

Names of the Months.

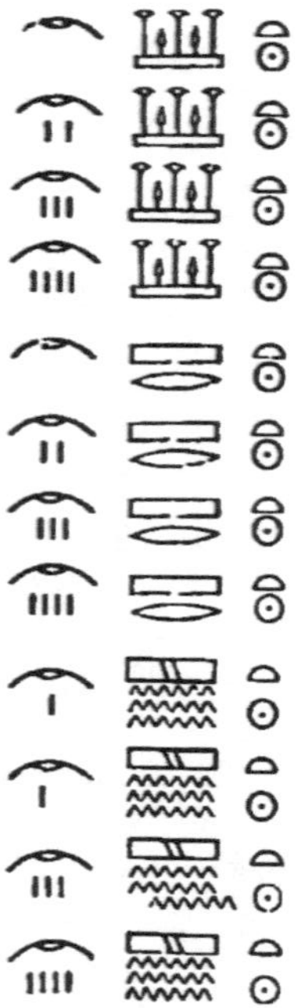

Egyptian.		Alexandrian Months (Coptic Forms).		
àbeṭ uā śat	Month one of sowing	ⲑⲱⲟⲩⲧ	August	29 *
àbeṭ sen śat	Month two of sowing	ⲡⲁⲟⲡⲓ	September	28
àbeṭ chemt śat	Month three of sowing	ⲁⲑⲱⲣ	October	28
àbeṭ fṭu śat	Month four of sowing	ⲭⲟⲓⲁⲕ	November	27
àbeṭ uā pert	Month one of growing	ⲧⲱⲃⲓ	December	27
àbeṭ sen pert	Month two of growing	ⲙⲉⲭⲓⲣ	January	26
àbeṭ chemt pert	Month three of growing	ⲫⲁⲙⲉⲛⲱⲑ	February	25
àbeṭ fṭu pert	Month four of growing	ⲫⲁⲣⲙⲟⲩⲑⲓ	March	27
àbeṭ uā śet	Month one of inundation	ⲡⲁⲭⲟⲛ	April	26
àbeṭ sen śet	Month two of inundation	ⲡⲁⲱⲛⲓ	May	26
àbeṭ chemt śet	Month three of inundation	ⲉⲡⲏⲡ	June	25
àbeṭ fṭu śet	Month four of inundation	ⲙⲉⲥⲱⲣⲏ	July	25

* The days for the beginnings of these months were first fixed at Alexandria about B.C. 30.

The ancient Egyptians had: I. the vague or civil year, which consisted of 365 days; it was divided into twelve months of thirty days each, and five intercalary days were added at the end; II. the Sothic year of 365¼ days. The first year of a Sothic period began with the rising of Sirius or the dog-star, on the 1st of the month Thoth, when it coincided with the beginning of the inundation; III. the Egyptian solar year* was treated as if it were a quarter of a day shorter than the Sothic year, an error which corrected itself in 1460 fixed years or 1461 vague years. The true year was estimated approximately by the conjunction of the sun with Sirius. Dr. Brugsch thinks (*Egypt under the Pharaohs*, Vol. I., p. 176) that as early as B.C. 2500 *five* different forms of the year were already in use, and that the "little year" corresponded with the lunar year, and the "great year" with a lunar year having intercalated days. Each month was dedicated to a god.† The Egyptians dated their stelæ and documents by the day of the month and the year of the king who was reigning at the time. The Copts first dated their documents according to the years of the INDICTION; the indictions were periods of fifteen years, and the first began A.D. 312. In later times the Copts made use of the era of the Martyrs, which was reckoned from the 29th of August, A.D. 284. About the ninth century after Christ they began to adopt the Muḥammadan era of the Hijrah or "flight," which was reckoned from A.D. 622.

* It was practically the same as the civil year.

† Some of the Coptic names of the months show that they have been derived from the ancient Egyptian: thus Thôth is from , *Teḥuti*, Pachôn from  *Chensu*, Athôr from , *Ḥet-Ḥeru*, Mesôre from  *mes-Ḥeru*, "the birth of Horus" festival, etc. The Copts have I. an agricultural year, and II. an ecclesiastical year; the latter consists of twelve months of thirty days, with a thirteenth month called Nissi of five or six intercalary days.

THE RELIGION AND GODS OF EGYPT.

The religion of the ancient Egyptians is one of the most difficult problems of Egyptology, and though a great deal has been written about it during the last few years, and many difficulties have been satisfactorily explained, there still remain unanswered a large number of questions connected with it. In all religious texts the reader is always assumed to have a knowledge of the subject treated of by the writer, and no definite statement is made on the subject concerning which very little, comparatively, is known by students to-day. For example, in the texts inscribed inside the pyramids of Unȧs, Tetȧ, and Pepi (B.C. 3300–3233), we are brought face to face with religious compositions which mention the acts and relationships of the gods, and refer to beliefs, and give instructions for the performance of certain acts of ritual which are nowhere explained. It will be remembered that Ptolemy II. Philadelphus instructed Manetho to draw up a history of the religion of the ancient Egyptians. If such a work was needed by the cultured Greek who lived when the religion of ancient Egypt, though much modified, was still in existence, how much more is it needed now? The main beliefs of the Egyptian religion were always the same. The attributes of one god might be applied to another, or one god might be confused with another; the cult of one god might decline in favour of another, or new gods might arise and become popular, but the foundation of the religion of Egypt remained unchanged. Still, it is asserted by some that the religion of the dynasties of the Early Empire was simpler and more free from speculation than that of the Middle and New Empires, in which the nature and mutual relationships of the gods were discussed and theogonies formulated. Speaking generally the gods of Egypt were the everlasting and unalterable powers of nature, *i.e.*, 'day and night,' 'light and darkness,' etc. The great god of the Egyptians, Rā, or Ȧmen-Rā, as he was called in the Middle Empire, was said to be the maker of all things; the various gods Horus, Ȧtmu, etc., were merely forms of him. Rā was self-begotten, and hymns to him never cease to proclaim his absolute and perfect unity in terms which resemble those of the Hebrew Scriptures. It will be seen from the translation of a hymn given in the following pages that he is made to possess every attribute, natural and spiritual, which Christian peoples ascribe to God Almighty. The one doctrine, however, which lived persistently and unchanged in the Egyptian mind for five thousand years, is that of a future life. During the earliest dynasties beautiful and enduring tombs* were built in order that the bodies which were placed in them might be preserved until such time as the resurrection of the body should take place. It is clear from the papyri that man was supposed to possess a body, a soul,  *ba*, a 'genius'  *ka*, and an intelligence,  *χu*. The body, freed from all its most corruptible portions, was preserved by being filled with bitumen, spices, and

* "Les belles tombes que l'on admire dans les plaines de Thèbes et de Saḳḳârah ne sont donc pas dues à l'orgueil de ceux qui les ont érigées. Une pensée plus large a présidé à leur construction. Plus les matériaux sont énormes, plus on est sûr que les promesses faites par la religion recevront leur exécution. En ces sens, les Pyramides ne sont pas des monuments 'de la vaine ostentation des rois'; elles sont des obstacles impossibles à renverser, et les preuves gigantesques d'un dogme consolant." (Mariette, *Notices des Principaux Monuments*, p. 44.)

aromatic drugs, and having been bandaged in many a fold of linen, lay in its tomb, ready to take part in the life which was inherited by those who were deemed worthy of it.

Of the funeral procession we are able to gain some idea from the vignettes which are given in hieroglyphic copies of the Book of the Dead. In the centre of p. 75 the dead man is seen lying on a bier in a chest mounted on a boat with runners, which is drawn by oxen. In the rear is a sepulchral ark or chest surmounted by a figure of Anubis, the god of the dead. In front of the boat are a group of women (p. 76) beating their faces and wailing, and a youth carrying the staff, chair, and box of the deceased. At the head of the procession is the *kher ḥeb* or master of funereal ceremonies, who reads from an open roll of papyrus the funereal service. The scene on page 76 represents the ceremony of "opening the mouth," which takes place at the door of the tomb. Before the tomb stands the mummy of Hu-nefer to receive the final honours; behind him, and embracing him, stands Anubis, the god of the dead, and at his feet in front kneel his wife Nasha and her daughter to take a last farewell of the body. By the side of a table of offerings stand three priests: the *sem* priest, who wears a panther's skin, holding in his right hand a libation vase, and in the left a censer; a priest who offers vases of unguents to the deceased; and a priest who holds in one hand the instrument *ur-ḥeka* 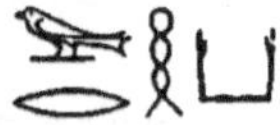 with which he is about to touch the eyes and mouth of the mummy, and in the other the instrument  for "opening the mouth." On the rounded stele , at the door of the tomb, is inscribed:—"Hail, Osiris, chief of Amenta, the lord of eternity, spreading out in everlastingness, lord of adorations, chief of the cycle of his gods; and hail, Anubis [dweller] in

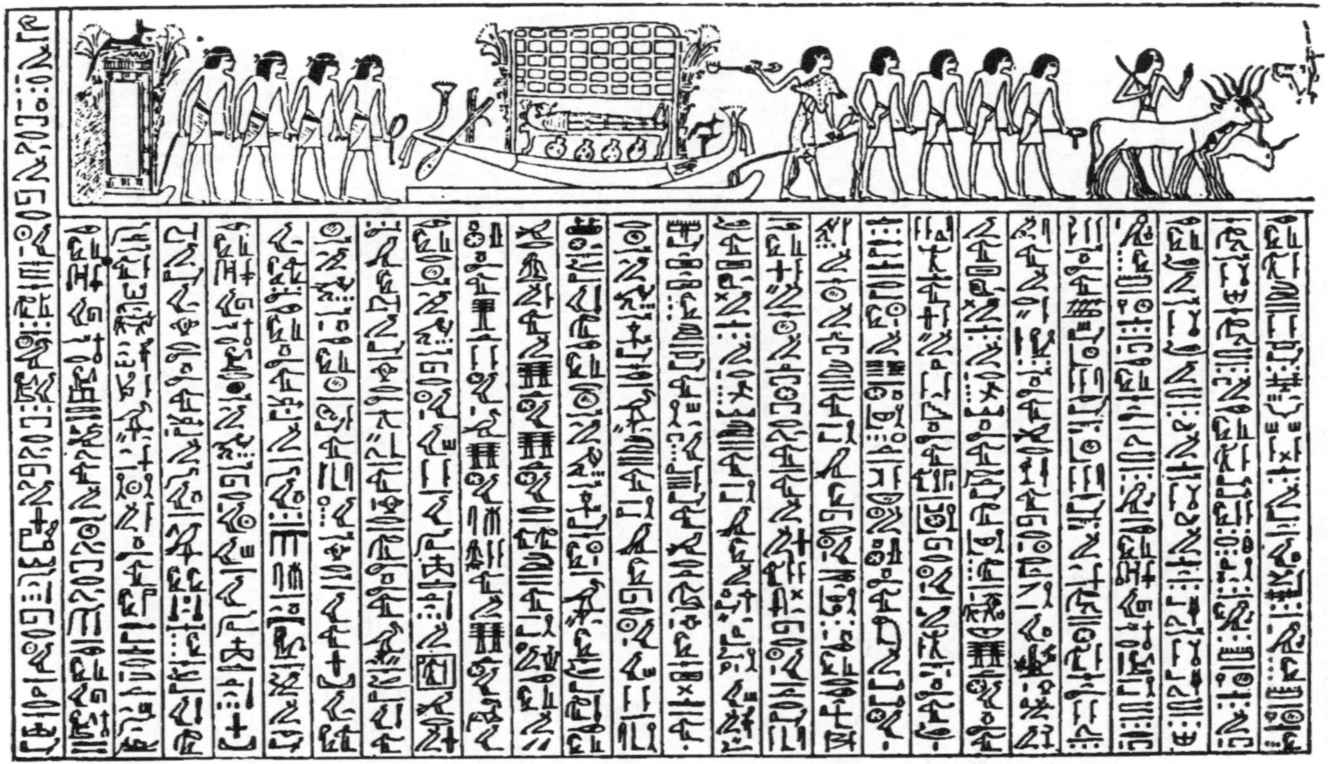

An Egyptian Funeral Procession. The hieroglyphic text beneath is the First Chapter of the Book of the Dead.
(From British Museum Papyrus, No. 9,901.)

An Egyptian Funeral Procession and the Performance of the Ceremony of "Opening the Mouth" at the Door of the Tomb. (From British Museum Papyrus, No. 9,901.)

the tomb, great god, chief of the divine dwelling. May they grant that I may go in and come out from the underworld; that I may follow Osiris in all his festivals at the beginning of the year; that I may receive cakes, and that I may come forth in the presence of [Osiris], I the *ka* of Osiris, the greatly favoured of his god, Hu-nefer."

In the lower register are a cow and calf, a priest holding a vase, a priest carrying a haunch of a bull, a table of offerings, a sepulchral box, and a table upon which are arranged the instruments employed in the ceremony of opening the mouth, *viz.*, the *Pesh-en-kef*, the haunch, the libation vases, the feather, the instruments, the *ur-ḥeka*, the boxes of purification, the bandlet, *etc.*

After the death of a man it was thought that he was taken into the hall of the god Osiris, judge of the dead, and that his conscience, symbolized by the heart, was weighed in the balance before him. An excellent idea of what the Egyptians believed in this matter may be gathered from the two following scenes in the Papyrus of Ani. Ani and his wife Thuthu are entering the Hall of Double Truth, wherein the heart is to be weighed against the feather, emblematic of Right and Truth, or Law. This ceremony is being performed in the presence of the gods "Ḥeru-khuti (Harmachis) the great god within his boat"; Temu; Shu; "Tefnut, lady of heaven,"; Seb; "Nut, lady of heaven,"; Isis; Nephthys; "Horus, the great god,"; "Hathor,

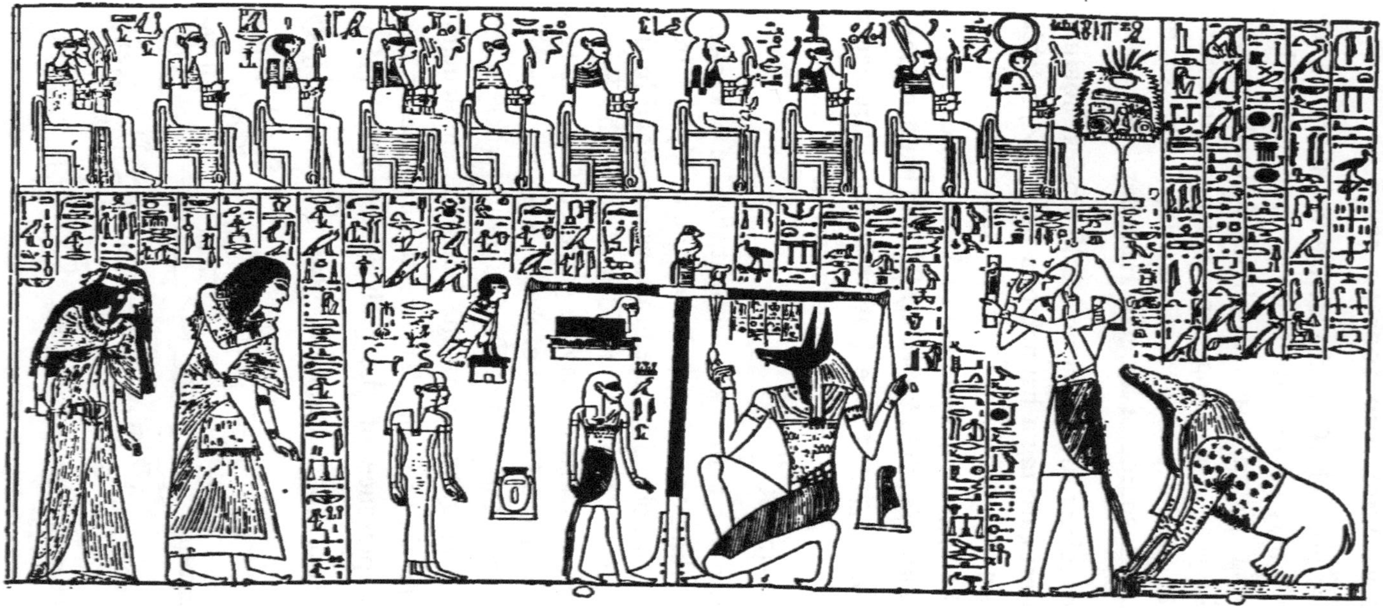

The Heart of Ani being Weighed in the Balance.

(From British Museum Papyrus, No. 10,470.)

Horus introducing Ani to the God Osiris.

(From British Museum Papyrus, No. 10,470.)

lady of Amenta," ; Ḥu ; and Sa . Upon the beam of the scales is the dog-headed ape , the companion or attendant of Thoth, "the scribe of the gods." The god Anubis, jackal-headed, is kneeling to examine the indicator of the balance, which is suspended from a projection made in the form of . The inscription above the head of Anubis reads:—"Saith he who is in the abode of the dead, 'Turn thy face, O just and righteous weigher [who weighest] the heart in the balance, to stablish it.'" Facing Anubis, the god of the dead, stands Ani's "Luck" or "Destiny," *Shai* , and above is a human-headed object resting upon a pylon which is supposed to be connected with the place where he was born. Behind these stand the goddesses Meskhenet  and Renenet , who were the deities who presided over the birth and education of children. Near these is the soul of Ani in the form of a human-headed bird , standing upon a pylon . On the right of the balance, behind Anubis, stands Thoth, the scribe of the gods, with his reed-pen and palette containing black and red ink, with which to record the result of the trial. Behind Thoth is the female monster Āmām 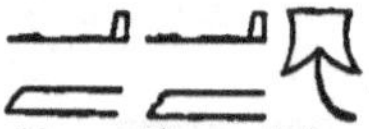, the "Devourer," called also Ām-mit   the "Eater of the Dead." She has the fore-part of a crocodile, the hind-quarters of a hippopotamus, and the middle part of a lion. Ani says:—

"My heart my mother, my heart my mother, my heart my coming into being. May there be no resistance to me in [my] judgment; may there be no opposition to me from the divine chiefs; may there be no parting of thee from me in the presence of him who keepeth the scales! Thou art my *ka* (double) within my body which knitteth and strengtheneth my limbs. Mayest thou come forth to the place of happiness to which we advance. May the divine chiefs (*Shenit*) not make my name to stink, and may no lies be spoken against me in the presence of the god. It is good for thee to hear [glad tidings of joy at the weighing of words. May no false accusation be made against me in the presence of the great god. Verily, exceedingly mighty shalt thou be when thou risest]."

Thoth, the righteous judge of the great cycle of the gods who are in the presence of the god Osiris, saith, "Hear ye this judgment. The heart of Osiris hath in very truth been weighed and his soul hath stood as a witness for him; his trial in the Great Balance is true. There hath not been found any wickedness in him; he hath not wasted the offerings in the temples; he hath not harmed any by his works; and he uttered not evil reports while he was upon earth."

Next the great cycle of the gods reply to Thoth dwelling in Khemennu (Hermopolis): "That which cometh forth from thy mouth cannot be gainsaid. Osiris, the scribe Ani, the victorious one in judgment, is just and righteous. He hath not committed sin, neither hath he done evil against us. The Devourer shall not be allowed to prevail over him; he shall be allowed to enter into the presence of the god Osiris, and offerings of meat and drink shall be given unto him, together with an abiding habitation in Sekhet-ḥetepu, as unto the followers of Horus."

In the second part of this scene we have Ani being led into the presence of the god Osiris. On the left the hawk-headed god Horus , the son of Isis, wearing the crowns

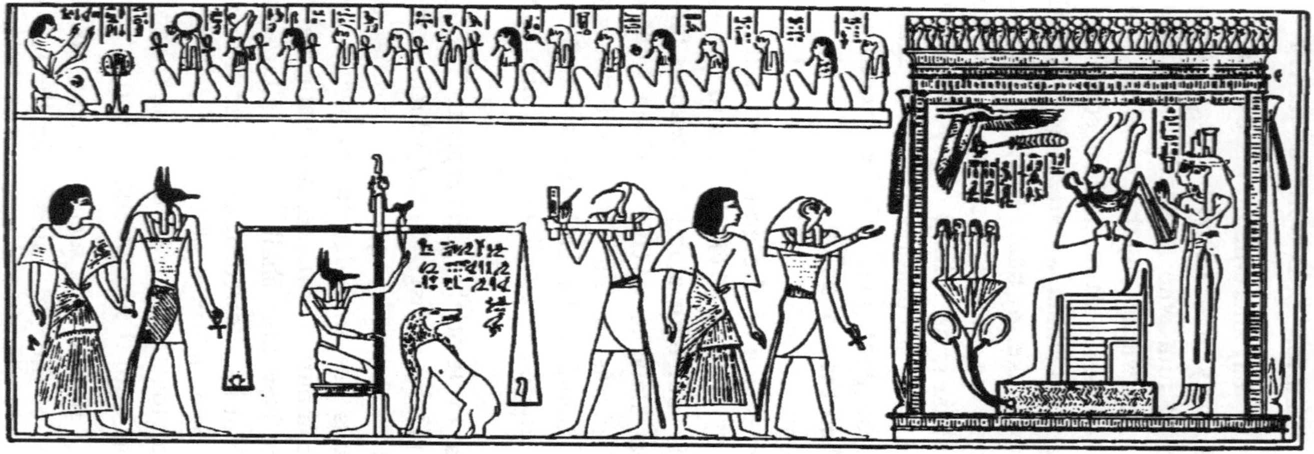

Scene of the Weighing of the Heart in the Hall of Osiris.
(From British Museum Papyrus, No. 9901.)

of the North and South , holding Ani by the hand, leads him into the presence of "Osiris, the lord of eternity,"  *Ȧusȧr neb t'etta.* This god is seated within a shrine in the form of a funereal chest, and he wears the *atef* crown , with plumes; at the back of his neck hangs a *menȧt* , the emblem of joy and happiness. In his hands he holds the crook , sceptre , and the flail , emblems of rule, sovereignty and dominion. On the side of his throne  are depicted the doors of the tomb with bolts, . Behind him stand Nephthys on his right and Isis on his left. Standing upon a lotus flower which springs from the ground, are the four deities generally known as "the children of Horus" (or Osiris); they represent the cardinal points. The first, Mesthȧ 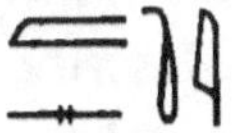, has the head of a man ; the second, Ḥāpi , the head of an ape ; the third, Ṭuamāutef , the head of a jackal ; and the fourth, Qebḥsennuf, , the head of a hawk . Suspended near the lotus flower is a bullock's hide, into which the deceased, or the person who represented him at funereal ceremonies, was supposed to enter. The roof of the shrine rests upon pillars with lotus capitals, and is ornamented with a cornice of uræi; the hawk-headed figure above represents the god Horus-Sept or Horus-Seker.

At the foot of steps leading to the throne of Osiris, kneels Ani upon a mat made of fresh reeds; his right hand is raised in adoration, and in his left he holds the *kherp* sceptre. He wears a whitened wig surmounted by a "cone," the signification of which is unknown. Round his neck is the collar. Close by are a table of offerings of meat, fruit, flowers, *etc.*, and a number of vases containing wine, beer, unguents, , , , *etc.*; with these are trussed ducks, flowers, cakes and loaves of bread, , O, *etc.* The inscription above the table of offerings reads, "Osiris, the scribe Ani." . The inscription above Ani reads: "O Lord of Amenta (the underworld), I am in thy presence. There is no sin in my body, I have uttered no lie wilfully, and I have done nothing with a double motive. Grant that I may be like unto those favoured beings who [stand] about thee, and that I may be an Osiris greatly favoured of the beautiful god and beloved of the lord of the world—[I] who am in truth a royal scribe loving him, Ani, victorious in judgment before the god Osiris."

To Osiris Horus says:—"I have come to thee, O Unnefer, and I have brought the Osiris Ani to thee. His heart is righteous coming forth from the balance, and it hath not committed sin against any god or any goddess. Thoth hath weighed it according to the directions spoken to him by the cycle of the gods; and it is very true and righteous. Grant unto him offerings of meat and drink, permit him to enter into the presence of Osiris, and grant that he may be like unto the followers of Horus for ever."

An interesting vignette in the papyrus of Neb-seni (British Museum, No. 9900) shows the deceased being weighed against his own heart in the presence of the god Osiris:

If the result of the weighing of the heart was unfavourable, the Devourer stepped forward and claimed the dead man as his. Annihilation was the result.

The following is a specimen of the hymns which the deceased addresses to Rā :—

A HYMN TO RĀ [TO BE SUNG] WHEN HE RISETH IN THE EASTERN SKY.

(*From British Museum Papyrus, No.* 9901.)

"Homage to thee, O thou who art Rā when thou risest and Tmu when thou settest. Thou risest, thou risest; thou shinest, thou shinest, O thou who art crowned king of the gods. Thou art the lord of heaven, thou art the lord of earth, thou art the creator of those who dwell in the heights, and of those who dwell in the depths. Thou art the ONE god who came into being in the beginning of time. Thou didst create the earth, thou didst fashion man, thou didst make the watery abyss of the sky, thou didst form Ḥāpi (Nile); thou art the maker of all streams and of the great deep, and thou givest life to all that is therein. Thou hast knit together the mountains, thou, thou hast made mankind and the beasts of the field, thou hast created the heavens and the earth. Worshipped be thou whom the goddess Maāt embraceth at morn and at eve. Thou stridest across the sky with heart expanded with joy; the Lake of Testes is at peace. The fiend Nȧk hath fallen and his two arms are cut off. The boat of the rising sun hath a fair wind, and the heart of him that is in its shrine rejoiceth. Thou art crowned with a heavenly form, thou the Only ONE art provided [with all things] Rā cometh forth from Nu [sky] in triumph. O thou mighty youth, thou everlasting son, self-begotten, who didst give birth to thyself; O thou mighty One of myriad forms and aspects, King of the world, Prince of Ȧnnu (Heliopolis), lord of eternity, and ruler of the everlasting; the company of the gods rejoice when thou risest, and when thou sailest across the sky, O thou who art exalted in the *sektet* boat. Homage to thee, O Ȧmen-Rā, thou who dost rest upon Maāt, thou who passest over heaven, [from] every face that seeth thee. Thou dost wax great as thy Majesty doth advance, and thy rays are upon all faces. Thou art unknown and inscrutable . . . . ; thou art the Only One. [Men] praise thee in thy name [Rā], and they swear by thee, for thou art lord over them. Thou hast heard with thine ears and thou hast seen with thine eyes. Millions of years have gone over the world; those through which thou hast passed I cannot count. Thy heart hath decreed a day of happiness in thy name [of Rā]. Thou dost pass over and travellest through untold spaces of millions and hundreds of thousands of years, thou settest in peace and thou steerest thy way across the watery abyss to the place which thou lovest; this thou doest in one little moment of time, and thou dost sink down and makest an end of the hours. Hail my lord, thou that passest through eternity and whose being is everlasting. Hail thou Disk, lord of beams of light, thou risest and thou makest all mankind to live. Grant thou that I may behold thee at dawn each day."

From the scene on p. 87, we may form an idea of how the deceased was supposed to employ his time in the "islands of the blessed," which the Egyptians called "Seχet-

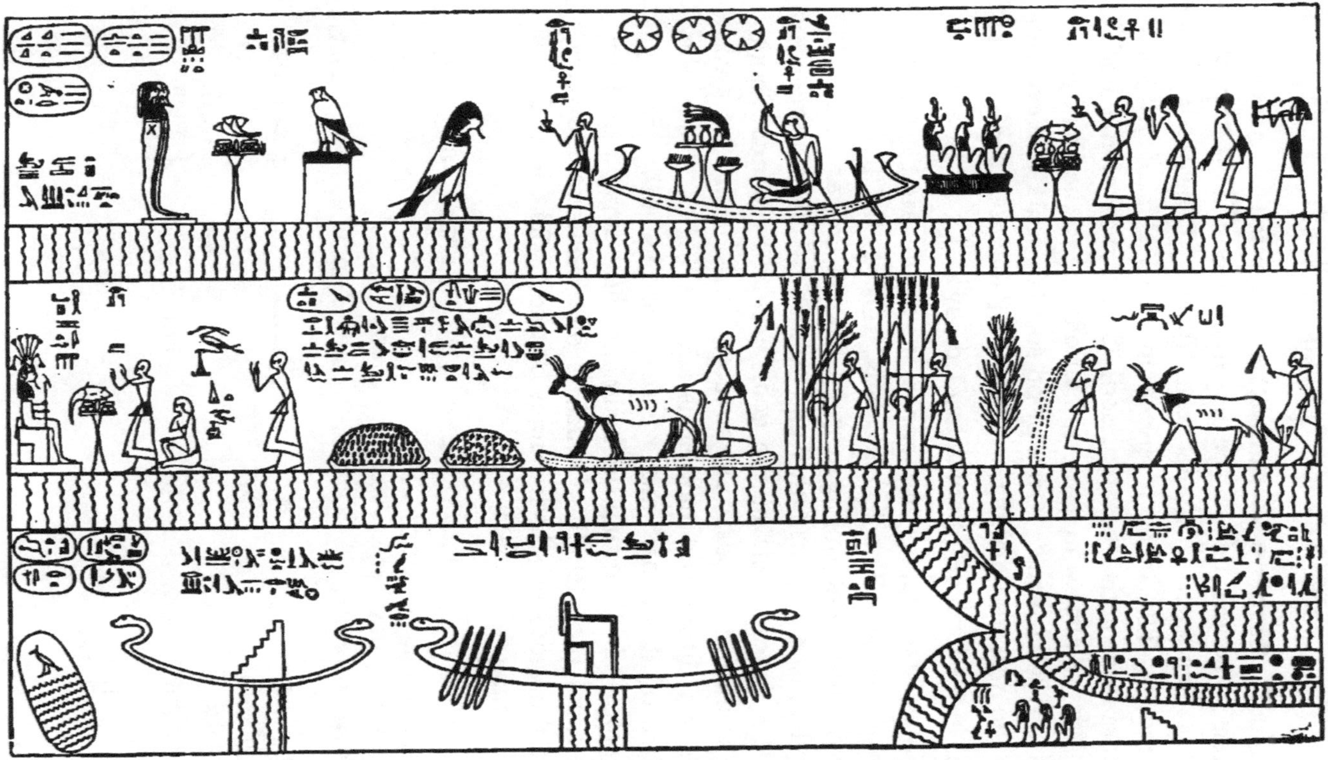

THE SEKHET-HETEPU OR ELYSIAN FIELDS OF THE EGYPTIANS.

Ḥetepu." Here we have an estate intersected by canals of waters. To the left in the upper division are three pools called Qenqenet, Ȧnttenet and Nut-ur. Beneath is the legend :—"The being in peace in the Fields of Air (?)." Before three gods who are described as "gods of the horizon," is an altar with flowers, "an offering to the great god, the lord of heaven." On a pylon stands a hawk. Next we see the deceased making an offering of incense to his own soul in the form of a human-headed hawk . In a boat, in which stand tables of offerings, sits the deceased paddling himself along. The legend reads, "Osiris, the living one, the victorious one sailing over the Lake of Peace." Behind, the deceased and his father and mother are offering incense to the "great cycle of the gods"; close by stands Thoth the scribe of the gods. In the second division the deceased, with his father and mother, is adoring "Ḥāpi (Nile), the father of the gods," and we see him ploughing, sowing, reaping and winnowing the luxuriant wheat along a track by he canal the "length of which is one thousand measures, and the width of which cannot be told." The legend says concerning this canal :—

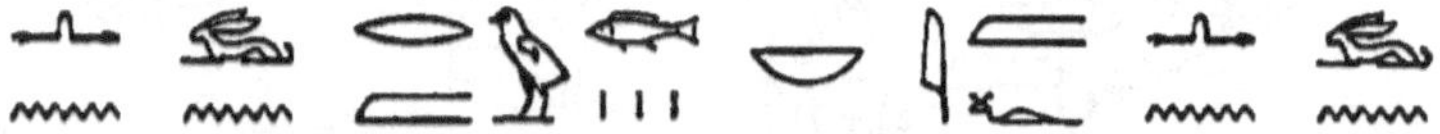

ȧn	*un*	*remu*	*neb*	*ȧm-f*	*ȧn*	*un*
"Not	exist	fishes	any	in it,	not	exist

ȧu	*neb*	*ȧm-f*	*ȧn*	*un*	*ḥefi*
ȧu fishes	any	in it,	not	exist	{ worms snakes

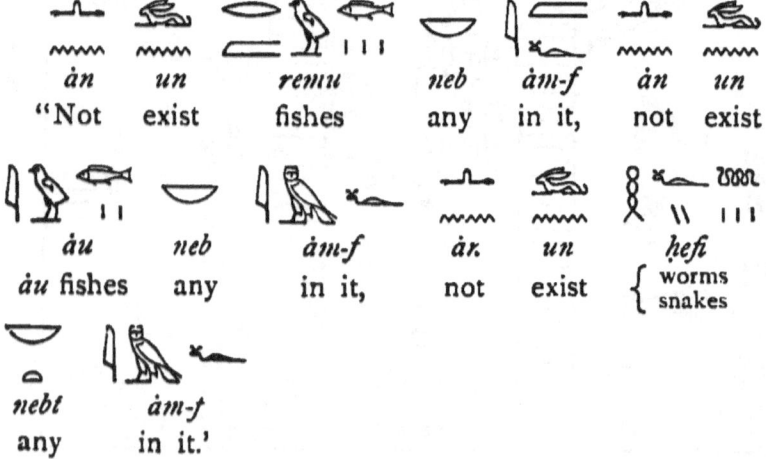

nebt	*ȧm-f*
any	in it.'

In the third division are:—five islands (?); "the boat of Rā-Harmachis when he goeth forth to Sekhet-Åanre"; a boat the master of which is the god Un-nefer; and three small divisions formed by the "water of the sky." In the first are "beatified beings seven cubits high, and wheat three cubits high for spiritual beings who are made perfect"; the second is the place where the gods refresh themselves; and in the third live the gods Seb, Shu and Tefnut.

After death the soul of the dead man was supposed to have many enemies to combat, just as the sun was supposed to spend the time between his rising and setting in fighting the powers of mist, darkness, and night. These he vanquished by the knowledge and use of certain "words of power." The deceased was also supposed to be condemned to perform field labours in the nether-world, but to avoid this, stone, wooden, or Egyptian porcelain figures were placed in his tomb to do the work for him. After undergoing all these troubles and trials the soul went into

THE SOUL REVISITING THE BODY IN THE TOMB.
(From the Papyrus of Neb-seni, British Museum, No. 9900.)

the abode of beatified spirits, and there did everything wished by it, and remained in bliss until it rejoined its body in the tomb. During its wanderings it might enter successively into a phœnix (*bennu*), a heron, a swallow, a snake, a crocodile, etc.

In the hall of Osiris the soul was supposed to affirm before forty-two gods that it had not committed any of the forty-two sins which are detailed in good papyri at full length as follows:—

1. O thou that stridest, coming forth from Heliopolis, I have done no wrong.*
2. O thou that embracest flame, coming forth from Cher-āba, I have not committed theft.
3. O Fenṭiu, who comest forth from Hermopolis, I have committed no act of violence.
4. O Eater of Shadows, who comest forth from Qernet, I have never slain men.
5. O Neḥa-ḥrȧ, who comest forth from Re-stau, I have never filched from the measures of corn.
6. O ye double lions, who come forth from the sky, I have committed no fault.
7. O Eyes of Flame, who come forth from Seaut, I have never stolen the property of the gods.
8. O Neba (*i.e.*, Fire), who comest forth in retreating, I have never spoken falsehood.
9. O Seizer of Bones, who comest forth from Suten-ḥenen, I have never stolen food to eat.
10. O Breath of Flame, who comest forth from the Ḥet-ka-Ptaḥ (Memphis), I have spoken no evil.
11. O Qererti, who comest forth from the underworld, I have committed no act of uncleanness.
12. O thou god whose face is turned behind thee, who comest forth from thy shrine, I have never caused any one to weep tears of sadness.

* From the Papyrus of Ani, Brit. Mus. No. 10,470, plates 31, 32. For a complete translation of the 125th Chapter of the *Book of the Dead*, to which this Confession belongs, see my *Papyrus of Ani*, London, 1895, pp. 344 ff.

13. O Basti, who comest forth from the tomb (?), I have never eaten my heart (*i.e.*, lied).
14. O Legs of Flame, who come forth from the darkness of night, I have never made an attack upon any man.
15. O Eater of Blood, who comest forth from the block of sacrifice, I have never meditated upon iniquity.
16. O Eater of the intestines, who comest forth from the Abode of the Thirty, I have never stolen tilled ground.
17. O Lord of Law, who comest forth from the abode of Law, I have never entered into a conspiracy.
18. O thou that stridest backwards, who comest forth from Bubastis, I have never accused any man of crime.
19. O Serṭiu, who comest forth from Heliopolis, I have never been angry without cause.
20. O god of two-fold evil, who comest forth from the nome Atchi,* I have never committed adultery.
21. O Uamemti, who comest forth from Chebt, I have never committed adultery.
22. O thou that observest what hath been brought into the Temple of Åmsu, I have never defiled myself.
23. O ye Chiefs, who come forth from the persea trees, I have never caused terror.
24. O Chemi, who comest forth from Ḳu, I have never transgressed.
25. O Reciter of words, who comest forth from Urit, I have never spoken in hot anger.
26. O Babe, who comest forth from Uab,† I have never made my ear (*literally*, face) deaf to the sound of words of truth.
27. O Kenememti, who comest forth from Kenemmet, I have never uttered curses.
28. O thou that bringest thy offering, who comest forth from Seut, I have never put out my hand in a quarrel.

* The ninth nome of Lower Egypt.

† The 19th nome of Upper Egypt, capital Oxyrhynchos.

29. O thou that orderest words, who comest forth from Unaset, I have never been an excitable and contentious person.
30. O Lord of [various] aspects, who comest forth from Netchefet, I have never been precipitate in judgment.
31. O Secheriu, who comest forth from Uten, I have never stirred up conspiracy.
32. O Lord of the double horns, who comest forth from Senti, I have never multiplied my words against those of others.
33. O Nefer-Tmu, who comest forth from Ḥet-ka-Ptaḥ (Memphis), I have never meditated evil, and I have never done evil.
34. O Tmu in his seasons, who comest forth from Ṭaṭṭu, I have never committed an act of wrong against the king.
35. O thou that workest in thy heart, who comest forth from Sahu, I have never turned running water out of its course.
36. O Akhi, who comest forth from Nu, I have never been arrogant in speech.
37. O thou who verdifiest mankind, who comest from Seu, I have never blasphemed God.
38. O Neḥebka, who comest forth from thy shrine, I have never committed fraud.
39. O thou who art dowered with splendours, who comest forth from thy shrine, I have never defrauded the gods of their offerings.
40. O Ser-ṭep, who comest forth from [thy] shrine, I have never robbed the dead.
41. O thou that bringest thy arm, who comest forth from the place of double truth, I have never robbed the child nor defiled the god of [my] town.
42. O Illuminator of the lands, who comest forth from Tashe (Fayyûm), I have never slain the animals sacred to the gods.

It is tolerably evident then that grand tombs were not built as mere objects of pride, but as "everlasting habitations" which would serve to preserve the body from decay, and keep it ready to be re-inhabited by the soul at the proper season. Greek authors have written much about the beliefs of the Egyptians; but the greater number of their statements are to be received with caution. They wrote down what they were told, but were frequently misinformed.

The papyri which have come down to us show that the moral conceptions of the Egyptians were of a very high order: and works like the Maxims of Ptaḥ-ḥetep and the Maxims of Ani* show clearly that a man's duty to his god and to his fellow-man was laid down in a distinct manner. Such works will compare very favourably with the Proverbs of Solomon and the Wisdom of Jesus the son of Sirach.

The religious literature of the Egyptians includes a large number of works, of which the most important is the collection of chapters generally called the **Book of the Dead**; in Egyptian its name is *per em hru*, "Coming forth by day." Selections from this work were written in the hieratic character upon coffins as early as the XIIth dynasty (B.C. 2500), and this practice was continued down to the second century of our era. The walls of tombs were covered with extracts from it, and scribes and people of rank had buried with them large rolls of papyrus inscribed with its principal chapters, and ornamented with vignettes explanatory of the text which ran beneath. Some of the chapters in the work are of very great antiquity; and so far back as B.C. 3500 the text was so old, and had been copied so often, that it was already not to be understood. Many parts of it are obscure, and many utterly corrupt; but the discovery from time to time of ancient papyri with accurate readings tends to clear up many doubtful points, and to bring out the right meaning of certain parts of the work.

* See page 191.

The following is a list of the most important gods with their names in hieroglyphs; it will be readily seen how very many of them are merely forms of the sun-god Rā, and how many of them have the same attributes:—

CHNEMU,* the 'Moulder,' , is represented with the head of a ram, and is one of the oldest gods of the Egyptian religion. He was thought to possess some of the attributes of Åmen, Rā, and Ptaḥ, and shared with the last-named god the attribute of "maker of mankind." At Philæ he is represented making man out of clay on a potter's wheel. Chnemu put together the scattered limbs of the dead body of Osiris, and it was he who constructed the beautiful woman who became the wife of Bata in the Tale of the Two Brothers. Like Åmen-Rā he is said to be the father of the gods. His cult had great vogue in the regions round about the first cataract, where he was always associated with Aneq and Sati. In bas-reliefs he is usually coloured green, and wears the *atef* crown† with uræi, etc.

CHNEMU.

* The authorities for the figures of the gods are given by Lanzone in his *Dizionario di Mitologia Egizia.*

† The following are the crowns most commonly met with on the monuments:—

PTAḤ, the 'Opener,' perhaps the oldest of all the gods of Egypt, was honoured with a temple and worshipped at Memphis from the time of the Ist dynasty. He is said to be the father of the gods, who came forth from his eye, and of men, who came forth from his mouth. He is represented in the form of a mummy, and he holds a sceptre composed of *usr*, 'strength,' *ānch*, 'life,' and *ṭeṭ*, 'stability.' With reference to his connection with the resurrection and the nether-world, he is called PTAḤ-SEKER-ÅUSÅR, and is then represented as a little squat boy, at times wearing a beetle on his head. He is at times represented with Isis and Nephthys, and then appears to be a form of Osiris.

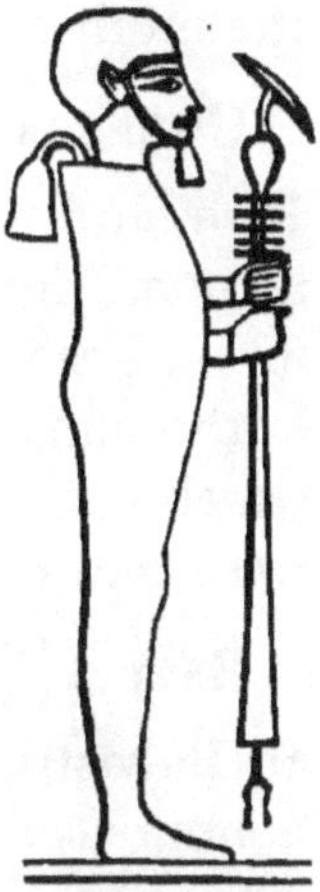

PTAḤ.

TMU, or ÅTMU, was the 'Closer' of the day or night.

TMU.

MUT.

MUT, the 'Mother,' was one of the divinities of the Theban triad; she was supposed to represent Nature, the mother of all things.

CHEPERÅ, the 'Creator,' was associated with Ptaḥ, and was supposed to be the god who caused himself to come into existence. He is represented with a beetle for his head. In later days he was supposed to be the father of the gods and creator of the universe, and the attributes which had been applied to Rā during the Middle Empire were transferred to him. (*See* pp. 200–202.)

BAST was principally worshipped in Lower Egypt at Bubastis, where a magnificent temple was built in her honour (see p. 130); she is represented with the head of a cat, and was associated with Ptaḥ. The correct reading of her name appears to be Sechet, and she represents the flame of the Sun.

BAST.

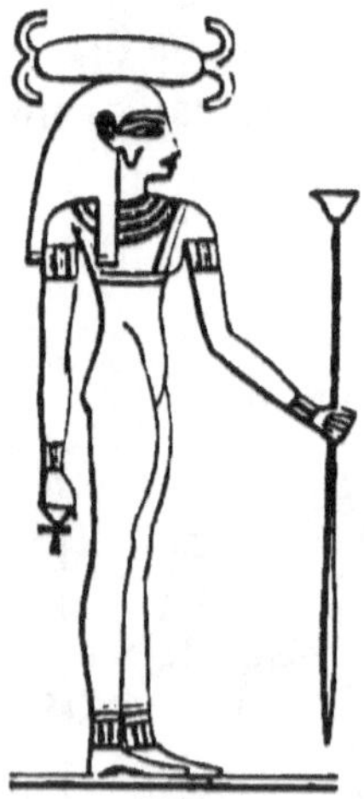
NIT.

NIT, , the 'Weaver,' was a counterpart of the goddess Mut; she is also identified with Hathor. She was the goddess of hunting, and is represented holding bows and arrows; she is usually coloured green.

RĀ, , the Sun-god, was the creator of gods and men; his emblem was the sun's disk. His worship was very ancient, and he was said to be the offspring of Nut, or the sky. He assumed the forms of several other gods, and is at times represented by the lion, cat, and hawk. In papyri and on bas-reliefs he is represented with the head of a hawk and wearing a disk, in front of which is an uræus . He was particularly adored at Thebes. When he rose in the morning he was called Ḥeru-chuti or Harmachis; and at night, when he set, he was called Ȧtmu, or 'the closer.' During the night he was supposed to be engaged in fighting Āpepi, the serpent, who, at the head of a large army of fiends, personifications of mist, darkness, and cloud, tried to overthrow him. The battle was fought daily, but Rā always conquered, and appeared day after day in the sky.

HORUS, , Ḥeru, is the morning sun, and is also represented as having the head of a hawk; he was said to be the son of Isis and Osiris, and is usually called the "avenger of his father," in reference to his defeat of Set.

RĀ.

HORUS.

ÅMEN-RĀ 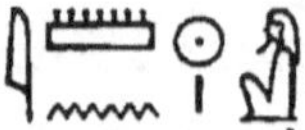, Mut, and Chonsu formed the great triad of Thebes. Åmen-Rā was said to be the son of Ptaḥ, and he seems to nave usurped the attributes of many of the gods. The word Åmen means 'hidden.' His chief titles were "lord of the thrones of the two lands," and "king of the gods." He is represented as wearing horns and feathers, and holding  'rule,'  'dominion,'  'power,' and  'stability.' The god ÅMSU  was a form of Åmen-Rā. The exalted position which Åmen-Rā, originally a mere local deity, occupied at Thebes, will be best understood from the translation of a hymn to him written in hieratic during the XVIIIth or XIXth dynasty :—

ÅMEN-RĀ.

"Adoration* of Åmen-Rā, the bull in Heliopolis, president of all the gods, beautiful god, beloved one, the giver of the life of all warmth to all beautiful cattle!

"Hail to thee, Åmen-Rā, lord of the thrones of the two lands, at the head of the Åpts.† The bull of his mother, at the head of his fields, the extender of footsteps, at the head of the "land of the South,"‡ lord of the Mat'au, § prince of Araby, lord of the sky, eldest son of earth, lord

* A French version of this hymn is given by Grébaut in his *Hymne à Ammon-Rā*, Paris, 1875. The hieratic text is published by Mariette, *Les Papyrus Egyptiens du Musée du Boulaq*, pl. 11–13.

† The great temple at Karnak.

‡ Ethiopia and Asia.

§ A country in Asia.

of things which exist, establisher of things, establisher of all things.

"One in his times, as among the gods. Beautiful bull of the cycle of the gods, president of all the gods, lord of Law, father of the gods, maker of men, creator of beasts, lord of things which exist, creator of the staff of life, maker of the green food which makes cattle to live. Form made by Ptaḥ, beautiful child, beloved one. The gods make adorations to him, the maker of things which are below, and of things which are above. He shines on the two lands sailing through the sky in peace. King of the South and North, the SUN (Rā), whose word is law, prince of the world! The mighty of valour, the lord of terror, the chief who makes the earth like unto himself. How very many more are his forms than those of any (other) god! The gods rejoice in his beauties, and they make praises to him in the two great horizons, at (his) risings in the double horizon of flame. The gods love the smell of him when he, the eldest born of the dew,* comes from Araby, when he traverses the land of the Mat'au, the beautiful face coming from Neter-ta.† The gods cast themselves down before his feet when they recognize their lord in his majesty, the lord of fear, the mighty one of victory, the mighty of Will, the master of diadems, the verdifier of offerings (?), the maker of *t'efau* food.

"Adorations to thee, O thou maker of the gods, who hast stretched out the heavens and founded the earth! The untiring watcher, Åmsu-Åmen, lord of eternity, maker of everlasting, to whom adorations are made (literally, lord of adorations), at the head of the Åpts, established with two horns, beautiful of aspects; the lord of the uræus crown,

* Compare Psalm cx. 3.

† *I.e.*, "Divine land," a name frequently given on the monuments to indicate the lands which lie to the south of Egypt between the Nile and the Red Sea.

exalted of plumes, beautiful of tiara, exalted of the white crown; the serpent *meḥen* and the two uræi are the (ornaments) of his face; the double crown, helmet and cap are his decorations in (his) temple. Beautiful of face he receives the *atef* crown ; beloved of the south and north is he, he is master of the *sechti* crown . He receives the åmsu sceptre , (and is) lord of the. . . . . . and of the whip. Beautiful prince, rising with the white crown , lord of rays, creator of light! The gods give acclamations to him, and he stretches out his hands to him that loves him. The flame makes his enemies fall, his eye overthrows the rebels, it thrusts its copper lance into the sky and makes the serpent Nâk* vomit what it has swallowed.

* Nák is one of the names of Āpepi, the demon of mist, cloud, and night, who was supposed to swallow up the sun daily; he was the enemy, *par excellence*, whom the Sun-god Rā was supposed to fight against and overcome. Āpepi was represented under the form of a serpent with knives stuck in his back . Compare the following extract from the service for his destruction which was recited daily in the temple of Amen-Rā, at Thebes: "Fall down upon thy face, Āpepi, enemy of Rā! The flame coming forth from the eye of Horus comes against thee, a mighty flame which comes forth from the eye of Horus, comes against thee. Thou art thrust down into the flame of fire which rushes out against thee, a flame which is fatal to thy soul, thy intelligence, thy words of power, thy body and thy shade. The flame prevails over thee, it drives darts into thy soul, it makes an end of whatever thou hast, and sends goads into thy form. Thou hast fallen by the eye of Horus, which is mighty over its enemy, which devours thee, and which leads on the mighty flame against thee; the eye of Rā prevails over thee, the flame devours thee, and nothing of thee remains. Get thee back, thou art hacked in pieces, thy soul is parched, thy name is buried in oblivion, silence covers it, it is overthrown; thou art put an end to and buried under threefold oblivion. Get thee back, retreat thou, thou art cut in pieces and removed from him that is in his shrine. O Āpepi, thou doubly crushed one, an end to thee, an end to thee! Mayest thou never rise up again! The eye of Horus prevails over thee

"Hail to thee, Rā, lord of Law, whose shrine is hidden, master of the gods, the god Cheperȧ in his boat; by the sending forth of (his) word the gods spring into existence. Hail god Ȧtmu, maker of mortals. However many are their forms he causes them to live, he makes different the colour of one man from another. He hears the prayer of him that is oppressed, he is kind of heart to him that calls unto him, he delivers him that is afraid from him that is strong of heart, he judges between the mighty and the weak.

"The lord of intelligence, knowledge (?) is the utterance of his mouth. The Nile cometh by his will, the greatly beloved lord of the palm tree comes to make mortals live. Making advance every work, acting in the sky, he makes to come into existence the sweet things of the daylight; the gods rejoice in his beauties, and their hearts live when they see him. O Rā, adored in the Ȧpts, mighty one of risings in the shrine; O Ȧni,* lord of the festival of the new moon, who makest the six days' festival and the festival of the last quarter of the moon; O prince, life, health, and strength! lord of all the gods, whose appearances are in the horizon, president of the ancestors of Auḳer;† his name is hidden from his children in his name 'Ȧmen.'

"Hail to thee, O thou who art in peace, lord of dilation of heart (*i.e.*, joy), crowned form, lord of the *ureret* crown, exalted of the plumes, beautiful of tiara, exalted of the white crown, the gods love to look upon thee; the double crown of Upper and Lower Egypt is established upon thy brow. Beloved art thou in passing through the two lands.

and devours thee daily, according to that which Rā decreed should be done to thee. Thou art thrown down into the flame of fire which feeds upon thee; thou art condemned to the fire of the eye of Horus which devours thee, thy soul, thy body, thy intelligence and thy shade."—British Museum Papyrus, 10188, col. xxiv.

* 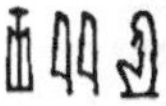, a form of Rā.

† A common name for a necropolis.

Thou sendest forth rays in rising from thy two beautiful eyes. The *pāt* (ancestors, *i.e.*, the dead) are in raptures of delight when thou shinest, the cattle become languid when thou shinest in full strength; thou art loved when thou art in the sky of the south, thou art esteemed pleasant in the sky of the north. Thy beauties seize and carry away all hearts, the love of thee makes the arms drop; thy beautiful creation makes the hands tremble, and (all) hearts to melt at the sight of thee.

"O Form, ONE, creator of all things, O ONE, ONLY, maker of existences! Men came forth from his two eyes, the gods sprang into existence at the utterance of his mouth. He maketh the green herb to make cattle live, and the staff of life for the (use of) man. He maketh the fishes to live in the rivers, the winged fowl in the sky; he giveth the breath of life to (the germ) in the egg, he maketh birds of all kinds to live, and likewise the reptiles that creep and fly; he causeth the rats to live in their holes, and the birds that are on every green twig. Hail to thee, O maker of all these things, thou ONLY ONE.

"He is of many forms in his might! He watches all people who sleep, he seeks the good for his brute creation. O Åmen, establisher of all things, Åtmu and Harmachis,* all people adore thee, saying, 'Praise to thee because of thy resting among us; homage to thee because thou hast created us.' All creatures say 'Hail to thee,' and all lands praise thee; from the height of the sky, to the breadth of the earth, and to the depths of the sea art thou praised. The gods bow down before thy majesty to exalt the Will of their creator; they rejoice when they meet their begetter, and say to thee, Come in peace, O father of the fathers of all the gods, who hast spread out the sky and hast founded the earth, maker of things which are,

* These three names are the names of the Sun-god at mid-day, evening and morning respectively.

creator of things which exist, prince, life, health, strength! president of the gods. We adore thy will, inasmuch as thou hast made us, thou hast made (us) and given us birth, and we give praises to thee by reason of thy resting with us.

"Hail to thee, maker of all things, lord of Law, father of the gods, maker of men, creator of animals, lord of grain, making to live the cattle of the hills! Hail Åmen, bull, beautiful of face, beloved in the Apts, mighty of risings in the shrine, doubly crowned in Heliopolis, thou judge of Horus and Set in the great hall.* President of the great cycle of the gods, ONLY ONE,† without his second, at the head of the Åpts, Åni at the head of the cycle of his gods, living in Law every day, the double horizoned Horus of the East! He has created the mountain (or earth), the silver, the gold, and genuine lapis lazuli at his Will . . . . Incense and fresh *ānti* ‡ are prepared for thy nostrils, O beautiful face, coming from the land of the Māt'au, Åmen-Rā, lord of the thrones of the two lands, at the head of the Åpts, Åni at the head of his shrine. King, ONE among the gods, myriad are his names, how many are they is not known; shining in the eastern horizon and setting in the western horizon, overthrowing his enemies by his birth at dawn every day. Thoth exalts his two eyes, and makes him to set in his splendours; the gods rejoice in his beauties which those who are in his . . . . . . exalt. Lord of the *sekti* § boat, and of the *āṭet* || boat, which travel over the sky for thee in peace. Thy sailors rejoice when they see Nåk overthrown, his limbs stabbed with the knife, the fire devouring him, his foul soul beaten out of his foul body, and his feet carried away. The gods rejoice, Rā is satisfied,

* See page 113.

† Compare "The Lord our God is ONE," Deut. vi. 4.

‡ A perfume brought into Egypt from the East.

§ The boat in which Rā sailed to his place of setting in the West.

|| The boat in which Rā sailed from his place of rising in the East.

Heliopolis is glad, the enemies of Åtmu are overthrown, and the heart of Nebt-ānch * is happy because the enemies of her lord are overthrown. The gods of Cher-āba are rejoicing, those who dwell in the shrines are making obeisance when they see him mighty in his strength (?) Form (?) of the gods of law, lord of the Åpts in thy name of 'maker of Law.' Lord of *t'efau* food, bull . . . . . . in thy name of 'Åmen bull of his mother.' Maker of mortals, making . . . . . become, maker of all things that are in thy name of Åtmu Cheperȧ. Mighty Law making the body festal, beautiful of face, making festal the breast. Form of attributes (?), lofty of diadem; the two uræi fly by his forehead. The hearts of the *pātu* go forth to him, and unborn generations turn to him; by his coming he maketh festal the two lands. Hail to thee, Åmen-Rā, lord of the thrones of the two lands! his town loves his shining."

Another hymn to Amen-Rā reads as follows:—

1. Hail, prince coming forth from the womb!
2. Hail, eldest son of primeval matter!
3. Hail, lord of multitudes of aspects and evolutions!
4. Hail, golden circle in the temples!
5. Hail, lord of time and bestower of years!
6. Hail, lord of life for all eternity!
7. Hail, lord of myriads and millions!
8. Hail, thou who shinest in rising and setting!
9. Hail, thou who makest beings joyful!
10. Hail, thou lord of terror, thou fearful one!
11. Hail, lord of multitudes of aspects and divinities!
12. Hail, thou who art crowned with the white crown; thou master of the *urerer* crown!
13. Hail, thou sacred baby of Horus, praise!
14. Hail, son of Rā who sittest in the boat of millions of years!
15. Hail, restful leader, come to thy hidden places!

* *I.e.*, "the lady of life," a name of Isis.

16. Hail, lord of terror, self-produced !
17. Hail, thou restful of heart, come to thy town !
18. Hail, thou that causest cries of joy, come to thy town
19. Hail, thou darling of the gods and goddesses !
20. Hail, thou dipper in the sea, come to thy temple !
21. Hail, thou who art in the Nether-world, come to thy offerings !
22. Hail, thou that protectest them, come to thy temple !
23. Hail, Moon-god, growing from a crescent into an illuminated disk !
24. Hail, sacred flower of the mighty house !
25. Hail, thou that bringest the sacred cordage of the Sekti* boat !
26. Hail, thou lord of the Ḥennu† boat who becomest young again in the hidden place !
27. Hail, thou perfect soul in the Nether-world !
28. Hail, thou sacred visitor of the north and south !
29. Hail, thou hidden one, unknown to mankind !
30. Hail, thou illuminator of him that is in the Nether world, that causest him to see the disk !

* The *Sektet*  was the boat of the sun in the morning, just as the *Māti* 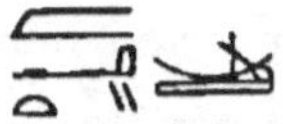 was the boat of the sun in the evening. A hymn to the sun-god says :—

χā - k *em* *ṭuau* *em* *sekti*
Risest thou in the morning in the *sekti* boat ;

ḥetep-k *em* *māti* *em* *māsher*
Settest thou in the *māti* boat in the evening.

† The *ḥennu* 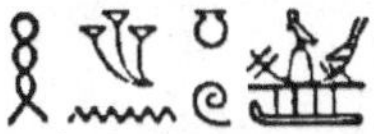 was the boat which was drawn around the sanctuaries of the temples at dawn. Drawings of it are given by Lanzone, *Dizionario*, plates CCLXV-CCCLXVII.

31. Hail, lord of the *atef* crown, thou mighty one in Ḥet-suten-ḥenen ! *
32. Hail, mighty one of terror !
33. Hail, thou that risest in Thebes, flourishing for ever !
34. Hail, Åmen-Rā, king of the gods, who makest thy limbs to grow in rising and setting !
35. Hail, ... offerings and oblations in Ru-stau (*i.e.*, the passages of the tomb) !
36. Hail, thou that placest the uræus upon the head of its lord!
37. Hail, stablisher of the earth upon its foundations !
38. Hail, opener of the mouth of the four mighty gods who are in the Nether-world !
39. Hail, thou living soul of Osiris, who art diademed with the moon !
40. Hail, thou that hidest thy body in the great coffin at Heliopolis !
41. Hail, hidden one, mighty one, Osiris in the Netherworld !
42. Hail, thou that unitest his soul to heaven, thine enemy is fallen !

ISIS, , Åuset, the mother of Horus and wife of Osiris, , Åusår, was the daughter of Nut, or the sky ; she married her brother Osiris. Her sister Nephthys and her brother Set likewise married one another. This last couple conspired against Isis and Osiris, and Set having induced his brother Osiris to enter a box, closed the lid down and threw it into the Nile ; the box was carried down by the river and finally cast up on the sea shore. Set having found the box once more, cut the body of Osiris into fourteen pieces, which he cast over the length and breadth of the land. As soon as

ISIS.

* Heracleopolis, the metropolis of the 20th nome of Upper Egypt.

Isis heard what had happened, she went about seeking for the pieces, and built a temple over each one; she found all save one. Osiris, however, had become king of the netherworld, and vengeance was taken by his son Horus upon his brother Set. Osiris is usually represented in the form of a mummy, holding in his hands 'dominion,' 'life,' 'rule,' and 'power.' He is called 'the lord of Abydos,' 'lord of the holy land, lord of eternity and prince of everlasting,' 'the president of the gods,' 'the head of the corridor of the tomb,' 'bull of the west,' 'judge of the dead,' etc., etc.

The writers of Egyptian mythological texts always assume their readers to possess a knowledge of the history of the murder of Osiris by Set, and of the wanderings and troubles of his disconsolate wife Isis. The following extracts from Plutarch's work on the subject will supply certain information not given in the Egyptian texts.

"Osiris, being now become king of Egypt, applied himself towards civilizing his countrymen by turning them from their former indigent and barbarous course of life; he moreover taught them how to cultivate and improve the fruits of the earth; he gave them a body of laws to regulate their conduct by, and instructed them in that reverence and worship which they were to pay to the gods; with the same good disposition he afterwards travelled over the rest of the world, inducing the people everywhere to submit to his discipline; not indeed compelling them by force of arms, but persuading them to yield to the strength of his reasons, which were conveyed to them in the most agreeable manner, in hymns and songs accompanied with instruments of music; from

OSIRIS.

which last circumstance the Greeks conclude him to have been the same person with their Dionysus or Bacchus. During the absence of Osiris from his kingdom, Typhon had no opportunity of making any innovations in the State, Isis being extremely vigilant in the government, and always upon her guard. After his return, however, having first persuaded seventy-two other persons to join with him in the conspiracy, together with a certain queen of Ethiopia named Aso, who chanced to be in Egypt at that time, he contrived a proper stratagem to execute his base designs. For having privily taken the measure of Osiris's body, he caused a chest to be made exactly of the same size with it, as beautiful as might be, and set off with all the ornaments of art. This chest he brought into his banqueting room; where after it had been much admired by all who were present, Typhon, as it were in jest, promised to give it to any one of them whose body upon trial it might be found to fit. Upon this the whole company, one after another, go into it. But as it did not fit any of them, last of all Osiris lays himself down in it; upon which the conspirators immediately ran together, clapped the cover upon it, then fastened it down on the outside with nails, pouring likewise melted lead over it. After this they carried it away to the river-side, and conveyed it to the sea by the Tanaïtic mouth of the Nile; which, for this reason, is still held in the utmost abomination by the Egyptians, and never named by them but with proper marks of detestation. These things, say they, were thus executed upon the 17th day of the month Athôr, when the sun was in Scorpio, in the 28th year of Osiris's reign; though there are others who tell us that he was no more than twenty-eight years old at this time.

"The first who knew of the accident which had befallen their king, were the Pans and Satyrs who inhabited the country round Chemmis (Panopolis or Aḥmîm); and they immediately acquainting the people with the news, gave the first occasion to the name of Panic Terrors, which has ever since been made use of to signify any sudden affright or amazement of a multitude. As to Isis, as soon as the report reached her, she immediately cut off one of the locks of her hair, and put on mourning apparel upon the very spot where she then happened to be, which accordingly from this accident has ever since been called Coptos, or the *City of Mourning*, though some are of opinion that this word rather signifies *Deprivation*. After this she wandered everywhere about the country full of disquietude and perplexity in search of the chest, enquiring of every person she met with, even of some children whom she chanced to see, whether they knew what was become of it. Now it so happened that these children had seen what Typhon's accomplices had done with the body, and accordingly acquainted her by what mouth of the Nile it had been conveyed into the sea . . . . .

"At length she received more particular news of the chest, that it had been carried by the waves of the sea to the coast of Byblos, and there gently lodged in the branches of a bush of Tamarisk, which in a short time had shot up into a large and beautiful tree, growing round the chest and enclosing it on every side, so that it was not to be seen; and further, that the king of the country, amazed at its unusual size, had cut the tree down, and made that part of the trunk wherein the chest was concealed a pillar to support the roof of his house. These things, say they, being made known to Isis in an extraordinary manner, by the report of demons, she immediately went to Byblos;* where, setting herself down by the side of a fountain, she refused to speak to any body excepting only to the queen's women who chanced to be there; these she saluted and caressed in the kindest manner possible, plaiting their hair for them, and transmitting

* *I.e.*, the papyrus swamps.

into them part of that wonderfully grateful odour which issued from her own body ..... The queen therefore sent for her to court, and after a further acquaintance with her, made her nurse to one of her sons ..... The goddess, discovering herself, requested that the pillar which supported the roof of the king's house might be given to her; which she accordingly took down, and then easily cutting it open, after she had taken out what she wanted, she wrapt up the remainder of the trunk in fine linen, and pouring perfumed oil upon it, delivered it into the hands of the king and queen ...... When this was done, she threw herself upon the chest, making at the same time such a loud and terrible lamentation over it as frighted the younger of the king's sons who heard her out of his life. But the elder of them she took with her, and set sail with the chest for Egypt .....

"No sooner was she arrived in a desert place, where she imagined herself to be alone, but she presently opened the chest, and laying her face upon her dead husband's, embraced his corpse, and wept bitterly.

"Isis intending a visit to her son Horus, who was brought up at Butus, deposited the chest in the meanwhile in a remote and unfrequented place; Typhon, however, as he was one night hunting by the light of the moon accidentally met with it; and knowing the body which was enclosed in it, tore it into several pieces, fourteen in all, dispersing them up and down in different parts of the country. Upon being made acquainted with this event, Isis once more sets out in search of the scattered fragments of her husband's body, making use of a boat made of the reed papyrus in order the more easily to pass through the lower and fenny parts of the country. For which reason, say they, the crocodile never touches any persons who sail in this sort of vessel, as either fearing the anger of the goddess, or else respecting it on account of its having once carried her. To this occasion, therefore, it is to be imputed that there are so many different sepulchres of Osiris shewn in Egypt; for we are told that wherever Isis met with any of the scattered limbs of her husband, she there buried it. There are others, however, who contradict this relation, and tell us that this variety of sepulchres was owing rather to the policy of the queen, who, instead of the real body, as was pretended, presented these several cities with the image only of her husband; and that she did this not only to render the honours which would by this means be paid to his memory more extensive, but likewise that she might hereby elude the malicious search of Typhon; who, if he got the better of Horus in the war wherein they were going to be engaged, distracted by this multiplicity of sepulchres, might despair of being able to find the true one. . . . . .

"After these things Osiris, returning from the other world, appeared to his son Horus, encouraged him to the battle, and at the same time instructed him in the exercise of arms. He then asked him, 'what he thought the most glorious action a man could perform?' to which Horus replied, 'to revenge the injuries offered to his father and mother.' This reply much rejoiced Osiris . . . . We are moreover told that amongst the great numbers who were continually deserting from Typhon's party was the goddess Thoueris, and that a serpent pursuing her as she was coming over to Horus, was slain by his soldiers. Afterwards it came to a battle between them, which lasted many days: but victory at length inclined to Horus, Typhon himself being taken prisoner. Isis, however, to whose custody he was committed, was so far from putting him to death, that she even loosed his bonds and set him at liberty. This action of his mother so extremely incensed Horus, that he laid hands upon her and pulled off the ensign of royalty which she wore on her head; and instead thereof Hermes clapt on an helmet made in the shape of an ox's head.

. . . . After this there were two other battles fought between them, in both of which Typhon had the worst. . . . . . .

"Such, then, are the principal circumstances of this famous story, the more harsh and shocking parts of it, such as the cutting in pieces of Horus and the beheading of Isis, being omitted." (Plutarch, *De Iside et Osiride*, xii–xx. Squire's translation.)

The following is an extract from a hymn addressed to Osiris by Isis and Nephthys (Brit. Mus. Papyrus No. 10,188):—

"O beloved of his father, lord of rejoicings, thou delightest the hearts of the cycle of the gods, and thou illuminatest thy house with thy beauties; the cycle of the gods fear thy power, the earth trembleth through fear of thee.

I am thy wife who maketh thy protection, the sister who protecteth her brother; come, let me see thee, O lord of my love.

O twice exalted one, mighty of attributes, come, let me see thee; O baby who advancest, child, come, let me see thee.

Countries and regions weep for thee, the zones weep for thee as if thou wert Sesheta, heaven and earth weep for thee, inasmuch as thou art greater than the gods; may there be no cessation of the glorifying of thy *Ka*.

Come to thy temple, be not afraid, thy son Horus embraces the circuit of heaven.

O thou sovereign, who makest afraid, be not afraid. Thy son Horus avenges thee and overthrows for thee the fiends and the devils.

Hail, lord, follow after me with thy radiance, let me see thee daily; the smell of thy flesh is like that of Punt (*i.e.*, the spice land of Arabia).

Thou art adored by the venerable women, in peace; the entire cycle of the gods rejoice.

Come thou to thy wife in peace, her heart flutters through her love for thee, she will embrace thee and not let thee depart from her; her heart is oppressed because of her anxiety to see thee and thy beauties. She has made an end of preparations for thee in the secret house; she has destroyed the pain which is in thy limbs and the sickness as if it never existed. Life is given to thee by the most excellent wife.

Hail, thou protectest the inundation in the fields of Aphroditopolis this day.

The cow (*i.e.*, Isis) weeps aloud for thee with her voice, thy love is the limit of her desire. Her heart flutters because thou art shut up from her.

She would embrace thy body with both arms and would come to thee quickly.

She avenges thee on account of what was done to thee, she makes sound for thee thy flesh on thy bones, she attaches thy nose to thy face for thee, she gathers together for thee all thy bones."

In the calendar of the lucky and unlucky days of the Egyptian year, the directions concerning the 26th day of the month of Thoth, which is marked , or "thrice unlucky," say, "Do nothing at all on this day, for it is the day on which Horus fought against Set. Standing on the soles of their feet they aimed blows at each other like men, and they became like two bears of hell, lords of Cher-āba. They passed three days and three nights in this manner, after which Isis made their weapons fall. Horus fell down, crying out, 'I am thy son Horus,' and Isis cried to the weapons, saying, 'Away, away, from my son Horus' . . . . Her brother Set fell down and cried out, saying, 'Help, help!' Isis cried out to the weapons, 'Fall down.' Set cried out several times, 'Do I not wish to honour my mother's brother?' and Isis cried out to the weapons, 'Fall down—set my elder brother free'; then the weapons fell away from him. And Horus and Set stood up like two men, and each paid no attention to what they had said. And the majesty of Horus was enraged against his mother Isis like a panther of the south, and she fled before him. On that day a terrible struggle took place, and Horus cut off the head of Isis; and Thoth transformed this head by his incantations, and put it on her again in the form of a head of a cow." (Chabas, *Le Calendrier*, p. 29.)

NEPHTHYS, , Nebt-ḥet, sister of Osiris and Isis, is generally represented standing at the bier of Osiris lamenting him. One myth relates that Osiris mistook her for Isis, and that ANUBIS, the god of the dead, was the result of the union.

SET, , the god of evil, appears to have been worshipped in the earliest times. He was the opponent of Horus in a three days' battle, at the end of which he was defeated. He was worshipped by the Hyksos, and also by the Cheta; but in the later days of the Egyptian empire he was supposed to be the god of evil, and was considered to be the chief fiend and rebel against the sun-god Rā.

ANUBIS, , Ȧnpu, the god of the dead, is usually represented with the head of a jackal.

SEB, , was the husband of Nut, the sky, and father of Osiris, Isis, and the other gods of that cycle.

NEBT-ḤET.

ANUBIS.

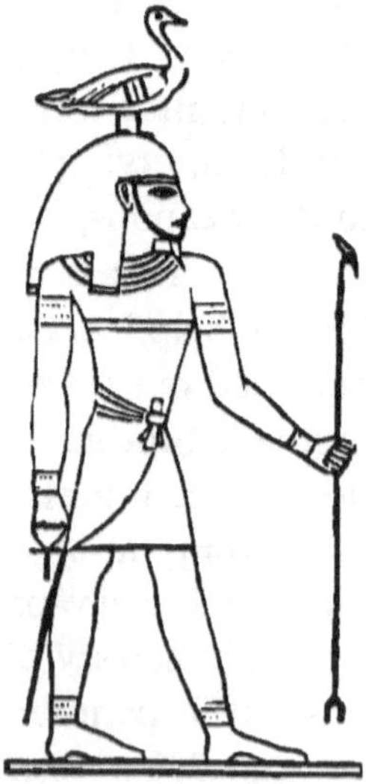

SEB.

THOTH, , Teḥuti, 'the measurer,' was the scribe of the gods, and the measurer of time and inventor of numbers. In the judgment hall of Osiris he stands by the side of the balance holding a palette and reed ready to record the result of the weighing as announced by the dog-headed ape which sits on the middle of the beam of the scales. In one aspect he is the god of the moon, and is represented with the head of an ibis.

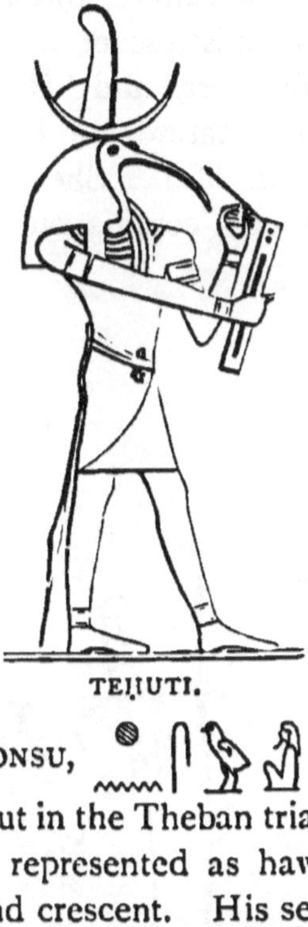
TEḤUTI.

CHONSU.

CHONSU, , was associated with Ȧmen-Rā and Mut in the Theban triad. He was the god of the moon, and is represented as hawk-headed and wearing the lunar disk and crescent. His second name was Nefer-ḥetep, and he was worshipped with great honour at Thebes.

SEBEK, , the crocodile-headed god, was worshipped at Kom-Ombos and in the Fayyûm.

Ȧ-EM-ḤETEP (Imouthis), , was the son of Ptaḥ.

SHU, , and TEFNUT, , were the children of Seb and Nut, and represented sunlight and moisture respectively.

ATHOR, or HATHOR, , Ḥet-Ḥeru, 'the house of Horus,' is identified with Nut, the sky, or place in which she brought forth and suckled Horus. She was the wife of Åtmu, a form of Rā. She is represented as a woman wearing a headdress in the shape of a vulture, and above it a disk and horns. She is called 'mistress of the gods,' 'lady of the sycamore,' 'lady of the west,' and 'Hathor of Thebes.' She is the female power of nature, and has some of the attributes of Isis, Nut, and Mut. She is often represented under the form of a cow coming out of the Theban hills.

HATHOR.

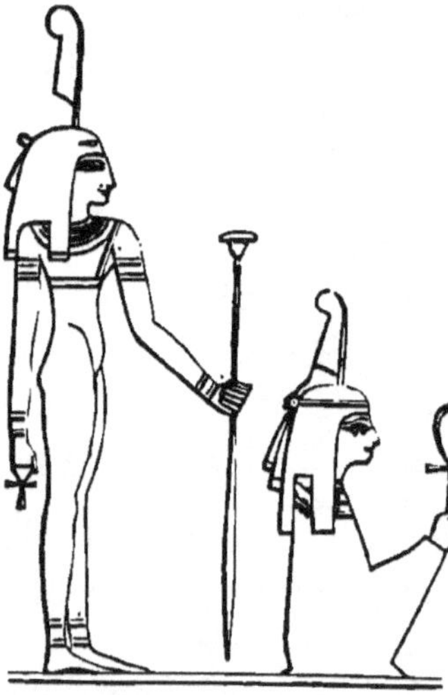

MAĀT.

MAĀT, , the goddess of 'Law,' was the daughter of the Sun-god Rā; she is represented as wearing the feather , emblematic of law .

ḤĀPI, 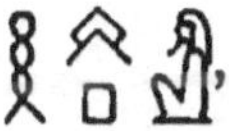, the god of the Nile, is represented wearing a cluster of flowers on his head ; he is coloured red and green, probably to represent the colours of the water of the Nile immediately before and just after the beginning of the inundation.

SERAPIS, *i.e.*, Osiris-Apis, 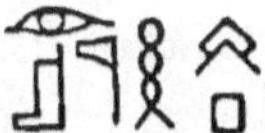, was a god introduced into Egypt during the reign of the Ptolemies;* he is represented with the head of a bull wearing a disk and uræus. He is said to be the second son of Ptaḥ. The worship of Apis at Memphis goes back to the earliest times; the Serapeum, discovered there by M. Mariette, contained the tombs of Apis bulls from the time of Amenophis III. (about B.C. 1550) down to the time of the Roman Empire. See page 244.

* ". . . . . the Lagids, as well as the Seleucids, were careful of disturbing the foundations of the old religion of the country; . . . . . they introduced . . . . . the Greek god of the lower world, Pluto, into the native worship, under the hitherto little mentioned name of the Egyptian god Serapis, and then gradually transferred to this the old Osiris worship." (Mommsen, *Provinces of the Roman Empire*, Vol. II., p. 265.)

LOWER EGYPT.

ALEXANDRIA.

Alexandria was founded B.C. 332 by Alexander the Great, who began to build his city on the little town of Rakoti, just opposite to the island of Pharos. King Ptolemy I. Soter made this city his capital: and having founded the famous library and museum, he tried to induce the most learned men of his day to live there. His son and successor Ptolemy II. Philadelphus, continued the wise policy of his father, and Alexandria became famous as a seat of learning. The keeper of the museum during the reign of Ptolemy III. Euergetes I. was Aristophanes of Byzantium. During the siege of the city by the Romans in the time of Cæsar, B.C. 48, the library of the museum was burnt; but Antony afterwards gave Cleopatra a large collection of manuscripts which formedthe nucleus of a second library.* In the early centuries of our era the people of Alexandria quarrelled perpetually among themselves,† the subjects of dispute

* This collection numbered 200,000 MSS., and formed the famous Pergamenian library founded by Eumenes II., king of Pergamus, B.C. 197.

† ". . . . . the Alexandrian rabble took on the slightest pretext to stones and to cudgels. In street uproar, says an authority, himself Alexandrian, the Egyptians are before all others; the smallest spark suffices here to kindle a tumult. On account of neglected visits, on account of the confiscation of spoiled provisions, on account of exclusion from a bathing establishment, on account of a dispute between the slave of an Alexandrian of rank and a Roman foot-soldier as to the value or non-value of their respective slippers, the legions were under the necessity of charging among the citizens of Alexandria . . . . . In these riots the Greeks acted as instigators . . . . . but in the further course o the matter the spite and savageness of the Egyptian proper came into the conflict. The Syrians were cowardly, and as soldiers the Egyptians were so too; but in a street tumult they were able to develope a courage worthy of a better cause." (Mommsen, *Provinces of the Roman Empire*, Vol. II., p. 265.)

being matters connected with Jews and religious questions. St. Mark is said to have preached the Gospel here. Meanwhile the prosperity of the town declined and the treasury became empty.

Alexandria was captured by Chosroes (A.D. 619), and by 'Amr ibn el-'Âṣi, a general of 'Omar, A.D. 641. The decline of Alexandria went on steadily, until it became in the Middle Ages little more, comparatively, than a moderate sized seaport town, with a population of some thousands of people. In the present century a little of its prosperity was restored by Muḥammad 'Ali, who in 1819 built the Maḥmûdîyeh canal to bring fresh water to the town from the Rosetta arm of the Nile. Its population to-day is about 300,000, and includes large and wealthy colonies of Jews and Greeks.

The Christians were persecuted at Alexandria with great severity by Decius (A.D. 250), by Valerianus (A.D. 257), and by Diocletian (A.D. 304). For a large number of years the city was disturbed by the fierce discussions on religious dogmas between Arius and Athanasius, George of Cappadocia and Athanasius, the Anthropomorphists and their opponents, and Cyril and Nestorius. The Christian sects supported their views by violence, and the ordinary heathen population of the town rebelled whenever they could find a favourable opportunity.

The most important ancient buildings of Alexandria were :—

The **Lighthouse** or **Pharos**, one of the seven wonders of the world, was built by Sostratus of Cnidus, for Ptolemy Philadelphus, and is said to have been about 600 feet high. All traces of this wonderful building have now disappeared. The embankment or causeway called the HEPTASTADIUM * (from its length of seven stades), was made either by Ptolemy Philadelphus or his father Ptolemy Soter; it divided the

* The Heptastadium joined the ancient town and the Island of Pharos; a large part of the modern town is built upon it.

harbour into two parts. The eastern port is only used by native craft, on account of its sandy shoals; the western port is the Eunostos Harbour, which at present is protected by a breakwater about one mile and three-quarters long. The MUSEUM and **Library of Alexandria** were founded by Ptolemy I., and greatly enlarged by his son Ptolemy Philadelphus. When this latter king died the library was said to contain 100,000 manuscripts. These were classified, arranged, and labelled by Callimachus; when it was burnt down in the time of Julius Cæsar, it is thought that more than 750,000 works were lost. Copies of works of importance were made at the expense of the State, and it is stated that every book which came into the city was seized and kept, and that a copy only of it was returned to the owner. Antony handed over to Cleopatra about 200,000 manuscripts (the Pergamenian Library), and these were made the foundation of a second library. Among the famous men who lived and studied in this library were Eratosthenes, Strabo, Hipparchus, Archimedes, and Euclid. The **Serapeum** was built by Ptolemy Soter, and was intended to hold the statue of a god from Sinope, which was called by the Egyptians 'Osiris-Apis,' or Serapis. It stood close by Rakoti to the east of Alexandria near 'Pompey's Pillar,' and is said to have been one of the most beautiful buildings in the world; it was filled with remarkable statues and other works of art. It was destroyed by the Christian fanatic Theophilus,* Patriarch of Alexandria, during the reign of Theodosius II. The LIBRARY of the Serapeum is said to have contained about 300,000 manuscripts, which were burnt by 'Amr ibn el-'Âṣi at the command of the Khalif 'Omar, A.D. 641; these were sufficiently numerous, it is said, to heat the public baths of Alexandria for six

* ". . . the perpetual enemy of peace and virtue; a bold, bad man, whose hands were alternately polluted with gold and with blood." (Gibbon, *Decline*, Chap. xxvii.)

months.* The SÔMA formed a part of the Cæsareum, and contained the bodies of Alexander the Great and the Ptolemies, his successors. The Theatre, which faced the island of Antirhodus, the Sôma, and the Museum and Library, all stood in the royal buildings in the Bruchium quarter of the town, between Lochias and the Heptastadium. The stone sarcophagus (now in the British Museum, No. 10), which was thought to have belonged to Alexander the Great, was made for Nectanebus I., the first king of the XXXth

* "The spirit of Amrou ('Amr ibn el-'Âṣi) was more curious and liberal than that of his brethren, and in his leisure hours the Arabian chief was pleased with the conversation of John, the last disciple of Ammonius, and who derived the surname of *Philoponus* from his laborious studies of grammar and philosophy. Emboldened by this familiar intercourse, Philoponus presumed to solicit a gift, inestimable in *his* opinion, contemptible in that of the Barbarians: the royal library, which alone, among the spoils of Alexandria, had not been appropriated by the visit and the seal of the conqueror. Amrou was inclined to gratify the wish of the grammarian, but his rigid integrity refused to alienate the minutest object without the consent of the caliph; and the well-known answer of Omar was inspired by the ignorance of a fanatic. 'If these writings of the Greeks agree with the book of God, they are useless and need not be preserved: if they disagree, they are pernicious and ought to be destroyed.' The sentence was executed with blind obedience: the volumes of paper or parchment were distributed to the 4,000 baths of the city; and such was their incredible multitude that six months were barely sufficient for the consumption of this precious fuel." (Gibbon, *Decline and Fall*, chap. li.) The chief authority for this statement is Bar-Hebraeus (born A.D. 1226, died at Marâghah in Âdhôrbâîjân, July 30th, 1286), and it has been repeated by several Arabic writers. Both Gibbon and Renaudot thought the story incredible, but there is no reason why it should be. Gibbon appears to have thought that the *second* Alexandrian library was pillaged or destroyed when Theophilus, Patriarch of Alexandria, destroyed the image of Serapis; there is, however, no proof that it was, and it seems more probable that it remained comparatively unhurt until the arrival of 'Amr ibn el-'Âṣi. See the additional notes in Gibbon, ed. Smith, Vol. III., p. 419, and Vol. VI., p. 338.

dynasty, B.C. 378. The PANEUM, or temple of Pan, is probably represented by the modern Kôm ed-Dîk. The JEWS' QUARTER lay between the sea and the street, to the east of Lochias. The NECROPOLIS was situated at the west of the city. The GYMNASIUM stood a little to the east of the Paneum, on the south side of the street which ends, on the east, in the Canopic Gate.

Pompey's Pillar was erected by Pompey, a Roman prefect, in honour of Diocletian, some little time after A.D. 302.* It is made of granite brought from Aswân; the shaft is about 70 feet, and the whole monument, including its pedestal, is rather more than 100 feet high. The fragments of the columns which lie around the base of this pillar are thought to have belonged to the Serapeum.

A few years ago there were to be seen in Alexandria the two famous granite obelisks called **Cleopatra's Needles.** They were brought from Heliopolis during the reign of the Roman Emperor Augustus, and set up before the Temple of Cæsar. Until quite lately one of them remained upright; the other had fallen. They are both made of Aswân granite; one measured 67 feet in height, the other 68½ feet; the diameter of each is about 7½ feet. The larger obelisk was given by Muḥammad 'Ali to the English early in this century, but it was not removed until 1877, when it was transported to England at the expense of Sir Erasmus Wilson, and it now stands on the Thames Embankment. The smaller obelisk was taken to New York a few years later. The inscriptions show that both were made during the reign of Thothmes III., about B.C. 1600, and that Rameses II. who lived about 250 years later, added lines of inscriptions recording his titles of honour and greatness.

* The Greek inscription recording this fact is published in Boeckh, *Corpus Inscriptionum Graecarum*, t. iii., p. 329, where it is also thus restored: **Τὸν [ὁσ]ιώτατον Αὐτοκράτορα, τὸν πολιοῦχον 'Αλεξανδρείας, Διοκλητιανὸν τὸν ἀνίκητον πο[μπήϊ]ος ἔπαρχος Αἰγύπτου. . . . .**

The **Catacombs**, which were built early in the fourth century of our era, are on the coast near the harbour and on the coast near the new port.

The **Walls** of the city were built by Muḥammad 'Ali, and appear to have been laid upon the foundation of ancient walls.

On the south side of Alexandria lies Lake Mareotis, which in ancient days was fed by canals running from the Nile. During the middle ages the lake nearly dried up, and the land which became available for building purposes in consequence was speedily covered with villages. In the year 1801, the English dug a canal across the neck of land between the lake and the sea, and flooded the whole district thus occupied. During the last few years an attempt has been made to pump the water out; it would seem with considerable success.

Between Alexandria and Cairo are the following important towns:—

I. DAMANHÛR*(Eg.,  Ṭemâien-Ḥeru, 'Town of Horus,' the capital of the Mudîrîyeh of Beḥêreh. This was the Hermopolis Parva of the Romans.

II. KAFR EZ-ZAIYÂT, on the east side of the river, situated among beautiful and fertile fields.

III. ṬANṬA, the capital of Gharbîyeh, situated between the Rosetta and Damietta arms of the Nile. This town is celebrated for three *Fairs*, which are held here in January, April, and August, in honour of the Muḥammadan saint Seyyid el-Bedawi, who was born at Fez about A.D. 1200, and who lived and died at Ṭanṭa. Each fair lasts eight days, and the greatest day in each fair is the Friday; the most important fair is that held in August.

IV. BENHA el-'Asal, 'Benha of the Honey,' the capital of

* It is called ϯⲙⲁⲓⲛϩⲱⲣ by the Copts.

Ḳalyûb. It obtained this name because a Copt called Maḳawḳas * sent, among other gifts, a jar of honey to Muḥammad the Prophet. The Arabic geographers state that the best honey in Egypt comes from Benha. Quite close to this town are the ruins of the ancient city of Athribis.

About forty miles to the east of Alexandria lies the town of Rosetta, not far from the ancient Bolbitane. It was founded towards the end of the ninth century, and was once a flourishing seaport; it has become famous in modern times on account of the trilingual inscription, called the '**Rosetta Stone**,' which was found here in 1799 by a French officer called Boussard. This inscription was inscribed on a block of basalt, and contained a decree by the Egyptian priests in honour of Ptolemy V., Epiphanes, dated in the eighth year of his reign (B.C. 196). The hieroglyphic, demotic, and Greek texts enabled Young and Champollion to work out the phonetic values of a number of the hieroglyphic characters employed to write the names of the Greek rulers. The stone is preserved in the British Museum.

* Maḳawḳas was "Prince of the Copts," and "Governor of Alexandria and Egypt"; he was a Jacobite, and a strong hater of the Melchites or "Royalists." He was invited to become a follower of Muḥammad the Prophet, but he declined. When Egypt was captured by 'Amr ibn el-'Âṣi he betrayed the Copts, but by means of paying tribute he secured to himself the liberty of professing the Christian religion, and he asked that, after his death, his body might be buried in the church of St. John at Alexandria. He sent, as gifts to the Prophet, two Coptic young women, sisters, called Maryam and Shîrîn; two girls, one eunuch, a horse, a mule, an ass, a jar of honey, an alabaster jar, a jar of oil, an ingot of gold, and some Egyptian linen. (Gagnier, *La vie de Mahomet*, pp. 38, 73.) Maḳawḳas, مقوقس, appears to be the Arabic transcription of the Greek μεγαυχής "famous," a title which was bestowed upon George, the son of Menas Parkabios, who was over the taxes of Egypt, and who was addressed by Muḥammad the Prophet as "Prince of the Copts."

SUEZ AND THE SUEZ CANAL.

The town of Suez practically sprang into existence during the building of the Suez Canal, which was opened in 1869; before that time it was an insignificant village with a few hundred inhabitants. Ancient history is almost silent about it, even if it be identified with Clysma* Praesidium. It is situated at the north end of the Gulf of Suez, and is now important from its position at the south end of the Suez Canal. A fresh-water canal from Cairo to Suez was built in 1863, but before the cutting of this canal the inhabitants obtained their water either from the Wells of Moses (about eight miles from Suez) or Cairo. It was at one time considered to be near the spot where the Israelites crossed the 'Sea of Sedge'; there is little doubt, however, that the passage was made much nearer the Mediterranean.

The neck of land which joins Asia to Africa, or the Isthmus of Suez, is nearly one hundred miles wide; on the south side is the Gulf of Suez, on the north the Mediterranean. The Red Sea and the Mediterranean appear to have been united in ancient days. Modern investigations have proved that so far back as the time of Rameses II. or earlier a canal was cut between Pelusium and Lake Timsaḥ, and it is almost certain that it was well fortified. The Asiatics who wished to invade Egypt were compelled to cross the Isthmus of Suez, and a canal would not only serve as a water barrier against them, but be useful

* Clysma, in Arabic Ḳulzum, is said by the Arab geographers to have been situated on the coast of the sea of Yemen, on the Egyptian side, at the far end, three days from Cairo and four days from Pelusium. (Juynboll, *Lex. Geog. Arab.*, t. ii., p. ٣٤٤.)

as a means of transport for troops from one point to another. The name of the place Ḳanṭara, 'a bridge,' a little to the north of Isma'ilîya, seems to point to the fact of a ford existing here from very early times. Nekau (B.C. 610) began to make a canal at Bubastis, between the Nile and the Red Sea, but never finished it; it was continued in later times by Darius, and Ptolemy Philadelphus made a lock for it; still later we know that the Mediterranean and Red Seas were joined by a canal. The emperor Trajan made a canal from Cairo to the Red Sea, which, having become impassable, was re-opened by 'Omar's general, 'Amr ibn el-'Âṣi, after his capture of Egypt.

In the Middle Ages various attempts were made in a half-hearted manner to cut a new canal across the Isthmus, but although several royal personages in and out of Egypt were anxious to see the proposed work begun, nothing was seriously attempted until 1798, when Napoleon Bonaparte directed M. Lepère to survey the route of a canal across the Isthmus. M. Lepère reported that the difference between the levels of the Red Sea and Mediterranean was thirty-three feet, and, that, therefore, the canal was impossible.* Although several scientific men doubted the accuracy of M. Lepère's conclusion, the fact that the level of the two seas is practically the same was not proved until M. Linant Bey, Stephenson, and others examined the matter in 1846. It was then at once evident that a canal *was* possible. M. de Lesseps laid the plans for a canal before Sa'îd Pasha in 1854; two years afterwards they were sanctioned, and two years later the works began. The original plan proposed to make a

* This was the opinion of some classical writers: compare Aristotle, *Meteorologica*, i. 14, 27; Diodorus, i. 23; and Strabo, xvii. 1, 25. The Arab writer Mas'ûdi relates that a certain king tried to cut a canal across this isthmus, but that on finding that the waters of the Red Sea stood at a higher level than those of the Mediterranean, he abandoned his project. (*Les Prairies d'Or*, t. iv. p. 97.)

canal from Suez to Pelusium, but it was afterwards modified, and by bringing the northern end into the Mediterranean at Port Sa'îd, it was found possible to do away with the lock at each end, which would have been necessary had it embouched at Pelusium. The **fresh-water canal** from Bûlâḳ to Suez, with an aqueduct to Port Sa'îd, included in the original plan, was completed in 1863. The filling of the Bitter Lakes with sea-water from the Mediterranean was begun on the 18th March, 1869, and the whole canal was opened for traffic on November 16th of the same year. The cost of the canal was about £19,000,000.

The buoyed channel which leads into the canal at the Suez end is 300 yards across in the widest part. The average width of the dredged channel is about 90 feet, and the average depth about 28 feet. At Shalûf et-Terrâbeh the excavation was very difficult, for the ground rises about twenty feet above the sea-level, and the elevation is five or six miles long. A thick layer of hard rock 'cropped' up in the line of the canal, and the work of removing it was of no slight nature. On a mound not quite half-way between Suez and Shalûf are some granite blocks bearing traces of cuneiform and hieroglyphic inscriptions recording the name of Darius. They appear to be the remains of one of a series of buildings erected along the line of the old canal which was restored and probably completed by Darius. At Shalûf the width of the canal is about 90 feet, and shortly after leaving this place the canal enters the Small Bitter Lake, which is about seven miles long. Before reaching the end of it is, on the left, another mound on which were found the ruins of a building which was excavated by M. de Lesseps. Granite slabs were found there inscribed with the name of Darius in Persian cuneiform characters and in hieroglyphics. The canal next passes through the Great Bitter Lake (about fifteen miles long), and a few kilomètres farther along it passes through the rock, upon which was built by Darius another monument to tell passers-by that he it was who made the canal. The track of the canal through the Bitter Lakes is marked by a double row of buoys; the distance between each buoy is 330 yards, and the space between the two rows is about thirty yards. At a little distance to the north of the Bitter Lake is Ṭusân, which may be easily identified by means of the tomb of the Muḥammadan saint Ennedek. Shortly after Lake Timsaḥ, or the 'Crocodile Lake,' is reached, on the north side of which is the town of Isma'îlîya, formerly the head-quarters of the staff in charge of the various works connected with the construction of the canal. The canal channel through the lake is marked by buoys as in the Bitter Lakes. Soon after re-entering the canal the plain of El-Gisr, or the 'bridge,' is entered; it is about fifty-five feet above the level of the sea. Through this a channel about eighty feet deep had to be cut. Passing through Lake Balâḥ, el-Ḳanṭara, 'the bridge,' a place situated on a height between the Balâḥ and Menzaleh Lakes, is reached. It is by this natural bridge that every invading army must have entered Egypt, and its appellation, the 'Bridge of Nations,' is most appropriate. On the east side of the canal, not far from el-Ḳanṭara, are some ruins of a building which appears to have been built by Rameses II., and a little beyond Ḳanṭara begins Lake Menzaleh. About twenty miles to the east are the ruins of Pelusium. The canal is carried through Lake Menzaleh in a perfectly straight line until it reaches Port Sa'îd.

The town of Port Sa'îd is the product of the Suez Canal, and has a population of about 12,000. It stands on the island which forms part of the narrow tract of land which separates Lake Menzaleh from the Mediterranean. The first body of workmen landed at the spot which afterwards became Port Sa'îd in 1859, and for many years the place was nothing but a factory and a living-place for workmen.

The harbour and the two breakwaters which protect it are remarkable pieces of work; the breakwater on the west is lengthened yearly to protect the harbour from the mud-carrying current which always flows from the west, and would block up the canal but for the breakwater. Near the western breakwater is the lighthouse, about 165 feet high; the electric light is used in it, and can be seen for a distance of twenty miles. The port is called Sa'îd in honour of Sa'îd Pasha. The fresh water used is brought in iron pipes laid along the western side of the canal from Isma'îlîya. The choice fell upon this spot for the Mediterranean end of the canal because water sufficiently deep for ocean-going ships was found within two miles of the shore. The total length of the canal, including the buoyed channel at the Suez end, is about one hundred miles. The Suez Canal Company's light railway, carrying passengers, runs directly to Isma'îlîya at 9 A.M., to connect with the midday train from Suez to Cairo.

CAIRO TO SUEZ.

On the line between Cairo and Suez the following important places are passed :—

I. **Shibîn el-Kanâṭir,** the stopping place for those who wish to visit the 'Jewish Hill' or Tell el-Yahûdîyyeh, where Onia, the high priest of the Jews, built a temple by the permission of Ptolemy Philometor, in which the Egyptian Jews might worship. The site of the town was occupied in very early times by a temple and other buildings which were set up by Rameses II. and Rameses III.; a large number of the tiles which formed parts of the walls of these splendid works are preserved in the British Museum.

II. **Zakâzîḳ,** the capital of the Sherḳîyeh province, is a town of about 40,000 inhabitants; the railway station stands about one mile from the mounds which mark the site of the famous old city of Bubastis,* or **Tell Basṭa.** The chief article of commerce here is cotton. Not far from Zaḳâzîḳ flows the Fresh-water Canal from Cairo to Suez, which in many places exactly follows the route of the old canal which was dug during the XIXth dynasty.

Bubastis, Bubastus, or Tell Basṭa (the Pibeseth=" House of Bast" of Ezekiel xxx. 17), was the capital of the Bubastites nome in the Delta, and was situated on the eastern side of the Pelusiac arm of the Nile. The city was dedicated to the goddess Bast, the animal sacred to whom was the cat, and was famous for having given a dynasty of kings (the XXIInd) to Egypt. To the south of the city were the lands which Psammetichus I. gave to his Ionian and Carian mercenaries, and on the north side was the canal which Nekau (Necho) dug between the Nile and the Red Sea. The city was captured by the Persians B.C. 352, and the walls, the entire circuit of which was three miles, were dismantled. Recent excavations, by M. Naville, have shown beyond doubt that the place was inhabited during the earliest dynasties, and that many great kings of Egypt delighted to build temples there. The following description by Herodotus of the town and the festival celebrated there will be found of interest:—

"Although other cities in Egypt were carried to a great height, in my opinion, the greatest mounds were thrown up about the city of Bubastis, in which is a temple of Bubastis well worthy of mention; for though other temples may be larger and more costly, yet none is more pleasing to look at than this. Bubastis, in the Greek language, answers to Diana. Her sacred precinct is thus situated: all except the entrance is an island; for two canals from the Nile extend to it, not mingling with each other, but each reaches

* From the hieroglyphic 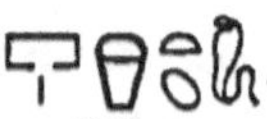 *Pa-Bast*, Coptic ⲠⲞⲨⲂⲀⲤϮ; it was the metropolis of the 18th nome of Lower Egypt, "where the soul of Isis lived in [the form] of Bast."

as far as the entrance of the precinct, one flowing round it on one side, the other on the other Each is a hundred feet broad, and shaded with trees. The portico is sixty feet in height, and is adorned with figures six cubits high, that are deserving of notice. This precinct, being in the middle of the city, is visible on every side to a person going round it: for as the city has been mounded up to a considerable height, but the temple has not been moved, it is conspicuous as it was originally built. A wall sculptured with figures runs round it; and within is a grove of lofty trees, planted round a large temple in which the image is placed. The width and length of the precinct is each way a stade [600 feet]. Along the entrance is a road paved with stone, about three stades in length [1800 feet], leading through the square eastward; and in width it is about four plethra [400 feet]: on each side of the road grow trees of enormous height; it leads to the temple of Mercury."*

The goddess Bast who was worshipped there is represented as having the head of a lioness or cat. She wore a disk, with an uræus, and carried the sceptre  or . She was the female counterpart of Ptaḥ, and was one of the triad of Memphis. Properly speaking her name is Sechet . She is called 'Lady of Heaven,' and 'The great lady, beloved of Ptaḥ.'† The nature of the ceremony on the way to Bubastis, says Herodotus,‡ is this:—

"Now, when they are being conveyed to the city Bubastis, they act as follows: for men and women embark together,

* Herodotus, ii. 137, 138 (Cary's translation).

† She is a form of Hathor, and as wife of Ptaḥ, was the mother of Nefer-Ȧtmu and I-em-ḥetep. She was the personification of the power of light and of the burning heat of the sun; it was her duty to destroy the demons of night, mist and cloud, who fought against the sun.

‡ Book II. 60.

and great numbers of both sexes in every barge; some of the women have castanets on which they play, and the men play on the flute during the whole voyage; the rest of the women and men sing and clap their hands together at the same time. When in the course of their passage they come to any town, they lay their barge near to land, and do as follows: some of the women do as I have described; others shout and scoff at the women of the place; some dance, and others stand up and behave in an unseemly manner; this they do at every town by the river-side. When they arrive at Bubastis, they celebrate the feast, offering up great sacrifices; and more wine is consumed at this festival than in all the rest of the year. What with men and women, besides children, they congregate, as the inhabitants say, to the number of seven hundred thousand."

The fertile country round about Zaḳâzîḳ is probably a part of the Goshen of the Bible.

III. Abu Ḥammâd, where the Arabian desert begins.

IV. Tell el-Kebîr, a wretched village, now made famous by the victory of Lord Wolseley over 'Arabi Pasha in 1882.

V. Maḥsamah, which stands on the site of a town built by Rameses II. Near this place is Tell el-Maskhûta, which some have identified with the Pithom which the Israelites built for the king of Egypt who oppressed them.

VI. Isma'îlîya (see p. 128).

VII. Nefîsheh. Here the fresh water canal divides into two parts, the one going on to Suez, and the other to Isma'îlîya.

TANIS.

The town which the Greeks called *Tanis*, and the Copts ⲦⲀⲚⲈⲰⲤ or ϪⲀⲚⲎ was named by the ancient Egyptians

 *Sekhet Tchā*, or 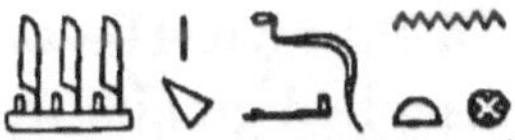 *Sekhet Tchānt* (which is accurately translated "Field of Zoan,"* שְׂדֵה־צֹעַן, in Psalm lxxviii. 12, 43) and  *Tchar*; it was the capital of the fourteenth nome of Lower Egypt,  Chent-âbṭ. The two determinatives  indicate that the place was situated in a swampy district, and that foreigners dwelt there. The Arabs have adopted the shorter name of the town, and call it Ṣân. Dr. H. Brugsch endeavoured to show that Tanis represented the town of Rameses, which was built by the Israelites, but his theory has not been generally accepted, although there is no doubt whatever that Tchar and Tanis are one and the same town. The other names of Tanis given by Dr. Brugsch in his great *Dictionnaire Géographique* are "Mesen, Mesen of the North, Teb of the North, and Beḥuṭet of the North." Tanis was situated on the right or east bank of the Tanaïtic branch of the Nile, about thirty miles nearly due west of the ancient Pelusium; and as it was near the north-east frontier of Egypt, it was always one of the towns which formed the object of the first attack of the so-called Hyksos, Syrians, Assyrians, Greeks, Arabs, and Turks. The excavations which have been made in the ruins round about Ṣân by Mariette and Petrie prove that Tanis must have been one of the largest and most important cities in the Delta. The earliest monuments found here date from the time of Pepi I., VIth dynasty, about B.C. 3233; the next oldest are the black granite statues of Usertsen I. and

* Zoan must have been considered a place of great importance by the Hebrews, for they date the founding of Hebron by it (Numbers, xiii. 22), and Isaiah, describing the future calamities of Egypt, says "Surely the princes of Zoan are fools." (Isaiah xix. 11.)

Ȧmenemḥāt II., a sandstone statue of Usertsen II., an inscribed granite fragment of Usertsen III., and two statues of Sebek-ḥetep III. Following these come the most interesting black granite sphinxes, which are usually said to be the work of the so-called Hyksos (see pp. 174–175), but which are, in my opinion, older than the period when these people ruled over Lower Egypt. The cartouches inscribed upon them only prove that many kings were anxious to have their names added to these monuments. The greatest builder at Tanis was Rameses II., who erected a temple with pylons, colossal statues, obelisks and sphinxes. Pasebkhānu, Shashanq I. and Shashanq III. repaired and added to the buildings in Tanis, and they took the opportunity of usurping sphinxes, obelisks, etc., which had been set up by earlier kings. The famous red granite "Tablet of four hundred years" was found at Ṣân. The inscription upon it, which is of the time of Rameses II., is dated in the four hundredth year of a Hyksos king named "Āa-peḥ-peḥ-Set, son of the Sun, Nub-Set (?)" 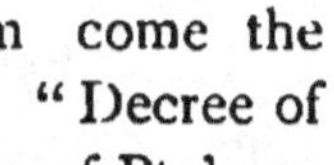 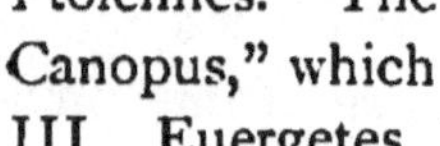, which appears to prove that this king reigned 400 years before the time of Rameses II.

The last native king of Egypt whose name is mentioned at Tanis is Nectanebus II., and after him come the Ptolemies. The stele, commonly called the "Decree of Canopus," which was set up in the ninth year of Ptolemy III., Euergetes I. (B.C. 238), was found here. The trilingual inscription in hieroglyphics, Greek, and Demotic, mentions at some length the great benefits which this king had conferred upon Egypt, and states what festivals are to be celebrated in his honour and in that of Berenice. The priests assembled at Canopus from all parts of Egypt resolved that these things should be duly inscribed upon stelæ, of which one should be placed in every large temple in Egypt to commemorate their resolution.

Under the Roman Empire Tanis still held a high position among the towns of the Delta, and the Egyptians considered it of sufficient importance to make it an episcopal see. In the list of the bishops who were present at the Council of Chalcedon (A.D. 451), the name of Apollonius, Bishop of Tanis, is found. Tanis must not be confounded with Tennis, the sea-port town which grew and increased in importance as Tanis declined; and it is difficult to understand why Tanis should have dwindled away, considering that Arab writers have described its climate as being most salubrious, and its winter like summer. Water was said to flow there at all times, and the inhabitants could water their gardens at their will ; no place in all Egypt, save the Fayyûm, could be compared with it for fertility, and for the beauty of its gardens and vines. In the sixth century of our era the sea invaded a large portion of Tanis territory, and it went on encroaching each year little by little, until all its villages were submerged. The inhabitants removed their dead to Tennis, and established themselves there ; Tennis was evacuated by its inhabitants A.D. 1192, and the town itself was destroyed A.D. 1226.

CAIRO.

Cairo (from the Arabic Ḳâhira, 'the Victorious,' because the planet Ḳâhir or Mars was visible on the night of the foundation of the city) is situated on the right or eastern bank of the Nile, about ten miles south of the division of the Nile into the Rosetta and Damietta branches. It is called in Arabic Maṣr *: it is the largest city in Africa, and its population must be now about half a million souls. Josephus says that the fortress of the Babylon of Egypt, which stood on the spot occupied by old Cairo or Fosṭâṭ, was founded by the Babylonian mercenary soldiers of Cambyses, B.C. 525; Diodorus says that it was founded by Assyrian captives in the time of Rameses II., and Ctesias is inclined to think that it was built in the time of Semiramis. The opinions of the two last mentioned writers are valuable in one respect, for they show that it was believed in their time that Babylon of Egypt was of very ancient foundation. During the reign of Augustus it was the headquarters of one of the legions that garrisoned Egypt, and remains of the town and fortress which these legionaries occupied are still to be seen a little to the north of Fosṭâṭ. The word Fosṭâṭ † means a 'tent,' and the place is so called from the tent of 'Amr ibn el-'Âṣi, which was pitched there when he invaded Egypt, A.D. 638, and to which he returned after his capture of Alexandria. Around his tent lived a large number of his followers, and

* Maṣr is a form of the old name Miṣri (Hebrew *Misraim*), by which it is called in the cuneiform tablets, B.C. 1450.

† Arab. فُسْطَاط, another form of فُسَّاط, = Byzantine Greek φοσσάτον.

these being joined by new comers, the city of Fosṭâṭ at length arose. It was enlarged by Aḥmed ibn Ṭulûn, who built a mosque there; by Khamarûyeh, who built a palace there; but when the Fâṭimite Khalif Mu'izz conquered Egypt (A.D. 969), he removed the seat of his government from there, and founded Maṣr el-Ḳâhira, "Maṣr the Victorious," near Fosṭâṭ. Fosṭâṭ, which was also known by the name of Maṣr, was henceforth called Maṣr el-'Atiḳa. During the reign of Ṣalâḥeddîn the walls of the new city were thoroughly repaired and the citadel was built. Sulṭân after Sulṭân added handsome buildings to the town, and though it suffered from plagues and fires, it gained the reputation of being one of the most beautiful capitals in the Muḥammadan empire. In 1517 it was captured by Selim I., and Egypt became a pashalik of the Turkish empire, and remained so until its conquest by Napoleon Bonaparte in 1798. Cairo was occupied by Muḥammad 'Ali in 1805. and the massacre of the Mamelukes took place March 1, 1811.

COPTIC CHURCHES IN CAIRO.*

The Church of MÂR MÎNÂ lies between Fosṭâṭ and Cairo; it was built in honour of St. Menas, an early martyr, who is said to have been born at Mareotis, and martyred during the persecution of Galerius Maximinus at Alexandria. The name Mînâ, or Menâ, probably represents the Coptic form of Menâ, 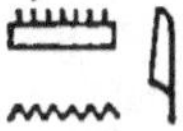, the name of the first historical king of Egypt. The church was probably founded during the fourth century, and it seems to have been restored in the eighth century; the first church built

* The authorities for the following facts relating to Coptic Churches are Butler's *Coptic Churches of Egypt*, 2 vols., 1884; and Curzon, *Visits to Monasteries in the Levant*.

to Mâr Mînâ was near Alexandria. The church measures 60 feet × 50 feet; it contains some interesting pictures, and a very ancient bronze candelabrum in the shape of two winged dragons, with seventeen sockets for lighted tapers. On the roof of the church is a small bell in a cupola.

About half-a-mile beyond the Dêr * containing the church of St. Menas, lies the Dêr of Abu's Sêfên, in which are situated the churches al-'Aḏra (the Virgin), Anba Shenûti, and Abu's Sêfên. The last-named church was built in the tenth century, and is dedicated to St. Mercurius, who is called "Father of two swords," or Abu's Sêfên. The church measures 90 feet × 50 feet, and is built chiefly of brick; there are no pillars in it. It contains a fine ebony partition dating from A.D. 927, some interesting pictures, an altar casket dating from A.D. 1280, and a marble pulpit. In this church are chapels dedicated to Saints Gabriel, John the Baptist, James, Mâr Buḳṭor, Antony, Abba Nûb, Michael, and George. Within the Dêr of Abu's Sêfên is the "Convent of the Maidens;" the account of Mr. Butler's discovery of this place is told by him in his *Coptic Churches of Egypt*, Vol. I, p. 128. The church of the Virgin was founded probably in the eighth century.

The church of Abu Sargah, or Abu Sergius, stands well towards the middle of the Roman fortress of Babylon in Egypt. Though nothing is known of the saint after whom it was named, it is certain that in A.D. 859 Shenûti was elected patriarch of Abu Sargah; the church was most probably built much earlier, and some go so far as to state that the crypt (20 feet × 15 feet) was occupied by the Virgin and her Son when they fled to Egypt to avoid the wrath of Herod. "The general shape of the church is, or was, a nearly regular oblong, and its general structure is basilican. It consists of narthex, nave, north and south

* Arabic دير "convent, monastery."

aisle, choir, and three altars eastward each in its own chapel: of these the central and southern chapels are apsidal, the northern is square ended . . . . . . Over the aisles and narthex runs a continuous gallery or triforium, which originally served as the place for women at the service. On the north side it stops short at the choir, forming a kind of transept, which, however, does not project beyond the north aisle . . . . . . On the south side of the church the triforium is prolonged over the choir and over the south side-chapel. The gallery is flat-roofed while the nave is covered with a pointed roof with framed principals like that at Abu's Sêfên . . . . . . Outside, the roof of Abu Sargah is plastered over with cement showing the king-posts projecting above the ridge-piece. Over the central part of the choir and over the haikal the roof changes to a wagon-vaulting; it is flat over the north transept, and a lofty dome overshadows the north aisle chapel . . . . . . The twelve monolithic columns round the nave are all, with one exception, of white marble streaked with dusky lines . . . . . . The exceptional column is of red Assuân granite, 22 inches in diameter . . . . . . The wooden pulpit . . . . . . is of rosewood inlaid with designs in ebony set with ivory edgings . . . . . . The haikal-screen projects forward into the choir as at Al 'Aḍra . . . . . . and is of very ancient and beautiful workmanship; pentagons and other shapes of solid ivory, carved in relief with arabesques, being inlaid and set round with rich mouldings . . . . . . The upper part of the screen contains square panels of ebony set with large crosses of solid ivory, most exquisitely chiselled with scrollwork, and panels of ebony carved through in work of the most delicate and skilful finish." (Butler, *Coptic Churches*, Vol. I., pp. 183–190, ff.) The early carvings representing St. Demetrius Mâr George, Abu's Sêfên, the Nativity, and the Last Supper are worthy of careful examination.

The Jewish synagogue near Abu Sargah was originally a Coptic church dedicated to St. Michael, which was sold to the Jews by a patriarch called Michael towards the end of the ninth century; it measures 65 feet × 35 feet, and is said to contain a copy of the Law written by Ezra.

A little to the south-east of Abu Sargah is the church dedicated to the Virgin, more commonly called El-Mu'allaḳah, or the 'hanging,' from the fact that it is suspended between two bastions, and must be entered by a staircase. The church is triapsal, and is of the basilican order. It originally contained some very beautiful screens, which have been removed from their original positions and made into a sort of wall, and, unfortunately, modern stained glass has been made to replace the old. The cedar doors, sculptured in panels, are now in the British Museum. The cedar and ivory screens are thought to belong to the eleventh century. The church is remarkable in having no choir, and Mr. Butler says it is "a double-aisled church, and as such is remarkable in having no transepts." The pulpit is one of the most valuable things left in the church, and probably dates from the twelfth century; in the wooden coffer near it are the bones of four saints. Authorities differ as to the date to be assigned to the founding of this church, but all the available evidence now known would seem to point to the sixth century as the most probable period; at any rate, it must have been before the betrayal of the fortress of Babylon to 'Amr by the Monophysite Copts in the seventh century.

A little to the north-east of Abu Sargah is the church of St. Barbara, the daughter of a man of position in the East, who was martyred during the persecution of Maximinus; it was built probably during the eighth century. In the church is a picture of the saint, and a chapel in honour of St. George. At the west end of the triforium are some mural paintings of great interest.

Within the walls of the fortress of Babylon, lying due north of Abu Sargah, are the two churches of Mâr Girgis and the Virgin.

To the south of the fortress of Babylon, beyond the Muḥammadan village on the rising ground, lie the Dêr of Bablûn and the Dêr of Tadrus. In Dêr el-Bablûn is a church to the Virgin, which is very difficult to see. It contains some fine mural paintings, and an unusual candlestick and lectern; in it also are chapels dedicated to Saints Michael and George. This little building is about fifty-three feet square. Dêr el-Tadrus contains two churches dedicated to Saints Cyrus and John of Damanhûr in the Delta; there are some fine specimens of vestments to be seen there.

A short distance from the Mûski is a Dêr containing the churches of the Virgin, St. George, and the chapel of Abu's Sêfên. The church of the Virgin occupies the lower half of the building, and is the oldest in Cairo. The chapel of Abu's Sêfên is reached through a door in the north-west corner of the building, and contains a wooden pulpit inlaid with ivory. The church of St. George occupies the upper part of the building, and is over the church of the Virgin.

In the Greek (Byzantine) quarter of Cairo is the Dêr el-Tadrus, which contains the churches of St. George and the Virgin.

The Coptic churches of Cairo contain a great deal that is interesting, and are well worth many visits. Though the fabrics of many of them are not older than the sixth, seventh, or eighth century of our era, it may well be assumed that the sites were occupied by Coptic churches long before this period.

The Mosques of Cairo.

Speaking generally there are three types of mosque * in

* The word "mosque" is derived from the Arabic مَسْجِد a "place of prayer."

Cairo: 1, the court-yard surrounded by colonnades, as in the Mosques of 'Amr and Ṭulûn; 2, the court yard surrounded by four gigantic arches, as in the Mosque of Sulṭân Ḥasan, etc.; and 3, the covered yard beneath a dome, as in the Mosque of Muḥammad 'Ali.

The Mosque of **'AMR** in Fosṭâṭ, or Old Cairo, is the oldest mosque in Egypt, its foundation having been laid A.H. 21 = A.D. 643. The land upon which it was built was given by 'Amr ibn el-'Âṣi and his friends after they had become masters of the fortress of Babylon. Of 'Amr's edifice very little remains, for nearly all the building was burnt down at the end of the ninth century. Towards the end of the third quarter of the tenth century the mosque was enlarged and rebuilt, and it was subsequently decorated with paintings etc.; the splendour of the mosque is much dwelt upon by Maḳrîzî. The court measures 350 feet × 400 feet. The building contains 366 pillars—one row on the west side, three rows on the north and south sides, and six rows on the east side; one of the pillars bears the name of Muḥammad. In the north-east corner is the tomb of 'Abdallah, the son of 'Amr.

The Mosque of **AḤMED IBN ṬULÛN** (died A.D. 884) is the oldest in Maṣr el-Ḳâhira or New Cairo, having been built A.D. 879, under the rule of Khalif Mu'tamid (A.D. 870–892). It is said to be a copy of the Ka'ba at Mecca, and to have taken two or three years to build. The open court is square, and measures about 300 feet from side to side; in the centre is the Ḥanafiyyeh (حَنَفِيَّة) or fountain for the Turks. On the north, west, and south sides is an arcade with walls pierced with arches; on the east side are five arcades divided by walls pierced with arches. The wooden pulpit is a famous specimen of wood carving, and dates from the thirteenth century. Around the outside of the minaret of this mosque is a spiral staircase, which is said to have been suggested by its founder. The mosque is called the "Fortress of the Goat," because it is said to mark the spot where Abraham offered up the ram; others say that the ark rested here.

The Mosque of **ḤÄKIM** (A.D. 996-1020), the third Fâṭimite Khalif, was built on the plan of the mosque of ibn Ṭulûn (see above); the date over one of the gates is A.H. 393 = A.D. 1003. The Museum of Arab art is located here.

The Mosque **EL-AZHAR** is said to have been founded by Jôhar, the general of Mu'izz, about A.D. 980. The plan of the principal part was the same as that of the mosque of 'Amr, but very little of the original building remains. It was made a university by the Khalif 'Aziz (A.D. 975–996), and great alterations were made in the building by different Sulṭâns in the twelfth, thirteenth, fifteenth, sixteenth, and eighteenth centuries; Sa'id Pasha made the last, A.D. 1848. The minarets belong to different periods; the mosque has six gates, and at the principal of these, the "Gate of the Barbers," is the entrance. On three of the sides of the open court are compartments, each of which is reserved for the worshippers who belong to a certain country. The Liwân of the mosque is huge, and its ceiling is supported upon 380 pillars of various kinds of stone; it is here that the greater part of the students of the university carry on their studies. The number of students varies from 10,000 to 13,000, and the education, from the Muḥammadan point of view, is perhaps the most thorough in the whole world.

In the Citadel are:—1. The Mosque of Yûsuf Ṣalâḥeddin, built A.D. 1171–1198; 2. The Mosque of Sulêmân Pasha or Sulṭân Selim, built A.H. 391 = A.D 1001.

The Muristân Ḳalaûn, originally a hospital, contains the tomb of El-Manṣûr Ḳalaûn (A.D. 1279–1290), which is decorated with marble mosaics.

The Mosque-tomb of Muḥammad en-Nâṣir (A.D. 1293–1341), son of Ḳalaûn, stands near that of Ḳalaûn.

The Mosque of **SULṬÂN ḤASAN**, built of stone taken from the pyramids of Gîzeh, is close to the citadel, and is generally considered to be the grandest in Cairo. It was built by Ḥasan, one of the younger sons of Sulṭân Nâṣir, and its construction occupied three years, A.D. 1356–1358. It is said that when the building was finished the architect's hands were cut off to prevent his executing a similar work again. This story, though probably false, shows that the mosque was considered of great beauty, and the judgment of competent critics of to-day endorses the opinion of it which was prevalent in Ḥasan's time. Ḥasan's tomb is situated on the east side of the building. The remaining minaret* is about 280 feet high, the greatest length of the mosque is about 320 feet, and the width about 200 feet. In the open court are two fountains which were formerly used, one by the Egyptians, and one by the Turks. On the eastern side are still to be seen a few of the balls which were fired at the mosque by the army of Napoleon.

The Mosque of Barḳûḳ (A.D. 1382–1399) contains the tomb of the daughter of Barḳûḳ.

The Mosque of **MUAIYAD**, one of the Circassian Mamelukes, was founded between the years 1412–1420; it is also known as the "Red Mosque," from the colour of the walls outside. "Externally it measures about 300 feet by 250, and possesses an internal court, surrounded by double colonnades on three sides, and a triple range of arches on the side looking towards Mecca, where also are situated—as in that of Barḳûḳ—the tombs of the founder and his family. A considerable number of ancient columns have been used in the erection of the building, but the superstructure is so light and elegant, that the effect is agreeable." † The bronze gate in front belonged originally to the mosque of Sulṭân Ḥasan.

* From the Arabic مَنَارَة "place of light."

† Fergusson, *Hist. of Architecture*, Vol. II., p. 516.

The Mosque of **ḲAIT** Bey (A.D. 1468–1496), one of the last independent Mameluke sulṭâns of Egypt, is about eighty feet long and seventy feet wide; it has some fine mosaics, and is usually considered the finest piece of architecture in Cairo.

The Mosque el-Ghûri was built by the Sulṭân Kanṣuweh el-Ghûri early in the sixteenth century; it is one of the most beautiful mosques in Cairo.

The Mosque of Sittah Zênab was begun late in the last century; it contains the tomb of Zênab, the granddaughter of the Prophet.

The Mosque begun by Muḥammad 'Ali in the Citadel was finished in 1857 by Sa'îd Pasha, after the death (in 1849) of that ruler; it is built of alabaster from the quarries of Beni Suêf. As with nearly all mosques built by the Turks, the church of the Hagia Sophia at Constantinople served as the model, but the building is not considered of remarkable beauty. The mosque is a square covered by a large dome and four small ones. In the south-east corner is the tomb of Muḥammad 'Ali, and close by is the mimbar (مِنْبَر) or pulpit; in the recess on the east side is the Ḳiblah (قِبْلَة), or spot to which the Muḥammadan turns his face during his prayers. The court is square, with one row of pillars on each of its four sides, and in the centre is the fountain for the Turks; the clock in the tower on the western side was presented to Muḥammad 'Ali by Louis Philippe.

The Mosque of el-Ḥasanên, *i.e.*, the mosque of Ḥasan and Ḥusên, the sons of 'Ali the son-in-law of the Prophet, is said to contain the head of Ḥusên who was slain at Kerbela A.D. 680; the head was first sent to Damascus and afterwards brought to Cairo.

In the Mosque of el-Akbar the **dancing dervishes** perform.

The Tombs of the Khalifs.*

These beautiful buildings are situated on the eastern side of the city, and contain the tombs of the members of the families of the Circassian Mameluke Sulṭâns who reigned from A.D. 1382–1517. The tomb-mosques of Yûsuf, el-Ashraf, and the tomb of el-Ghûri (A.D. 1501–1516) are to the north-east of the Bâb en-Naṣr; the tomb-mosques of Yûsuf and el-Ashraf are only to be seen by special permission. In the tomb-mosque of Barḳûḳ are buried that sulṭân, his son the Sulṭân Farag (A.D. 1399–1412), and various other members of the family. The limestone pulpit and the two minarets are very beautiful specimens of stone work. To the west of this tomb-mosque is the tomb of Sulṭân Sulêmân, and near that are the tombs of the Seven Women, the tomb-mosque of Bursbey (A.D. 1422–1438), the Ma'bed er-Rifâ'i, and the tomb of the mother of Bursbey. The most beautiful of all these tombs is the tomb-mosque of Ḳait Bey (A.D. 1468–1496), which is well worthy of more than one visit.

The Tombs of the Mamelukes.†

Of the builders of these tombs no history has been preserved; the ruins, however, show that they must have been very beautiful objects. Some of the minarets are still very fine.

The Citadel.

The Citadel was built by Ṣalâḥeddîn, A.D. 1166, and the

* The word "Khalif," Arabic, خَلِيفَة *Khalîfah*, means "successor" (of Muḥammad) or "vicar" (of God upon earth), and was a title applied to the head of the Muslim world. The last Khalifah died in Egypt *about* A.D. 1517.

† The word "Mameluke" means a "slave," Arabic مَمْلُوك, plur. مَمَالِيك.

stones used were taken from the pyramids of Gîzeh; it formed a part of the large system of the fortifications of Cairo which this Sulṭân carried out so thoroughly. Though admirably situated for commanding the whole city, and as a fortress in the days before long range cannon were invented, the site was shown in 1805 to be ill chosen for the purposes of defence in modern times by Muḥammad 'Ali, who, by means of a battery placed on the Moḳaṭṭam heights, compelled Khurshîd Pasha to surrender the citadel. In the narrow way, with a high wall, through the Bâb el-Azab, which was formerly the most direct and most used means of access to it, the massacre of the Mamelukes took place by the orders of Muḥammad 'Ali, A.D. 1811. The single Mameluke who escaped is said to have made his horse leap down from one of the walls of the Citadel; he refused to enter the narrow way.

Joseph's Well.

This well is not called after Joseph the Patriarch, as is usually supposed, but after the famous Ṣalâḥeddîn (Saladin), whose first name was Yûsuf or Joseph. The shaft of this well, in two parts, is about 280 feet deep, and was found to be choked up with sand when the Citadel was built; Saladin caused it to be cleared out, and from his time until 1865 its water was regularly drawn up and used. This well was probably sunk by the ancient Egyptians.

The Library.

This valuable institution was founded by Isma'îl in 1870, and contains the library of Muṣṭafa Pasha; the number of works in the whole collection is said to be about 24,000. Some of the copies of the Ḳorân preserved there are among the oldest known.

Ezbekîyeh Garden.

This garden or "place," named after the Amir Ezbeki,

the general of Ḳait Bey (A.D. 1468—1496), was made in 1870 by M. Barillet, and has an area of about twenty acres.

THE NILOMETER IN THE ISLAND OF RÔḌA.

The Nilometer here is a pillar, which is divided into seventeen parts, each representing a cubit, *i.e.*, 21⅓ inches, and each cubit is divided into twenty-four parts. This pillar is placed in the centre of a well about sixteen feet square; the lower end is embedded in the foundations, and the upper end is held in position by a beam built into the side walls. The well is connected with the Nile by a channel. The first Nilometer at Rôḍa is said to have been built by the Khalif Sulêmân (A.D. 715—717), and about one hundred years later the building was restored by Mâmûn (A.D. 813—833). At the end of the eleventh century a dome resting upon columns was built over it. When the Nile is at its lowest level it stands at the height of seven cubits in the Nilometer well, and when it reaches the height of 15⅔ cubits, the shêkh of the Nile proclaims that sufficient water has come into the river to admit of the cutting of the dam which prevents the water from flowing over the country. The difference between the highest rise and the lowest fall of the Nile at Cairo is about twenty-five feet. The cutting of the dam takes place some time during the second or third week in August, at which time there are general rejoicings. When there happens to be an exceptionally high Nile, the whole island of Rôḍa is submerged, and the waters flow over the Nilometer to a depth of two cubits, a fact which proves that the bed of the Nile is steadily rising, and one which shows how difficult it is to harmonize all the statements made by Egyptian, Greek, and Arab writers on the subject. As the amount of taxation to be borne by the people has always depended upon the height of the inundation, attempts were formerly made by the governments of Egypt to prove to the people that there never was a low Nile.

THE EGYPTIAN MUSEUM AT GÎZEH.

The Khedevial collection of Egyptian antiquities, formerly exhibited in the Museum at Bûlâḳ, is now arranged in a large number of rooms in the **Palace at Gizeh**, a building which is said to have been built at a cost of nearly five millions sterling. This edifice, which is pleasantly situated in spacious grounds close to the river, was opened by H.H. the Khedive on January 12, 1890.

For many years the condition and arrangement of the antiquities exhibited in the Bûlâḳ and Gîzeh Museums have been notorious subjects for complaint on the part of the Egyptologist and the tourist. The Egyptologist could obtain no trustworthy information about the antiquities which he knew were being acquired year by year, and the tourist visited the collection time after time and winter after winter, and went away on each occasion feeling that nothing had been done to help him to understand the importance of a number of objects which guide-books and experts told him were famous and of the greatest value to the artist, ethnographer, philologist, and historian. That marvellous man Mariette had gathered together from all parts a series of unique specimens of Egyptian sculpture and art of the earliest dynasties, and had, owing to the parsimony of the Egyptian government, been obliged to house them in the buildings of an old post-office at Bûlâḳ, and thither, for several years, the curious of all nations bent their steps. As his great excavations went on, the collection at Bûlâḳ became larger, until at last it was found necessary to store coffins, sarcophagi, mummies, stelæ, stone statues, *etc.*, in the sheds attached to the buildings like boxes of preserved meats in a grocer's shop. With the arrival of the Dêr el-Baḥari mummies and coffins the crowding of objects became greater, for the civilized world demanded that a

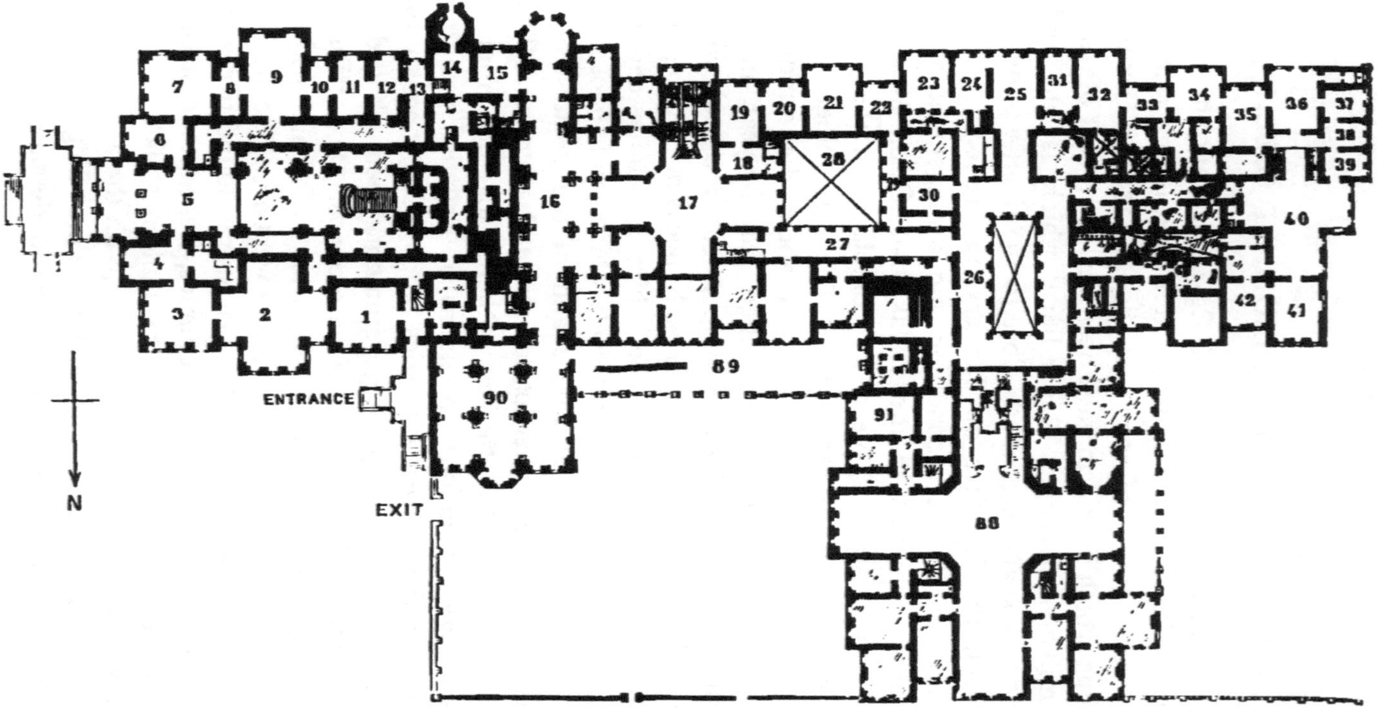

PLAN OF THE GROUND FLOOR OF THE GÎZEH MUSEUM.

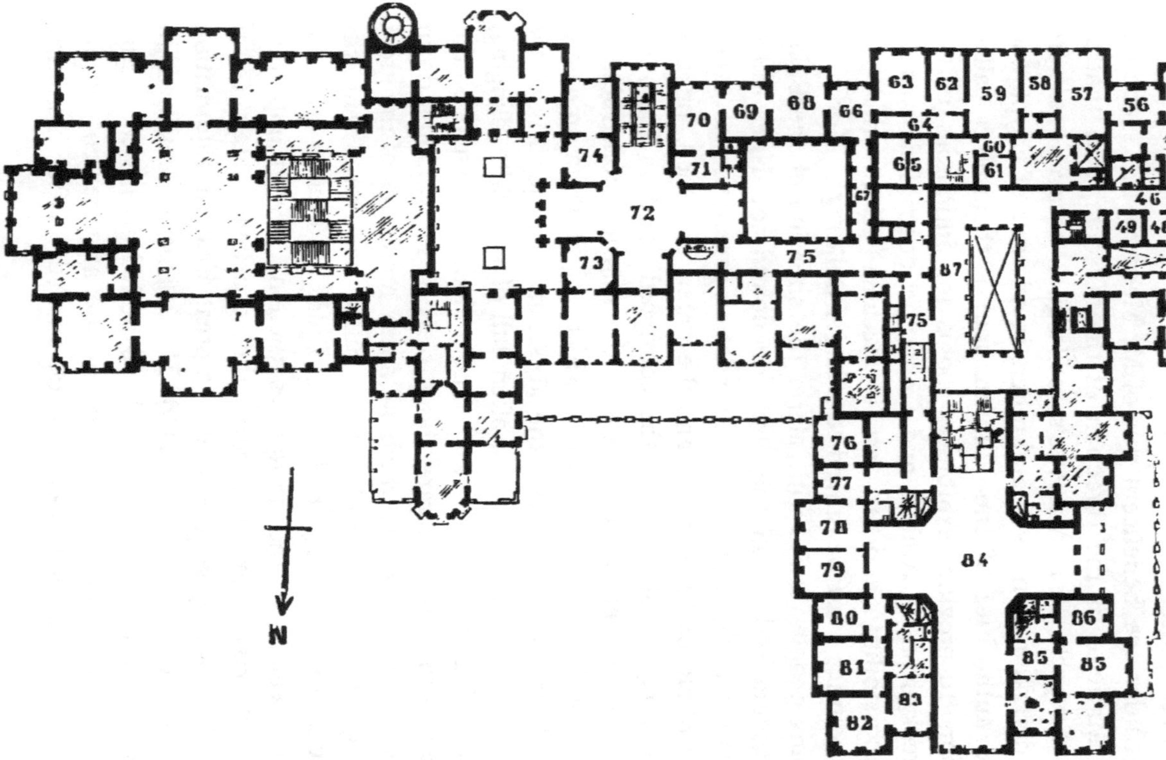

PLAN OF THE FIRST FLOOR OF THE GÎZEH MUSEUM.

place of honour should be afforded to the well-preserved mummy of Rameses the Great, and to those of the mighty kings who were his ancestors and successors. For one object laid by in the "magazine" two new ones arrived to claim its place.

Under the beneficent rule of M. Maspero, the successor of Mariette in the direction of the Museum, and that of E. Brugsch Bey, Mariette's colleague, excavations were undertaken by natives and others in all parts of Egypt, and the authorities of the Museum found themselves called upon to provide exhibition rooms for antiquities of the Greek, Roman, Arabic, and Coptic periods. This was an impossibility, and at last it became certain that the antiquities must be moved to a larger building. Moreover, many people viewed with alarm the situation of the Bûlâḳ Museum itself. On the one side flowed the Nile, which more than once during the inundation threatened to sweep the whole building away, and the waters of which, on one occasion, actually entered the courtyard; and on the other were a number of warehouses of the flimsiest construction, filled with inflammable stores which might at any moment catch fire and burn down the Museum. In the early winter mornings the building was often full of the white, clinging, drenching mist which is common along the banks of the river, and it was no rare thing to see water trickling down inside the glass cases which held the mummies of the great kings of Egypt. With all its faults, however, there was much to be said for the old Bûlâḳ Museum, and the arrangement of the antiquities therein. Every important object was numbered, and the excellent catalogue of M. Maspero gave the visitor a great deal of information about the antiquities. Had M. Maspero remained in Egypt he would, no doubt, have added to his catalogue, and every important change in the arrangement of the rooms would have been duly chronicled. After his retirement, however, a policy was inaugurated which is difficult either to understand or describe. The influx of objects during Maspero's reign at Bûlâḳ was great—so great that it would have been impossible for him to incorporate them all, even if he had had the necessary space; we now know that many of them were exceedingly fine, yet after his departure no attempt was made to exhibit them. This might, in many cases, have been done easily, for poor specimens could have been relegated to the "magazine," and fine ones exhibited in their stead.

With the increase of accommodation for tourists and of facilities for travelling after the occupation of Egypt by the British, public opinion grew and waxed strong, and the advisers of the late Khedive found it necessary to consider the task of the removal of the Egyptian antiquities from Bûlâḳ to a safer and larger resting-place. The Egyptian Government had no funds at their disposal with which to build a new Museum, and after much discussion it was decided to transfer the antiquities to the large palace at Gîzeh, which is said to have cost five millions sterling. The usual irresponsible opposition to the scheme was offered by those who should have known better, but there seems to be little doubt that this decision was the best that could have been arrived at under the circumstances in which the Egyptian Government was placed. The fabric of the Gîzeh palace seems to be flimsy, and the appearance of the building is not that which those who are acquainted with European museums are accustomed to associate with Egyptian antiquities; it is, nevertheless, a large building, and the fact that it would cost nothing must have been a great inducement to transform the palace into a museum. Much was said at first about danger to the antiquities from fire, but it is quite certain that the danger from fire at Bûlâḳ was greater than it is at Gîzeh. Some excellent alterations in the building and arrangements to prevent fire were made by Sir Francis Grenfell, and when the further contemplated precautions are taken the Museum will be as safe from fire as any building, half French, half Oriental, can be in the East. It cannot however be doubted that a specially arranged fire-proof building constructed in some suitable open place in Cairo would more effectually protect the priceless relics of a great early civilization. Here the antiquities would be better guarded in every way, and it is probable that the income which would be derived from the increased number of visits made by tourists, would in a short time form an important contribution towards the original outlay.

The decision to remove the antiquities from Bûlâḳ to Gîzeh was carried out in 1889 in the most praiseworthy manner. Gangs of men toiled from morning till night, and behind the trucks or carts containing the most precious objects M. Grébaut, the director of the Museum, and Brugsch Bey might be seen directing the workmen. During the hottest months of the summer and during the hottest hours of the day, under an exposure to the sun such as the ancient Coptic monks considered to be an adequate preparation for the lake of fire in Gehenna, the work went on; nothing of value was injured or broken, and the authorities declare that no object was lost. When the antiquities had been moved from Bûlâḳ, every lover of Egyptian art hoped that the statues, etc., which had been acquired during the last seven or eight years would be incorporated with those with which he was familiar, that each object would be numbered, that brief labels would be added, and that a chronological arrangement would be attempted. Owing to ill-health, however, M. Grébaut failed to continue the good work which he had begun, and for a long period but little new was done. Early in the year 1892 it was reported that M. Grébaut was about to resign, and for once rumour was correct. M. Grébaut was succeeded by M. Jacques de

Morgan, who at once began the task of re-arranging the collection and of examining the contents of the "magazine" with the view of increasing the number of exhibited objects. During the past year the work has been pushed on with great energy, and we believe that the visitors to the Gîzeh Museum will greatly appreciate what the staff has done. It will be remembered that of the rooms in the palace, only some thirty-eight contained antiquities two years ago; now, however, about eighty-seven are used for exhibition purposes, and, for the first time, it is possible to see of what the Egyptian collection really consists. On the ground floor the positions of several of the large monuments have been changed, and the chronological arrangement is more accurate than before. In one large handsome room are exhibited for the first time several fine maṣṭăba stelæ, which have been brought from Saḳḳârah during the past year. The brightness of the colours, the vigour of the figures, and the beauty of the hieroglyphics upon these fine monuments of the early dynasties, will, we believe, make them objects of general interest and attraction. On the same floor the visitor will also examine with wonder two splendid colossal statues of the god Ptaḥ which were excavated by M. de Morgan at Memphis in 1892. In a series of rooms are arranged the coffins and mummies of the priests of Ȧmen which M. Grébaut brought down from Thebes in the winter of 1890–91. The coffins are of great interest, for they are ornamented with mythological scenes and figures of the gods which seem to be peculiar to the period immediately following the rule of the priests kings of Thebes, *i.e.*, from about B.C. 1000–800.

A new and important feature in the arrangement of the rooms on the upper floor is the section devoted to the exhibition of papyri. Here in flat glazed cases are shown at full length fine copies of the Book of the Dead, hieratic texts, including the unique copy of the "Maxims of Ani," and many other papyri which have been hitherto inaccessible to the ordinary visitor. Now that these precious works cannot be reached by damp, their exhibition in a prominent place is a wise act on the part of the direction of the Museum. To certain classes of objects, such as scarabs, blue-glazed *faïence*, linen sheets, mummy bandages and clothing, terra-cotta vases and vessels, alabaster jars, *etc.*, special rooms are devoted, and the visitor or student can see at a glance which are the most important specimens of each class. The antiquities which, although found in Egypt, are certainly not of Egyptian manufacture, *e.g.*, Greek and Phœnician glass, Greek statues, tablets inscribed in cuneiform, found at Tell el-Amarna, are arranged in groups in rooms set apart for them; and the monuments of the Egyptian Christians or Copts are also classified and arranged in a separate room. The antiquities have now been arranged and numbered on an intelligent system by the exertion of MM. de Morgan and Brugsch, and the excellent work which has been done during the past years is, we hope and believe, an earnest of what will be done in the immediate future. The growing prosperity of Egypt is an accomplished fact,* and it seems that the Museum of

* The following table shows the revenue from 1887–1897:—

	Revenue from direct taxation.	Revenue from indirect taxation.	Revenue from Railways, Telegraphs, Post Office, etc.	Total.
	£	£	£	£
1887	5,474,503	2,246,182	1,579,719	9,616,358
1888	5,456,791	2,277,217	1,551,158	9,661,436
1889	5,463,470	2,354,275	1,597,303	9,718,958
1890	5,480,752	2,712,551	1,688,813	10,236,612
1891	5,272,667	3,003,623	1,905,439	10,539,460
1892	5,224,378	2,741,300	1,974,717	10,297,312
1893	5,121,648	2,854,917	1,907,731	10,241,866
1894	4,747,487	3,072,298	2,033,978	10,161,318
1895	5,080,442	3,029,171	1,983,046	10,431,265
1896	5,023,697	3,219,939	2,074,013	10,693,577
1897	5,049,386	3,398,854	2,225,686	11,092,564

From Lord Cromer, *Egypt*, No. 1 (1898), p. 51.

Gîzeh should participate in this prosperity and receive a larger grant of money, both for making purchases and excavations, for the attraction of the antiquities of the country is a very real and genuine matter, and induces travellers to visit it again and again. Whether the antiquities remain in their present position, or whether the authorities decide to remove them to a more suitable building in Cairo, it is equally certain that the English advisers of the Khedive will never allow the progress of an institution which draws much money into the country, and which is now doing splendid work, to be hampered for the sake of a few thousand pounds a year.

The founding of the Bûlâḳ Museum is due to the marvellous energy and perseverance of **F. Auguste Ferdinand Mariette.** This distinguished Frenchman was born at Boulogne-sur-Mer on February 11th, 1821.* His grandfather was the author of several poetical works, short plays, etc., but his father was only an employé in the Registrar's Office of his native town. He was educated at Boulogne, and was made professor there when he was twenty years of age; here too he lived until 1848. Side by side with the duties of his professorship he devoted himself in turn to journalism, painting, novel-writing, etc., and in addition to these matters he found time to study archæology. Some of his early studies were devoted to classical archæology, and here, according to M. Maspero, he exhibited "power of discussion, clearness and vigour of style, and keen penetration," qualities for which in after-life he was famous.

* For full accounts of the life of Mariette, see *Inauguration du Monument élevé à Boulogne-sur-Mer en l'honneur de l'Égyptologue Auguste Mariette*, le 16 Juillet, 1882, par Aug. Huguet, Mayor of Boulogne, Boulogne, 1882; and Wallon, *Notice sur la vie et les travaux de F. A. F. Mariette Pasha*, Paris, 1883, 4to., with portrait of Mariette as frontispiece; and Maspero, *Guide au Musée de Boulaq*, Cairo, 1884, pp. 12–23.

His attention was first drawn to the study of Egyptian archæology by the examination of a collection of Egyptian antiquities which had been made by Vivant Denon, one of the artists attached to the French Expedition in Egypt, and his first work on Egyptian archæology seems to have been a notice of a coffin in this collection, which he drew up for the instruction of those who came to inspect it in the municipal buildings where it was exhibited. Soon after this he wrote a paper on the classification of the cartouches inscribed upon the **Tablet of Karnak,*** a most valuable monument which was discovered at Karnak by Burton, and taken by Prisse d'Avennes to Paris, where it is now preserved in the Bibliothèque Nationale. This work was addressed to Charles Lenormant, a pupil of the famous Champollion, and this gentleman, together with Maury, de Saulcy and Longpérier, advised him to come to Paris, where by the kind intercession of Janron, he obtained an appointment on the staff of the Louvre in 1848. As the salary paid to the young man was not sufficient to keep him, he resolved to ask the French Government to provide him with the necessary funds to go to Egypt, where he wished to try his fortune. In his application to the Government he stated that the object of his proposed mission was to study the Coptic and Syriac manuscripts† which still remained in the monasteries of the Nitrian desert, and if possible to acquire them for the nation, and with his application he sent in an essay on Coptic bibliography. The petition was favourably received, and he set out for Egypt in the summer of 1850. Having arrived in Egypt, he found that it was not easy to obtain access to the libraries of the

* See page 3.

† The reader interested in the history of Dr. Tattam's acquisition of MSS. from the Monastery of St. Mary Deipara, in the Natron Valley, should read the article in the Quarterly Review for December, 1845, and the preface to Cureton, *Festal Letters of Athanasius*, London, 1848.

monasteries, for the Patriarch had insisted that they should be carefully guarded from strangers. Profiting by the delays caused by the Patriarch's orders, he began to visit the sites of ancient Egyptian buildings in the neighbourhood of Cairo. While at Saḳḳârah one day he discovered by accident a sphinx, on which were inscribed the names of Ȧusȧr-Ḥāpi or Osiris-Apis (Serapis), similar to one he had seen at Cairo. He remembered that the Serapeum at Memphis was described by ancient authors as standing on a sandy plain,* and he believed that he had really found the spot where it stood and its ruins. Neglecting the original object of his expedition, he collected workmen, and in 1850 set to work to dig; two months' work revealed one hundred and forty sphinxes, two chapels, a semi-circular space ornamented with Greek statues, etc. Through the jealousy of certain people who united the profession of politics with wholesale trading in antiquities, the Egyptian Government of the day issued an order to suspend the excavations, and the work was stopped. Soon after, however, the French National Assembly voted 30,000 francs for excavation purposes, and towards the end of the year Mariette was enabled to enter the Serapeum, where he found sixty-four Apis bulls, stelae, etc. As the dates when the bulls were placed in the Serapeum are stated, they afford a valuable help in fixing the chronology of Egypt as far back as the XVIIIth dynasty. The year 1852 was spent in clearing out the Serapeum, and early in 1853 he came to the Pyramids of Gîzeh, where he carried on excavations for the Duc de Luynes; in the latter year he discovered a granite temple near Gîzeh. About this time he was appointed Assistant-Curator at the Louvre.

In 1854, 'Abbâs Pasha, who had suspended Mariette's excavations two or three years before, died; he was succeeded by Sa'îd Pasha, who at once conferred the honour

* *Ἔστι δὲ καὶ Σαράπιον ἐν ἀμμώδει τόπῳ σφόδρα*, Strabo, xvii. i. 32.

of Bey upon Mariette, and commissioned him to found an Egyptian Museum at Bûlâḳ. Mariette proceeded to work out a plan for the complete excavation of ancient Egyptian sites, and it is said that he began to work at thirty-seven places at once; his work literally extended from "Rakoti (Alexandria) to Syene." At Tanis he brought to light valuable monuments belonging to the XIIIth, XIVth, XIXth and XXIst dynasties, among which must be specially mentioned the statues and the sphinx which he attributed to the Hyksos; he explored hundreds of maṣṭăbas in the cemeteries at Gîzeh, Saḳḳârah, and Mêdûm; he opened the *Maṣṭăbat el-Far'ûn* (see p. 242); at Abydos, which he practically discovered, he cleared out the temple of Seti I., two temples of Rameses II., and a large number of tombs; at Denderah, a temple of Hathor; at Thebes he removed whole villages and mountains of earth from above the ruins of the temples at Karnak, Medînet-Habû and Dêr el-Baḥari; and at Edfû he removed from the roof of the temple a village of huts, and cleared out its interior. Mariette was appointed Commissioner of the Paris Exhibition of 1867, and upon him devolved the task of removing to Paris several of the most beautiful and valuable antiquities from the collection under his charge at Bûlâḳ. In 1870 he was overtaken by severe domestic troubles, and a disease which had some years before fastened upon him now began to show signs of serious progress. Notwithstanding his infirmities, however, he continued to edit and publish the texts from the monuments which he had discovered, and remained hard at work until his death, which took place at Cairo on January 17th, 1881. His body was entombed in a marble sarcophagus which stood in the court-yard of the Bûlâḳ Museum, and which has since been removed to Gizeh, together with the antiquities of the Museum.

The following is a list of the most important of Mariette's works:—

Abydos, description des fouilles exécutées sur l'emplacement de cette ville. 3 tom. Paris, 1869–1880. Fol.

Album du Musée de Boulaq. Cairo, 1871. Fol.

Aperçu de l'histoire d'Égypte. Cairo, 1874. 8vo.

Choix de Monuments et de dessins découverts ou exécutés pendant le déblaiement du Sérapéum de Memphis. Paris, 1856. 4to.

Deir el-bahari. Leipzig, 1877. 4to.

Dendérah—Description générale. Paris, 1875.

Dendérah—Planches. Paris. 5 tom. 1870–74.

Itinéraire de la Haute-Égypte. Alexandria, 1872.

Karnak—Étude Topographique. Leipzig, 1875. 4to.

Karnak—Planches. Leipzig, 1875. 4to.

Les Mastaba de l'ancien empire. Paris, 1889. Fol.

Les Papyrus Égyptiens du Musée de Boulaq. Paris, 1872.

Monuments divers. Paris, 1872. Fol.

Le Sérapéum de Memphis. Paris, 1857. Fol.

Voyage dans la Haute Égypte. Cairo, 1878. Fol.

Mariette was succeeded as Director of the Bûlâḳ Museum by **M. Maspero,** who proved an able administrator, and who carried on many of the works which Mariette had left unfinished at his death. Mariette had formulated a theory that none of the pyramids was ever inscribed inside, and consequently never attempted to open the Pyramids of Saḳḳârah, although he lived at their feet for some thirty years; M. Maspero, however, dug into them, and was rewarded by finding inscribed upon the walls a series of religious texts of the greatest importance for the history of the religion of Egypt. M. Maspero was, in 1886, succeeded by **M. Grébaut,** who, in turn, was, in 1892, succeeded by **M. de Morgan.**

Jacques Jean Marie de Morgan, Ingénieur civil des Mines, was born on June 3rd, 1857, at the Château de Bion, Loir-et-Cher, and is descended from a family which came originally from Wales. For more than twenty years he has devoted himself to the study of archæology, but he is, nevertheless, a distinguished pupil of the School of Mines at Paris, and is eminent as a geologist and mathematician. To the exactness induced by the study of mathematics, and to his scientific training as a geologist and observer of nature, his works entirely owe their value, for he arranges his historical, geographical, and other facts in a logical manner, and never confounds fact with theory or assumption with evidence. In 1882 he made a tour through India for scientific purposes, and in the same year he published his *Géologie de la Bohême*, 8vo. In 1884 he undertook an expedition to Siam and the neighbouring countries, and in the following year he published some account of his work in *Exploration dans la presqu'île Malaisie*, Rouen, 1885. In this year we also find him contributing articles to the newspaper *L'Homme;* and in 1886 he published in the *Annales des Mines* an important article entitled, *Note sur la géologie et l'industrie minière du royaume de Perak.* During the years 1886–1889 he was employed on a mission to Turkey-in-Asia, the Caucasus and Armenia, and he published the scientific results of his travels in two volumes, large 8vo., entitled, *Mission Scientifique au Caucase. Études archéologiques et historiques*, Paris, 1889. In this work M. de Morgan shows that he is well acquainted with the statements about these countries made by classical writers, that he is familiar with the best works upon general archæology, such as those of Sir John Evans, Montelius and Mourier, and also that he knows well the works of Brugsch, Maspero, George Smith, and of other scholars of Assyriology and Egyptology at first hand. From 1889 to the beginning of 1892 M. de Morgan made an expedition to Persia, Kurdistan and Luristan, and the results of his travels in these countries will appear in due course.

During the first years of his work as Director of Antiquities, M. de Morgan carried out the following works:—At **Aswân** the sand has been cleared away from the tombs which were discovered by Sir Francis Grenfell, G.C.B., and the tomb of Se-renput has been entirely cleared. At **Kom Ombos** the whole temple has been excavated; at **Luxor** the works have been carried on with great activity: at **Saḳḳârah** the tomb of Ti has been restored and cleared; at **Dahshûr** two brick pyramids and several *maṣṭâba* tombs have been excavated (see p. 395 ff.); and at **Gîzeh** and **Memphis** important excavations have been made. M. de Morgan was, in 1897, succeeded by **M. Loret.**

Victor Loret was born at Paris on September 1, 1859. He has been a Member of *Institut Français d'archéologie Orientale au Caire* since its foundation in 1879; and he was "Maître de conférences d'Égyptologie à l'Université de Lyon" in April, 1886. He is the author of *Manuel de la langue Égyptienne* (Paris, 1891); *La Flore pharaonique* (Paris, 1892); and of articles in the various publications devoted to Egyptology. The various Directors of the Museum have been most ably seconded in all their endeavours by **Emil Brugsch Bey,** the Conservator of the Museum, to whom the arrangement and classification of the collections therein is chiefly due. He holds the traditions of the great Mariette, having been his fellow-worker, and possesses an unrivalled knowledge of sites and of matters relating to excavations; his learning and courtesy are too well known to need further mention.

The national **Egyptian collection at Gîzeh** surpasses every other collection in the world, by reason of the number of the monuments in it which were made during the first six dynasties, and by reason of the fact that the places from which the greater number of the antiquities come are well ascertained. It contains also a large number of *complete* monuments and statues, which it owes chiefly to the fact that MM. Mariette, Maspero, E. Brugsch-Bey and Grébaut were present at the sites when they were found, and superintended their transport to the Museum. The collection of scarabs is of little importance, and many a private collector, not to mention the great museums of Europe, now possesses collections of more importance historically, and of more value intrinsically.

In the **Garden of the Museum** are exhibited :—

6008. Red granite **Sphinx,** inscribed with the cartouches of Rameses II.; excavated by Mariette at Tanis in the Delta. The Egyptians called the Sphinx *ḥu* , and he represented the god Harmachis, "*i.e.*, Horus in the horizon." (See p. 233.)

6628. Upper portion of an **obelisk** or pyramidion of the XVIIth dynasty, before B.C. 1700; from Karnak.

Marble sarcophagus on a pedestal of masonry, containing the body of **F. A. F. Mariette,** the founder of the Egyptian Museum at Bûlâḳ; the sphinxes round about it come from the Serapeum.

Among the most interesting of the antiquities in the Museum are :—

Ground Floor. Room I.—Monuments of the first six Dynasties.

261. Table of offerings of the scribe **Setu,** sculptured with grapes, bread, chickens, etc., in relief; the hollow for

holding the libations offered is divided into a series of cubits to represent the height of the water in the Nilometer at Memphis: 22 cubits in the spring, 23 in the autumn, and 25 in the winter.

VIth dynasty. From Dahshûr.

1. Black granite statue of a priest kneeling. A remarkable example of early work, probably before the IVth dynasty. From Saḳḳârah.

2. Panels of wood for inlaying upon the false doors of the tomb of **Ḥesi-Rā**; they are splendid examples of the delicate and accurate work executed by Egyptian carvers in wood during the IVth dynasty. From Saḳḳârah.

962. Round, white alabaster table of offerings made for **Khu-ḥetep-heres**, prophet of the goddess Maāt of Nekhen. Vth dynasty. From Saḳḳârah.

3. Layer of clay and plaster painted in water colours, with a scene in which geese are represented walking along. The artist has depicted the birds with great fidelity to nature, and was evidently a very accomplished draughtsman. This fragile object was brought from a ruined maṣṭăba at Mêdûm by M. Vassali, and dates probably from the IVth dynasty.

4, 5. Two libation tables found in a tomb near the Step Pyramid (see page 241) of Saḳḳârah. A slab, resting on the backs of a pair of lions, has a trench cut in it for carrying off the liquid into a bowl, which stands between the tails of the two lions.

IVth dynasty. From Saḳḳârah.

6. Double statue of **Rā-ḥetep** and his wife Nefert, "a royal connexion," found in a maṣṭăba near the Pyramid of Mêdûm, which is generally thought to have been built by Seneferu the first king of the IVth dynasty. The eyes are filled with quartz or rock crystal. Mariette placed the period when this statue was made in the IIIrd dynasty, but Maspero thinks that it belongs to the XIIth dynasty.

8, 9. Stelæ of **Setu.** IVth dynasty. From Gîzeh.

11, 12. Two door-posts from the tomb of **Seker-khā-baiu,** inscribed with figures of the lady Hathor-nefer-ḥetep, who was surnamed Tepes.
Before the IVth dynasty. From Saḳḳârah.

13. Stele, in the form of a false door, from the tomb of **Sherȧ,** a priest who lived during the reign of **Senṭ,** the fifth king of the IInd dynasty, about B.C. 4000. A stele of this Sherȧ is preserved in the Ashmolean Museum at Oxford. From Saḳḳârah.

16. Stele in the form of a door from the tomb of **Seker-khā-baiu.** Before the IVth dynasty. From Saḳḳârah.

Room II.—Monuments of Dynasties IV.–VI.

17. Limestone statue of **Rā-nefer,** a priest with shaven head. Vth dynasty. From Saḳḳârah.

18. Limestone statue of **Rā-nefer,** a priest wearing a wig. These two statues are generally admitted to be the best examples of the work of the Vth dynasty, and they exhibit an amount of skill in sculpture which was never surpassed at any subsequent period in the history of Egyptian art. From Saḳḳârah.

19. Wooden statue of a man, originally covered with a thin layer of plaster and painted; the feet are restored. His hair is cut short, his eyes are formed of pieces of quartz set in bronze lids, each having a piece of bright metal driven through it to hold it in position and to give the rock-crystal pupil in front of it an animated appearance; he wears an apron only, and holds in one hand an unpeeled stick. It is quite evident that we have here a portrait statue which possesses the greatest possible fidelity to life, and a startling example of what the ancient Egyptian artist could attain to when he shook off the fetters of conventionality. The countenance possesses the peaceful look of the man who is satisfied with himself, and contented with the world. This statue is commonly known by the name of **Shêkh el-Beled,** or "Shêkh of the Village," because of the likeness which it was thought to bear to a native shêkh at Saḳḳârah by Mariette's workmen when they found it in the tomb of the man in whose honour it was made.

Vth dynasty.   From Saḳḳârah.

20. Statue of **Antkha,** a priest.

21. Statue of **Atep,** a master of funereal ceremonies.

23, 28. Stelæ of **Rā-en-kau.**

Vth dynasty.   From Saḳḳârah.

24. Statue of **Ḥeses,** an overseer of public works.

From Saḳḳârah.

25. Stele of **Sesha.**   VIth dynasty.   From Abydos.

29, 30. Portions of the shrine from the tomb of **Sabu,** a large land-owner.   On No. 881 are represented Sabu receiving funereal offerings, statues of the deceased being brought to the tomb, the slaughter of animals for the funereal feast, boats bringing furniture for the tomb, etc.   On No. 1046 are given the names of the various foods which are to form the meal of the deceased, and Sabu is seen sitting at a table loaded with offerings.

Vth dynasty.   From Saḳḳârah.

35. Upper part of a wooden statue of a female which was found in the tomb with the **Shêkh el-Beled.**

Vth dynasty.   From Saḳḳârah.

Room III.—Monuments of Dynasties IV.–VI.

33. Diorite statue of **Mycerinus,** builder of the third pyramid at Gizeh, IVth dynasty, B.C. 3633.

From Mit-Rahîneh.

37. Alabaster statue of a king, name unknown.
From Mît-Rahîneh.

38. Alabaster statue of **Men-kau-Ḥeru**, Vth dynasty, B.C. 3400. From Mît-Rahîneh.

39. Red granite statue of **User-en-ka**, Vth dynasty, B.C. 3433. From Mît-Rahîneh.

41. Alabaster statue of **Khephren**, builder of the second pyramid at Gîzeh, IVth dynasty, B.C. 3666.
From Mît-Rahîneh.

42. Green basalt statue of **Khephren**, IVth dynasty. B.C. 3666. Found in a well in the temple at Gîzeh.

43. Limestone statue of **Ȧteṫȧ**, surnamed Ānkhares.
Vth or VIth dynasty. From Saḳḳârah.

48. Portion of a grey granite shrine, inscribed with the name of **Saḥu-Rā**. Vth dynasty.

49. Limestone slab from the tomb of **Unȧ**, a high official who served under the kings **Tetȧ**, **Pepi I. and Mer-en-Rā**, of the VIth dynasty, about B.C. 3300–3233. Unȧ was a man of humble birth, and began life in the royal service as a "crown bearer"; he was next made overseer of the workmen, and was soon after sent to Ṭurrah to bring back a block of stone for the sarcophagus of the king. He was then made governor of the troops, and was set at the head of an expedition against the Āāmu and the Ḥerushā. On five different occasions did Unȧ wage war successfully against Egypt's foes, and having wasted their countries with fire and sword, he returned to Memphis crowned with glory. The inscription is of the greatest importance for the history of the period, and is interesting as showing that a man of very humble birth could attain to the highest dignities at the Egyptian court. From Abydos.

51. Slab from the tomb of **Tchāu**, the uncle of Pepi II.
VIth dynasty. From Abydos

54. Limestone stele, inscribed with a text recording the **building of the temple of Isis**, lady of the pyramid, by Khufu, or Cheops, the builder of the Great Pyramid, IVth dynasty, B.C. 3733. This stele is not a contemporaneous monument, but was probably set up by a later king after the XXth dynasty.

55. Black granite stele of **User.** From Karnak.

Room IV.—Stelæ, etc., of Dynasties IV.–VI.

In this room are arranged stelæ found at Gîzeh and Saḳḳârah.

62. In the centre of the room is a seated limestone statue of Heken, a lady belonging to the royal family.

Room V.—Statues, etc., of Dynasties IV.–VI.

64. Green diorite statue of **Khephren**, the builder of the second Pyramid at Gîzeh. This full-sized portrait statue of the king is one of the most remarkable pieces of Egyptian sculpture extant. Khephren is seated upon a throne, the arms of which are ornamented with lions' heads; on the sides are depicted the papyrus, , and the lotus, , intertwined about , forming the device  emblematic of the union of Upper and Lower Egypt. The king holds in his hand a roll of papyrus, and above his head is a hawk, the visible emblem of the god Horus, his protector, with outspread, sheltering wings. On the pedestal, by the feet, is inscribed, "The image of the Golden Horus, Khephren, beautiful god, lord of diadems." IVth dynasty.

Found in a well in the granite temple at Gizeh.

65. Limestone stele from the tomb of **Ankheftka**; see Room VII., No. 86.

Vth dynasty. From Saḳḳârah.

66. Stele of **Ankhmȧka,** a priest of the kings Saḥu-Rā and User-ka-f. From Saḳḳârah.

70. Limestone stele of **Ptaḥ-ḥetep.**
Vth dynasty. From Saḳḳârah.

74. Granite sarcophagus of **Ḥeru-baf,** a descendant or relative of Cheops. IVth dynasty. From Gîzeh.

926. Red granite seated statue of **Ma-nefer,** a scribe.
Vth dynasty. From Gîzeh.

The seated statues of the **scribes** near the door are good examples of the work of this period.

Room VI.—Stelæ of Dynasties IV.–VI.

In this room are arranged stelæ and statues found at Gîzeh and Saḳḳârah.

Room VII.—Statues, etc., of Dynasties IV.–VI.

77. Limestone statue of **Ti.** Found in her tomb.
Vth dynasty. From Saḳḳârah.

78. Statue of the dwarf **Khnum-ḥetep.**
IVth dynasty. From Saḳḳârah.

79. Limestone statue of **Nefer.**
Vth dynasty. From Saḳḳârah.

81. Limestone statues of **Nefer-ḥetep** and the lady **Tentetȧ.** Vth dynasty. From Saḳḳârah.

1033. Limestone statue of **Seten-Maāt.**
Vth dynasty. From Saḳḳârah.

82. Limestone bas-relief on which the high official **Apa,** seated in a chair, making a tour of inspection of his farm, is depicted. The operations of harvest, and the slaughter of animals for the funereal meal are also represented. At the table Apa is accompanied by his wife **Senbet** and daughter **Pepi-ānkh-nes.**
VIth dynasty. From Saḳḳârah.

83. Limestone slab, sculptured with scenes in which are depicted the threshing and winnowing of wheat, the baking of bread, the carving of a statue, glass blowing, and working in gold.

85. Limestone group of three figures. The decoration of the woman is curious and worthy of note.

86. Bas-relief from the tomb of **Ānkheftka.**
From Saḳḳârah.

87. Statue of a man carrying a sack or bag over his left shoulder. Vth dynasty. From Saḳḳârah.

88. Limestone figures of a man and woman kneading dough.
IVth dynasty. From Saḳḳârah.

89. Limestone statue of a scribe kneeling.
Vth dynasty. From Saḳḳârah.

All the small statues exhibited in the wall-cases of this room are worth careful study.

Room VIII.—Bas-reliefs, etc., from Gîzeh and Saḳḳârah.

95. Wooden statue of **Tep-em-ānkh.**
Vth dynasty. From Saḳḳârah.

Among the bas-reliefs should be noticed :—quarrel of boatmen; servants making bread and bottling wine; flocks crossing a river or canal; bulls being led to slaughter; ape biting a man's leg; pasturing of flocks, etc.; cleaning and grinding of corn (Nos. 91, 92, 93, 94).
All these are from Saḳḳârah.

Room IX.—Sarcophagi, Wooden Objects, etc.

96. Red granite sarcophagus of **Khufu-Ānkh,** a priest of Isis, and "Clerk of the Works." The cover is rounded, and at each end are "ears" or projections for lifting it on

and off; its sides are inscribed with the usual prayer to the god **Ȧp-uat,** and record the names of a large number of festivals. The sides of the sarcophagus are ornamented with false doors, etc., and resemble the architectural decorations of the maṣṭăbas.

IVth dynasty. Found near the Great Pyramid.

97. Red granite sarcophagus of the royal son **Ka-em-sekhem.** IVth dynasty. From Gîzeh.

98. Limestone stele of **Tep-em-ānkh,** a priestly official who held offices connected with the pyramids of Cheops, Chephren, Mycerinus, Seneferu, Saḥu-Rā, and Userkaf.

From Saḳḳârah.

99. Stele of **Sebu,** a minister of art education under king Tetȧ. From Saḳḳârah.

100. Limestone stele of **Ptaḥ-kepu,** who lived in the reign of king Assȧ. From Saḳḳârah.

103. Models of granaries. The grain was carried on to the roof and poured into the different chambers through holes therein; in the front are rectangular openings with sliding shutters through which it could be taken out.

From Akhmîm (Panopolis).

104. Model of a house. From Akhmîm (Panopolis).

105. Box containing models of an altar, vases, a granary, boats, etc. VIth dynasty. From Saḳḳârah.

6229. Small ivory statue. Vth dynasty. From Gîzeh.

6235. Model of a boat for carrying the dead.

From Akhmîm.

Room X.—Royal Mummies, etc.

106. **Mummy** of king **Mentu-em-sa-f.**

VIth dynasty. Found in a pyramid at Saḳḳârah, 1881.

107. Fragments of the **mummy** of King **Unȧs.**
Vth dynasty. Found in his pyramid at Saḳḳarah.

109. Portion of the tomb of **Tesher** (re-constructed).
VIth dynasty. From Dahshûr.

Rooms XI.-XIII.—Stelæ, etc., belonging to Dynasties IV.-XI., from Upper Egypt.

In these rooms are arranged a number of stelæ chiefly from Abydos, Akhmîm and Thebes. The stelæ from each place have their special characteristics, and afford most valuable information for dating the period of each step in the development of the decoration of the funereal stele from its oldest and simplest to its full and final form. They afford excellent material for hieroglyphic palæography.

The three wooden sarcophagi (Nos. 6301, 6302, 6608). from Akhmîm (Panopolis) are very interesting as examples of local art and decoration.

Rooms XIV.-XVI.—Stelæ, Royal Statues, Hyksos Monuments.

111. Limestone stele of a prince called **Ȧntefȧ.**
XIth dynasty (or earlier). From Thebes.

112. Stele of **Ȧntef IV.**, sculptured with a figure of his son, and five dogs. XIth dynasty. From Thebes.

113. Bas-relief in which king **Mentu-ḥetep** is represented slaying the Sati (Asiatics), the Tahennu (Lybians), and other peoples. From Gebelên.

114. Tomb of **Ḥeru-ḥetep.** This interesting monument was discovered and broken into in the early part of this century; it was brought to Bûlâḳ in 1883 by M. Maspero.
XIth dynasty. From Dêr el-Baḥari.

115. Mummy of **Ament,** priestess of Hathor. The body of the deceased is in the attitude in which it was when overtaken by death. It was found by M. Grébaut in a stone chest at the bottom of a small uninscribed chamber at Dêr el-Bahâri; the necklaces and rings which were upon it are exhibited in Room LXX, case E.

116, 117. Outer and inner coffins of Ament, priestess of Hathor.

118. Stele of **Men-khāu-Rā**; the king adoring the god Ȧmsu. XIVth dynasty. From Abydos.

122. Granite seated statue of **Nefert,** wife of Usertsen I. XIIth dynasty. From Tanis.

123. Sandstone table of offerings inscribed with the name of **Ȧmeni-Ȧntef-Ȧmenemḥāt.**
XIIIth dynasty. From Karnak.

125. Grey granite bust of a colossal statue of a king usurped by Meneptah. Middle Empire. From Alexandria.

127. Stele of Se-ḥetep-ȧb, an officer of Ȧmenemḥāt III. XIIth dynasty. From Abydos.

128. Granite statue of **Sebek-em-sa-f.**
XIIIth dynasty. From Abydos.

129. Statue of King **Ī-ȧn-Rā,** excavated at Zaḳâziḳ in 1888 by M. Naville. XIVth or XVth dynasty.

130. Alabaster table of offerings made for the princess Neferu-Ptaḥ. From the Pyramid of Hawâra.

131. Grey granite altar inscribed with the name of Usertsen III. XIIth dynasty. From Thebes.

132. Two figures making offerings of water-fowl, fish, and flowers. This interesting monument is supposed to be the work of the period of the "Shepherd Kings," although the cartouche of Pa-seb-khā-nut is found upon it.

133. Black granite table of offerings dedicated to the temple at Tanis by **Àpepà.**

XVIIth dynasty. From Tanis.

134. Black granite **Sphinx** excavated at Tanis by Mariette in 1863. The face of this remarkable monument has given rise to much discussion, and the theories propounded on the subject of the origin of the monument have been many. Mariette believed it to have been made by the so-called Hyksos, or "Shepherd Kings," and saw in the strange features of the face, and short, thick-set lion's body, a proof of their Asiatic origin. Some have seen a likeness to a Turanian original in the features, and others have insisted, probably rightly, that the king for whom the monument was originally made was a foreigner. Judging from the style of the work and the form of the lion's body, we should probably attribute it to a period anterior to B.C. 2000; that the name of the so-called Hyksos king Àpepà is inscribed upon it proves nothing except that this king, in common with many others, had his name inscribed on the statue. On the right shoulder, almost effaced, is the name of Àpepà; on the left shoulder is the name of Meneptah I.; on the right-hand side and front of the pedestal are the cartouches of Rameses II.; and on the breast is the cartouche of Pasebkhānet.

135. Head of a sphinx, similar to No. 107, inscribed with the name of **Meneptah.** This object is older than the time of the king whose name it bears.

136. Black granite table of offerings dedicated to the temple at Luxor by Usertsen III. From Thebes.

137. Grey granite head of a king. From the Fayyûm.

139. Limestone fragments of a sphinx. XIIth dynasty (?). From El-Ḳâb.

140. Limestone sarcophagus of Tagi.

XIth dynasty. From Thebes.

Room XVII.—Rectangular wooden sarcophagi of the XIth and XIIth dynasties.

142. Wooden sarcophagus of Kheper-ka.

143. Alabaster table of offerings bearing the cartouches of Usertsen I. Found near the Pyramid of Mêdûm.

Room XVIII.—Panels of a sarcophagus of the Middle Empire.

Room XIX.—Sarcophagi from Akhmîm and stelæ from Abydos.

Rooms XX and XXI.—Sarcophagi, stelæ, etc.

144. Black granite sphinx inscribed with the name of Sebek-ḥetep III. XIIIth dynasty.

Room XXII.—Stelæ, etc.

145. Fragment of a limestone bas-relief inscribed with the name of Rameses II. The hieroglyphics are painted blue, and the figures of the gods are decorated with gold. XIXth dynasty. From Abydos.

146, 147. Red granite fore-arms of a colossus. XIXth dynasty. From Luxor.

148. Colossal red granite scarab.

Room XXIII.—Stelæ, reliefs, etc.

149. Limestone bas-relief in which Amenophis IV. is represented making an offering to the solar disk. XVIIIth dynasty. From Tell el-Amarna.

153. Red granite seated figures of the god Harmachis and his beloved, Rameses II. Excavated at Memphis by M. de Morgan in 1892.

154. Red granite statue of a man carrying offerings. From Karnak.

Room XXIV.

155. Colossal red granite model of the sacred boat of Ptaḥ. A remarkably fine object.

Excavated at Memphis by M. de Morgan in 1892.

Room XXV.—Stelæ from Ethiopia, etc.

160. Red granite **Stele of Piānkhi**, King of Ethiopia, about B.C. 750. The text gives a detailed account of the expedition of this king into Egypt and of his conquest of that country. It was reported to Piānkhi in the 21st year of his reign, that the governors of the northern towns had made a league together and had revolted against his authority. He set out for Egypt with his soldiers, and when he arrived at Thebes he made offerings to Àmen-Rā, and commanded his soldiers to pay proper homage to the god. Passing northwards from Thebes, he captured city after city, and finally besieged Memphis, which he soon captured, and thus made himself master of Egypt. The details of the capture of the towns, the speeches of the king and of his vassal princes, and the general information contained in the narrative, give this inscription an importance possessed by few others.

From Gebel Barkal.

161. Greygranite **Stele of Ḥeru-se-àtef**, King of Ethiopia, about B.C. 580, dated in the 35th year of his reign. The text records that this king made war expeditions in the 3rd, 5th, 6th, 11th, 16th, 23rd and 33rd years of his reign against various peoples living to the south and east of Nubia, and that he returned from them in triumph. It also sets forth at great length a list of the various articles which he dedicated to the temple of Àmen-Rā at Napata, or Gebel Barkal, on his return from each expedition. From Gebel Barkal.

162. Grey granite **Stele of the Dream.** The text here inscribed records that an Ethiopian king, whose name is read provisionally Nut-meri-Åmen, and who reigned about B.C. 650, had a dream one night in which two snakes appeared to him, one on his right hand, and the other on his left. When he awoke he called upon his magicians to explain it, and they informed him that the snakes portended that he should be lord of the lands of the North and South. His majesty went into the temple of Åmen-Rā at Napata, or Gebel Barkal, and having there made rich offerings to the god, he set out for the north. Sailing down the river he made offerings to Khnemu-Rā, the god of Elephantine, and to Åmen-Rā of Thebes, and the people on both sides of the river shouted "Go in peace." When he arrived at Memphis the people thereof made war upon him, but he defeated them and entered the town. He went into the temple of Ptaḥ and made rich offerings to Ptaḥ-Seker and to Sekhet, and gave orders to build a temple to Åmen He then set out to conquer the chiefs in the Delta, and having succeeded by the help of Åmen, he returned to Nubia. From Gebel Barkal.

163. Grey granite **Stele of the Coronation.** The text gives an account of the ceremonies which were performed at the coronation of a king of Ethiopia, whose names are erased; this king was probably called **Åspaleta** 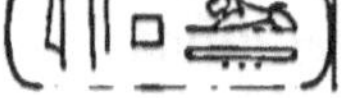. From Gebel Barkal.

164. Black granite head of **Tirhakah**, King of Ethiopia. XXVth dynasty; about B.C. 693.

165. Red granite **Stele of the Excommunication.** The text records that a king of Ethiopia, whose name has been carefully chiselled out, went into the temple of Åmen-Rā of Napata to drive out a set of people whose

custom was to eat the sacrificial meat raw, and who had made a resolve to kill all those who ate it cooked. The king passed an edict forbidding these men and their posterity to enter the temple for ever, and it seems that he burnt some of the heretics with fire.

From Gebel Barkal.

166. Black granite head of a colossal statue of **Rameses II.**

From Luxor.

167. Group inscribed with the name of **Meneptah.**

168. Limestone stele of **Rameses IV.** From Abydos.

169, 171, 172. Bas reliefs from the tomb of **Ptaḥ-mai.**

XVIIIth dynasty. From Saḳḳârah.

174. Alabaster statue of **Àmenàrṭās** , daughter of Kashta , sister of Shabaka , wife of Piānkhi , and mother of Shep-en-àpt 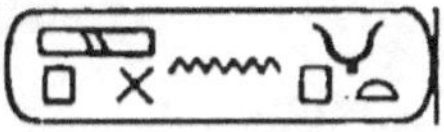, the wife of Psammetichus I. A very beautiful piece of sculpture.

XXVth dynasty. From Karnak.

Room XXVI.

177. Granite bust of Rameses IV.

XXth dynasty. From Bubastis.

178. Granite dog-headed ape from the foundations of the obelisk of Luxor. XIXth dynasty.

179. Seated group, brother and sister. Fine work.

XIXth dynasty. From Memphis.

180. Alabaster shaft of a column from the temple of Rameses III. at Tell el-Yahûdiyyeh.

182. Grey granite pillar inscribed on its four faces with scenes representing Rameses II. making offerings to Àmen and Mentu-Rā.

184. Limestone stele inscribed with a prayer of Rameses IV. to the gods of Abydos.

185, 186. Two sandstone colossal statues of Ptaḥ, one of the primeval gods of Egypt: they were set up by Rameses II., and in the inscriptions upon them the god promises to give to the king "all life, health, and strength," and long years of existence and an unlimited posterity. These wonderful objects are as beautiful for the delicacy of their work as for their size. They were discovered by M. de Morgan in the temple of Ptaḥ of Memphis, in 1892.

188. Grey granite fragment of a statue of Amenophis II.
From Karnak.

190. Granite head of a statue of a nobleman.
XIIIth dynasty. From Karnak.

192. Red granite bust of Thothmes III.
XVIIIth dynasty. From Karnak.

193. Limestone stele of Åmen-mes.
XVIIIth dynasty. From Saḳḳârah.

196. Grey granite colossal statue usurped by Rameses II.
XII–XVth dynasty. From Tanis.

198. Limestone head, thought by Mariette to belong to a statue of Queen Thi.
XVIIIth dynasty. From Karnak.

200. Black granite shrine, containing a figure of Ptaḥ-Mes, a priest who lived in the reign of Thothmes III.

202. Red granite statue of Thothmes III. From Karnak.

205. Limestone statue of a scribe, seated, reading from a roll of papyrus spread out upon his knees.
XVIIIth dynasty. From Ḳûrnah.

206. Limestone statue of Amenophis II.

210. Grey granite statue of the lion-headed goddess Sekhet, who represented the destructive heat of the sun; this monument bears the name of Amenophis III.
From the temple of Mut at Karnak.

213. Black granite stele inscribed with a poetical account of the victories of Thothmes III. The text is a speech of the god Åmen-Rā addressed to Thothmes. After describing the glory and might which he has attached to his name, he goes on to mention the countries which he had made his son Thothmes to conquer. The countries enumerated include Tchah and Ruthen in northern Syria, Phœnicia and Cyprus, Mathen or Mitani on the borders of Mesopotamia by the Euphrates, the countries along the Red Sea, the land of Nubia and the countries lying to the south of it, and the northern parts of Africa. Although Thothmes wasted and destroyed these lands, it cannot be said that he was successful in imposing the yoke of Egypt upon them permanently, for history shows that on the accession to the throne of each of his successors it was necessary to re-conquer them. Many of the phrases are stereotyped expressions which we find repeated in the texts of other kings. This monument was found at Karnak, on the site of the famous temple of Åmen of the Apts, and shows marks of erasures made by the order of Amenophis IV., the king who vainly tried to upset the national religion of Egypt. XVIIIth dynasty.

214. Black granite seated statue of **Thothmes III.**
XVIIIth dynasty.

Room XXVII. The Tablet of Saḳḳârah, Stelæ, etc.

218. The **Tablet of Saḳḳârah** was found by Mariette in the tomb of a high official named Tanurei, at Saḳḳârah, in 1861. It is a precious document, for it contained when complete the names of fifty-six kings; this list agrees tolerably well with that on the Tablet of Abydos, but there are many omissions. The list begins with Merbapen, the sixth king of the Ist dynasty, instead of with Mená, and ends with Rameses II.

Courtyard XXVIII.—Sphinxes and Colossal Statues.

221, 222. Red granite sphinxes inscribed with the names and titles of **Thothmes III.**

XVIIIth dynasty. From Karnak.

223. Colossal statue of **Usertsen I.** From Abydos.

224. Red granite statue usurped by Rameses II.

From Tanis.

225. Red granite statue usurped by Rameses II.

From Abûkîr.

226. Black granite seated statue of a king, usurped by **Rameses II.** XIVth dynasty. From Tanis.

Gallery XXIX.—Bas-reliefs of the XVIIIth and XXth dynasties.

228, 229. Limestone slabs from the tomb of Ḥeru-em-ḥeb.

XIXth dynasty. From Saḳḳârah.

Room XXX.

231. Painted limestone statue of Mut-nefert, the mother of Thothmes II.

From the ruins of a little temple near the Ramesseum.

232. Limestone funereal box made for the lady Ta-maut.

XVIIIth dynasty. Excavated by M. de Morgan at Memphis in 1892.

234. Limestone fragment of a stele in which Thothmes III. pays honour to his father Thothmes I.

236. Limestone wall fragment upon which is a figure of the Queen of Punt. From Dêr el-Baḥari.

237. The donkey of the Queen of Punt.

Room XXXI.—Monuments of the Saïte Period.

241. Granite sarcophagus inscribed with the cartouches of Psammetichus II. From Damanhûr.

242. Limestone table of offerings inscribed with the cartouches of Hophra.

243. Red granite slab inscribed with the cartouches of Ānput.

245. Black granite shrine inscribed with the name of Shabaka, King of Ethiopia. From the temple of Esneh

246. Red granite bas-relief inscribed with the cartouches of Nectanebus I. From Bubastis.

249. Black granite shrine inscribed with the cartouches of Nectanebus II. XXXth dynasty.

250. Black granite headless statue inscribed with the names of Shabataka and Tirhakah. XXVth dynasty.

Room XXXII.

253. Black granite shrine inscribed with the name of Nectanebus I.

256. Sandstone bas-relief inscribed with the cartouche of Queen Nitocris. XXVIth dynasty. From Karnak.

257. Sandstone cornice inscribed with the cartouches of Queens Shep-en-àp and Amenartas.. XXVIth dynasty. From Karnak.

Room XXXIII.—Stelæ from Saḳḳârah, Heliopolis, Abydos, etc.

261. Sandstone shrine inscribed with the cartouches of Psammetichus I., Shep-en-àp, and Nitocris; for the green basalt statue of the goddess Thoueris, which was found in it, see Room LXXII (p. 205).

262. Basalt statue of the god Osiris. XXVIth dynasty. From Saḳḳârah.

Room XXXIV.—Stelæ, chiefly from Abydos.

Room XXXV.—Antiquities of late Periods.

271. Fragment of a granite obelisk set up in honour of Åmen-Rā at Napata in Nubia by the Ethiopian king Atalnarsa.

Room XXXVI.

278. "Stele of Pithom." Excavated at Tell el-Maskhuta by M. Naville.

283. Black granite stele dated in the seventh year of Alexander II., son of Alexander the Great, and set up by Ptolemy Lagus. The text records victories in Syria and on the North coast of Africa, and the restoration of the temple of Buto.

284. Limestone stele of the Ram of Mendes, discovered by E. Brugsch Bey on the site of the ancient city of Mendes.

Room XXXVII.—Monuments inscribed in Demotic.

Room XXXVIII.—Stelæ from about B.C. 100—A.D. 300.

Room XXXIX.—Græco-Roman Antiquities.

Room XL.

290. White limestone stele generally known as the "Stele of Canopus." It is inscribed in hieroglyphics, Demotic and Greek, with a decree made at Canopus by the priesthood assembled there from all parts of Egypt, in honour of Ptolemy III., Euergetes I. It mentions the great benefits which he had conferred upon Egypt, and states what festivals are to be celebrated in his honour and in that of Berenice, *etc.*, and concludes with a resolution ordering that a copy of this inscription in hieroglyphics, Greek, and Demotic shall be placed in every large temple of Egypt.

291. White limestone stele of Canopus (duplicate). A third copy of the decree is in the Louvre at Paris.

304. Black granite "Stele of Menshiah," inscribed with the name of the emperor Trajan.

306. White marble head of Jupiter Olympus.
From Crocodilopolis.

308. Red granite colossal statue of a Macedonian king.
From Karnak.

Rooms XLI, XLII.

The monuments exhibited in these rooms illustrate the work of the Egyptian Christians or Copts.

Room XLIII.

In five cases in this room are exhibited Græco-Roman terra-cotta figures of Harpocrates, Bes, Aphrodite, Isis, Serapis, *etc.*; moulds for casting figures; lamps, pieces of glass, *etc.*

Room XLIV.—Mummies, from Akhmîm, the Fayyûm, etc.

334. Mummy with portrait painted upon linen.

335. Mummy with portrait painted upon wood.

337. Mummy, with portrait, from the Fayyûm. IIIrd century A.D.

350. Glazed faïence "mummy label."

355. Mummy of Artemidora. From the Fayyûm.

359. Fine gilded mummy mask inlaid with enamel. From Meir.

All the mummies in this room are of interest.

Room XLV.—Græco-Roman Antiquities.

363. Black granite inscribed slabs from the temple of Coptos.

395. Wooden sarcophagus ornamented with some curious paintings.

Gallery XLVI.—Coptic Linen Work.

Room XLVII.

Here are exhibited Coptic inscriptions upon papyrus, leather, wood, terra-cotta, *etc.;* bronze lamps, candlesticks, censers, basins, cymbals and other objects employed in Coptic churches; bottles bearing upon them figures of Saint Mina; and many small objects of Coptic work.

Room XLVIII.

This room contains Coptic pottery and inscriptions, and three remarkable Coptic mummies.

Room XLIX.

431. Wooden coffin with an inscription in the Himyaritic character.

The **Tell el-Amarna Tablets** exhibited in this room are a portion of a collection of about 320 documents which were found at Tell el-Amarna, the site of the town built by **Khu-en-àten** or Amenophis IV., which is situated about 180 miles south of Memphis. The Berlin Museum * ac-

* The cuneiform texts of the tablets at Berlin and Gîzeh are published by Abel and Winckler, *Der Thontafelfund von El-Amarna*, Berlin, 1889–1890; and the texts of those in the British Museum by Bezold, with an introduction and summary of contents by Bezold and Budge, *The Tell el-Amarna Tablets in the British Museum.* Printed by Order of the Trustees, 1892.

quired 160, a large number being fragments, the British Museum 82, and the Gizeh Museum 55. These documents were probably written between the years B.C. 1500–1450.

The Tell el-Amarna tablets supply entirely new information concerning the political relations which existed between the kings of Egypt and the kings of Western Asia, and prove that an important trade between the two countries existed from very early times. They also supply facts concerning treaties, alliances, religious ceremonies, etc., which cannot be derived from any other source, and they give us for the first time the names of Artatama, Artashumara, and Tushratta, kings of Mitani (the Māthen of the Egyptian inscriptions), and of Kallimma-Sin, King of Karaduniyash. The dialect in which these inscriptions are written has a close affinity to the language of the Old Testament.

The first conquest of Syria by the Egyptians took place in the reign of Amāsis I., B.C. 1700. Thothmes I., B.C. 1633, conquered all Palestine and Syria, and set up a tablet at Ruthen to mark the boundary of Egypt. Thothmes III., B.C. 1600, marched through Palestine and Syria and made himself master of all the country from Gaza to the Euphrates. At Tunip he established the Egyptian religion, and at Ruthen, in the 33rd year of his reign, he set up a tablet by the side of that of Thothmes I. The cuneiform tablets call him

D.P. Ma - na - akh - bi - ir - ya

a very close imitation of the pronunciation of this king's prenomen Men-Kheper-Rā 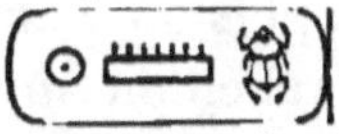.

Amenophis II., B.C. 1566, marched to Nî on the Euphrates, and slew seven kings in Ruthen, and brought their bodies to Egypt. Amenophis III. was not a great conqueror in the strict sense of the word, but he was proclaimed conqueror of Kadesh, Tunip, Sanḳar, and north western Mesopotamia, to which country he was in the habit of going to shoot lions. Now we know from a scarab that a lady called Thi , the daughter of Iuâa  and Thuâa , came to Egypt to become the wife of Amenophis in the tenth year of his reign. We know also that she became the "great Queen of Egypt," and as she is depicted with a fair complexion and blue eyes, there is no doubt that she is to be identified with the lady called Tî 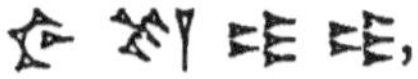, in the inscriptions on the Tell el-Amarna tablets, who came from the country to the north-east of Syria. Tî was the mother of Amenophis IV., the "heretic king." Besides this lady, we learn from the tablets that Amenophis married at least five other ladies from Mesopotamia, viz., a sister and two daughters of Kallimma-Sin, King of Karaduniyash, and a sister and daughter of Tushratta, King of Mitani; but none of these ladies was acknowledged "Queen of Egypt." In the time of Amenophis III., a Mesopotamian princess was honoured by marriage with the King of Egypt, but when Kallimma-Sin wished to marry an Egyptian princess, Amenophis replied haughtily, "the daughter of the King of the land of Egypt hath never been given to a nobody"; yet in the reign of Khu-en-âten we learn that an Egyptian princess was given in marriage to Burraburiyash, King of Karaduniyash, a proof that the Egyptian power was waning in Mesopotamia. The greater number of the tablets are addressed to "the King of Egypt," either Amenophis III. or his son Amenophis IV., and they reveal a state of disorganization and rebellion in the Egyptian dependencies in Palestine and Syria which cannot be understood unless we assume that for some years before the death of Amenophis III. the Semitic peoples of Western Asia were being encouraged to reject the rule of the Egyptians by their kinsfolk living in Egypt.

A list of the letters preserved at Gîzeh is as follows :—

*1. Letters from [Kal]-limma-Sin.
9. Letter from Ashur-uballiṭ, King of Assyria, B.C. 1400.
10. Letter from Amenophis III. to Tarḫundaradush, King of Arzapi.
11, 12, 14. Letters from the King of Alashiya.
40. Letter from Aziru.
60, 61, 62, 63, 65, 78, 79, 83. Letters from Rib-Adda.
94. Letter from Zatadna.
96. Letter from Namyawiza.
98, 99. Letters from Abu-Milki.
100. Letter from Shuardata.
109. Letter from Milkili.
115. Letter from Biridiwi.
116, 117. Letters from Shubandi
118, 121. Letters from Widya.
124. Letter from Yabnî-ili.
125. Letter from Arzawya.
127. Letter from Dashru.
131. Letter from Shamu-Adda.
138. Letter from the lady 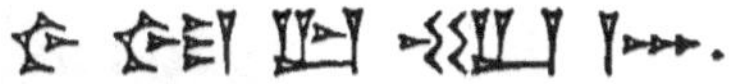.
150. Letter from Nurtuwi . . . . (?)
151. Letter from the governor of the city of Nazima.
152. Letter from Ara . . . . . of the city of Kumiṭi.
153. Letter from Pu-Addu.
154. Letter from Addu-asharid.
195. Letter from Bayawi.
196. Letter from Aba . . . . zi.
239. Part of a legend.
5, 17, 18, 20, 197-209. Letters from unknown writers.

436. Table of offerings with Meroïtic inscription.

441, 442. Phœnician and Aramean papyri.

* These numbers refer to Winckler's edition of the texts.

443. Terra-cotta cylinders of Nebuchadnezzar II., King of Babylon, B.C. 605–562.

445. The Lord's Prayer in Syriac.

Room L.—Weights, Measures, etc.

446. Alabaster vase, of the capacity of 21 *hin*, inscribed with the cartouches of Thothmes III.

447. Grey granite weight of 300 *uten*, in the form of a calf's head; the cartouches are those of Seti I.

449-451. Squares and plumb-line from the tomb of Sennetchem. XXth dynasty. From Thebes.

455. Goldsmith's scales.

In Case B are masons' and carpenters' mallets, models of houses, a window-screen, *etc.*

467. Painted wooden door from the tomb of Sennetchem.

Room LI.

The cases in this room contain fine examples of glazed *faïence* from Tell el-Yahûdîyyeh; bricks stamped with royal names; a collection of bronzes from Saïs, *etc.*

Room LII.

The cases in this room contain wooden beds, chairs, stools and boxes; plaques inlaid with ivory; granite, limestone, and *faïence* legs of beds, or couches; a pillow; wooden spindles and distaffs; hanks of thread, cushions, *etc.*

Room LIII.—Chairs, Stools and other furniture.

Room LIV.

This room contains a large number of thin slices of limestone upon which are traced in black and red curious and interesting designs of royal personages, gods, animals, etc.

Room LV.—Sculptors' Models, terra-cotta Moulds, etc.

Room LVI.—Inscribed Ostraka, etc.

Room LVII.—Inscribed Papyri.

587. Papyrus of Ḥerub, a priestess of Mut, daughter of Pai-netchem and Åuset-em-khebit.

XXIst dynasty. From Dêr el-Baḥari.

589. Copy of a work written by a scribe called **Ani**, who gives his son Khensu-ḥetep advice as to judicious behaviour in all the varied scenes of life; the following are taken from his precepts:—

"If a man cometh to seek thy counsel, let this drive thee to books for information.

"Enter not into the house of another; if a man maketh thee to enter his house it is an honour for thee.

"Spy not upon the acts of another from thy house.

"Be not the first to enter or to leave an assembly lest thy name be tarnished.

"The sanctuary of God abhorreth noisy declamations. Pray humbly and with a loving heart, whose words are spoken silently. God will then protect thee, and hear thy petitions, and accept thy offerings.

"Consider what hath been. Set before thee a correct ule of life as an example to follow. The messenger of death will come to thee as to all others to carry thee away; yea, he standeth ready. Words will profit thee nothing, for he cometh, he is ready! Say not, 'I am a child, wouldst thou in very truth bear me away?' Thou knowest not how thou wilt die. Death cometh to meet the babe at his mother's breast, even as he meeteth the old man who hath finished his course.

"Take heed with all diligence that thou woundest no man with thy words.

"Keep one faithful steward only, and watch his deeds, and let thy hand protect the man who hath charge of thy house and property.

"The man who having received much giveth little, is as one who committeth an injury.

"Be not ungrateful to God, for He giveth thee existence.

"Sit not while another standeth if he be older than thou, or if he is thy superior.

"Whosoever speaketh evil receiveth no good.

"When thou makest offerings to God, offer not that which He abominateth. Dispute not concerning His mysteries. The god of the world is in the light above the firmament, and his emblems are upon earth; it is unto those that worship is paid daily.

"When thou hast arrived at years of maturity, and art married and hast a house, forget never the pains which thou hast cost thy mother, nor the care which she hath bestowed upon thee. Never give her cause to complain of thee, lest she lift up her hands to God in heaven, and He listen to her complaint.

"Be watchful to ḳeep silence."

This work has much in common with the Maxims of Ptaḥ-ḥetep * and the Book of Proverbs.

590. Papyrus inscribed with a treatise on the geography of the Fayyûm and of the country round about. The concluding part is in the possession of a Mr. Hood, residing in England. Greek period. From Dêr el-Medîneh.

In the wall cases are exhibited the Egyptian scribes' palettes of wood, ivory, limestone, *etc.*, and specimens of the reeds and colours with which they wrote.

* The maxims of Ptaḥ-ḥetep are inscribed upon the Prisse papyrus, which was written about B.C. 2500; they were composed during the reign of Ȧssa, the eighth king of the Vth dynasty, about B.C. 3366.

Room LVIII.—Funereal Objects.

In this room are exhibited :—Network for placing upon mummies ; painted and gilded masks for mummies ; hypocephali in terra-cotta, bronze and cartonnage, the object of which, by means of the texts inscribed upon them, was to preserve some heat in the body until the day of the resurrection ; linen shrouds inscribed with funereal scenes ; pads for the feet of the dead ; sandals ; wooden figures of the god Osiris in which papyri were deposited : pectorals in the form of pylons in which scarabs are embedded between figures of the goddesses Isis and Nephthys ; symbolic eyes or *utchats* ; green basalt scarabs inscribed with Chapter 30B of the Book of the Dead, *etc.*

Room LIX.

In Case A are arranged a fine collection of small sepulchral figures called in Egyptian *ushabtiu.* They are made of stone, alabaster, wood, glazed *faïence*, and are in the form of the god Osiris, who is here represented in the form of a mummy. They were placed in the tomb to do certair agricultural works for the deceased, who was supposed to be condemned to sow the fields, to fill the canals with water, and to carry sand from the West to the East. They are usually inscribed with the VIth Chapter of the Book of the Dead. As many travellers buy *ushabtiu* figures in Egypt, the following version of the chapter may be of interest to them.

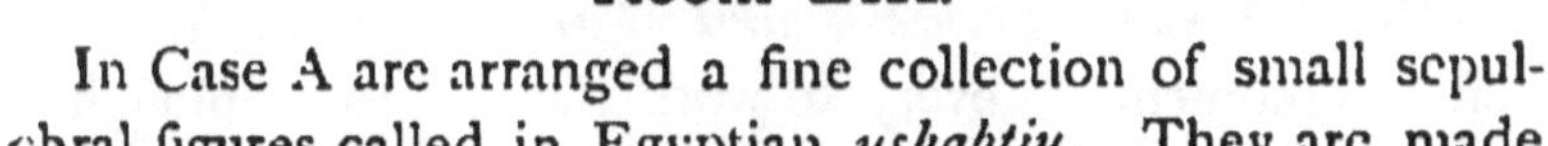

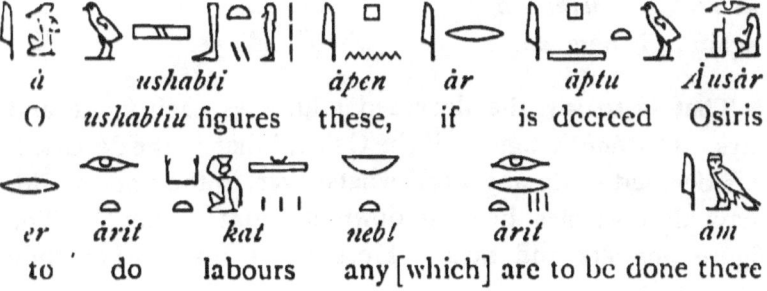

à *ushabti* *àpen* *àr* *àptu* *Àusàr*

O *ushabtiu* figures these, if is decreed Osiris

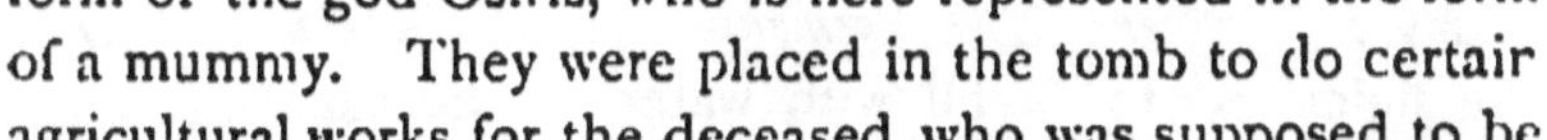

er *àrit* *kat* *nebt* *àrit* *àm*

to do labours any [which] are to be done there

o

em neter χert åstu ḥu - nej

in the underworld, behold, be there smitten down for him

set'ebu åm em se er χert - f

obstructions there for a person beneath him.

māku - å ka - ten åp - tu - ten

Here am I [when] call ye. Watch ye

er ennu neb årit åm er seruṭet

at moment every to work there, to plough

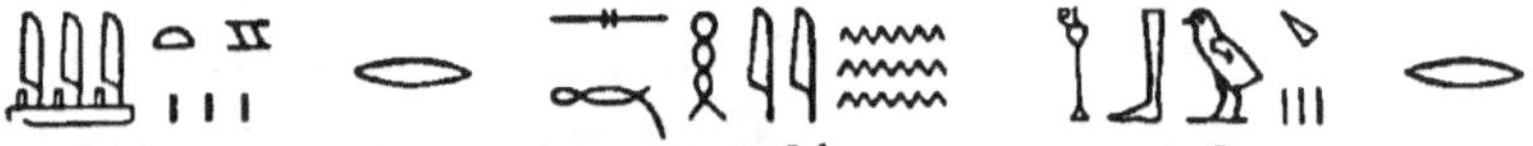

seχet er semeḥi utebu er

he fields, to fill with water the canals, to

χen šā en Abtet er Åmentet

carry sand of the east to west.

θes rer māku - å ka - ten

Again here am I [when] call ye.

That is to say, the deceased addresses each figure and says, "O *ushabtiu* figures, if the Osiris," that is, the deceased, "is decreed to do any work whatsoever in the underworld, may all obstacles be cast down in front of him!" The figure answers and says, "Here am I ready when thou callest." The deceased next says, "O ye figures, be ye ever watchful to work, to plough and sow the fields, to water the canals, and to carry sand from the east to the west." The figure replies, "Here am I ready when thou callest."

In Case D are an interesting set of collection of wooden tablets, pillows, *etc.*

In Case G are a collection of sets of limestone and alabaster "Canopic Jars."

Each jar of a set was dedicated to one of the four genii of the underworld, who represented the cardinal points, and each jar was provided with a cover which was made in the shape of the deity to whom it was dedicated. The jar of Mesthà is man-headed; that of Ḥāpi is dog-headed; that of Ṭuamāutef is jackal-headed; and that of Qebḥsennuf is hawk-headed. They represented the south, north, east, and west respectively, and in them were placed the stomach and large intestines, the small intestines, the lungs and heart, and the liver and gall-bladder.

Room LX.

Here are arranged funereal figures from the "find" of the priests of Àmen at Dêr el-Baḥari.

Room LXI.—Funereal Figures, Canopic Vases, etc.

Room LXII.—Papyri.

683. Fragment of a Book of the Dead written for Mapui.

684. Papyrus of Tchet-Khonsu-auf-ānkh. From Dêr el-Baḥari.

685. Papyrus of the Princess Nesi-Khonsu, inscribed in fine hieratic characters. From Dêr el-Baḥari

687. Papyrus of Queen Maāt-ka-Rā. From Dêr el-Baḥari.

Room LXIII.

688. Green basalt slab of Tirhaka.

694. Blue glazed *faïence* sistrum, inscribed with the cartouche of Darius.

698. Limestone figure of Amenophis I. Fine work.
From Medînet-Habu.

700. Four alabaster vases found with the mummy of Queen Åāḥ-ḥetep. XVIIIth dynasty.

701a. Stele of Hophra, with Carian (?) inscription.

710. Blue glazed faïence *ushabti* figure of Rameses IV.

716. *Ushabti* figure of Nectanebus I.

717. *Ushabti* figure of Nectanebus II.

721. Bronze lion, inscribed with the name of Hophra.

738. Papyrus of Pi-netchem.

740. Blue paste scarab, inscribed with the cartouches of Hophra.

742. Steatite scarab, made to celebrate the marriage of Amenophis III. with the Mesopotamian lady Thi.

742a. Steatite scarab, recording the slaughter by Amenophis III. of 102 lions during the first ten years of his reign.

743. Blue paste scarab inscribed with the name of Nekau (Necho). XXVIth dynasty.

744. Bronze axe-head, inscribed with the cartouches of Kames, a king of the XVIIth dynasty; it is set in a horn handle.

In this room are also exhibited a series of amulets, the principal of which are as follows :—

1. The **Buckle** or Tie, , usually made of some red stone, the colour of which was intended to represent the blood of Isis, was placed on the neck of the mummy, which it

was supposed to protect. It was often inscribed with the 156th chapter of the Book of the Dead.

2. The **Tet,** , which had sometimes plumes, disk and horns, , attached to it, was also placed on the neck of the mummy, and was often inscribed with the 155th chapter of the Book of the Dead.

3. The **Vulture,** , was placed upon the neck of the mummy on the day of the funeral, and brought with it the protection of the "mother" Isis.

4. The **Collar,** , was placed upon the neck of the mummy on the day of the funeral.

5. The **Papyrus Sceptre,** , was placed upon the neck of the mummy, and typified the green youth which it was hoped the deceased would enjoy in the nether world.

6. The **Pillow,** , usually made of hæmatite, was generally inscribed with the 166th chapter of the Book of the Dead.

7. The **Heart,** , represented the "**soul of Kheperȧ.**"

8. The **Ankh,** , represented "Life."

9. The **Utchat,** or Symbolic Eye, , typified "good health and happiness," and was a very popular form of amulet in Egypt.

10. The **Nefer,** , represented "good-luck."

11. The **Sam,** , represented "union."

12. The **Menȧt,** , represented "virility."

13. The **Neha,** , represented "protection."

14. The **Serpent's Head,** , was placed in mummies to prevent their being devoured by worms.

15. The **Frog**, , represented "fertility" and "abundance."

16. The **Stairs**, , the meaning of which is unknown to me.

17. The **Fingers**, index and medius, found inside mummies, represented the two fingers which the god Horus stretched out to help the deceased up the ladder to heaven.

Rooms LXIV, LXV.

Here are exhibited tables of offerings; models of boats and rowers (see particularly No. 760, a boat with a sail); boxes for *ushabtiu* figures; mummies of animals sacred to the gods *; models of funereal bread in terra-cotta, *etc.*

Room LXVI.—Vessels in alabaster, bronze, etc.

Room LXVII.—Weapons and Tools.

Room LXVIII.—Pottery, etc.

Room LXIX.—Articles of Clothing.

Room LXX.

In this room are exhibited bronze mirrors, musical instruments, draught boards, dolls, necklaces of precious stones, vases of coloured glass, statuettes of fine work, spoons, perfume boxes, a broken ivory figure from a tomb of the Vth dynasty (No. 912), fans, *etc.*

922. Collection of silver vases found among the ruins of Mendes.

* The principal animals sacred to the gods were the ape to Thoth, the hippopotamus to Thoueris, the cow to Hathor, the lion to Horus, the sphinx to Harmachis, the bull to Apis or Mnevis, the ram to Åmen-Rā, the cat to Bast, the jackal to Anubis, the hare to Osiris, the sow to Set, the crocodile to Sebek, the vulture to Mut, the hawk to Horus, the ibis to Thoth, the scorpion to Serqet, and the beetle to Kheperå.

The jewellery of Âāḥ-ḥetep, the wife of Seqenen-Rā, mother of Kames, and grandmother of Amāsis I., the first king of the XVIIIth dynasty, was found in the coffin of that queen by the fellâḥîn at Drah abu'l-Neḳḳa in 1860. Among the most beautiful objects of this find are:—

943. Gold bracelet, inlaid with lapis-lazuli, upon which Amāsis I. is shown kneeling between Seb and other gods.

944. Gold head-dress, inlaid with precious stones, inscribed with the name of Amāsis I.

945. Gold chain, terminated at each end by a goose's head; from the chain hangs a scarab made of gold and blue paste.

948. Part of a fan made of wood covered with gold, upon which Kames is shown making an offering to Khonsu.

949. Mirror of Âāḥ-ḥetep set in an ebony handle.

950. Cedar haft of an axe, plated with gold, into which a bronze axe, also plated with gold, inscribed with the cartouche of Amāsis I., has been fastened with gold wire.

951. Gold dagger, inscribed with the cartouche of Amāsis I. (?), and gold sheath inlaid with lapis-lazuli and other precious stones.

953. Gold pectoral, inlaid with precious stones, upon which Amāsis I. is represented standing in a sacred bark between the gods Ȧmen and Rā, who pour water upon him.

955. Gold model of the sacred bark of the dead, in the centre of which is seated Amāsis I. The rowers are made of silver, the body of the chariot of wood, and the wheels of bronze.

956. Silver bark and seven men found with the jewellery of Âāḥ-ḥetep.

958. Bronze dagger, set in a silver handle in the form of a circle.

962. Gold necklace.

963. Gold bracelet inlaid with lapis-lazuli, carnelian, and other precious stones.

963a. Gold bracelet inlaid with lapis-lazuli, carnelian, and other precious stones, inscribed with the prenomen of Amāsis I.

965. Bronze head of a lion inscribed with the prenomen of Amāsis I.

966. Nine small gold and silver axes.

967. Gold chain and three flies.

982. Gold figure of Ptaḥ.

983. Gold figure of Åmen.

All the other ornaments in this case are worth careful examination.

Room LXXI.—Scarabs, Amulets, etc.

Scarab or scarabæus (from the Greek σκάραβος) is the name given by Egyptologists to the myriads of models of a certain beetle, which are found in mummies and tombs and in the ruins of temples and other buildings in Egypt, and in other countries the inhabitants of which, from a remote period, had intercourse with the Egyptians. M. Latreille considered the species which he named *Ateuchus Aegyptiorum*, or ἡλιοκάνθαρος, and which is of a fine greenish colour, as that which especially engaged the attention of the early Egyptians, and Dr. Clarke affirmed that it was eaten by the women of Egypt because it was considered to be an emblem of fertility. In these insects a remarkable peculiarity exists in the structure and situation of the hind legs, which are placed so near the extremity of the body, and so far from each other, as to give them a most extraordinary appearance when walking. This peculiar formation is, nevertheless, particularly serviceable to its possessors in rolling the balls of excrementitious matter in which they enclose their eggs. These balls are at first irregularly shaped and soft, but by degrees, and during the process of rolling along, become rounded and harder; they are propelled by means of the hind legs. Sometimes these balls are an inch and a half or two inches in diameter, and in rolling them along the beetles stand almost upon their heads, with the heads turned from the balls. They do this in order to bury their balls in holes which they have already dug for them, and it is upon the dung thus deposited that the larvæ when hatched feed. Horapollo thought that the beetle was self-produced, but he made this mistake on account of the females being exceedingly like the males, and because both sexes appear to divide the care of the preservation of their offspring equally between them.

The Egyptians called the scarabæus Kheperá  , and the god represented by this insect also Kheperá . The god Kheperá was supposed to be the "father of the gods," and the creator of all things in heaven and earth; he made himself out of matter which he himself had made. He was identified with the rising sun and thus typified resurrection. The verb *Kheper* , which is usually translated "to exist, to become," also means "to roll," and "roller," or "revolver," was a fitting name for the sun. In a hieratic papyrus in the British Museum (No. 10, 188), the god Khepera is identified with the god Neb-er-tcher, who, in describing the creation of gods, men, animals and things says:—"I am he who evolved himself under the form of the god Kheperá. I, the evolver of evolutions, evolved myself, the evolver of all evolutions, after a multitude of evolutions and developments* which came forth from my mouth (or at my command). There was no heaven, there was no earth, animals which move upon the earth and reptiles existed not at all in that place. I constructed their forms out of the inert mass of watery matter. I found no place there where I could stand. By the strength which was in my will I laid the foundation [of things] in the form of the god Shu [see page 116], and I created for them every attribute which they have. I alone existed, for I had not as yet made Shu to emanate from me, and I had not ejected the spittle which became the god Tefnut; there existed none other to work with me. By my own will I laid the foundations of all things, and the evolutions of the things, and the evolutions which took place from the evolutions of their births which took place through the evolutions of their offspring, became multiplied. My shadow was united with me, and I produced Shu and Tefnut from the emanations of my body, ... thus from being one god I became three gods . . . . I gathered together my members and wept over them, and men and women sprang into existence from the tears which fell from my eye." Scarabs may be divided into three classes :—1. Funereal scarabs; 2. Scarabs worn for ornament; 3. Historical scarabs. Of **funereal scarabs**

* The duplicate copy of this chapter reads, "I developed myself from the primeval matter which I made. My name is Osiris, the germ of primeval matter. I have worked my will to its full extent in this earth, I have spread abroad and filled it . . . . . . I uttered my name as a word of power, from my own mouth, and I straightway developed myself by evolutions. I evolved myself under the form of the evolutions of the god Khepera, and I developed myself out of the primeval matter which has evolved multitudes of evolutions from the beginning of time. Nothing existed on this earth [before me], I made all things. There was none other who worked with me at that time. I made all evolutions by means of that soul which I raised up there from inertness out of the watery matter."

the greater number found measure from half an inch to two inches, and are made of steatite glazed green, or blue, or brown; granite, basalt, jasper, amethyst, lapis-lazuli, carnelian, and glass. The flat base of the scarab was used by the Egyptians for engraving with names of gods, kings, priests, officials, private persons, monograms and devices. Scarabs were set in rings and worn on the fingers by the dead or living, or were wrapped up in the linen bandages with which the mummy was swathed, and placed over the heart. The best class of funereal scarabs were made of a fine, hard, green basalt, which, when the instructions of the rubric concerning them in the Book of the Dead were carried out, were set in a gold border, and hung from the neck by a fine gold wire. Such scarabs are sometimes joined to a heart on which is inscribed, "life, stability, and protection" 𓋹𓊽𓎬. Funereal scarabs were also set in pectorals, and were in this case ornamented with figures of the deceased adoring Osiris. Scarabs of all kinds were kept in stock by the Egyptian undertaker, and spaces were left blank in the inscriptions * to add the names of the persons for whom they were bought. **Scarabs worn for ornament** exist in many thousands. By an easy transition, the custom of placing scarabs on the bodies of the dead passed to the living, and men and women wore the scarab probably as a silent act of homage to the creator of the world, who was not only the god of the dead, but of the living also. **Historical scarabs** appear to be limited to a series of four, which were made during the reign of **Amenophis III.** to commemorate certain historical events, *viz.*, 1. The slaughter of 102 lions by Amenophis during the first ten years of his reign. 2. A description of the boundaries of the Egyptian Empire, and the names of the

* The chapter usually inscribed upon these scarabs is No. 30 B.

parents of Queen Thi. 3. The arrival of Thi and Gilukhipa in Egypt together with 317 women. 4. The construction of a lake in honour of Queen Thi.

Room LXXII.—Figures of the Gods and of Animals sacred to them.

1006. Black granite vase in the shape of a heart, dedicated to the god Thoth by Hophra.

1007. Bronze figure of a goddess.

1008. Bronze *lepidotus* fish.

In the standard and wall cases are arranged a very fine collection of **figures of the gods** of Egypt, and of the animals, birds, and reptiles, sacred to them. These interesting objects are made of glazed faïence, hard stone, bronze, glass, etc., and among them are some splendid specimens of excellent design and workmanship. Figures of gods are found among the ruins of houses, and in tombs and temples. Those found in the ruins were either placed in shrines, and represented the gods worshipped by the family, or were buried in niches in the walls, and were supposed to be able to protect the family by their supernatural influence. It is thought that the Egyptians believed that the gods inhabited the statues placed in the temples in their honour. Figures of gods were also buried in the sand round about houses and tanks with the view of guarding them from the influences of demons. The principal gods exhibited in this room are Ȧmen, Ȧmen-Rā, Ȧmsu, Anhur, Anubis, Apis, Ȧtmu, Bast, Bes, Ḥāpi, Harpocrates, Hathor, Horus, Horus-beḥuṭet, Ī-em-ḥetep (Imouthis), Isis, Khnemu (Chnoumis), Khensu, Maāt, Mahes, Mehit, Meḥ-urit, Mentu, Mut, Neḥebka, Nephthys, Nit (Neith), Nefer-Ȧtmu, Osiris, Ptaḥ, Ptaḥ-Seker-Osiris, Rā, Rā-Harmachis, Sebek, Set, Serqet, Shu, Ta-urt (Thoueris), and Thoth.

1015. Bronze statatues of the goddess Sekhet. From Saïs.

1016. Green basalt figure of the goddess **Ta-urt** (Thoueris), in the form of a hippopotamus; this is one of the finest examples of the work of the period.

1017. Green basalt table of offerings inscribed with the name of **Psammetichus**, an official.
XXVIth dynasty. From Karnak.

1018. Green basalt seated statue of **Osiris**, judge of the dead. XXVIth dynasty.

1019. Green basalt seated statue of **Isis**, wife of Osiris.
XXVIth dynasty.

1020. Green basalt statue of a cow, sacred to **Hathor**, the goddess of Àmentet or the underworld, in front of which stands the official **Psammetichus**, in whose honour this beautiful group was made. XXVIth dynasty.

Room LXXIII.—Collection of Egyptian Plants, Seeds, etc., classified and arranged by Dr. Schweinfurth.

Room LXXIV.

In this room M. de Morgan himself intends to arrange a mineralogical collection.

Galleries LXXV.—Sarcophagi of the XXVIth dynasty.

Room LXXVI.—Priests of Àmen.

1135. Cartonnage of Pameshon, high-priest of Àmen.

1136. Case inscribed with the name of Khonsu-em-ḥeb, "divine father" and scribe of the estates of Àmen-Rā at Thebes.

Room LXXVII.—Priests of Åmen.

1137, 1138. Coffins of children.

1140. Coffin of Ānkhes-nesit, a lady in the college of Åmen-Rā at Thebes.

1141. Coffin of Tanneferef, a "divine father" of Åmen.

Room LXXVIII.—Priests of Amen.

1142. Coffin of Nesi-neb-taui, a lady in the college of Åmen-Rā at Thebes.

Room LXXIX.—Priests of Åmen.

1144. Coffin of Peṭā-Åmen, a "divine father" and priest of the highest rank.

1145. Coffin of Ṭirpu, a lady in the college of Åmen-Rā.

1146. Coffin of Ānkh-f-en-Mut, a "divine father," which originally belonged to a lady whose name still stands upon it.

1147. Coffin of Ānkh-f-en-Mut, a priest of Mut, and scribe of the estates of Åmen, and priest of the Queen Åāḥ-ḥetep.

1148 a and b. Covers of coffins of Peṭā-Åmen, a scribe of the granaries of Åmen-Rā.

Room LXXX.—Priests of Åmen.

1150. Cover of a coffin of Pa-khare, surnamed Kha-nefer-Åmen, a "divine father."

1151 a and b. Coffins of Nesesta-pen-her-tahat, fourth prophet of Åmen.

1152. Coffin of Peṭā-Åmen, an official of Åmen, Mut and Khonsu.

Room LXXXI.—Priests of Åmen.

1153. Coffin of Ānkh-f-en-Khonsu, chief of the metal-workers of Åmen.

1154. Coffin of Nes-pa-nefer-ḥrå, a "divine father" of Åmen and Mut.

1155. Cartonnage of Åmen-nut-nekhtu, a metal-worker of Åmen.

1156. Cartonnage of Mert-Åmen, a lady in the college of Åmen-Rā.

1157 a and b. Covers of the inner coffin of Mert-Åmen.

1158. Coffin of Nesi-Åmen-åpt, a high-priest of Åmen, director of the offerings in the chamber of Anubis, *etc.*

Room LXXXII.—Priests of Åmen.

1160. Coffin of Peta-Åmen, a priest who held many high offices at Thebes.

1161. Coffin of Masha-sebeket, a lady attached to the service of Åmen-Rā, Mut, Hathor and Khonsu.

1162. Coffin of Pennest-taui, a scribe of the estates of Åmen.

1163. Coffin of Ta-nefer, a "divine father" of the goddess Maāt.

1164. Cartonnage of Khonsu-en-renp, a priest, "divine father," and scribe.

1165. Coffin of Nesi-pa-her-an, a "divine father" of Åmen, and scribe.

Room LXXXIII.—Priests of Åmen.

1156. Coffin of Ta-nefer, third prophet of Åmen-Rā, prophet of Mentu and Khnum, superintendent of the "flocks of the sun," *etc.*

1167 a and b. Cartonnage and coffin of Maāt-ka-Rā, a lady of the college of Åmen.

1168. Coffin of Heru, prophet of Åmen-Rā, Hathor, Khonsu, Anubis, *etc.*

1169. Coffin of Katsheshni, daughter of the first prophet of Åmen.

1170. Coffin of Men-kheper-Rā, son of Tcha-nefer, third prophet of Åmen.

1171. Coffin of Herub, second prophetess of the goddess Mut, *etc.*, daughter of Men-Kheper-Rā and Āuset-em-khebit.

Room LXXXIV.—The Der el-Baḥari Mummies.*

XVIITH DYNASTY, BEFORE B.C. 1700.

1174. Coffin and mummy of **Seqenen-Rā**. This king was killed in battle.

XVIIITH DYNASTY, B.C. 1700–1400.

1172. Cartonnage mummy-case, inscribed with the name of Åāḥmes-nefert-åri, wife of Amāsis I.

1173. Mummy-case of Queen Åāḥ-ḥetep, wife of Amenophis I.

1175. Mummy and coffin of Amāsis I.

1176. Mummy and coffin of Se-Åmen, son of Amāsis I.

1177. Mummy and coffin of Amenophis I.

1178, 1188a. Coffin and mummy of Thothmes II.

1179, 1188. Coffin of **Thothmes III.** The mummy of this king when brought up from the pit at Dêr el-Baḥari was found to be in a very bad condition, and examination showed that it had been broken in three places in ancient times. The large scarab which was laid over the heart when the body of the king was being mummified is now in the British Museum.

* For an account of finding the mummies, see pp. 306–312.

XIXTH DYNASTY, B.C. 1400–1200.

1180. Coffin and **mummy of Seti I.**, father of Rameses II.

1181. Coffin and **mummy of Rameses II.**

XXTH DYNASTY, B.C. 1200–1100.

1182. Mummy of Rameses III., found in the coffin of Queen Ȧāḥmes-nefert-ȧri.

XXIST DYNASTY, B.C. 1100–1000.

1183. Coffin of Pinetchem I.

1184. Coffin of Queen Ȧuset-em-khebit 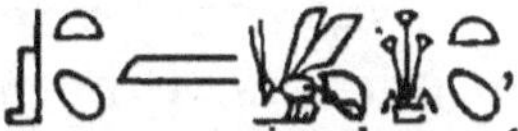, the daughter of Masaherthȧ. The mummy is that of Nessu (*or* Nesi) Khensu.

1185. Coffin of Set-Ȧmen, daughter of Amāsis I.

1187, 1190. Coffins of Masaherthȧ 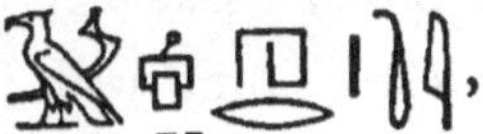, high-priest of Ȧmen, and son of Pinetchem II.

1189. Coffins of Tcheṭ-Ptaḥ-ȧuf-ānkh , priest and "divine father" of Ȧmen-Rā.

1191. Outer coffin of Ȧuset-em-khebit.

1192. Outer coffin of Maāt-ka-Rā (see No. 1198).

1193. Coffin and mummy of Nebseni , a scribe, the son of Pa-ḥeri-ȧb , and Ta-mesu .

1194. An excellent reproduction of the leather canopy of Ȧuset-em-khebit by E. Brugsch Bey and M. Bouriant.*

1195. Coffin of Netchemet , mother of the priest-king "Ḥer-Ḥeru, the son of Ȧmen" 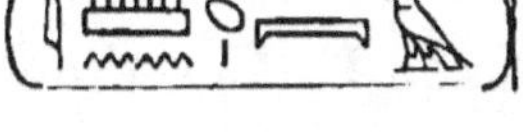.

* This interesting object is reproduced in Maspero, *Les Momies Royales de Déir el-Baharî* (*Mémoires de la Mission Archéologique Française*, Paris, 1887, p. 585).

1196. Coffin of Nessu-Khensu 

1198. Coffin and mummies of Queen Maāt-ka-Rā, daughter of Pa-seb-khā-nut, and her infant daughter Mut-em-ḥāt 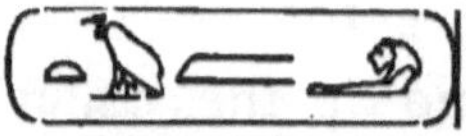. It is thought that the queen died in giving birth to her daughter.

1199. Coffins of Nesi-ta-neb-åsher  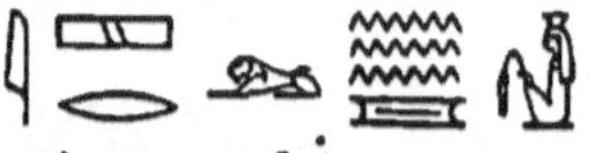, daughter of Nesi-Khensu, and priestess of Åmen.

1204. Cover of the coffin of Queen Netchemet.

1206. Box containing the wig of Princess Åuset-em-khebit.

1208. Small chest inscribed with the name of Rameses IX.

1212. Oars found with the mummy of Thothmes III.

1214. Coffin of Pi-netchem II., son of Åuset-em-khebit.

1216. Coffin, which originally belonged to Thothmes I., and mummy of Pi-netchem I.

1217. Gilded cover of the outer coffin of Queen Åuset-em-khebit.

Case E. Cover of the coffin of Thothmes I.

Case F. Cover of the coffin of Masaherthå.

1225. Wooden plaque inscribed in hieratic with the assurances of the god Åmen concerning the welfare of the Princess Nesi-Khonsu. A duplicate of this plaque is preserved in the British Museum.

Case H. Cover of the coffin of Maāt-ka-Rā.

Case I. Cover of the coffin of Nesi-Khonsu.

Case K. Cover of the outer coffin of Nesi-ta-neb-åsher.

Case L. Cover of the coffin of Amenophis I.

1234, 1235. Cover and cartonnage of the coffin of Pi-netchem II.

1236. Cover of the coffin of Queen Ḥent-taui.

1237. Coffin of Rameses II.

1238. Mummy of Åuset-em-khebit.

Case O. Cover of the coffin of Rameses II.

Rooms LXXXV and LXXXVI.—Mummies of the Priests of Amen.

On the landing of the staircase leading to Room LXXXVII, is:

1251. Gilded cover of the coffin of Åāḥ-ḥetep I., the queen whose jewellery is exhibited in Room No. LXX.

Room LXXXVII.

1252. Gilded coffin of Ḥeru-se-Åuset, prophet of Horus of Beḥuṭet.

1253. Coffin of Åuset, mother of Sen-netchem.

1254. Funereal sledge of Khonsu, found in the coffin of Sen-netchem.

1256. Coffin and mummy of Tripi (?).
1st century A.D. From Thebes.

1258. Coffin of Amenårṭās.

1259. Funereal sledge of Sennetchem.

1260. Coffin of Sennetchem. From Dêr el-Medîneh.

1261. Mummy of a woman. Greek period.

1264, 1265. Portraits painted upon wax laid upon pieces of wood, which were fastened by bandages over the faces of mummies. From the Fayyûm.

1265. Portrait painted on a mummy wrapping.

1272. Painted wooden mummy-bier.

The other coffins exhibited in this room are worthy of careful examination.

Room LXXXVIII.

1278. Granite sarcophagus of Queen Nitocris.
From Dêr el-Medîneh

1280. Grey granite sarcophagus inscribed with the name of Psammetichus.

1281–1284. Sarcophagi of the Greek period.

1285. Grey granite sarcophagus of Ānkh-Ḥāpi.
From Saḳḳârah.

1286. Limestone Sarcophagus of Tche-ḥrá.

1299, 1300. Grey granite sarcophagi of two brothers, each of whom was called Tchaho.

1302 a and b. Basalt sarcophagus of Ḥeru-em-ḥeb.

1304. Black granite sarcophagus of Un-nefer.

1305. Grey basalt sarcophagus of Ī-em-ḥetep, a priest.

1308. Grey basalt sarcophagus of Bataita, mother of the brothers Tchaho.

Whether the art of mummifying was known to the aboriginal inhabitants of Egypt, or whether it was introduced by the newcomers from Asia, is a question which is very difficult to decide. We know for a certainty that the stele of a dignitary preserved at Oxford was made during the reign of Senṭ, the fifth king of the IInd dynasty, about B.C. 4000. The existence of this stele, with its figures and inscriptions, points to the fact that the art of elaborate sepulture had reached a high pitch in those early times. The man for whom it was made was called  Sherá, and he held the dignity of 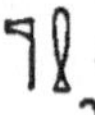 *neter ḥen*, or "prophet"; the stele also tells us that he was  *suten reχt*, or "royal kinsman." The inscriptions contain prayers asking for the deceased in the nether-world "thousands of oxen, linen bandages, cakes, vessels of wine, incense, etc.," which fact shows that religious belief, funereal ceremonies, and a hope for a life after death had already become a part of the life of the people of Egypt. During the reign of King Sent the redaction of a medical papyrus was carried out. As this work presupposes many years of experiment and experience, it is clear that the Egyptians possessed ample anatomical knowledge for mummifying a human body. Again, if we consider that the existence of this king is proved by papyri and contemporaneous monuments, and that we know the names of some of the priests who took part in funereal ceremonies during his reign, there is no difficulty in acknowledging the great antiquity of such ceremonies, and that they presuppose a religious belief in the actual revivification of the body, for which hoped-for event the Egyptian took the greatest possible care to hide and preserve his body.

"Mummy" is the term which is generally applied to the body of a human being or animal which has been preserved from decay by means of bitumen, spices, gums, and natron. As far as can be discovered, the word is neither a corruption of the ancient Egyptian word for a preserved body, nor of the more modern Coptic form of the hieroglyphic name. The word "mummy" is found in Byzantine Greek and in Latin, and indeed in almost all European languages. It is derived from the Arabic مُومِيَا *mûmîâ*, "bitumen"; the Arabic word for mummy is مُومِيَّة *mûmîyyet*, and means a "bitumenized thing," or a body preserved by bitumen.

We obtain our knowledge of the way in which the ancient Egyptians mummified their dead from Greek historians, and from an examination of mummies. According to Herodotus (ii. 86) the art of mummifying was carried on by a special guild of men who received their appointment by law. These men mummified bodies in three different ways, and the price to be paid for preserving a body varied according to the manner in which the work was done. In the first and most expensive method the brain was extracted through the nose by means of an iron probe, and the intestines were removed entirely from the body through an incision made in the side with a sharp Ethiopian stone. The intestines were cleaned and washed in palm wine, and, having been covered with powdered aromatic gums, were placed in jars. The cavity in the body was filled up with myrrh and cassia and other fragrant and astringent substances, and was sewn up again. The body was next laid in natron for seventy days,* and when these were over, it was carefully washed, and afterwards wrapped up in strips of fine linen smeared on their sides with gum. The cost of mummifying a body in this fashion was a talent of silver, *i.e.*, about £240, according to Diodorus (i. 91, 92).

In the second method of mummifying the brain was not removed at all, and the intestines were simply dissolved and removed in a fluid state. The body was also laid in salt or natron which, it is said, dissolved everything except the skin and bones. The cost of mummifying in this manner was 20 minae, or about £80.

The third method of embalming was employed for the poor only. It consisted simply of cleaning the body by injecting some strong astringent, and then salting the body for seventy days. The cost in this case was very little.

The account given by Diodorus agrees generally with that of Herodotus. He adds, however, that the incision was made on the left side of the body, and that the "dissector" having made the incision fled away, pursued and stoned by those who had witnessed the ceremony. It would seem that the dissector merely fulfilled a religious obligation in fleeing away, and that he had not much to fear. Diodorus goes on to say that the Egyptians kept the

* In Genesis l. 3, the number is given as forty.

bodies of their ancestors in splendid chambers, and that they had the opportunity of contemplating the faces of those who died before their time. In some particulars he is right, and in others wrong. He lived too late (about B.C. 40) to know what the well-made Theban mummies were like, and his experience therefore would only have familiarised him with the Egypto-Roman mummies, in which the limbs were bandaged separately, and the contour of their faces, much blunted, was to be seen through the thin and tightly drawn bandages which covered the face. In such examples the features of the face can be clearly distinguished underneath the bandages.

An examination of Egyptian mummies will show that the accounts given by Herodotus and Diodorus are generally correct, for mummies with and without ventral incisions are found, and some are preserved by means of balsams and gums, and others by bitumen and natron. The skulls of mummies which may be seen by hundreds in caves and pits at Thebes contain absolutely nothing, a fact which proves that the embalmers were able not only to remove the brain, but also to take out the membranes without injuring or breaking the nose in any way. The heads of mummies are found, at times, to be filled with bitumen, linen rags, or resin. The bodies which have been filled with resin or some such substance are of a greenish colour, and the skin has the appearance of being tanned. Such mummies, when unrolled, perish rapidly and break easily. Usually, however, the resin and aromatic gum process is favourable to the preservation of the teeth and hair. Bodies from which the intestines have been removed and which have been preserved by being filled with bitumen, are quite black and hard. The features are preserved intact, but the body is heavy and unfair to look upon. The bitumen penetrates the bones so completely that it is sometimes difficult to distinguish what is bone and what is bitumen. The arms, legs, hands, and feet of such mummies break with a sound like the cracking of chemical glass tubing; they burn freely. Speaking generally, they will last for ever.

When a mummy has been preserved by natron, that is, a mixture of carbonate, sulphate, and muriate of soda, the skin is found to be very hard, and it hangs loosely from the bones in much the same way as it hangs from the skeletons of the dead monks preserved in the crypt beneath the Capuchin convent at Floriana in Malta. The hair of such mummies usually falls off when touched.

When the friends of a dead Egyptian were too poor to pay for the best method of embalmment, the body could be preserved by two very cheap methods; one method was to soak it in salt and hot bitumen, and the other in salt only. In the salt and bitumen process every cavity of the body was filled with bitumen, and the hair disappeared. Clearly it is to the bodies which were preserved in this way that the name "mummy," or bitumen, was first applied.

The salted and dried body is easily distinguishable. The skin is like paper, the features and hair have disappeared, and the bones are very brittle and white.

The art of mummifying arrived at the highest pitch of perfection at Thebes. The mummies of the first six dynasties drop to pieces on exposure to the air, and smell slightly of bitumen; those of the XIth dynasty are of a yellowish colour and very brittle; those of the XIIth dynasty are black. The method of embalming varied at different periods and places. From the XVIIIth to the XXIst dynasties the Memphis mummies are black, while those made at Thebes during the same period are yellowish in colour, and have the nails of the hands and feet dyed yellow with the juice of the *henna* plant. After the XXVIth dynasty the mummies made at both places are quite black and shapeless; they are also very heavy and tough, and can only be broken with difficulty.

What the mummies which were made three or four hundred years after Christ are like I am unable to say, for I have never seen one unrolled. About B.C. 100 the Greeks began to paint the portrait of the dead upon the wrappings which covered the face.

The art of mummifying was carried on in Egypt for nearly five hundred years after the birth of Christ, for the Greeks and Romans adopted the custom freely. We may then say that we know for a certainty that the art of embalming was known and practised for about five thousand years.

In the account of embalming given us by Herodotus, we are told that the internal organs of the body were removed, but he omits to say what was done with them. We now know that they also were mummified and preserved in four jars, the covers of which were made in the shape of the heads of the four children of Horus, the genii of the dead, whose names were Mesthȧ, Ḥāpi, Ṭuamāutef, and Qebḥsennuf. These genii have been compared with the four beasts in the Revelation (chap. iv. 7). The jars and the genii to which they were dedicated were under the protection of Isis, Nephthys, Neith, and Serk respectively. They are called "Canopic" jars, because they resemble the vase shape of Osiris called Canopus, and they are made of Egyptian porcelain, marble, calcareous stone, terra-cotta, wood, etc. The jar of Mesthȧ received the stomach, that of Ḥāpi the smaller intestines, that of Ṭuamāutef the heart, and that of Qebḥsennuf the liver. Each jar was inscribed with a legend stating that the genius to which it was dedicated protected and preserved the part of the dead body that was in it. In the case of poor people, who could not afford a set of canopic jars, it was usual to have a set of wax figures made in the shape of the four genii of the dead, and to place them in the dead body with the intestines, which were put back. In the time of the XXVIth dynasty, and later, poverty or laziness made people consider the interior parts of the body to be sufficiently well guarded if figures of these genii were roughly drawn on the linen bandages. It was sometimes customary to lay a set of these figures, made of porcelain or bead-work, upon the chest of the mummy.

It was the fashion some years ago to state in books of history that the ancient Egyptian was a negro, and some distinguished historians still make this statement, notwithstanding Prof. Owen's distinct utterance, "taking the sum of the correspondence notable in collections of skulls from Egyptian graveyards as a probable indication of the hypothetical primitive race originating the civilised conditions of cranial departure from the skull-character of such race, that race was certainly not of the Australoid type, is more suggestive of a northern Nubian or Berber basis. But such suggestive characters may be due to intercourse or 'admixture' at periods later than [the] XIIIth dynasty; they are not present, or in a much less degree, in the skulls, features, and physiognomies of individuals of from the IIIrd to the XIIth dynasties."* The character of the ancient Egyptian,

* *Journal of the Anthropological Institute of Great Britain and Ireland*, vol. iv., p. 239. The most important scientific examinations of the skeletons of mummified Egyptians in England have been made by the late Sir Richard Owen, Prof. Sir W. Flower, and Prof. Macalister of Cambridge. Within the last few years I have collected for this last-named *savant* beween six and seven hundred Egyptian skulls from Thebes and Aswân (Syene). The greater part of these reached England in excellent condition, and they are now being measured and examined by craniological experts. On some of them the skin of the face and neck remains in a perfect condition, and Prof. Macalister has found a means whereby he is able to make these dry and withered faces fill out and resume something of the appearance which they wore in life. As all these skulls are of great antiquity, and belonged to high-class Egyptians, priests, and others, the results of his work may be anticipated with great interest by both the ethnographist and Egyptologist.

and of the race to which he belonged, has been vindicated by examinations of the skulls of Egyptian mummies.

If the pure ancient Egyptian, as found in mummies and represented in paintings upon the tombs, be compared with the negro, we shall find that they are absolutely unlike in every important particular. The negro is prognathous, but the Egyptian is orthognathous; the bony structure of the negro is heavier and stronger than that of the Egyptian; the hair of the negro is crisp and woolly, while that of the Egyptian is smooth and fine.

It must be pointed out clearly that the Egyptians took trouble to preserve the bodies of the dead because they believed that after a series of terrible combats in the underworld, the soul, triumphant and pure, would once more return to the clay in which it had formerly lived. It was necessary, then, to preserve the body that it might be ready for the return of the soul. It was also necessary to build large and beautiful tombs, in order that the triumphant soul, having revivified its ancient house of clay, might have a fit and proper abode in which to dwell. The pyramid tombs built by the kings of the earlier dynasties, and the vast many-chambered sepulchres hewn in the sides of the Theban hills during the XVIIIth and XIXth dynasties, were not, in my opinion, built to gratify the pride of their owners. They are the outcome of the belief that the soul would revivify the body, and they are the result of a firm assurance in the mind of the ancient Egyptians of the truth of the doctrine of immortality, which is the foundation of the Egyptian religion, and which was as deeply rooted in them as the hills are in the earth.

HELIOPOLIS.*

About five miles to the north-east of Cairo stands the little village of Maṭariyyeh †, built upon part of the site of Heliopolis, where may be seen the sycamore tree, usually called the "Virgin's Tree," under which tradition says that the Virgin Mary sat and rested during her flight to Egypt; it was planted some time towards the end of the XVIIth century, and was given to the Empress Eugénie by Ismaʻîl on the occasion of the opening of the Suez Canal. Beyond the "Virgin's Tree" is the fine Aswân granite obelisk which marks the site of the ancient town of Heliopolis, called "On" in Gen. xli. 45, "House of the Sun" in Jeremiah

* Called in Egyptian , *Ànnu meḥt*, "Annu of the North," to distinguish it from , *Ànnu Qemāu*, "Annu of the South," *i.e.*, Hermonthis.

† مَطَرِيَّة, Juynboll, *op. cit.*, t. iii., p. 110. At this place the balsam trees, about which so many traditions are extant, were said to grow. The balsam tree was about a cubit high, and had two barks; the outer red and fine, and the inner green and thick. When the latter was macerated in the mouth, it left an oily taste and an aromatic odour. Incisions were made in the barks, and the liquid which flowed from them was carefully collected and treated; the amount of balsam oil obtained formed a tenth part of all the liquid collected. The last balsam tree cultivated in Egypt died in 1615, but two were seen alive in 1612; it is said that they would grow nowhere out of Egypt. They were watered with the water from the well at Maṭariyyeh in which the Virgin Mary washed the clothes of our Lord when she was in Egypt. The oil was much sought after by the Christians of Abyssinia and other places, who thought it absolutely necessary that one drop of this oil should be poured into the water in which they were baptized. See Wansleben, *L'Histoire de l'Église d'Alexandrie*, pp. 88–93; *Abd-al-Laṭîf* (ed. de Sacy), p. 88.

xliii. 13, and "Eye or Fountain of the Sun" by the Arabs. Heliopolis was about twelve miles from the fortress of Babylon, and stood on the eastern side of the Pelusiac arm of the Nile, near the right bank of the great canal which passed through the Bitter Lakes and connected the Nile with the sea. Its ruins cover an area three miles square. The greatest and oldest Egyptian College or University for the education of the priesthood and the laity stood here, and it was here that Ptolemy II. Philadelphus, sent for Egyptian manuscripts when he wished to augment the library which his father had founded.

The **obelisk** is sixty-six feet high, and was set up by Usertsen I.  about B.C. 2433; a companion obelisk remained standing in its place until the seventh century of our era, and both were covered with caps of *smu* (probably copper) metal. During the XXth dynasty the temple of Heliopolis was one of the largest and wealthiest in all Egypt, and its staff was numbered by thousands. When Cambyses visited Egypt the glory of Heliopolis was well on the wane, and after the removal of the priesthood and sages of the temple to Alexandria by Ptolemy II. its downfall was well assured. When Strabo visited it (B.C. 24), the greater part of it was in ruins; but we know from Arab writers that many of the statues remained *in situ* at the end of the twelfth century. Heliopolis had a large population of Jews, and it will be remembered that Joseph married the daughter of Pa-ṭā-pa-Rā (Potiphar) a priest of On (Ånnu), or Heliopolis. It lay either in or very near the Goshen of the Bible. The Mnevis bull, sacred to Rā, was worshipped at Heliopolis, and it was here that the phœnix or palm-bird brought its ashes after having raised itself to life at the end of each period of five hundred years. Alexander the Great halted here on his way from Pelusium to Memphis. Macrobius says that the Heliopolis of Syria, or Baalbek, was founded by a body of priests who left the ancient city of Heliopolis of Egypt.

THE PYRAMIDS OF GÎZEH.

On the western bank of the Nile, from Abu Roâsh on the north to Mêdûm on the south, is a slightly elevated tract of land, about twenty-five miles long, on the edge of the Libyan desert, on which stand the pyramids of Abu Roâsh, Gîzeh, Zâwyet el-'Aryân, Abuṣîr, Saḳḳârah, and Dahshûr. Other places in Egypt where pyramids are found are El-lâhûn* in the Fayyûm, and Kullah near Esneh. The pyramids built by the Ethiopians at Meroë and Gebel Barkal are of a very late date (B.C. 600–100), and are mere copies, in respect of form only, of the pyramids in Egypt. It is well to state at once that the pyramids were tombs and nothing else. There is no evidence whatever to show that they were built for purposes of astronomical observations, and the theory that the Great Pyramid was built to serve as a standard of measurement is ingenious but worthless. The significant fact, so ably pointed out by Mariette, that pyramids are only found in cemeteries, is an answer to all such theories. Tomb-pyramids were built by kings and others until the XIIth dynasty. The ancient writers who have described and treated of the pyramids are given by Pliny (Nat. Hist., xxxvi. 12, 17). If we may believe some of the writers on them during the Middle Ages, their outsides must have been covered with inscriptions; these were probably of a religious nature.† In modern times they have been examined by Shaw (1721),

* *I.e.*,  *Le-ḥen*, "mouth of the canal," Coptic λεϩωnι.

† "......... their surfaces exhibit all kinds of inscriptions written in the characters of ancient nations which no longer exist. No one knows what this writing is or what it signifies." Mas'ûdi (ed. Barbier de Meynard), t. ii., p. 404.

Pococke (1743), Niebuhr (1761), Davison (1763), Bruce (1768), Denon and Jomard (1799), Hamilton (1801), Caviglia (1817), Belzoni (1817), Wilkinson (1831), Howard Vyse and Perring (1837–38), Lepsius (1842–45), and Petrie (1881).

It appears that before the actual building of a pyramid was begun a suitable rocky site was chosen and cleared, a mass of rock if possible being left in the middle of the area to form the core of the building. The chambers and the galleries leading to them were next planned and excavated. Around the core a truncated pyramid building was made, the angles of which were filled up with blocks of stone. Layer after layer of stone was then built around the work, which grew larger and larger until it was finished. Dr. Lepsius thought that when a king ascended the throne, he built for himself a small but complete tomb-pyramid, and that a fresh coating of stone was built around it every year that he reigned; and that when he died the sides of the pyramids were like long flights of steps, which his successor filled up with right-angled triangular blocks of stone. The door of the pyramid was walled up after the body of its builder had been laid in it, and thus remained a finished tomb. The explanation of Dr. Lepsius may not be correct, but at least it answers satisfactorily more objections than do the views of other theorists on this matter. It has been pointed out that near the core of the pyramid the work is more carefully executed than near the exterior, that is to say, as the time for the king's death approached the work was more hurriedly performed.

During the investigations made by Lepsius in and about the pyramid area, he found the remains of about seventy-five pyramids, and noticed that they were always built in groups.

The pyramids of Gîzeh were opened by the Persians during the fifth and fourth centuries before Christ; it is probable that they were also entered by the Romans. Khalif Mâmûn (A.D. 813–833) entered the Great Pyramid, and found that others had been there before him. The treasure which is said to have been discovered there by him is probably fictitious. Once opened, it must have been evident to every one what splendid quarries the pyramids formed, and very few hundred years after the conquest of Egypt by the Arabs they were laid under contribution for stone to build mosques, etc., in Cairo. Late in the twelfth century Melik el-Kâmil made a mad attempt to destroy the third pyramid at Gîzeh built by Mycerinus; but after months of toil he only succeeded in stripping off the covering from one of the sides. It is said that Muḥammad 'Ali was advised to undertake the senseless task of destroying them all.

THE GREAT PYRAMID.

This, the largest of the three pyramids at Gizeh, was built by Chufu 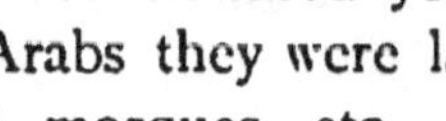 or Cheops, the second king of the IVth dynasty, B.C. 3733, who called it 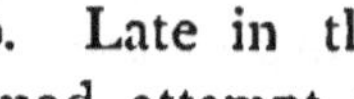 *Chut.* His name was found written in red ink upon the blocks of stone inside it. All four sides measure in greatest length about 755 feet each, but the length of each was originally about 20 feet more; its height now is 451 feet, but it is said to have been originally about 481 feet. The stone used in the construction of this pyramid was brought from Ṭurra and Moḳaṭṭam, and the contents amount to 85,000,000 cubic feet. The flat space at the top of the pyramid is about thirty feet square, and the view from it is very fine.

The entrance (A) to this pyramid is, as with all pyramids, on the north side, and is about 45 feet above the ground. The passage A B C is 320 feet long, $3\frac{1}{4}$ feet high, and 4 feet

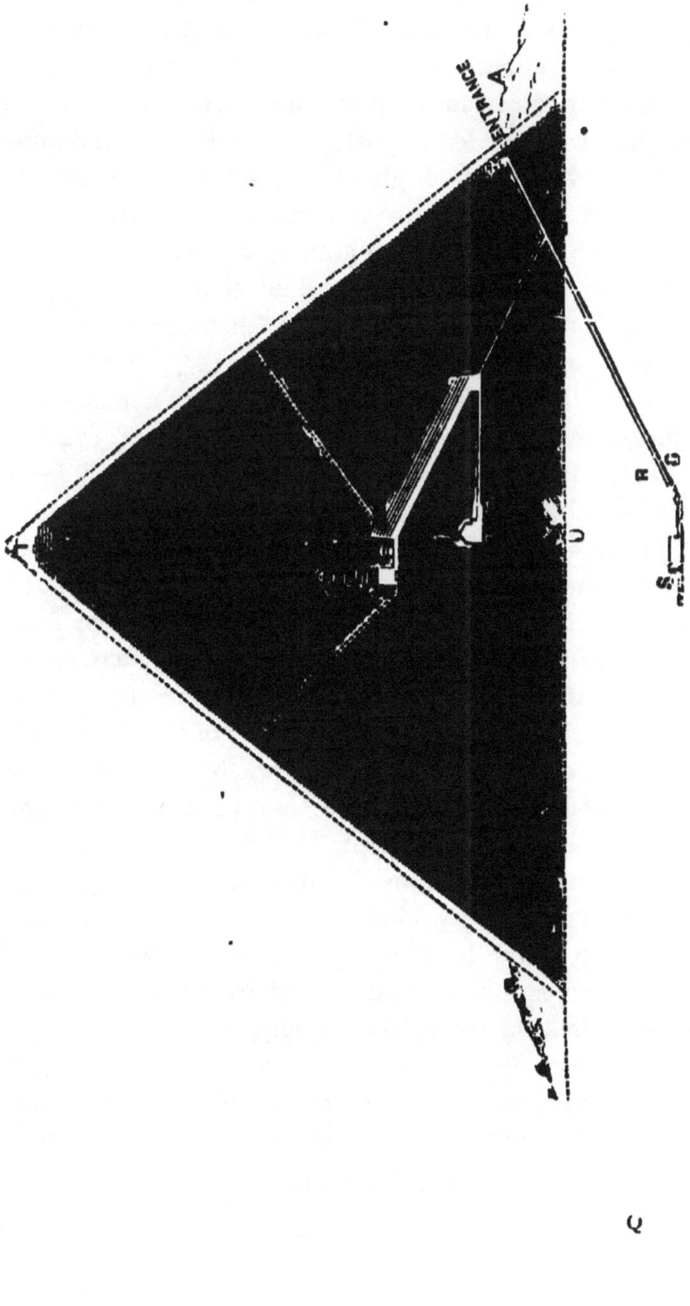

Section of the Pyramid of Cheops at Gîzeh. From Vyse, *Pyramids of Gizeh*, Vol. I., p. 2.

wide; at B is a granite door, round which the path at D has been made. The passage at D E is 125 feet long, and the large hall E F is 155 feet long and 28 feet high; the passage E G leads to the pointed-roofed Queen's Chamber H, which measures about 17 × 19 × 20 feet. The roofing in of this chamber is a beautiful piece of mason's work. From the large hall E F there leads a passage 22 feet long, the ante-chamber in which was originally closed by four granite doors, remains of which are still visible, into the King's Chamber, J, which is lined with granite, and measures about 35 × 17 × 19 feet. The five hollow chambers K, L, M, N, O were built above the King's Chamber to lighten the pressure of the superincumbent mass. In chamber O the name Chufu was found written. The air shafts P and Q measure 234 feet × 8 inches × 6 inches, and 174 feet × 8 inches × 6 inches respectively. A shaft from E to R leads down to the subterranean chamber S, which measures 46 × 27 × 10½ feet. The floor of the King's Chamber, J, is about 140 ft. from the level of the base of the pyramid, and the chamber is a little to the south-east of the line drawn from T to U. Inside the chamber lies the empty, coverless, broken red granite sarcophagus of Cheops, measuring 7½ × 3¼ × 3⅓ feet. The account of the building of this pyramid is told by Herodotus* as follows: "Now, they told me, that to the reign of Rhampsinitus there was a perfect distribution of justice, and that all Egypt was in a high state of prosperity; but that after him Cheops, coming to reign over them, plunged into every kind of wickedness. For that, having shut up all the temples, he first of all forbade them to offer sacrifice, and afterwards he ordered all the Egyptians to work for himself; some, accordingly, were appointed to draw stones from the quarries in the Arabian mountain down to the Nile, others he ordered to receive the stones when transported in vessels across the river, and to drag

* Bk. ii. 124–126.

them to the mountain called the Libyan. And they worked to the number of 100,000 men at a time, each party during three months. The time during which the people were thus harassed by toil, lasted ten years on the road which they constructed, along which they drew the stones, a work in my opinion, not much less than the pyramid; for its length is five stades (3,051 feet), and its width ten orgyæ (60 feet), and its height, where it is the highest, eight orgyæ (48 feet); and it is of polished stone, with figures carved on it: on this road these ten years were expended, and in forming the subterraneous apartments on the hill, on which the pyramids stand, which he had made as a burial vault for himself, in an island, formed by draining a canal from the Nile. Twenty years were spent in erecting the pyramid itself: of this, which is square, each face is eight plethra (820 feet), and the height is the same; it is composed of polished stones, and jointed with the greatest exactness; none of the stones are less than thirty feet. This pyramid was built thus; in the form of steps, which some call crossæ, others bomides. When they had first built it in this manner, they raised the remaining stones by machines made of short pieces of wood: having lifted them from the ground to the first range of steps, when the stone arrived there, it was put on another machine that stood ready on the first range; and from this it was drawn to the second range on another machine; for the machines were equal in number to the ranges of steps; or they removed the machine, which was only one, and portable, to each range in succession, whenever they wished to raise the stone higher; for I should relate it in both ways, as it is related. The highest parts of it, therefore, were first finished, and afterwards they completed the parts next following; but last of all they finished the parts on the ground and that were lowest. On the pyramid is shown an inscription, in Egyptian characters, how much was expended in radishes, onions, and garlic, for the workmen; which the interpreter,* as I well remember, reading the inscription, told me amounted to 1,600 talents of silver. And if this be really the case, how much more was probably expended in iron tools, in bread, and in clothes for the labourers, since they occupied in building the works the time which I mentioned, and no short time besides, as I think, in cutting and drawing the stones, and in forming the subterraneous excavation. [It is related] that Cheops reached such a degree of infamy, that being in want of money, he prostituted his own daughter in a brothel, and ordered her to extort, they did not say how much; but she exacted a certain sum of money, privately, as much as her father ordered her; and contrived to leave a monument of herself, and asked every one that came in to her to give her a stone towards the edifice she designed: of these stones they said the pyramid was built that stands in the middle of the three, before the great pyramid, each side of which is a plethron and a half in length." (Cary's translation.)

THE SECOND PYRAMID.

The second pyramid at Gîzeh was built by Chā-f-Rā, , or Chephren, the third king of the IVth dynasty, B.C. 3666, who called it , *ur*. His name has not been found inscribed upon any part of it, but the fragment of a marble sphere inscribed with the name of Chā-f-Rā,

* Herodotus was deceived by his interpreter, who clearly made up a translation of an inscription which he did not understand. William of Baldensel, who lived in the fourteenth century, tells us that the outer coating of the two largest pyramids was covered with a great number of inscriptions arranged in lines. (Wiedemann, *Aeg. Geschichte*, p. 179.) If the outsides were actually inscribed, the text must have been purely religious, like those inscribed inside the pyramids of Pepi, Tetà, and Unàs.

which was found near the temple, close by this pyramid, confirms the statements of Herodotus and Diodorus Siculus, that Chephren built it. A statue of this king, now in the Gîzeh Museum, was found in the granite temple close by. This pyramid appears to be larger than the Great Pyramid because it stands upon a higher level of stone foundation; it was cased with stone originally and polished, but the greater part of the outer casing has disappeared. An ascent of this pyramid can only be made with difficulty. It was first explored in 1816 by Belzoni (born 1778, died 1823), the discoverer of the tomb of Seti I. and of the temple of Rameses II. at Abu Simbel. In the north side of the pyramid are two openings, one at the base and one about 50 feet above it. The upper opening led into a corridor 105 feet long, which descends into a chamber $46\frac{1}{2} \times 16\frac{1}{3} \times 22\frac{1}{2}$ feet, which held the granite sarcophagus in which Chephren was buried. The lower opening leads into a corridor about 100 feet long, which, first descending and then ascending, ends in the chamber mentioned above, which is usually called Belzoni's Chamber. The actual height is about 450 feet, and the length of each side at the base about 700 feet. The rock upon which the pyramid stands has been scarped on the north and west sides to make the foundation level. The history of the building of the pyramid is thus stated by Herodotus *: "The Egyptians say that this Cheops reigned fifty years; and when he died, his brother Chephren succeeded to the kingdom; and he followed the same practices as the other, both in other respects, and in building a pyramid; which does not come up to the dimensions of his brother's, for I myself measured them; nor has it subterraneous chambers; nor does a channel from the Nile flow to it, as to the other; but this flows through an artificial aqueduct round an island within, in which they say the body of

* Bk. ii. 127.

Cheops is laid. Having laid the first course of variegated Ethiopian stones, less in height than the other by forty feet, he built it near the large pyramid. They both stand on the same hill, which is about 100 feet high. Chephren, they said, reigned fifty-six years. Thus 106 years are reckoned, during which the Egyptians suffered all kinds of calamities, and for this length of time the temples were closed and never opened. From the hatred they bear them, the Egyptians are not very willing to mention their names; but call the pyramids after Philition, a shepherd, who at that time kept his cattle in those parts." (Cary's translation.)

THE THIRD PYRAMID.

The third pyramid at Gîzeh was built by Men-kau-Rā, 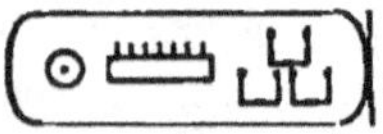, the fourth king of the IVth dynasty, about B.C. 3633, who called it , *Ḥer.* Herodotus and other ancient authors tell us that Men-kau-Rā, or Mycerinus, was buried in this pyramid, but Manetho states that Nitocris, a queen of the VIth dynasty, was the builder. There can be, however, but little doubt that it was built by Mycerinus, for the sarcophagus and the remains of the inscribed coffin of this king were found in one of its chambers by Howard Vyse in 1837. The sarcophagus, which measured 8 × 3 × 2½ feet, was lost through the wreck of the ship in which it was sent to England, but the venerable fragments of the coffin are preserved in the British Museum, and form one of the most valuable objects in the famous collection of that institution. The inscription reads: "Osiris, king of the North and South, Men-kau-Rā, living for ever! The heavens have produced thee, thou wast engendered by Nut (the sky), thou art the offspring of Seb (the earth). Thy mother Nut spreads herself over thee in her form as a divine mystery. She has granted thee to be a god, thou shalt nevermore have enemies, O king of the North and South, Men-kau-Rā, living for ever." This formula is one which is found upon coffins down to the latest period, but as the date of Mycerinus is known, it is possible to draw some interesting and valuable conclusions from the fact that it is found upon his coffin. It proves that as far back as 3,600 years before Christ the Egyptian religion was established on a firm base, that the doctrine of immortality was already deeply rooted in the human mind. The art of preserving the human body by embalming was also well understood and generally practised at that early date.

The pyramid of Men-kau-Rā, like that of Chephren, is built upon a rock with a sloping surface; the inequality of the surface in this case has been made level by building up courses of large blocks of stones. Around the lower part the remains of the old granite covering are visible to a depth of from 30 to 40 feet. It is unfortunate that this pyramid has been so much damaged; its injuries, however, enable the visitor to see exactly how it was built, and it may be concluded that the pyramids of Cheops and Chephren were built in the same manner. The length of each side at the base is about 350 feet, and its height is variously given as 210 and 215 feet. The entrance is on the north side, about thirteen feet above the ground, and a descending corridor about 104 feet long, passing through an ante-chamber, having a series of three granite doors, leads into one chamber about 40 feet long, and a second chamber about 44 long. In this last chamber is a shaft which leads down to the granite-lined chamber about twenty feet below, in which were found the sarcophagus and wooden coffin of Mycerinus, and the remains of a human body. It is thought that, in spite of the body of Mycerinus being buried in this pyramid, it was left unfinished at the death of this king, and that a succeeding ruler of

Egypt finished the pyramid and made a second chamber to hold his or her body. At a short distance to the east of this pyramid are the ruins of a temple which was probably used in connexion with the rites performed in honour of the dead king. In A.D. 1196 a deliberate and systematic attempt was made to destroy this pyramid by the command of the Muḥammadan ruler of Egypt.* The account of the character of Mycerinus and of his pyramid as given by Herodotus is as follows: "They said that after him, Mycerinus,† son of Cheops, reigned over Egypt; that the conduct of his father was displeasing to him; and that he opened the temples, and permitted the people, who were worn down to the last extremity, to return to their employments, and to sacrifices; and that he made the most just decisions of all their kings. On this account, of all the kings that ever reigned in Egypt, they praise him most, for he both judged well in other respects, and moreover, when any man complained of his decision, he used to make him some present out of his own treasury and pacify his anger. . . . . . . This king also left a pyramid much less than that of his father, being on each side twenty feet short of three plethra; it is quadrangular, and built half way up of Ethiopian stone. Some of the Grecians erroneously say that this pyramid is the work of the courtesan Rhodopis; but they evidently appear to me ignorant who Rhodopis was; for they would not else have attributed to her the building of such a pyramid, on which, so to speak, numberless thousands of talents were expended; besides, Rhodopis flourished in the reign of Amasis, and not at this time; for she was very many years later than those kings who left these pyramids." (Cary's translation.)

In one of the three small pyramids near that of Mycerinus the name of this king is painted on the ceiling.

* See p. 224. † Book ii. 129, 134.

THE SPHINX.

The age of the **Sphinx** is unknown, and few of the facts connected with its history have come down to these days. Some years ago it was generally believed to have been made during the rule of the kings of the Middle Empire over Egypt, but when the stele which recorded the repairs made in the temple of the sphinx by Thothmes IV., B.C. 1533, came to light, it became certain that it was the work of one of the kings of the Ancient Empire. The stele records that one day during an after-dinner sleep, Harmachis appeared to Thothmes IV., and promised to bestow upon him the crown of Egypt if he would dig his image, *i.e.*, the Sphinx, out of the sand. At the end of the inscription part of the name of Chā-f-Rā or Chephren appears, and hence some have thought that this king was the maker of the Sphinx; as the statue of Chephren was subsequently found in the temple close by, this theory was generally adopted. An inscription found by Mariette near one of the pyramids to the east of the pyramid of Cheops shows that the Sphinx existed in the time of Chufu or Cheops. The Egyptians called the Sphinx *ḥu* , and he represented the god Harmachis, *i.e.*, *Ḥeru-em-chut* , "Horus in the horizon," or the rising sun, the conqueror of darkness, the god of the morning. On the tablet erected by Thothmes IV., Harmachis says that he gave life and dominion to Thothmes III., and he promises to give the same good gifts to his successor Thothmes IV. The discovery of the steps which led up to the Sphinx, a smaller Sphinx, and an open temple, etc., was made by Caviglia, who first excavated this monument; within the last few years very extensive excavations have been made round it by the Egyptian Government, and several hitherto unseen parts of it have been brought to view. The Sphinx is hewn out of the living rock, but pieces of stone have been added where necessary; the body is about 150 feet long, the paws are 50 feet long, the head is 30 feet long, the face is 14 feet wide, and from the top of the head to the base of the monument the distance is about 70 feet. Originally there probably were ornaments on the head, the whole of which was covered with a limestone covering, and the face was coloured red; of these decorations scarcely any traces now remain, though they were visible towards the end of the last century. The condition in which the monument now appears is due to the savage destruction of its features by the Muḥammadan rulers of Egypt, some of whom caused it to be used for a target. Around this imposing relic of antiquity, whose origin is wrapped in mystery, a number of legends and superstitions have clustered in all ages; but Egyptology has shown I. that it was a colossal image of Rā-Harmachis, and therefore of his human representative upon earth, the king of Egypt who had it hewn, and II. that it was in existence in the time of, and was probably repaired by, Cheops and Chephren, who lived about three thousand seven hundred years before Christ.

The Temple of the Sphinx.

A little to the south-east of the Sphinx stands the large granite and limestone temple excavated by M. Mariette in 1853; statues of Chephren (now at Gizeh) were found in it, and hence it has been generally supposed that he was the builder of it. It is a good specimen of the solid simple buildings which the Egyptians built during the Ancient Empire. In one chamber, and at the end of the passage leading from it, are hewn in the wall niches which were probably intended to hold mummies.

The Tomb of Numbers.

This tomb was made for Chā-f-Rā-ānch, a "royal relative" and priest of Chephren (Chā-f-Rā), the builder of the second pyramid. It is called the "tomb of numbers" because the numbers of the cattle possessed by Chāf-Rā-ānch are written upon its walls.

Campbell's Tomb.

This tomb, named after the British Consul-General of Egypt at that time, was excavated by Howard Vyse in 1837; it is not older than the XXVIth dynasty. The shaft is about 55 feet deep; at the bottom of it is a small chamber in which were found three sarcophagi in niches.

The pyramids of Gîzeh are surrounded by a large number of tombs of high officials and others connected with the services carried on in honour of the kings who built the pyramids. Some few of them are of considerable interest, and as they are perishing little by little, it is advisable to see as many of the best specimens as possible.

The Pyramids of Abu Roâsh.

These pyramids lie about six miles north of the Pyramids of Gîzeh, and are thought to be older than they. Nothing remains of one except five or six courses of stone, which show that the length of each side at the base was about 350 feet, and a passage about 160 feet long leading down to a subterranean chamber about 43 feet long. A pile of stones close by marks the site of another pyramid; the others have disappeared. Of the age of these pyramids nothing certain is known. The remains of a causeway about a mile long leading to them are still visible.

The Pyramids of Abuṣir.

These pyramids, originally fourteen in number, were built by kings of the Vth dynasty, but only four of them are now standing, probably because of the poorness of the workmanship and the careless way in which they were put together. The most northerly pyramid was built by

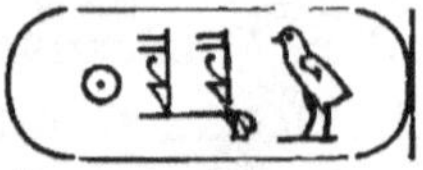 Saḥu-Rā, the second king of the Vth dynasty, B.C. 3533; its actual height is about 120 feet, and the length of each side at the base about 220 feet. The blocks of stone in the sepulchral chamber are exceptionally large. Saḥu-Rā made war in the peninsula of Sinai, he founded a town near Esneh, and he built a temple to Sechet at Memphis.

The pyramid to the south of that of Saḥu-Rā was built by 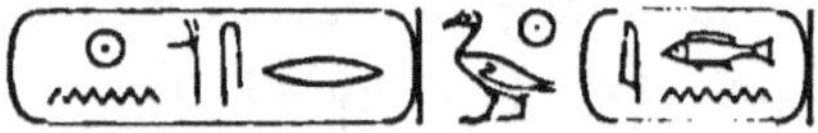 "*Usr-en-Rā, son of the Sun, An.*" This king, like Saḥu-Rā, also made war in Sinai. The largest of these three pyramids is now about 165 feet high and 330 feet square; the name of its builder is unknown. Abuṣir is the Busiris of Pliny.

BEDRASHÊN, MEMPHIS, AND SAḲḲÂRAH.

The ruins of **Memphis** and the antiquities at Saḳḳârah are usually reached by steamer or train from Cairo to Bedrashên. Leaving the river or station the village of Bedrashên is soon reached, and a short ride next brings the traveller to the village of Mît-Rahîneh. On the ground lying for some distance round about these two villages once stood the city of Memphis, though there is comparatively little left to show its limits. According to Herodotus (ii., 99), "Menes, who first ruled over Egypt, in the first place protected Memphis by a mound; for the whole river formerly ran close to the sandy mountain on the side of Libya; but Menes, beginning about a hundred stades above Memphis, filled in the elbow towards the south, dried up the old channel, and conducted the river into a canal, so as to make it flow between the mountains: this bend of the Nile, which flows excluded from *its ancient course*, is still carefully upheld by the Persians, being made secure every year; for if the river should break through and overflow in this part, there would be danger lest all Memphis should be flooded. When the part cut off had been made firm land by this Menes, who was first king, he in the first place built on it the city that is now called Memphis; for Memphis is situate in the narrow part of Egypt; and outside of it he excavated a lake from the river towards the north and the west; for the Nile itself bounds it towards the east. In the next place, *they relate* that he built in it the temple of Vulcan, which is vast and well worthy of mention." (Cary's translation.)

Whether Menes built the town or not, it is quite certain that the city of Memphis was of most ancient foundation.

The reason why the kings of Egypt established their capital there is obvious. From the peoples that lived on the western bank of the river they had little to fear, but on the eastern side they were always subject to invasions of the peoples who lived in Mesopotamia, Syria, and Arabia; with their capital on the western bank, and the broad Nile as a barrier on the east of it, they were comparatively safe. Added to this, its situation at the beginning of the Delta enabled it to participate easily of the good things of that rich country. The tract of land upon which Memphis stood was also fertile and well wooded. Diodorus speaks of its green meadows, intersected with canals, and of their pavement of lotus flowers; Pliny talks of trees there of such girth that three men with extended arms could not span them; Martial praises the roses brought from thence to Rome; and its wine was celebrated in lands remote from it. The site chosen was excellent, for in addition to its natural advantages it was not far from the sea-coast of the Delta, and holding as it were a middle position in Egypt, its kings were able to hold and rule the country from Philæ on the south to the Mediterranean on the north. In the inscriptions it is called  *Men-nefer,** "the beautiful dwelling," 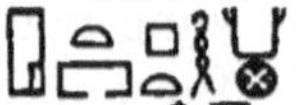 *Ḥet-Ptaḥ-ka,* "the temple of the double of Ptaḥ," and  Åneb-ḥet', "the white-walled city." The last name calls to mind the "White Castle" spoken of by classical writers. Tetå, son of Menes, built his palace there, and Ka-Kau , the second king of the IInd dynasty, B.C. 4100, established the worship of Apis there. During the rule of the IIIrd,

* The name Memphis is a corruption of Men-nefer; the city is called by the Arabs *Menûf*, and by the Copts Memfi, Menfi (ⲙⲉⲙϥⲓ, ⲙⲉⲛϥⲓ).

IVth, and VIth dynasties, the kings of which sprang from Memphis, that city reached a height of splendour which was probably never excelled. The most celebrated building there was the temple of Ptaḥ, which was beautified and adorned by a number of kings, the last of whom reigned during the XXVIth dynasty. The Hyksos ravaged, but did not destroy, the city; under the rule of the Theban kings, who expelled the Hyksos, the city flourished for a time, although Thebes became the new capital. When Rameses II. returned from his wars in the east, he set up a statue of himself in front of the temple of Ptaḥ there; Piānchi the Ethiopian besieged it; the Assyrian kings Esarhaddon and Assurbanipal captured it; Cambyses the Persian, having wrought great damage there, killed the magistrates of the city and the priests of the temple of Apis, and smote the Apis bull so that he died;* he established a Persian garrison there. After the founding of Alexandria, Memphis lost

* "When Cambyses arrived at Memphis, Apis, whom the Greeks call Epaphus, appeared to the Egyptians; and when this manifestation took place, the Egyptians immediately put on their richest apparel, and kept festive holiday. Cambyses seeing them thus occupied, and concluding that they made their rejoicings on account of his ill success, summoned the magistrates to Memphis; and when they came into his presence, he asked, 'why the Egyptians had done nothing of the kind when he was at Memphis before, but did so now, when he had returned with the loss of a great part of his army.' They answered, that their god appeared to them, who was accustomed to manifest himself at distant intervals, and that when he did appear, then all the Egyptians were used to rejoice and keep a feast. Cambyses, having heard this, said they lied, and as liars he put them to death. Having slain them, he next summoned the priests into his presence; and when the priests gave the same account, he said, that he would find out whether a god so tractable had come among the Egyptians; and having said this, he commanded the priests to bring Apis to him; they therefore went away to fetch him. This Apis, or Epaphus, is the calf of a cow incapable of conceiving another offspring; and the Egyptians say, that lightning descends upon the cow from heaven, and that from thence it brings

whatever glory it then possessed, and became merely the chief provincial city of Egypt. During the reign of Theodosius, a savage attack, the result of his edict, was made upon its temples and buildings by the Christians, and a few hundred years later the Muḥammadans carried the stones, which once formed them, across the river to serve as building materials for their houses and mosques. The circuit of the ancient city, according to Diodorus, was 150 stadia, or about thirteen miles.

THE COLOSSAL STATUE OF RAMESES II.

This magnificent statue was discovered by Messrs. Caviglia and Sloane in 1820, and was presented by them to the British Museum. On account of its weight and the lack of public interest in such matters, it lay near the road leading from Bedrashên to Mît-Rahîneh, and little by little became nearly covered with the annual deposit of Nile mud; during the inundation the greater part of it was covered by the waters of the Nile. During the winter of 1886–87 Sir Frederick Stephenson collected a sum of money in Cairo for the purpose of lifting it out of the hollow in which it

forth Apis. This calf, which is called Apis, has the following marks it is black, and has a square spot of white on the forehead; and on the back the figure of an eagle; and in the tail double hairs; and on the tongue a beetle. When the priests brought Apis, Cambyses, like one almost out of his senses, drew his dagger, meaning to strike the belly of Apis, but hit the thigh; then falling into a fit of laughter, he said to the priests, 'Ye blockheads, are there such gods as these, consisting of blood and flesh, and sensible to steel? This, truly, is a god worthy of the Egyptians. But you shall not mock me with impunity.' Having spoken thus, he commanded those whose business it was, to scourge the priests, and to kill all the Egyptians whom they should find feasting. . . . But Apis, being wounded in the thigh, lay and languished in the temple; and at length, when he had died of the wound, the priests buried him without the knowledge of Cambyses."—Herodotus, III, 27–29. (Cary's translation.)

lay, and the difficult engineering part of the task was ably accomplished by Major Arthur Bagnold, R.E. This statue is made of a fine hard limestone, and measures about forty-two feet in height; it is probably one of the statues which stood in front of the temple of Ptaḥ, mentioned by Herodotus and Diodorus. The prenomen of Rameses II. 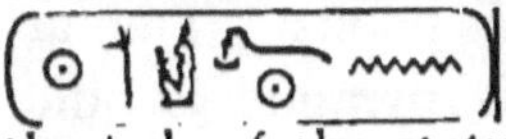 Rā-usr-māt-setep-en-Rā, is inscribed on the belt of the statue, and on the end of the roll which the king carries in his hand are the words "Rameses, beloved of Åmen." By the side of the king are figures of a daughter and son of Rameses. The famous temple of Ptaḥ founded by Menes was situated to the south of the statue.

SAḲḲÂRAH.

The name Saḳḳârah is probably derived from the name of the Egyptian god Seker , who was connected with the resurrection of the dead. The tract of land at Saḳḳârah which formed the great burial ground of the ancient Egyptians of all periods, is about four and a half miles long and one mile wide; the most important antiquities there are: I. the Step Pyramid; II. the Pyramids of Unås, Tetå, and Pepi, kings of the Vth and VIth dynasties; III. the Serapeum; and IV. the Tomb of Thi. Admirers of M. Mariette will be interested to see the house in which this distinguished *savant* lived.

I. The STEP PYRAMID is generally thought to have been built by the fourth king of the Ist dynasty (called Uenephes by Manetho, and 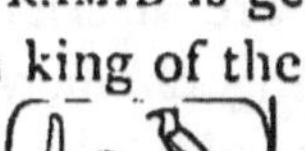 Åta in the tablet of Abydos), who is said to have built a pyramid at Kochome (*i.e.*, Ka-Kam) near Saḳḳârah. Though the date of this pyramid is not known accurately, it is probably right to assume that it is older than the pyramids of Gizeh. The door which led into the pyramid was inscribed with the name of a king called Rā-nub, and M. Mariette found the same name on one of the stelæ in the Serapeum. The steps of the pyramid are six in number, and are about 38, 36, 34½, 32, 31 and 29½ feet in height; the width of each step is from six to seven feet. The lengths of the sides at the base are: north and south 352 feet, east and west 396 feet, and the actual height is 197 feet. In shape this pyramid is oblong, and its sides do not exactly face the cardinal points. The arrangement of the chambers inside this pyramid is quite peculiar to itself.

II. The PYRAMID OF UNÀS , called in Egyptian Nefer-às-u, lies to the south-east of the Step Pyramid, and was reopened and cleared out in 1881 by M. Maspero, at the expense of Messrs. Thomas Cook and Son. Its original height was about 62 feet, and the length of its sides at the base 220 feet. Owing to the broken blocks and sand which lie round about it, Vyse was unable to give exact measurements. Several attempts had been made to break into it, and one of the Arabs who took part in one of these attempts, "Aḥmed the Carpenter," seems to have left his name inside one of the chambers in red ink. It is probable that he is the same man who opened the Great Pyramid at Gîzeh, A.D. 820. A black basalt sarcophagus, from which the cover had been dragged off, and an arm, a shin bone, some ribs and fragments of the skull from the mummy of Unàs, were found in the sarcophagus chamber. The walls of the two largest chambers and two of the corridors are inscribed with ritual texts and prayers of a very interesting character. Unàs, the last king of the Vth dynasty, reigned about thirty years. The Maṣṭabat el-Far'ûn was thought by Mariette to be the tomb of Unàs, but some scholars thought that the 'blunted pyramid' at Dahshûr was his tomb, because his name was written upon the top of it.

The PYRAMID OF TETÀ , called in Egyptian

Ṭeṭ-âsu, lies to the north-east of the Step Pyramid, and was opened in 1881. The Arabs call it the "Prison Pyramid," because local tradition says that it is built near the ruins of the prison where Joseph the patriarch was confined. Its actual height is about 59 feet; the length of each side at the base is 210 feet, and the platform at the top is about 50 feet. The arrangement of the chambers and passages and the plan of construction followed is almost identical with that of the pyramid of Unås. This pyramid was broken into in ancient days, and two of the walls of the sarcophagus chamber have literally been smashed to pieces by the hammer blows of those who expected to find treasure inside them. The inscriptions, painted in green upon the walls, have the same subject matter as those inscribed upon the walls of the chambers of the pyramid of Unås. According to Manetho, Tetå, the first king of the VIth dynasty, reigned about fifty years, and was murdered by one of his guards.

The Pyramid of Pepi I. or  'Rā-meri, son of the Sun, Pepi,' lies to the south-east of the Step Pyramid, and forms one of the central group of pyramids at Saḳḳârah, where it is called the Pyramid of Shêkh Abu Manṣûr; it was opened in 1880. Its actual height is about 40 feet, and the length of the sides at the base is about 250 feet; the arrangement of the chambers, etc., inside is the same as in the pyramids of Unås and Tetå, but the ornamentation is slightly different. It is the worst preserved of these pyramids, and has suffered most at the hands of the spoilers, probably because having been constructed with stones which were taken from tombs ancient already in those days, instead of stones fresh from the quarry, it was more easily injured. The granite sarcophagus was broken to take out the mummy, fragments of which were found lying about on the ground; the cover too, smashed in pieces, lay on the ground close by. A small rose granite box, containing alabaster jars, was also found in the sarcophagus chamber. The inscriptions are, like those inscribed on the walls of the pyramids of Unås and Tetå, of a religious nature; some scholars see in them evidence that the pyramid was usurped by another Pepi, who lived at a much later period than the VIth dynasty. The pyramid of Pepi I., the third king of the VIth dynasty, who reigned, according to Manetho, fifty-three years, was called in Egyptian by the same name as Memphis, *i.e.*, Men-nefer, and numerous priests were attached to its service. Pepi's kingdom embraced all Egypt, and he waged war against the inhabitants of the peninsula of Sinai. He is said to have set up an obelisk at Heliopolis, and to have laid the foundation of the temple at Denderah. His success as a conqueror was due in a great measure to the splendid abilities of one of his chief officers called Unå, who warred successfully against the various hereditary foes of Egypt on its southern and eastern borders.

III. The Serapeum or Apis Mausoleum contained the vaults in which all the Apis bulls that lived at Memphis were buried. According to Herodotus, Apis "is the calf of a cow incapable of conceiving another offspring; and the Egyptians say that lightning descends upon the cow from heaven, and that from thence it brings forth Apis. This calf, which is called Apis, has the following marks: it is black, and has a square spot of white on the forehead, and on the back the figure of an eagle; and in the tail double hairs; and on the tongue a beetle." Above each tomb of an Apis bull was built a chapel, and it was the series of chapels which formed the Serapeum properly so called; it was surrounded by walls like the other Egyptian temples, and it had pylons to which an avenue of sphinxes led. This remarkable place was excavated in 1850 by M. Mariette, who having seen in various parts of Egypt sphinxes upon which were written the names of Osiris–Apis, or Serapis, concluded that they must have come from the Serapeum or temple of Serapis spoken of by Strabo. Happening, by chance, to discover one day at Saḳḳârah a sphinx having the same characteristics, he made up his mind that he had lighted upon the remains of the long sought for building. The excavations which he immediately undertook, brought to light the Avenue of Sphinxes, eleven statues of Greek philosophers, and the vaults in which the Apis bulls were buried. These vaults are of three kinds, and show that the Apis bulls were buried in different ways at different periods: the oldest Apis sarcophagus laid here belongs to the reign of Amenophis III., about B.C. 1500. The parts of the Apis Mausoleum in which the Apis bulls were buried from the XVIIIth to the XXVIth dynasty are not visible; but the new gallery, which contains sixty-four vaults, the oldest of which dates from the reign of Psammetichus I., and the most modern from the time of the Ptolemies, can be seen on application to the guardian of the tombs. The vaults are excavated on each side of the gallery, and each was intended to receive a granite sarcophagus. The names of Amāsis II., Cambyses, and Chabbesha are found upon three of the sarcophagi, but most of them are uninscribed. Twenty-four granite sarcophagi still remain in position, and they each measure about 13 × 8 × 11 feet. The discovery of these tombs was of the greatest importance historically, for on the walls were found thousands of dated stelæ which gave accurate chronological data for the history of Egypt. These votive tablets mention the years, months, and days of the reign of the king in which the Apis bulls, in whose honour the tablets were set up, were born and buried. The Apis tombs had been rifled in ancient times, and only two of them contained any relics when M. Mariette opened them out.

IV. The Tomb of Thi lies to the north-east of the Apis

Mausoleum, and was built during the Vth dynasty, about B.C. 3500. Thi 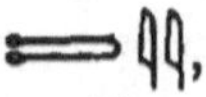, was a man who held the dignities of *smer*, royal councillor, superintendent of works, scribe of the court, confidant of the king, etc.; he held also priestly rank as prophet, and was attached to the service of the pyramids of Abuṣîr. He had sprung from a family of humble origin, but his abilities were so esteemed by one of the kings, whose faithful servant he was, that a princess called Nefer-ḥetep-s was given him to wife, and his children Thi and Tamut ranked as princes. Thi held several high offices under Kakaȧ  and User-en-Rā 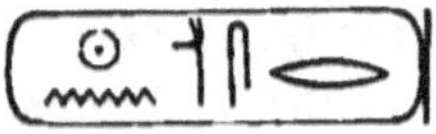 kings of the Vth dynasty. The tomb or maṣṭaba of Thi is now nearly covered with sand, but in ancient days the whole building was above the level of the ground. The chambers of the tomb having been carefully cleared, it is possible to enter them and examine the most beautiful sculptures and paintings with which the walls are decorated. To describe these wonderful works of art adequately would require more space than can be given here; it must be sufficient to say that the scenes represent Thi superintending all the various operations connected with the management of his large agricultural estates and farmyard, together with illustrations of his hunting and fishing expeditions.

The **Necropolis** of Saḳḳârah contains chiefly tombs of the Ancient Empire, that is to say, tombs that were built during the first eleven dynasties; many tombs of a later period are found there, but they are of less interest and importance, and in many cases small, but fine, ancient tombs have been destroyed to make them. As our knowledge of Egyptian architecture is derived principally from tombs and temples, a brief description of the most ancient tombs now known will not be out of place here; the following observations on them are based upon the excellent articles of M. Mariette in the *Revue Archéologique*, S. 2ième, t. xix. p. 8 ff. The tombs of the Ancient Empire found at Saḳḳârah belong to two classes, in the commoner of which the naked body was buried about three feet deep in the sand. When the yellowish-white skeletons of such bodies are found to-day, neither fragments of linen nor pieces of coffins are visible; occasionally one is found laid within four walls roughly built of yellow bricks made of sand, lime, and small stones. A vaulted brick roof covers the space between the walls; it is hardly necessary to say that such tombs represent the last resting places of the poor, and that nothing of any value is ever found inside them. The tombs of the better sort are carefully built, and were made for the wealthy and the great; such a tomb is usually called by the Arabs *maṣṭaba** (the Arabic word for 'bench'), because its length in proportion to its height is great, and reminded them of the long, low seat common in Oriental houses, and familiar to them. The maṣṭaba is a heavy, massive building, of rectangular shape, the four sides of which are four walls symmetrically inclined towards their common centre. Each course of stones, formed by blocks laid upon each other, is carried a little behind the other. The largest maṣṭaba measures about 170 feet long by 86 feet wide, and the smallest about 26 feet by 20 feet: they vary in height from 13 to 30 feet. The ground on which the maṣṭabas at Saḳḳârah are built is composed of rock covered with sand to the depth of a few feet; their foundations are always on the rock. Near the pyramids of Gîzeh they are arranged in a symmetrical manner; they are oriented astronomically to the true north, and their larger axes are always towards the north. Though they have, at first sight, the appearance of unfinished pyramids, still they have nothing in common with pyramids except their orientation towards the true north. Maṣṭabas are built of two kinds of stone and of bricks, and they are

* Pronounced *maṣṭăba*, Arabic مَصْطَبَة, compare Gr. *στιβάς*.

usually entered on the eastern side; their tops are quite flat. The interior of a maṣṭaba may be divided into three parts; the chamber, the *sirdâb*,* or place of retreat, and the pit. The entrance is made through a door in the middle of the eastern or northern side, and though the interior may be divided into many chambers, it is usual only to find one. The walls of the interior are sometimes sculptured, and in the lower part of the chamber, usually facing the east, is a stele; the stele alone may be inscribed and the walls unsculptured, but no case is known where the walls are sculptured and the stele blank. A table of offerings is often found on the ground at the foot of the stele. A little distance from the chamber, built into the thickness of the walls, more often to the south than the north, is a high, narrow place of retreat or habitation, called by the Arabs a *sirdâb*. This place was walled up, and the only communication between it and the chamber was by means of a narrow hole sufficiently large to admit of the entrance of the hand. One or more statues of the dead man buried in the maṣṭaba were shut in here, and the small passage is said to have been made for the escape of the fumes of incense which was burnt in the chamber. The pit was a square shaft varying in depth from 40 to 80 feet, sunk usually in the middle of the larger axis of the maṣṭaba, rather nearer the north than the south. There was neither ladder nor staircase, either outside or inside, leading to the funereal chamber at the bottom of the pit, hence the coffin and the mummy when once there were inaccessible. This pit was sunk through the maṣṭaba into the rock beneath. At the bottom of the pit, on the south side, is an opening into a passage, about four feet high, which leads obliquely to the south-east; soon after the passage increases in size in all directions, and becomes the sarcophagus chamber, which

* A سِرْدَاب is, strictly speaking, a lofty, vaulted, subterranean chamber, with a large opening in the north side to admit air in the hot season.

is thus exactly under the upper chamber. The sarcophagus, rectangular in shape, is usually made of limestone, and rests in a corner of the chamber; at Saḳḳârah they are found uninscribed. When the mummy had been laid in the sarcophagus, and the other arrangements completed, the end of the passage near the shaft leading to the sarcophagus chamber was walled up, the shaft was filled with stones, earth, and sand, and the friends of the deceased might reasonably hope that he would rest there for ever. When M. Mariette found a maṣṭaba without inscriptions he rarely excavated it entirely. He found three belonging to one of the first three dynasties; forty-three of the IVth dynasty; sixty-one of the Vth dynasty; twenty-three of the VIth dynasty; and nine of doubtful date. The Egyptians called the tomb "the house of eternity," , *pa t'etta.*

MARIETTE'S HOUSE.

This house was the headquarters of M. Mariette and his staff when employed in making excavations in the Necropolis of Saḳḳârah. It is not easy to properly estimate the value to science of the work of this distinguished man. It is true that fortune gave him the opportunity of excavating some of the most magnificent of the buildings of the Pharaohs of all periods, and of hundreds of ancient towns; nevertheless it is equally true that his energy and marvellous power of work enabled him to use to the fullest extent the means for advancing the science of Egyptology which had been put in his hands. It is to be hoped that his house will be preserved on its present site as a remembrance of a great man who did a great work.

The TOMB OF PTAḤ-ḤETEP, a priest who lived during the Vth century, is a short distance from Mariette's house, and well worthy of more than one visit.

THE PYRAMIDS OF DAHSHÛR.

These pyramids, four of stone and two of brick, lie about three and a half miles to the south of the Maṣṭabat el-Far'ûn, or Pyramid of Unas. The largest stone pyramid is about 326 feet high, and the length of each side at the base is about 700 feet; beneath it are three subterranean chambers. The second stone pyramid is about 321 feet high, and the length of its sides at the base is 620 feet; it is usually called the "Blunted Pyramid," because the lowest parts of its sides are built at one angle, and the completing parts at another. The larger of the two brick pyramids is about 90 feet high, and the length of the sides at the base is about 350 feet; the smaller is about 156 feet high, and the length of its sides at the base is about 343 feet. The brick pyramids have recently been excavated by M. de Morgan (see p. 395 ff.)

THE QUARRIES OF MA'ṢARA AND ṬURRA.

These quarries have supplied excellent stone for building purposes for six thousand years at least. During the Ancient Empire the architects of the pyramids made their quarrymen tunnel into the mountains for hundreds of yards until they found a bed of stone suitable for their work, and traces of their excavations are plainly visible to-day. The Egyptians called the Ṭurra quarry  Re-āu, or Ta-re-āu, from which the Arabic name Ṭurra is probably derived. An inscription in one of the chambers tells us that during the reign of Amenophis III. a new part of the quarry was opened. Unà, an officer who lived in the reign of Pepi I., was sent to Ṭurra by this king to bring back a white limestone sarcophagus with its cover, libation stone, etc., etc.

THE PYRAMID OF MÊDÛM.

This pyramid, called by the Arabs *El Haram el-Kaddab*, or "the False Pyramid," is probably so named because it is unlike any of the other pyramids known to them; it is said to have been built by Seneferu , the first king of the IVth dynasty, but there is little evidence for this statement. The pyramid is about 115 feet high, and consists of three stages: the first is 70, the second 20, and the third about 25 feet high. The stone for this building was brought from the Moḳaṭṭam hills, but it was never finished; as in all other pyramids, the entrance is on the north side. When opened in modern times the sarcophagus chamber was found empty, and it would seem that this pyramid had been entered and rifled in ancient days.* On the north of this pyramid are a number of maṣṭabas in which 'royal relatives' of Seneferu are buried; the most interesting of these are those of Nefermat, one of his feudal chiefs (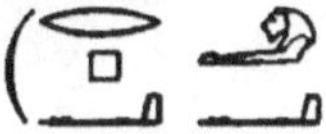 erpā ḥā), and of Atet his widow. The sculptures and general style of the work are similar to those found in the maṣṭabas of Saḳḳârah.

WASṬA.

At **Wasṭa**, a town 55 miles from Cairo, is the railway junction for the Fayyûm. The line from Wasṭa runs westwards, and its terminus is at Medînet el-Fayyûm, a large Egyptian town situated a little distance from the site of Arsinoë in the Heptanomis,† called Crocodilopolis‡ by the Greeks, because the crocodile was here worshipped. The Egyptians called the Fayyûm Ta-she  "the lake

* The results of Mr. Petrie's diggings here are given in his *Medum*, London, 1892.

† Heptanomis, or Middle Egypt, was the district which separated the Thebaïd from the Delta; the names of the seven nomes were: Memphites, Heracleopolites, Crocodilopolites or Arsinoites, Aphroditopolites, Oxyrhynchites, Cynopolites, and Hermopolites. The greater and lesser Oases were always reckoned parts of the Heptanomis.

‡ In Egyptian 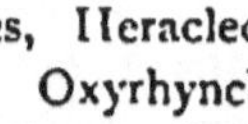, *Neter ḥet Sebek.*

district," and the name Fayyûm is the Arabic form of the Coptic ⲪⲒⲞⲘ,* "the water." The Fayyûm district has an area of about 850 square miles, and is watered by a branch of the Nile called the Baḥr-Yûsuf, which flows into it through the Libyan mountains. On the west of it lies the Birket el-Ḳurûn. This now fertile land is thought to have been reclaimed from the desert by Åmenemḥât III., a king of the XIIth dynasty. The Birket el-Ḳurûn was formerly thought to have been a part of Lake Moeris,† but more modern travellers place both it and the Labyrinth to the east of the Fayyûm district. The Baḥr-Yûsuf is said by some to have been excavated under the direction of the patriarch Joseph, but there is no satisfactory evidence for this theory; strictly speaking it is an arm of the Nile, which has always needed cleaning out from time to time, and the Yûsuf, or Joseph, after whom it is named, was probably one of the Muḥammadan rulers of Egypt. Herodotus says‡ of Lake Moeris, "The water in this lake does not spring from the soil, for these parts are excessively dry, but it is conveyed through a channel from the Nile, and for six months it flows into the lake, and six months out again into the Nile. And during the six months that it flows out it yields a talent of silver (£240) every day to the king's treasury from the fish; but when the water is flowing into it, twenty minæ (£80)." The Labyrinth§ stood on the bank of Lake Moeris, and a

* From the Egyptian , *Pa-iumā.*

† From the Egyptian  *mā-ur*, or  *mer ur.*

‡ Bk. II., 149.

§ "Yet the labyrinth surpasses even the pyramids. For it has twelve courts enclosed with walls, with doors opposite each other, six facing the north, and six the south, contiguous to one another; and the same exterior wall encloses them. It contains two kinds of rooms, number of its ruined chambers are still visible. During the years 1890, 1891 Mr. Petrie carried out some interesting excavations at Hawâra, Biyahmu, El-lâhûn, Mêdûm and other sites in the Fayyûm. The funds for the purpose were most generously provided by Mr. Jesse Haworth and Mr. Martyn Kennard.

Beni Suêf, 73 miles from Cairo, is the capital of the province bearing the same name, and is governed by a Mudîr. In ancient days it was famous for its textile fabrics, and supplied Aḥmîm and other weaving cities of Upper Egypt with flax. A main road led from this town to the Fayyûm.

---

some under ground and some above ground over them, to the number of three thousand, fifteen hundred of each. The rooms above ground I myself went through, and saw, and relate from personal inspection. But the underground rooms I only know from report; for the Egyptians who have charge of the building would on no account show me them, saying, that there were the sepulchres of the kings who originally built this labyrinth, and of the sacred crocodiles. I can therefore only relate what I have learnt by hearsay concerning the lower rooms; but the upper ones, which surpass all human works, I myself saw; for the passage through the corridors, and the windings through the courts, from their great variety, presented a thousand occasions of wonder as I passed from a court to the rooms, and from the rooms to the hall, and to the other corridors from the halls, and to other courts from the rooms. The roofs of all these are of stone, as also are the walls; but the walls are full of sculptured figures. Each court is surrounded with a colonnade of white stone, closely fitted. And adjoining the extremity of the labyrinth is a pyramid, forty orgyæ (about 240 feet) in height, on which large figures are carved, and a way to it has been made under ground." Herodotus, Bk. II., 148 (Cary's translation).

UPPER EGYPT.

Maghâghah, 106 miles from Cairo, is now celebrated for its large sugar manufactory, which is lighted by gas, and is well worth a visit; the manufacturing of sugar begins here early in January.

About twenty-four miles farther south, lying inland, on the western side of the Nile, between the river and the Baḥr Yûsuf, is the site of the town of Oxyrhyncus, so called by the Greeks on account of the fish which they believed was worshipped there. The Egyptian name of the town was 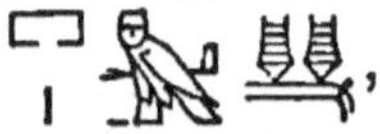, Pa-māt'et, from which came the Coptic Pemge, ⲡⲉⲙϫⲉ, and the corrupt Arabic form Behnesa.

A little above Abu Girgeh, on the west bank of the Nile, is the town of El-Kais, which marks the site of the ancient Cynopolis or "Dog-city;" it was the seat of a Coptic bishop, and is called Kais, Ⲕⲁⲓⲥ, in Coptic.

Thirteen miles from Abu Girgeh, also on the west bank of the Nile, is the town of Ḳlûṣanah, 134 miles from Cairo, and a few miles south, lying inland, is Samallût.

Farther south, on the east bank of the Nile, is Gebel eṭ-Ṭêr, or the "Bird mountain," so called because tradition says that all the birds of Egypt assemble here once a year, and that they leave behind them when departing one solitary bird, that remains there until they return the following year to relieve him of his watch, and to set another in his place. As there are mountains called Gebel eṭ-Ṭêr in all parts of Arabic-speaking countries, because of the number of birds which frequent them, the story is only one which springs from the fertile Arab imagination. Gebel eṭ-Ṭêr rises above the river to a height of six or seven hundred feet, and upon its summit stands a Coptic convent dedicated to Mary the Virgin, but called sometimes the "Convent of the Pulley," because the ascent to the convent is generally made by a rope and pulley. Leaving the river and entering a fissure in the rocks, the traveller finds himself at the bottom of a natural shaft about 120 feet long. When Robert Curzon visited this convent, he had to climb up much in the same way as boys used to climb up inside chimneys. The convent stands about 400 feet from the top of the shaft, and is built of small square stones of Roman workmanship; the necessary repairs have, however, been made with mud or sun-dried brick. The outer walls of the enclosure form a square which measures about 200 feet each way; they are 20 feet high, and are perfectly unadorned. Tradition says that it was founded by the Empress Helena,* and there is in this case no reason to doubt it. The church "is partly subterranean, being built in the recesses of an ancient stone quarry; the other parts of it are of stone plastered over. The roof is flat and is formed of horizontal beams of palm trees, upon which a terrace of reeds and earth is laid. The height of the interior is about 25 feet. On entering the door we had to descend a flight of narrow steps, which led into a side aisle about ten feet wide, which is divided from the nave by octagon columns of great thickness supporting the walls of a sort of clerestory. The columns were surmounted by heavy square plinths almost in the Egyptian style. I consider this church to be interesting from its being half a catacomb, or cave, and one of the earliest Christian buildings which has preserved its originality. . . . . it will be seen that it is constructed on the principle of a Latin basilica, as the buildings of the Empress Helena usually were." (Curzon, *Monasteries of the Levant*, p. 109.) In Curzon's time the convent possessed fifteen Coptic books with Arabic translations, and eight Arabic MSS. As the monks were, and are, extremely poor, they used to descend

* Died about A.D. 328, aged 80. (Sozomen, *Eccles. Hist.*, II., 2.)

the rock and swim out to any passing boat to beg for charity; the Patriarch has forbidden this practice, but it is not entirely discontinued. Two or three miles from the convent are some ancient quarries having rock bas-reliefs representing Rameses III. making an offering to the crocodile god Sebek  before Åmen-Rā.

Minyeh.

Minyeh, 156½ miles from Cairo, on the west bank of the Nile, is the capital of the province of the same name; its Arabic name is derived from the Coptic Mone, ⲙⲟⲛⲉ, which in turn represents the Egyptian  *Ment* in its old name Chufu-menāt. There is a large sugar factory here in which about 2,000 men are employed. A few miles south, on the eastern side of the river, are some tombs, which appear to have been hewn during the IIIrd or IVth dynasty.

BENI HASÂN.

Beni Hasân, 171 miles from Cairo, on the east bank of the Nile, is remarkable for the valuable historical tombs which are situated at a short distance from the site of the villages grouped under that name. The villages of the "Children of Hasân" were destroyed by order of Muḥammad 'Ali on account of the thievish propensities of their inhabitants. The **Speos Artemidos** is the first rock excavation visited here. The king who first caused this cavern to be hewn out was Thothmes III.; about 250 years later Seti I. made additions to it, but it seems never to have been finished. The cavern was dedicated to the lion-goddess Sechet, who was called Artemis by the Greeks; hence the name "cavern of Artemis." The portico had originally two rows of columns, four in each; the cavern is about 21 feet square, and the niche in the wall at the end was probably intended to hold a statue of Sechet.

There are about fifteen rock-tombs at Beni Hasân, but only two of them, those of Åmeni and Chnemu-ḥetep, are of interest generally speaking. They were all hewn during the XIIth dynasty, but have preserved the chief characteristics of the maṣṭabas of Saḳḳârah, that is to say, they consist of a chamber and a shaft leading down to a corridor, which ends in the chamber containing the sarcophagus and the mummy. As in the tombs at Aswân, a suitable layer of stone was sought for in the hill, and when found the tombs were hewn out. The walls were partly smoothed, and then covered with a thin layer of plaster upon which the scenes in the lives of the people buried there might be painted. The columns and the lower parts of some of the tombs are coloured red to resemble granite. The northern tomb is remarkable for columns somewhat resembling those subsequently termed **Doric.** Each of the four columns in the tomb is about 17 feet high, and has sixteen sides; the ceiling between each connecting beam, which runs from column to column, is vaulted. The columns in the southern tombs have lotus capitals, and are exceedingly graceful.

The **Tomb of Åmeni** belongs to the northern group of tombs; he is not the head of the family which was buried at Beni Hasân, as has been sometimes asserted, for he had no children. (*Recueil de Travaux*, I., p. 175.) Åmeni-Åmenemḥāt lived during the reign of Usertsen I., the second king of the XIIth dynasty; he was one of the feudal lords of Egypt, and chief of the nome of Meḥ or Antinoë, and chief president of the prophets. When quite a young man he was sent in the place of his father, who was too old for such work, to Ethiopia at the head of an army; he settled the frontiers of the country there, and came back to the king laden with spoil and tribute. In many other expeditions he was also perfectly successful. In the inscription on the tomb he says, "I have done all that I have said. I am a gracious and a compassionate man, and a ruler who loves his town. I have passed the course of years as the ruler of Meḥ, and all the labours of the palace have been carried out by my hands. I have given to the overseers of the temples of the gods of Meḥ 3,000 bulls with their cows, and I was in favour in the palace on account of it, for I carried all the products of the milk-bearing cows to the palace, and no contributions to the king's storehouses have been more than mine. I have never made a child grieve, I have never robbed the widow, I have never repulsed the labourer, I have never shut up a herdsman, I have never impressed for forced labour the labourers of a man who only employed five men; there was never a person miserable in my time, no one went hungry during my rule, for if there were years of scarcity I ploughed up all the arable land in the nome of Meḥ, up to its very frontiers on the north and south. By this means I made its people live and procured for them provisions, so that there was not a hungry person among them. I gave to the widow the same amount as I gave to the married woman, and I made no distinction between the great and the little in all that I gave. And, behold, when the inundation was great, and the owners of the land became rich thereby, I laid no additional tax upon the fields." The pictures on the walls represent scenes on the farm, the battle-field, the hunting ground and the river; the various domestic pursuits of women are portrayed with wonderful skill. Ȧmeni-Ȧmenemḥāt, 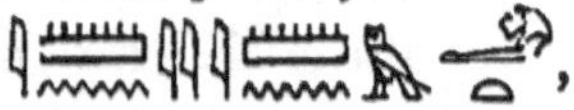, was the son of the lady Ḥennu; the name of his father is not given.

The **Tomb of Chnemu-Ḥetep** also belongs to the northern group of tombs. Chnemu-ḥetep  was one of the feudal lords of Egypt, a "royal relative," and the commandant of the land on the east side of the nome of Meḥ as far as the Arabian mountains; he lived during the reign of  "Nub-kau-Rā, son of the sun, Åmenemḥāt," the third king of the XIIth dynasty. Of the history of this Egyptian gentleman the following facts are known. During one of the expeditions which Åmenemḥāt I. made through Egypt, he raised to the rank of a feudal lord and "governor of the hilly land on the east of the nome of Meḥ," or Antinoë, the maternal grand-father of Chnemu-Ḥetep. In the reign of Usertsen I., the son of Åmenemḥāt I., the title of nobility conferred upon this man in the preceding reign was confirmed, and a large tract of land, lying between the Nile and the Libyan mountains, was added to his estates; higher titles were also bestowed upon him in addition to those which he already possessed. The lands on the east side of the river, together with all his titles, passed into the hands of his eldest son Necht. Necht had a sister called Beqt, who likewise had a right to inherit all titles and property. She married a man called Neḥerá, the son of Sebek-ānch, and bore to him an only son called Chnemuḥetep; it was for him that this tomb was built. After a time, for some reason not stated, the inheritance of Menāt-Chufu,* which had been held by his uncle Necht, became vacant, and Åmenemḥāt II. handed it over to the young man Chnemu-ḥetep, together with all the titles and honours which his grandfather had enjoyed by the command of Åmenemḥāt I. and Usertsen I. Chnemu-ḥetep married a lady called Chati, by whom he had seven children; one of whom, by the favour of Amenemḥāt II., became the ruler of Menāt-Chufu. It has been said that Chnemu-ḥetep's grand-father was the Åmeni-Åmenemḥāt whose tomb lies close by; it is, however, distinctly said in the inscription on Chnemu-ḥetep's tomb that he was called Sebek-ānch. This tomb is famous for a remarkable scene painted on the north wall,

* 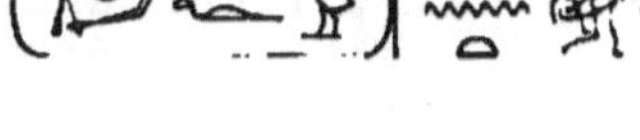.

which represents the arrival in Egypt of a family of thirty-seven persons belonging to the Āāmu, a Semitic race, who appear to have come thither to settle. The first person in the scene is the Egyptian "royal scribe, Nefer-ḥetep," who holds in his hands a piece of writing which states that in the sixth year of Usertsen II. thirty-seven people of the Āāmu brought to Chnemu-ḥetep, the son of a feudal lord, paint for the eyes called  *mest'emet.* Behind the scribe stands an Egyptian superintendent, and behind him the Āāmu chief Ȧbesha, "the prince of the foreign country," together with his fellow-countrymen and women, who have come with him; in addition to the eye-paint, they bring a goat as a present for Chnemu-ḥetep. The men of the Āāmu wear beards, and carry bows and arrows; both men and women are dressed in garments of many colours. The home of the Āāmu lay to the east of Palestine. In this picture some have seen a representation of the arrival of Jacob's sons in Egypt to buy corn; there is no evidence for the support of this theory. That the Āāmu were shepherds or Hyksos is another theory that has been put forth. The paintings in Chnemu-ḥetep's tomb are if anything more beautiful than those in that of Ȧmeni, and they represent with wonderful fidelity the spearing of fish, the netting of birds, the hunting of wild animals, etc., etc.

In the other tombs are most interesting scenes connected with the daily occupations and amusements of the ancient Egyptians. The results of the work carried on at Beni Hasân by the Egypt Exploration Fund are given by Messrs. Newberry and Fraser in *Beni-Hasan*, London, 1893, 1894.

Rôḍa.

Rôḍa, 182 miles from Cairo, and the seat of a large sugar manufactory, lies on the west bank of the river, just opposite Shêkh 'Abâdeh, or Antinoë, a town built by Hadrian, and named by him after Antinous,* who was drowned here in the Nile. To the south of Antinoë lies the convent of Abu Honnês (Father John), and in the districts in the immediate neighbourhood are the remains of several Coptic buildings which date back to the fifth century of our era. A little to the south-west of Rôḍa, lying inland, are the remains of the city of Hermopolis Magna, called in Egyptian 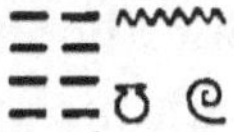 or 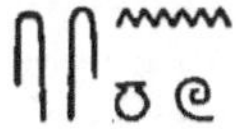, *Chemennu*, in Coptic Shmûn, ϣⲙⲟⲩⲛ, and in Arabic Eshmûnên; the tradition which attributes the building of this city to Eshmûn, son of Miṣr, is worthless. The Greeks called it Hermopolis, because the Egyptians there worshipped Thoth, , the scribe of the gods, who was named by the Greeks Hermes. A little distance from the town is the spot where large numbers of the ibis, a bird sacred to Thoth, were buried.

MELÂWÎ.

Melâwî, 188 miles from Cairo, is situated on the west bank of the river.

HAGGI ḲANDÎL.

Haggi Ḳandil, 195 miles from Cairo, lies on the east bank of the river, about five miles from the ruins of the city built by Chut-en-àten, , or Amenophis IV., the famous "heretic" king of the XVIIIth dynasty, whose prenomen was , Nefer-cheperu-Rā uā-en-Rā. Amenophis IV. was the son of Amenophis III., by a Mesopotamian princess called Thi, who came from the land of Mitani. When the young prince Amenophis IV. grew up,

* A Bithynian youth, a favourite of the Emperor Hadrian.

it was found that he had conceived a rooted dislike to the worship of Åmen-Rā, the king of the gods and great lord of Thebes, and that he preferred the worship of the disk of the sun to that of Åmen-Rā; as a sign of his opinions he called himself "beloved of the sun's disk," instead of the usual and time-honoured "beloved of Åmen." The native Egyptian priesthood disliked the foreign queen, and the sight of her son with his protruding chin, thick lips, and other characteristic features of the negro race, found no favour in their sight; that such a man should openly despise the worship of Åmen-Rā was a thing intolerable to the priesthood, and angry words and acts were, on their part, the result. In answer to their objections the king ordered the name of Åmen-Rā to be chiselled out of all the monuments, even from his father's names. Rebellion then broke out, and Chut-en-åten thought it best to leave Thebes, and to found a new city for himself at a place between Memphis and Thebes, now called Tell el-Amarna. The famous architect Bek, whose father, Men, served under Amenophis III., designed the temple buildings, and in a very short time a splendid town with beautiful granite sculptures sprang out of the desert. As an insult to the priests and people of Thebes, he built a sandstone and granite temple at Thebes in honour of the god Harmachis. When Chut-en-åten's new town, Chut-åten, "the splendour of the sun's disk," was finished, his mother Thi came to live there; and here the king passed his life quietly with his mother, wife, and seven daughters. He died leaving no male issue, and each of the husbands of his daughters became king. In 1887 a number of important cuneiform tablets, which confirmed in a remarkable manner many facts connected with this period of Egyptian history, were found at Tell el-Amarna (see page 187). The tombs in the rocks near Tell el-Amarna are of considerable interest. In 1892 Mr. Petrie uncovered a painted fresco pavement about 51 by 16 feet.

GEBEL ABU FADAH.

Seventeen miles south of Haggi Ḳandil, 212 miles from Cairo, on the east side of the river, is the range of low mountains about twelve miles long known by this name. Towards the southern end of this range there are some crocodile mummy pits.

MANFALÛṬ.

Manfalûṭ, 223½ miles from Cairo, on the west bank of the Nile, occupies the site of an ancient Egyptian town; Leo Africanus says that the town was destroyed by the Romans, and adds that it was rebuilt under Muḥammadan rule. In his time he says that huge columns and buildings inscribed with hieroglyphs were still visible. The Coptic name Manbalot, "place of the sack,"* is the original of its Arabic name to-day.

ASYÛṬ.

Asyûṭ, 249½ miles from Cairo, is the capital of the province of the same name, and the seat of the Inspector-General of Upper Egypt; it stands on the site of the ancient Egyptian city called  *Seut*, whence the Arabic name Siûṭ or Asyûṭ, and the Coptic ⲤⲒⲰⲞⲨⲦ. The Greeks called the city Lycopolis, or "wolf city," probably because the jackal-headed Anubis was worshipped there. Asyûṭ is a large city, with spacious bazaars and fine mosques; it is famous for its red pottery and for its market, held every Sunday, to which wares from Arabia and Upper Egypt are brought. The American Missionaries have a large establishment, and the practical, useful education of the natives by these devoted men is carried on here, as well as at Cairo, on a large scale. The Arabic geographers

* ⲙⲁ ⲛ̄ ⲃⲁⲗⲟⲧ.

described it as a town of considerable size, beauty, and importance, and before the abandonment of the Sûdân by the Khedive, all caravans from that region stopped there. In the hills to the west of the town are a number of ancient Egyptian tombs, which date back as far as the XIIIth dynasty. A large number have been destroyed during the present century for the sake of the limestone which forms the walls. When M. Denon stayed here he said that the number of hieroglyphic inscriptions which cover the tombs was so great that many months would be required to read, and many years to copy them. The disfigurement of the tombs dates from the time when the Christians took up their abode in them.

Fifteen miles farther south is the Coptic town of **Abu Tîg**, the name of which appears to be derived from ΑΠΟΘΗΚΗ, a "granary;" and 14½ miles beyond, 279 miles from Cairo, is Kâu el-Kebîr (the ⲔⲰⲞⲨ of the Copts), which marks the site of Antaeopolis, the capital of the Antaeopolite nome in Upper Egypt. The temple which formerly existed here was dedicated to Antaeus, the Libyan wrestler, who fought with Hercules. In the plain close by it was thought that the battle between Horus, the son of Osiris and Isis, and Set or Typhon, the murderer of Osiris, took place; Typhon was overcome, and fled away in the form of a crocodile. In Christian times Antaeopolis was the seat of a bishop.

Ṭahṭah, 291½ miles from Cairo, contains some interesting mosques, and is the home of a large number of Copts, in consequence of which, probably, the town is kept clean.

SÛHÂḲ (SOHAG), AND THE WHITE AND RED MONASTERIES.

Sûhâḳ, 317½ miles from Cairo, is the capital of the province of Girgeh; near it are the White and Red Monasteries.

The Dêr el-Abyaḍ or "**White Monastery**," so-called because of the colour of the stone of which it is built, but better known by the name of Amba Shenûdah, is situated on the west bank of the river near Sûhâḳ, 317½ miles from Cairo. "The peculiarity of this monastery is that the interior was once a magnificent basilica, while the exterior was built by the Empress Helena, in the ancient Egyptian style. The walls slope inwards towards the summit, where they are crowned with a deep overhanging cornice. The building is of an oblong shape, about 200 feet in length by 90 wide, very well built of fine blocks of stone; it has no windows outside larger than loopholes, and these are at a great height from the ground. Of these there are twenty on the south side and nine at the east end. The monastery stands at the foot of the hill, on the edge of the Libyan desert, where the sand encroaches on the plain. . . . . . . The ancient doorway of red granite has been partially closed up." (Curzon, *Monasteries of the Levant*, p. 131.) There were formerly six gates; the single entrance now remaining is called the "mule gate," because when a certain heathen princess came riding on a mule to desecrate the church, the earth opened and swallowed her up. The walls enclose a space measuring about 240 feet by 133 feet. The convent was dedicated to Shenûti, a celebrated Coptic saint who lived in the fourth century of our era.* Curzon says (*op. cit.*, p. 132) . . . . . . "The tall granite columns of the ancient church reared themselves like an avenue on either side of the desecrated nave, which is now open to the sky, and is used as a promenade for a host of chickens. . . . . The principal entrance was formerly at the west end, where there is a small vestibule, immediately within the door of which, on the left hand, is

* Shenûdah, Coptic ϣⲉⲛⲟⲩϯ Shenûti, was born A.D. 333; he died at midday on July 2, A.D. 451.

a small chapel, perhaps the baptistery, about twenty-five feet long, and still in tolerable preservation. It is a splendid specimen of the richest Roman architecture of the latter empire, and is truly an imperial little room. The arched ceiling is of stone; and there are three beautifully ornamented niches on each side. The upper end is semicircular, and has been entirely covered with a profusion of sculpture in panels, cornices, and every kind of architectural enrichment. When it was entire, and covered with gilding, painting, or mosaic, it must have been most gorgeous. The altar on such a chapel as this was probably of gold, set full of gems; or if it was the baptistery, as I suppose, it most likely contained a bath of the most precious jasper, or of some of the more rare kinds of marble, for the immersion of the converted heathen, whose entrance into the church was not permitted until they had been purified with the waters of baptism in a building without the door of the house of God" (p. 135). The library once contained over a hundred parchment books, but these were destroyed by the Mamelukes when they last sacked the convent.

The Dêr-el-Aḥmar or "**Red Monastery,**" so-called because of the red colour of the bricks of which it is built, was also built by the Empress Helena; it is smaller and better preserved than the White Monastery, and was dedicated to the Abba Bêsa, the disciple and friend of Shenûti. The pillars of both churches were taken from Athribis, which lay close by; the orientation of neither church is exact, for their axes point between N.E. and N.E. by E. The ruined church of Armant near Thebes is built on the same model.

Aḥmîm.

A few miles south of Sûhâḳ, on the east bank of the river, lies the town of **Aḥmîm**, called Shmin or Chmim, ϣⲙⲓⲛ, ϫⲙⲓⲙ, by the Copts, and Panopolis by the Greeks; Strabo and Leo Africanus say that it was one of the most ancient cities of Egypt. The ithyphallic god Åmsu, identified by the Greeks with Pan, was worshipped here, and the town was famous for its linen weavers and stone cutters. Its Egyptian name was  Åpu. In ancient days it had a large population of Copts, and large Coptic monasteries stood close by.

Menshiah, on the west bank of the river, 328½ miles from Cairo, stands on the site of a city which is said to have been the capital of the Panopolite nome; its Coptic name was Psôi, Ψⲱⲓ. In the time of Shenûti the Blemmyes, a nomad warlike Ethiopian tribe, invaded Upper Egypt, and having acquired much booty, they returned to Psôi or Menshiah, and settled down there.

Girgeh, on the west bank of the river, 341½ miles from Cairo, has a large Christian population, and is said to occupy the site of the ancient This, whence sprang the first dynasty of historical Egyptian kings.

ABYDOS.*

Abydos,† in Egyptian  Àbṭu, Coptic ⲉⲃⲱⲧ, Arabic Harabat el-Madfûnah, on the west bank of the Nile, was one of the most renowned cities of ancient Egypt; it was famous as the chief seat of the worship of Osiris in Upper Egypt, because the head of this god was supposed to be buried here. The town itself was dedicated to Osiris, and the temple in it, wherein the most solemn ceremonies connected with the worship of this god were celebrated, was more revered than any other in the land. The town and its necropolis were built side by side, and the custom usually followed by the Egyptians in burying their dead away from the town in the mountains was not followed in this case. Though the hills of fine white stone were there ready, the people of Abydos did not make use of them for funereal purposes; the sandy plain interspersed every here and there with rocks was the place chosen for burial. The town of Abydos, a small town even in its best time, was built upon a narrow tongue of land situated between the canal, which lies inland some few miles, and the desert. It owed its importance solely to the position it held as a religious centre, and from this point of view it was the second city in Egypt. Thebes, Abydos, and Heliopolis practically represented the homes of religious thought and learning in Egypt. The necropolis of Abydos is not much older than the VIth dynasty, and the tombs found there

* The Temples at Abydos are visited by Messrs. Cook's travellers on the return journey to Cairo.

† Greek Ἄβυδος; see Pape, *Wörterbuch*, p. 4. That the name was pronounced Abȳdos, and not Abўdos, is clear from:—

καὶ Σηστὸν καὶ Ἄβυδον ἔχον καὶ δῖαν Ἀρίσβην.

Iliad, ii., 836.

belonging to this period are of the maṣṭaba class. During the XIth and XIIth dynasties the tombs took the form of small pyramids, which were generally built of brick, and the ancient rectangular form of tomb was revived during the XVIIIth dynasty. Abydos attained its greatest splendour under the monarchs of the XIth and XIIth dynasties, and though its plain was used as a burial ground as late as Roman times, it became of little or no account as early as the time of Psammetichus I. It has often been assumed that the town of Abydos is to be identified with This, the home of Menes, the first historical king of Egypt; the evidence derived from the exhaustive excavations made by M. Mariette does not support this assumption. No trace of the shrine of Osiris, which was as famous in Upper Egypt as was the shrine of the same god at Busiris in Lower Egypt, has been found in the temple; neither can any trace be discovered of the royal tombs which Rameses II. declares he restored. Plutarch says that wealthy inhabitants of Egypt were often brought to Abydos to be buried near the mummy of Osiris, and curiously enough, the tombs close to certain parts of the temple of Osiris are more carefully executed than those elsewhere. Of Abydos Strabo says (Bk. XVII., cap. i., sec. 42), "Above this city (Ptolemaïs) is Abydos, where is the palace of Memnon, constructed in a singular manner, entirely of stone, and after the plan of the Labyrinth, which we have described, but not composed of many parts. It has a fountain situated at a great depth. There is a descent to it through an arched passage built with single stones of remarkable size and workmanship. There is a canal which leads to this place from the great river. About the canal is a grove of Egyptian acanthus, dedicated to Apollo. Abydos seems once to have been a large city, second to Thebes. At present it is a small town. But if, as they say, Memnon is called Ismandes by the Egyptians, the Labyrinth might be a Memnonium, and the work of the same person who constructed those at Abydos and at Thebes; for in those places, it is said, are some Memnonia. At Abydos Osiris is worshipped; but in the temple of Osiris no singer, nor player on the pipe, nor on the cithara, is permitted to perform at the commencement of the ceremonies celebrated in honour of the god, as is usual in rites celebrated in honour of the gods." (Bk. XVII. 1, 44, Falconer's translation.) The principal monuments which have been brought to light by the excavations of M. Mariette at Abydos are:—

I. The **Temple of Seti I.**,* and the **Temple of Rameses II.**

The **Temple of Seti I.**, better known as the **Memnonium**, is built of fine white calcareous stone upon an artificial foundation made of stone, earth and sand, which has been laid upon a sloping piece of land; it was called Men-māt-Rā,† after the prenomen of its builder. The Phœnician *graffiti* show that the temple must have ceased to be used at a comparatively early period. It would seem that it was nearly finished when Seti I. died, and that his son Rameses II. only added the pillars in front and the decoration. Its exterior consists of two courts, A and B, the wall which divides them, and the façade; all these parts were built by Rameses II. The pillars are inscribed with religious scenes and figures of the king and the god Osiris. On the large wall to the south of the central door is an inscription in which Rameses II. relates all that he has done for the honour of his father's memory, how he erected statues of

* The plans of the principal temples of Egypt printed in this book are copied from those which accompany the *Rapport sur les Temples Égyptiens adressé à S.E. Le Ministre des Travaux Publics* par Grand Bey. This gentleman's plans were made as recently as 1888, and are more complete than the more elaborate drawings given by Lepsius in his *Denkmäler*, and by other *savants*.

† 

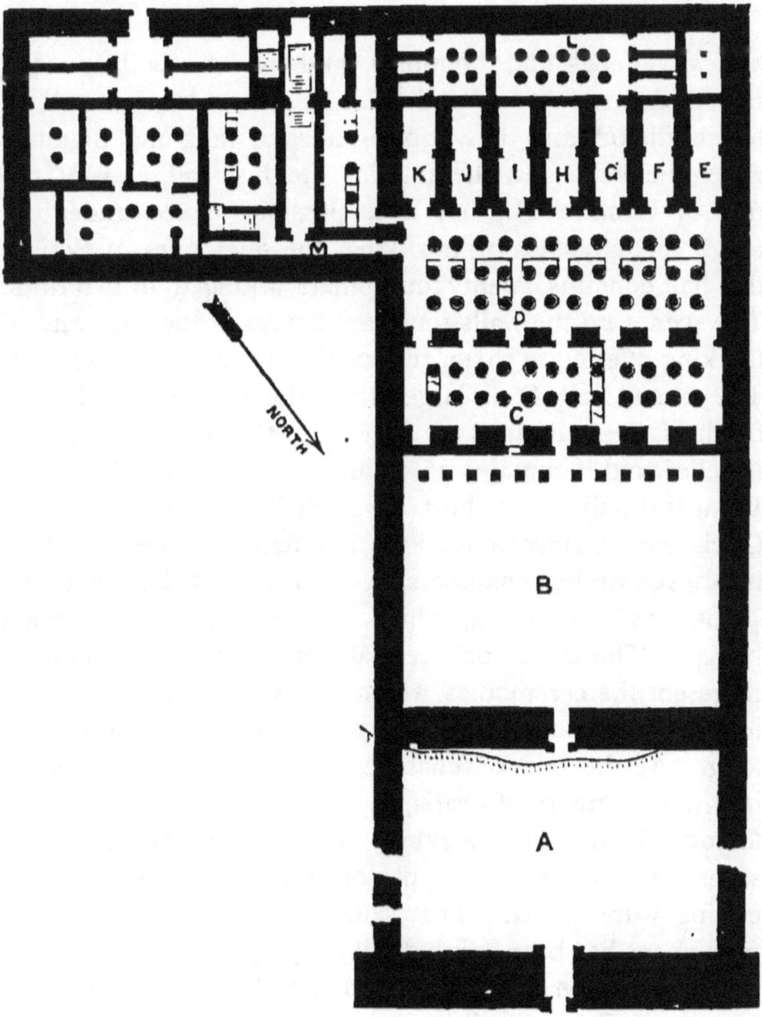

Plan of the Temple of Seti I. at Abydos.

him at Thebes and Memphis, and how he built up the sacred doors. At the end of it he gives a brief sketch of his childhood, and the various grades of rank and dignities which he held. In the interior the first hall, C, is of the time of Rameses II., but it is possible to see under the rough hieroglyphics of this king, the finer ones of Seti I.; this hall contains twenty-four pillars arranged in two rows. The scenes on the walls represent figures of the gods and of the king offering to them, the names of the nomes, etc., etc. The second hall, D, is larger than the first, the style and finish of the sculptures are very fine, the hieroglyphics are in relief, and it contains 36 columns, arranged in three rows. From this hall seven short naves dedicated to Horus, Isis, Osiris, Amen, Harmachis, Ptaḥ, and Seti I. respectively, lead into seven vaulted chambers, E, F, G, H, I, J, K, beautifully shaped and decorated, which are dedicated to the same beings. The scenes on the walls of six of these chambers represent the ceremonies which the king ought to perform in them; those in the seventh refer to the apotheosis of the king. At the end of chamber G is a door which leads into the sanctuary of Osiris, L, and in the corridor M is the famous TABLET OF ABYDOS, which gives the names of seventy-six kings of Egypt, beginning with Menes and ending with Seti I. The value of this most interesting monument has been pointed out on p. 3.

The **Temple of Rameses II.** was dedicated by this king to the god Osiris; it lies a little to the north of the temple of Seti I. Many distinguished scholars thought that this was the famous shrine which all Egypt adored, but the excavations made there by M. Mariette proved that it was not. It would seem that during the French occupation of Egypt in the early part of this century this temple stood almost intact; since that time, however, so much damage has been wrought upon it, that the portions of wall which now remain are only about eight or nine feet

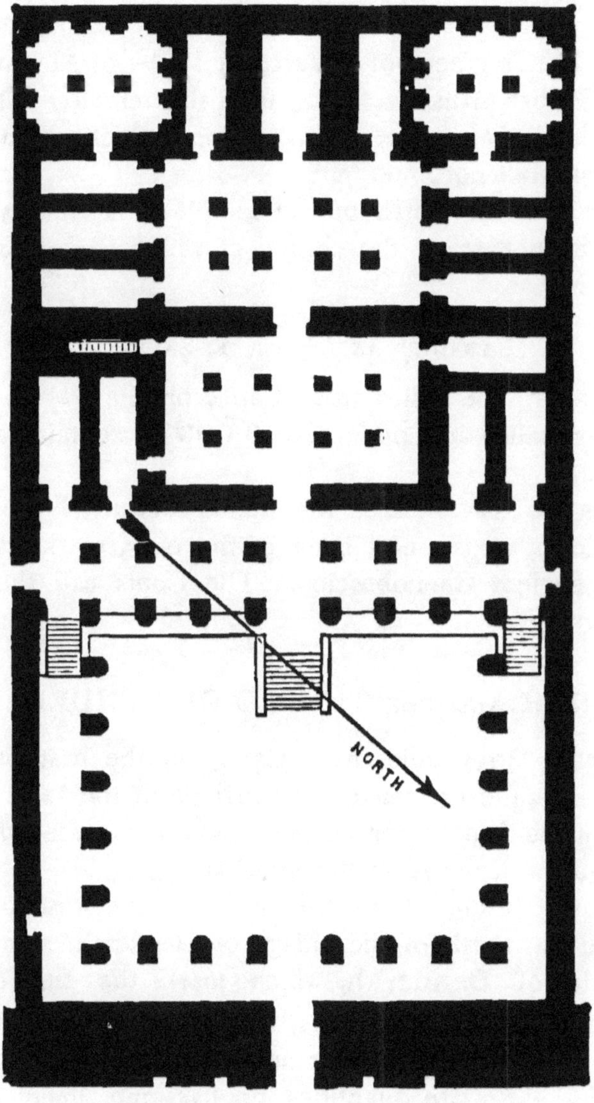

Plan of the Temple of Rameses II. at Abydos.

high. The fragment of the second Tablet of Abydos, now in the British Museum, came from this temple. The few scenes and fragments of inscriptions which remain are interesting but not important.

A little to the north of the temple of Rameses II. is a Coptic monastery, the church of which is dedicated to Amba Musas.

Farshût and Ḳaṣr eṣ-Ṣayyâd.

Farshût, 368 miles from Cairo, on the west bank of the river, called in Coptic Βερϭοογτ, contains a sugar factory.

Ḳaṣr eṣ-Sayyâd, or "the hunter's castle," 376 miles from Cairo, on the east bank of the river, marks the site of the ancient Chenoboscion. The Copts call the town ϣενεϲητ.

Ḳeneh and the Temple of Denderah.*

Keneh, 405½ miles from Cairo, on the east bank of the river, is the capital of the province of the same name. This city is famous for its dates, and the trade which it carries on with the Arabian peninsula.

A short distance from the river, on the west bank, a little to the north of the village of Denderah, stands the **Temple of Denderah**, which marks the site of the classical Tentyra or Tentyris, called Τεντωρε by the Copts, where the goddess Hathor was worshipped. During the Middle Empire quantities of flax and linen fabrics

* The Greek Tentyra, or Tentyris, is derived from the Egyptian 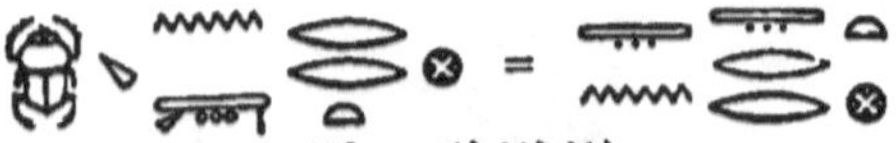 *Ta-en-ta-rert;* the name is also wrtten 

were produced at Tentyra, and it gained some reputation thereby. In very ancient times Chufu or Cheops, a king of the IVth dynasty, founded a temple here, but it seems never to have become of much importance,* probably because it lay so close to the famous shrines of Abydos and Thebes. The wonderfully preserved Temple now standing there is probably not older than the beginning of our era; indeed, it cannot, in any case, be older than the time of the later Ptolemies: hence it must be considered as the architectural product of a time when the ancient Egyptian traditions of sculpture were already dead and nearly forgotten. It is, however, a majestic monument, and worthy of careful examination.† Strabo says (Bk. xvii., ch. i. 44) of this town and its inhabitants: "Next to Abydos is ...... the city Tentyra, where the crocodile is held in peculiar abhorrence, and is regarded as the most odious of all animals. For the other Egyptians, although acquainted with its mischievous disposition, and hostility towards the human race, yet worship it, and abstain from doing it harm. But the people of Tentyra track and destroy it in every way. Some, however, as they say of the Psyllians of Cyrenæa, possess a certain natural antipathy to snakes, and the people of Tentyra have the same dislike to crocodiles, yet they suffer no injury from them, but dive and cross the river when no other person ventures to do so. When crocodiles were brought to Rome to be exhibited, they were attended by some of the Tentyritæ.

* M. Mariette thought that a temple to Hathor existed at Denderah during the XIIth, XVIIIth and XIXth dynasties.

† "Accessible comme il l'est aujourd'hui jusque dans la dernière de ses chambres, il semble se présenter au visiteur comme un livre qu'il n'a qu'à ouvrir et à consulter. Mais le temple de Dendérah est, en somme, un monument terriblement complexe. . . . Il faudrait plusieurs années pour copier tout ce vaste ensemble, et il faudrait vingt volumes du format (folio !) de nos quatre volumes de planches pour le publier." —Mariette, *Dendérah*, *Description Générale*, p. 10.

A reservoir was made for them with a sort of stage on one of the sides, to form a basking place for them on coming out of the water, and these persons went into the water, drew them in a net to the place, where they might sun themselves and be exhibited, and then dragged them back again to the reservoir. The people of Tentyra worship Venus. At the back of the fane of Venus is a temple of Isis; then follow what are called Typhoneia, and the canal leading to Coptos, a city common both to the Egyptians and Arabians." (Falconer's translation.) It will be remembered that Juvenal witnessed a fight between the crocodile worshippers of Kom Ombo and the crocodile haters of Tentyra.

On the walls and on various other parts of the temples are the names of several of the Roman Emperors; the famous portraits of Cleopatra and Cæsarion her son are on the end wall of the exterior. Passing along a dromos for about 250 feet, the portico, A, open at the top, and supported by twenty-four Hathor-headed columns, arranged in six rows, is reached. Leaving this hall by the doorway facing the entrance, the visitor arrives in a second hall, B, having six columns and three small chambers on each side. The two chambers C and D have smaller chambers on the right and left, E was the so-called sanctuary, and in F the emblem of the god worshipped in the temple was placed. From a room on each side of C a staircase led up to the roof. The purposes for which the chambers were used are stated by M. Mariette in his *Dendérah, Descrip. Gén. du Grand Temple de cette ville.* On the ceiling of the portico is the famous "Zodiac," which was thought to have been made in ancient Egyptian times; the Greek inscription = A.D. 35, written in the twenty-first year of Tiberius, and the names of the Roman Emperors, have clearly proved that, like that at Esneh, it belongs to the Roman time. The Zodiac from Denderah, now at Paris, was cut out, with the permis.

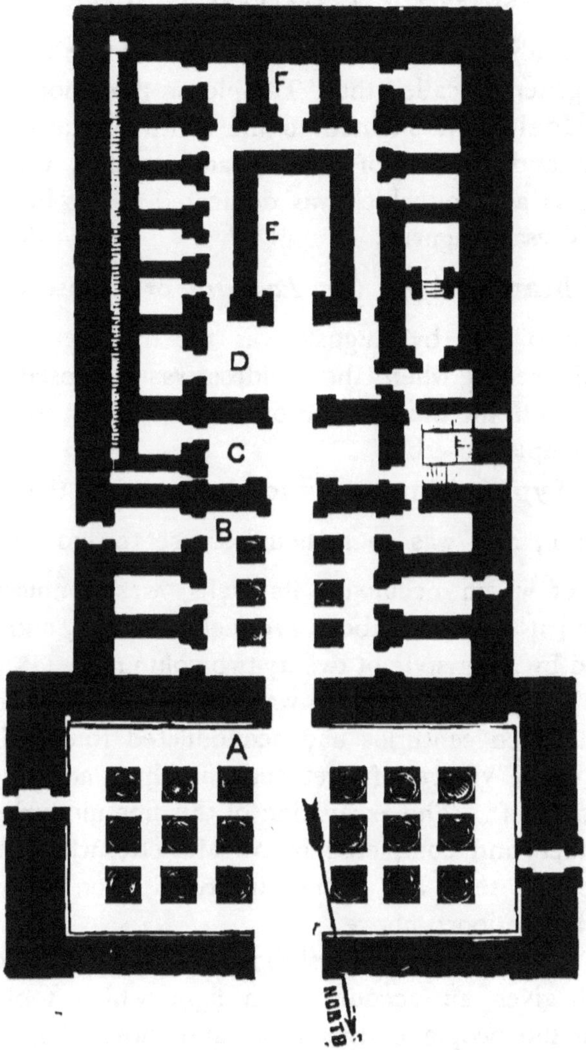

Plan of the Temple at Denderah.

sion of Muḥammad 'Ali, in 1821, from the small temple of Osiris, generally called the "Temple on the Roof."

The **Iseium** is situated to the south of the temple of Hathor, and consists of three chambers and a corridor; near by is a pylon which was dedicated to Isis in the 31st year of Cæsar Augustus.

The **Mammisi,** , *Pa-mestu*, or "house of giving birth," also built by Augustus, is the name given to the celestial dwelling where the goddess was supposed to have brought forth the third person of the triad which was adored in the temple close by.

The **Typhonium** stands to the north of the Temple of Hathor, and was so named because the god Bes , figures of whom occur on its walls, was confused with Typhon; it measures about 120 feet × 60 feet, and is surrounded by a peristyle of twenty-two columns.

The Temple of Denderah was nearly buried among the rubbish which centuries had accumulated round about it, and a whole village of wretched mud-huts actually stood upon the roof! The excavation of this fine monument was undertaken and completed by M. Mariette, who published many of the texts and scenes inscribed upon its walls in his work mentioned above.

The crocodile was worshipped at Kom Ombo, and Juvenal gives an account of a fight which took place between the people of this place and those of Denderah, in which one of the former stumbled, while running along, and was caught by his foes, cut up, and eaten.

A few miles beyond Denderah, on the east bank of the river, lies the town of **Ḳofṭ,** the 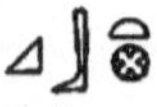 *Qebt* of the hieroglyphics, and ⲕⲉϥⲧ of the Copts; it was the principal city in the Coptites nome, and was the Thebaïs Secunda of the Itineraries. From Ḳofṭ the road which crossed the desert to Berenice on the Red Sea started, and the merchandise which passed through the town from the east, and the stone from the famous porphyry quarries in the Arabian desert must have made it wealthy and important. It held the position of a port on the Nile for merchandise from a very early period; and there is no doubt that every Egyptian king who sent expeditions to Punt, and the countries round about, found Ḳofṭ most usefully situated for this purpose. A temple dedicated to the ithyphallic god Âmsu, Isis and Osiris, stood here. It was nearly destroyed by Diocletian A.D. 292. A copy of a medical papyrus in the British Museum states that the work was originally discovered at Coptos during the time of Cheops, a king of the IVth dynasty; it is certain then that the Egyptians considered this city to be of very old foundation.

NAḲÂDAH (NAGADA).

NAḲÂDAH, 428 miles from Cairo, on the west bank of the river, nearly opposite the island of Maṭarah, was the home of a large number of Copts in early Christian times, and several monasteries were situated there. The four which now remain are dedicated to the Cross, St. Michael, St. Victor, and St. George respectively, and tradition says that they were founded by the Empress Helena; the most important of them is that of St. Michael. The church in this monastery "is one of the most remarkable Christian structures in Egypt, possessing as it does some unique peculiarities. There are four churches, of which three stand side by side in such a manner that they have a single continuous western wall. Two of the four have an apsidal haikal with rectagular side chapels, while the other two are entirely rectangular; but the two apses differ from all other apses in Egyptian churches by projecting . . . beyond the eastern wall and by showing an outward curvature. They form a solitary exception to the rule that the Coptic apse is merely internal, and so far belong rather to Syrian architecture than to Coptic. The principal church shows two other features which do not occur elsewhere in the Christian buildings of Egypt, namely, an external atrium surrounded with a cloister, and a central tower with a clerestory . . . . . Possibly the same remark may apply to the structure of the iconostasis, which has two side-doors and no central entrance, though this arrangement is not quite unparalleled in the churches of Upper Egypt, and may be a later alteration. It will be noticed that the church has a triple western entrance from the cloisters." (Butler, *Ancient Coptic Churches of Egypt*, Vol. I., p. 361.)

LUXOR (EL-ḲUṢUR) AND THEBES.

Luxor, 450 miles from Cairo, on the east bank of the river, is a small town with a few thousand inhabitants, and owes its importance to the fact that it is situated close to the ruins of the temples of the ancient city of Thebes. The name Luxor is a corruption of the Arabic name of the place, El-Ḳuṣûr, which means "the palaces." Ancient Thebes stood on both sides of the Nile, and was generally called in hieroglyphics , Uast; that part of the city which was situated on the east bank of the river, and included the temples of Karnak and Luxor, appears to have been called Àpet,* whence the Coptic ⲦⲀⲠⲈ and the name Thebes have been derived. The cuneiform inscriptions and Hebrew Scriptures call it No (Ezek. xxx. 14) and No-Amon † (Nahum iii. 8), and the Greek and Roman writers Diospolis Magna. When or by whom Thebes was founded it is impossible to say. Diodorus says that it is the most ancient city of Egypt; some say that, like Memphis, it was founded by Menes, and others, that it was a colony from Memphis. It is certain, however, that it did not become a city of the first importance until after the decay of Memphis, and as the progress of Egyptian civilization was from north to south, this is only what was to be expected. During the early dynasties no mention is made of Thebes, but we know that as early as the XIIth dynasty some kings were buried there.

The spot on which ancient Thebes stood is so admirably adapted for the site of a great city, that it

* *I.e.*, "throne city."

† In Revised Version, = *nut-Àmen.*

would have been impossible for the Egyptians to overlook it. The mountains on the east and west side of the river sweep away from it, and leave a broad plain on each bank of several square miles in extent. It has been calculated that modern Paris could stand on this space of ground. We have, unfortunately, no Egyptian description of Thebes, or any statement as to its size; it may, however, be assumed from the remains of its buildings which still exist, that the descriptions of the city as given by Strabo and Diodorus are on the whole trustworthy. The fame of the greatness of Thebes had reached the Greeks of Homer's age, and its "hundred gates" and 20,000 war chariots are referred to in Iliad IX, 381. The city must have reached its highest point of splendour during the rule of the XVIIIth and XIXth dynasties over Egypt, and as little by little the local god Åmen-Rā became the great god of all Egypt, his dwelling-place Thebes also gained in importance and splendour. The city suffered severely at the hands of Cambyses, who left nothing in it unburnt that fire would consume. Herodotus appears never to have visited Thebes, and the account he gives of it is not satisfactory; the account of Diodorus, who saw it about B.C. 57, is as follows: "Afterwards reigned Busiris, and eight of his posterity after him; the last of which (of the same name with the first) built that great city which the Egyptians call Diospolis, the Greeks Thebes; it was in circuit 140 stades (about twelve miles), adorned with stately public buildings, magnificent temples, and rich donations and revenues to admiration; and he built all the private houses, some four, some five stories high. And to sum up all in a word, made it not only the most beautiful and stateliest city of Egypt, but of all others in the world. The fame therefore of the riches and grandeur of this city was so noised abroad in every place, that the poet Homer takes notice of it. . . . . . Although there are some that say it had not a hundred gates; but that there were many large porches to the temples, whence the city was called *Hecatompylus*, a hundred gates, for many gates: yet that it was certain they had in it 20,000 chariots of war; for there were a hundred stables all along the river from Memphis to Thebes towards Lybia, each of which was capable to hold two hundred horses, the marks and signs of which are visible at this day. And we have it related, that not only this king, but the succeeding princes from time to time, made it their business to beautify this city; for that there was no city under the sun so adorned with so many and stately monuments of gold, silver, and ivory, and multitudes of colossi and obelisks, cut out of one entire stone. For there were there four temples built, for beauty and greatness to be admired, the most ancient of which was in circuit thirteen furlongs (about two miles), and five and forty cubits high, and had a wall twenty-four feet broad. The ornaments of this temple were suitable to its magnificence, both for cost and workmanship. The fabric hath continued to our time, but the silver and the gold, and ornaments of ivory and precious stones were carried away by the Persians when Cambyses burnt the temples of Egypt. . . . There, they say, are the wonderful sepulchres of the ancient kings, which for state and grandeur far exceed all that posterity can attain unto at this day. The Egyptian priests say that in their sacred registers there are 47 of these sepulchres; but in the reign of Ptolemy Lagus there remained only 17, many of which were ruined and destroyed when I myself came into those parts." (Bk. I., caps. 45, 46, Booth's translation, pp. 23, 24.)

Strabo, who visited Thebes about B.C. 24, says:—"Next to the city of Apollo is Thebes, now called Diospolis, 'with her hundred gates, through each of which issue 200 men, with horses and chariots,' according to Homer, who mentions also its wealth; 'not all the wealth the palaces of Egyptian Thebes contain.' Other writers use the same language, and consider Thebes as the metropolis of Egypt. Vestiges of its magnitude still exist, which extend 80 stadia (about nine miles) in length. There are a great number of temples, many of which Cambyses mutilated. The spot is at present occupied by villages. One part of it, in which is the city, lies in Arabia; another is in the country on the other side of the river, where is the Memnonium. Here are two colossal figures near one another, each consisting of a single stone. One is entire; the upper parts of the other, from the chair, are fallen down, the effect, it is said, of an earthquake. It is believed that once a day a noise as of a slight blow issues from the part of the statue which remains in the seat and on its base. When I was at those places with Ælius Gallus, and numerous friends and soldiers about him, I heard a noise at the first hour (of the day), but whether proceeding from the base or from the colossus, or produced on purpose by some of those standing around the base, I cannot confidently assert. For from the uncertainty of the cause, I am disposed to believe anything rather than that stones disposed in that manner could send forth sound. Above the Memnonium are tombs of kings in caves, and hewn out of the stone, about forty in number; they are executed with singular skill, and are worthy of notice. Among the tombs are obelisks with inscriptions, denoting the wealth of the kings of that time, and the extent of their empire, as reaching to the Scythians, Bactrians, Indians, and the present Ionia; the amount of tribute also, and the number of soldiers, which composed an army of about a million of men. The priests there are said to be, for the most part, astronomers and philosophers. The former compute the days, not by the moon, but by the sun, introducing into the twelve months, of thirty days each, five days every year. But in order to complete the whole year, because there is (annually) an excess of a part of a day, they form a period

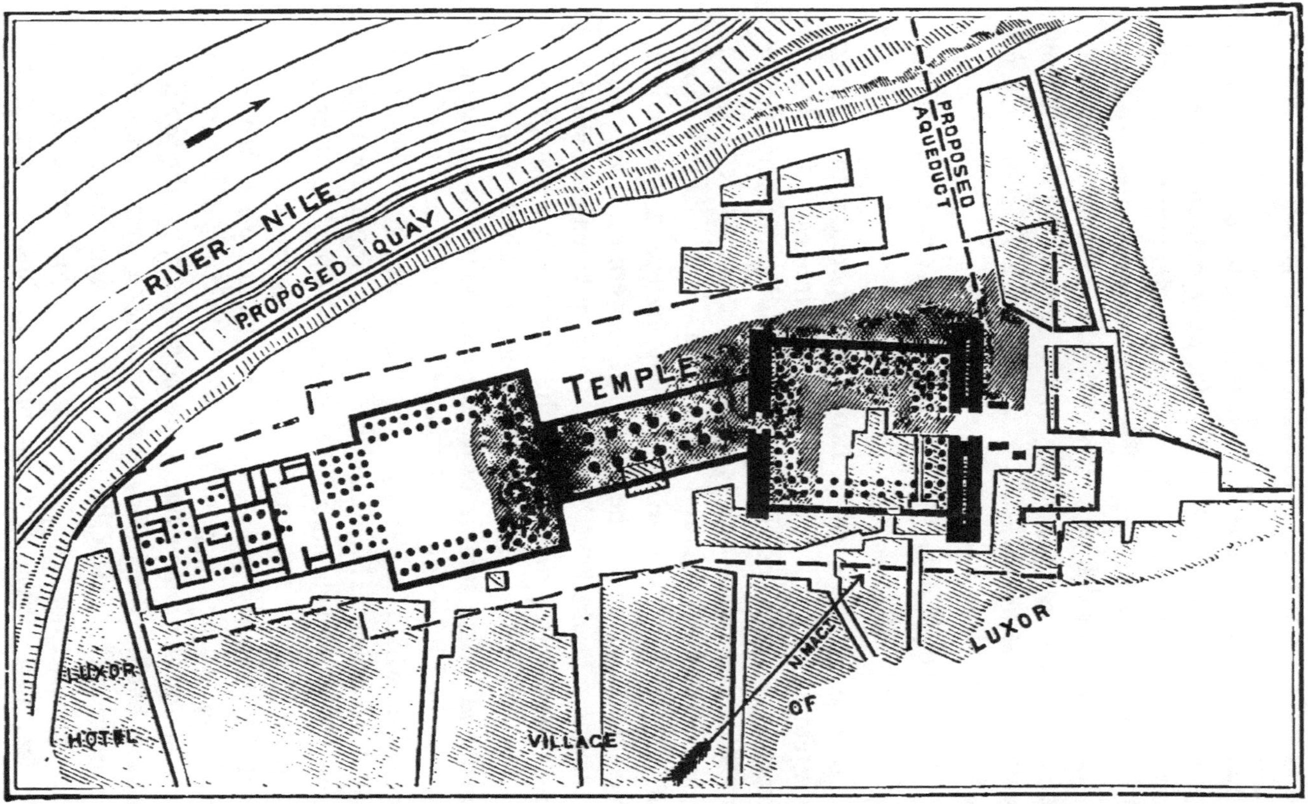

The Temple of Luxor. The shaded portions in the temple represent the amount of excavation which has been done during the winter of 1892–3.

from out of whole days and whole years, the supernumerary portions of which in that period, when collected together, amount to a day.* They ascribe to Mercury (Thoth) all knowledge of this kind. To Jupiter, whom they worship above all other deities, a virgin of the greatest beauty and of the most illustrious family (such persons the Greeks call pallades) is dedicated" . . . . (Bk. XVII, chap. 1, sec. 46, translated by Falconer.)

The principal objects of interest on the east or right bank of the river are :—

I. The **Temple of Luxor.** Compared with Karnak the temple of Luxor is not of any great interest. Until very recently a large portion of the buildings, connected in ancient days with the temple, was quite buried by the accumulated rubbish and earth upon which a large number of houses stood. During the last few years excavations have been made by the Egyptian Government, and some interesting results have been obtained. Among the antiquities thus brought to light may be mentioned a fine granite statue of Rameses II., the existence of which was never imagined. The temple of Luxor was built on an irregular plan caused by following the course of the river, out of the waters of which its walls, on one side, rose; it was founded by Amenophis III., about B.C. 1500. About forty years after, Ḥeru-em-ḥeb added the great colonnade, and as the name of Seti I., B.C. 1366, occurs in places, it is probable that he executed some repairs to the temple. His son Rameses II., B.C. 1333, set up two obelisks together with the colossi and the large pylon; the large court, nearly 200 feet square, behind the pylon, was surrounded by a double row of columns. The **Obelisk** now standing there records the names, titles, etc., of Rameses II., and stands about 82 feet high; it is one of the finest specimens of sculpture

* See page 71.

known. Its fellow obelisk stands in the Place de la Concorde, Paris.

After the burning and sacking of this temple by the Persians, some slight repairs, and rebuilding of certain chambers, were carried out by some of the Ptolemies, the name of one of whom (Philopator) is found inscribed on the temple. Certain parts of the temple appear to have been used by the Copts as a church, for the ancient sculptures have been plastered over and painted with figures of saints, etc.

II. The **Temple at Karnak.** The ruins of the buildings at Karnak are perhaps the most wonderful of any in Egypt, and they merit many visits from the traveller. It is probable that this spot was "holy ground" from a very early to a very late period, and we know that a number of kings from Thothmes III. to Euergetes II. lavished much wealth to make splendid the famous shrine of Åmen in the Åpts, and other temples situated there. The temples of Luxor and Karnak were united by an avenue about 6,500 feet long and 80 feet wide, on each side of which was arranged a row of sphinxes; from the fact that these monuments are without names, M. Mariette thought that the avenue was constructed at the expense of the priests or the wealthy inhabitants of the town, just as in later days the pronaos of the temple at Denderah was built by the people of that town. At the end of this avenue, to the right, is a road which leads to the so-called **Temple of Mut,** which was also approached by an avenue of sphinxes. Within the enclosure there stood originally two temples, both of which were dedicated to Åmen, built during the reign of Amenophis III.; Rameses II. erected two obelisks in front of the larger temple. To the north-west of these a smaller temple was built in Ptolemaic times, and the ruins on one side of it show that the small temples which stood there were either founded or restored by Rameses II., Osorkon,

PLANS OF KARNAK—1-3.

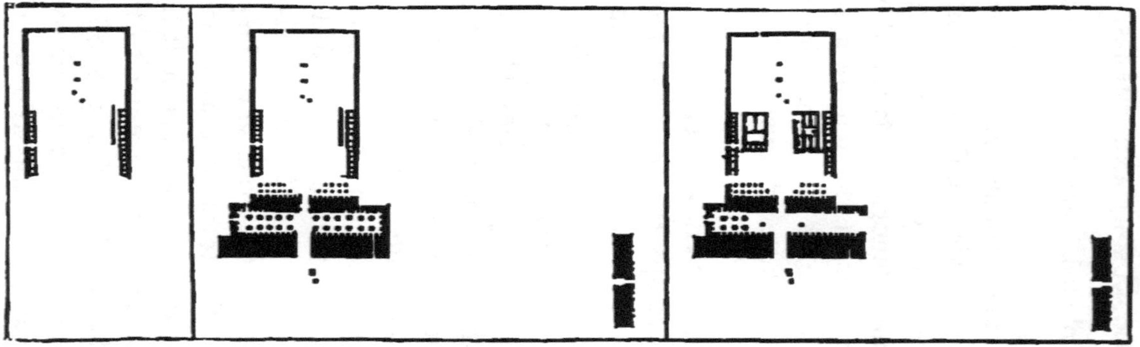

1. 2. 3.

1. Karnak before the time of Thothmes I., B.C. 1633.
2. Karnak during the reign of Thothmes I.
3. Karnak during the reign of Queen Ḥātshepset, B.C. 1600.

From Mariette, *Karnak*, Pl. VI.

Thekeleth, Sabaco, Nectanebus I., and the Ptolemies. Behind the temple enclosure are the remains of a temple dedicated to Ptaḥ of Memphis by Thothmes III.; the three doors behind it and the courts into which they lead were added by Sabaco, Tirhakah, and the Ptolemies.

Returning to the end of the avenue of sphinxes which leads from Luxor to Karnak, a second smaller avenue ornamented with a row of ram-headed sphinxes on each side is entered; at the end of it stands the splendid pylon built by Ptolemy IX. Euergetes II. Passing through the door, a smaller avenue of sphinxes leading to the temple built by Rameses III. is reached; the small avenue of sphinxes and eight of its columns were added by Rameses XIII. This temple was dedicated to Chensu, and appears to have been built upon the site of an ancient temple of the time of Amenophis III. To the west of this temple is a smaller temple built by Ptolemy IX. Euergetes II.

The great Temple of Karnak fronted the Nile, and was approached by means of a small avenue of ram-headed sphinxes which were placed in position by Rameses II. Passing through the first propylon, a court or hall, having a double row of pillars down the centre, is entered; on each side is a corridor with a row of columns. On the right hand (south) side are the ruins of a temple built by Rameses III., and on the left are those of another built by Seti II. This court or hall was the work of Shashanq, the first king of the XXIInd dynasty. On each side of the steps leading through the second pylon was a colossal statue of Rameses II.; that on the right hand has now disappeared. Passing through this pylon, the famous "**Hall of Columns**" is entered. The twelve columns forming the double row in the middle are about sixty feet high and about thirty-five feet in circumference; the other columns, 122 in number, are about forty feet high and twenty-seven feet in circumference. Rameses I. set up one column,

PLAN OF KARNAK—4.

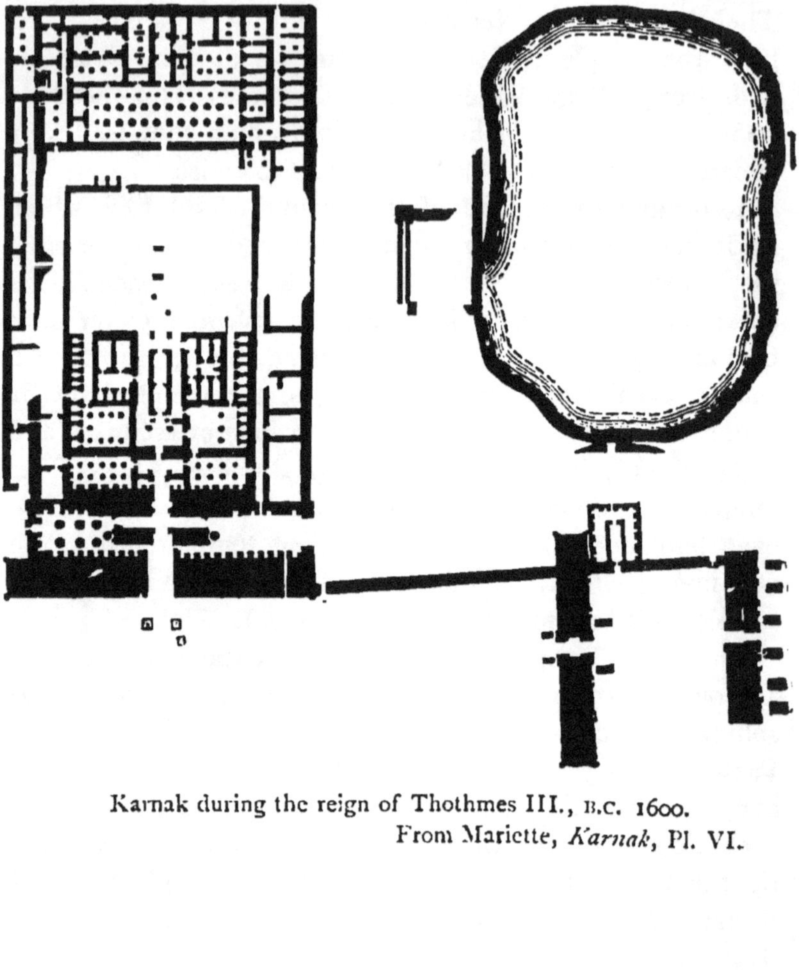

Karnak during the reign of Thothmes III., B.C. 1600.
From Mariette, *Karnak*, Pl. VI.

Seti I., the builder of this hall, set up seventy-nine, and the remaining fifty-four were set up by Rameses II. It is thought that this hall was originally roofed over. At the end of it is the third propylon, which was built by Amenophis III., and served as the entrance to the temple until the time of Rameses I. Between this and the next pylon is a narrow passage, in the middle of which stood two obelisks which were set up by Thothmes I.; the southern one is still standing, and bears the names of this king, but the northern one has fallen,* and its fragments show that Thothmes III. caused his name to be carved on it. At the southern end of this passage are the remains of a gate built by Rameses IX. The fourth and fifth pylons were built by Thothmes I. Between them stood fourteen columns, six of which were set up by Thothmes I., and eight by Amenophis II., and two granite obelisks; one of these still stands. These obelisks were hewn out of the granite quarry by the command of Ḥātshepset,† the daughter of Thothmes I., and sister of Thothmes II. and Thothmes III. This able woman set them up in honour of "father Åmen," and she relates in the inscriptions on the base of the standing obelisk that she covered their tops with *smu* metal, or copper, that they could be seen from a very great distance, and that she had them hewn and brought down to Thebes in about seven months. These obelisks were brought into their chamber from the south side, and were 98 and 105 feet high respectively; the masonry round their bases is of the time of Thothmes III. The sixth pylon and the two walls which

* It was standing when Pococke visited Egypt in 1737–1739.

† "Scarcely had the royal brother and husband of Hashop (*sic*) closed his eyes, when the proud queen threw aside her woman's veil, and appeared in all the splendour of Pharaoh, as a born king. For she laid aside her woman's dress, clothed herself in man's attire, and adorned herself with the crown and insignia of royalty." (Brugsch's *Egypt under the Pharaohs, Vol. I.*, p. 349.)

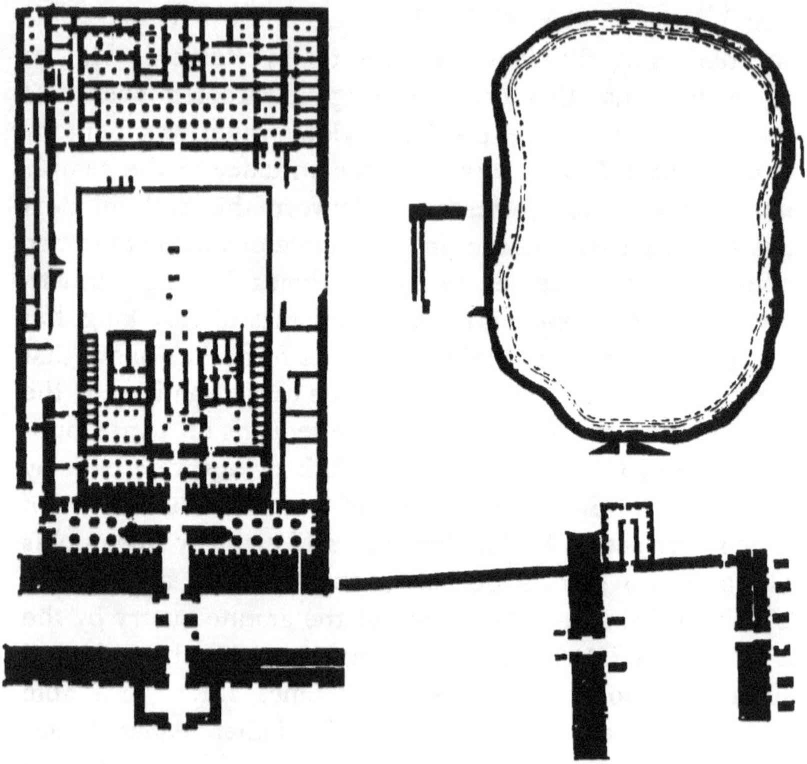

Karnak during the reign of Amenophis III., B.C. 1500.
From Mariette, *Karnak*, Pl. VI.

flank it on the north and south are the work of Thothmes III., but Seti II., Rameses III., and Rameses IV. have added their cartouches to them. On this pylon are inscribed a large number of geògraphical names of interest. Passing through it, the visitor finds himself in a vestibule which leads into a red granite oblong chamber, inscribed with the name of Philip III. of Macedon, which is often said to have formed the sanctuary. In the chambers on each side of it are found the names of Amenophis I., Thothmes I., Thothmes II., Ḥātshepset, and Thothmes III. The sanctuary stood in the centre of the large court beyond the two oblong red granite pedestals. In ancient days, when Thebes was pillaged by her conquerors, it would seem that special care was taken to uproot not only the shrine, but the very foundations upon which it rested. Some fragments of columns inscribed with the name of Usertsen I. found there prove, however, that its foundation dates from the reign of this king. Beyond the sanctuary court is a large building of the time of Thothmes III. In it was found the famous **Tablet of Ancestors,** now in Paris, where this king is seen making offerings to a number of his royal ancestors. On the north side of the building is the chamber in which he made his offerings, and on the east side is a chamber where he adored the hawk, the emblem of the Sun-god Rā; this latter chamber was restored by Alexander IV. Behind the great temple, and quite distinct from it, was another small temple. On the south side of the great temple was a lake which was filled by infiltration from the Nile; it appears only to have been used for processional purposes, as water for ablutionary and other purposes was drawn from the well on the north side of the interior of the temple. The lake was dug during the reign of Thothmes III., and its stone quays probably belong to the same period.

Passing through the gate at the southern end of tne

Plan of Karnak—6.

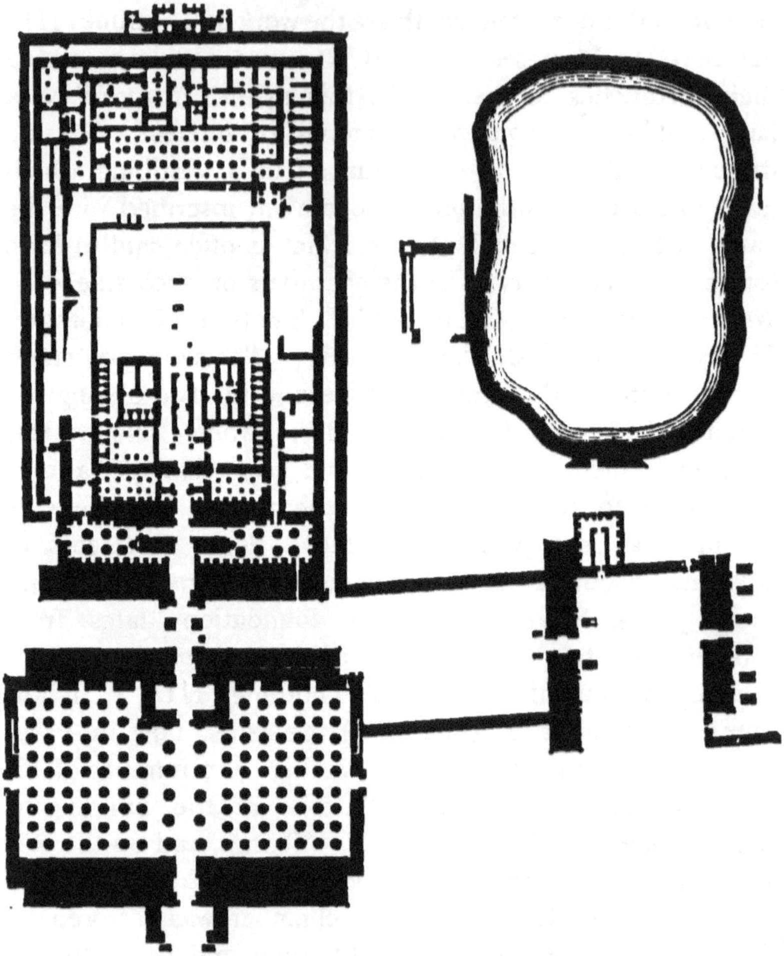

Karnak under Rameses II., B.C. 1333.
From Mariette, *Karnak*, Pl. VII.

passage in which stands the obelisk of Ḥātshepset, a long avenue with four pylons is entered; the first was built by Thothmes III., the second by Thothmes I., and the third and fourth by Ḥeru-em-ḥeb. Between these last two, on the east side stood a temple built by Amenophis II. On the north side of the Great Temple are the ruins of two smaller buildings which belong to the time of the XXVIth dynasty.

The outside of the north wall of the Great Hall of Columns is ornamented with some interesting scenes from the battles of Seti I. against the peoples who lived to the north-east of Syria and in Mesopotamia, called Shasu, Rutennu, and Charu. The king is represented as having conquered all these people, and returning to Thebes laden with much spoil and bringing many captives. It is doubtful if the events really took place in the order in which they are depicted; but the fidelity to nature, and the spirit and skill with which these bas-reliefs have been executed, make them some of the most remarkable sculptures known. The scene in which Seti I. is shown grasping the hair of the heads of a number of people, in the act of slaying them, is symbolic.

The outside of the south wall is ornamented with a large scene in which Shashanq (Shishak), the first king of the XXIInd dynasty, is represented smiting a group of kneeling prisoners; the god Åmen, in the form of a woman, is standing by presenting him with weapons of war. Here also are 150 cartouches, surmounted with heads, in which are written the names of the towns captured by Shishak. The type of features given to these heads by the sculptor shows that the vanquished peoples belonged to a branch of the great Semitic family. The hieroglyphics in one of the cartouches were supposed to read "the king of Judah," and to represent Jeroboam, who was vanquished by Shishak; it has now been proved conclusively that they form the name of a place called Iuta-melek. Passing along to the

PLAN OF KARNAK—7.

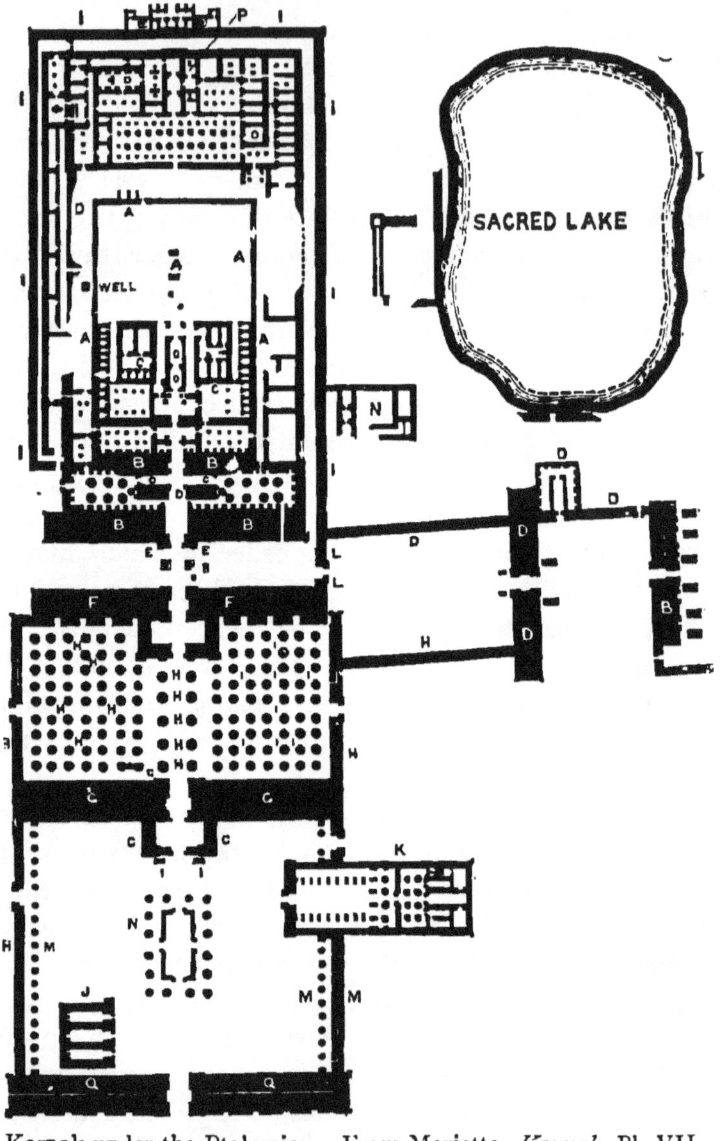

Karnak under the Ptolemies. From Mariette, *Karnak*, Pl. VII.

A. Walls standing before the time of Thothmes I.
B. Pylons built by Thothmes I.
C. Walls and obelisks of Hātshepset.
D. Walls, pylon, etc., of Thothmes III.
E. Gateway of Thothmes IV.
F. Pylon of Amenophis III.
G. Pylon of Rameses I.
H. Walls and columns of Seti I.
I. Columns, walls, and statues of Rameses II.
J. Temple of Seti II.
K. Temple of Rameses III.
L. Gateway of Rameses IX.
M. Pillars and walls of the XXIInd dynasty.
N. Pillars of Tirhakah.
O. Corridor of Philip III. of Macedon.
P. Chamber and shrine of Alexander II.
Q. Pylon built by the Ptolemies.

east, the visitor comes to a wall at right angles to the first, upon which is inscribed a copy of the poem of Pen-ta-urt, celebrating the victory of Rameses II. over the Cheta, in the fifth year of his reign; and on the west side of the wall is a stele on which is set forth a copy of the offensive and defensive treaty between this king and the prince of the Cheta.

The inscriptions on the magnificent ruins at Karnak show that from the time of Usertsen I., B.C. 2433, to that of Alexander IV., B.C. 312 (?), the religious centre* of Upper Egypt was at Thebes, and that the most powerful of the kings of Egypt who reigned during this period spared neither pains nor expense in adding to and beautifying the temples there.

The fury of the elements, the attacks of Egypt's enemies, and above all the annual inundation of the Nile, have helped to throw down these splendid buildings. The days are not far distant when, unless energetic measures are taken meanwhile, a large number of the columns in the wonderful hall of Seti I. must fall, and in their fall will do irreparable damage to the other parts of the building. It is much to be hoped that the public opinion of the civilized world will not allow these deeply interesting relics of a mighty nation to perish before their eyes. Steps should at once be taken to keep out the inundation, and if possible the tottering columns and walls should be strengthened.

* The short-lived heresy of the worship of the disk of the Sun instead of that of Àmen-Ṛā would not interfere with the general popularity of Theban temples.

On the **west bank** of the river the following are the most interesting antiquities :—

I. The **Temple of Ḳûrnah.** This temple was built by Seti I. in memory of his father Rameses I.; it was completed by Rameses II., by whom it was re-dedicated to the memory of his father Seti I. Two pylons stood before it, and between them was an avenue of sphinxes. This temple was to all intents and purposes a cenotaph, and as such its position on the edge of the desert, at the entrance to a necropolis, is explained. In the temple were six columns, and on each side were several small chambers. The sculptures on the walls represent Rameses II. making offerings to the gods, among whom are Rameses I. and Seti I. According to an inscription there, it is said that Seti I. went to heaven and was united with the Sun-god before this temple was finished, and that Rameses II. made and fixed the doors, finished the building of the walls, and decorated the interior. The workmanship in certain parts of this temple recalls that of certain parts of Abydos; it is probable that the same artists were employed.

II. The **Ramesseum.** This temple, called also the MEMNONIUM and the tomb of Osymandyas (Diodorus I., iv), was built by Rameses II., in honour of Ȧmen-Rā. As at Ḳûrnah, two pylons stood in front of it. The first court had a double row of pillars on each side of it; passing up a flight of steps, and through the second pylon, is a second court, having a double row of round columns on the east and west sides, and a row of pilasters, to which large figures of Rameses II. under the form of Osiris are attached, on the north and south sides. Before the second pylon stood a colossal statue of Rameses II., at least sixty feet high, which has been thrown down (by Cambyses?), turned over on its back, and mutilated. In the hall are twelve huge columns, arranged in two rows, and thirty-six smaller ones arranged in six rows. On the

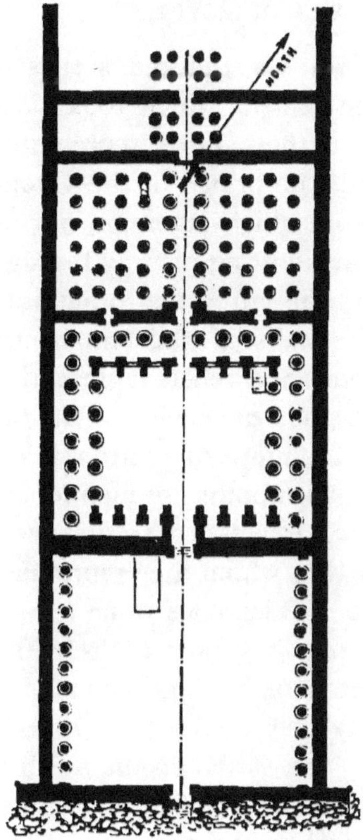

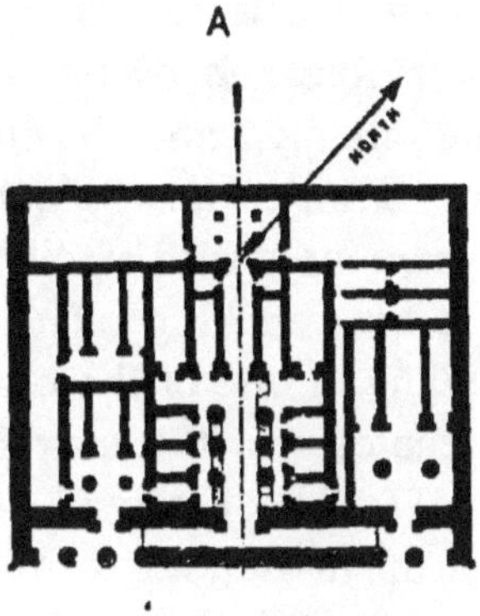

A. Plan of the Temple at Ḳûrnah.

B. Plan of the Ramesseum a Ḳûrnah.

interior face of the second pylon are sculptured scenes in the war of Rameses II. against the Cheta, which took place in the fifth year of his reign; in them he is represented slaying the personal attendants of the prince of the Cheta. Elsewhere is the famous scene in which Rameses, having been forsaken by his army, is seen cutting his way through the enemy, and hurling them one after the other into the Orontes near Kadesh. The walls of the temple are ornamented with small battle scenes and reliefs representing the king making offerings to the gods of Thebes. On the ceiling of one of the chambers is an interesting astronomical piece on which the twelve Egyptian months are mentioned.

III. The **Colossi**.—These two interesting statues were set up in honour of Amenophis III., whom they represent; they stood in front of the pylon of a calcareous stone temple which was built by this king; this has now entirely disappeared. They were hewn out of a hard grit-stone, and the top of each was about sixty feet above the ground; originally each was monolithic. The statue on the north is the famous **Colossus of Memnon**, from which a sound was said to issue every morning when the sun rose. The upper part of it was thrown down by an earthquake, it is said, about B.C. 27; the damage was partially repaired during the reign of Septimius Severus, who restored the head and shoulders of the figure by adding to it five ayers of stone. When Strabo was at Thebes with Ælius Gallus he heard "a noise at the first hour of the day, but whether proceeding from the base or from the colossus, or produced on purpose by some of those standing round the base, I cannot confidently assert." It is said that after the colossus was repaired no sound issued from it. Some think that the noise was caused by the sun's rays striking upon the stone, while others believe that a priest hidden in the colossus produced it by striking a stone. The inscriptions show that many distinguished Romans visited the "vocal Memnon" and heard the sound; one Petronianus, of a poetical turn of mind, stated that it made a sighing sound in complaining to its mother, the dawn, of the injuries inflicted upon it by Cambyses. The inscriptions on the back of the colossi give the names of Amenophis III.

IV. **Medinet Habû.**—This village lies to the south of the colossi, and its foundation dates from Coptic times. The early Christians established themselves around the ancient Egyptian temple there, and having carefully plastered over the wall sculptures in one of its chambers, they used it as a chapel. Round and about this temple many Greek and Coptic inscriptions have been found, which prove that the Coptic community here was one of the largest and most important in Upper Egypt. The temple here is actually composed of two temples; the older was built by Thothmes III., and the later by Rameses III. The first court of the temple of Thothmes III. was built during the time of the Roman occupation of Egypt, and the names of Titus, Hadrian, Antoninus, etc., are found on various parts of its walls. The half-built pylon at the end of this court is of the same period, although the door between them bears the names of Ptolemy X. Soter II. (Lathyrus) and Ptolemy XIII., Neos Dionysos (Auletes). The little court and pylon beyond are inscribed with the names of Tirhakah, B.C. 693, and Nectanebus II., B.C. 358. Passing through this last court and its pylon, the temple proper is reached. The oldest name found here is that of Thothmes II. The work begun by this king was completed by Thothmes III., and several subsequent kings restored or added new parts to it.

Before the Temple of Rameses III. there stood originally a building consisting of two square towers, the four sides of which were symmetrically inclined to a common centre. The interior chambers were ornamented with sculptures, on which were depicted scenes in the domestic (?) life of the

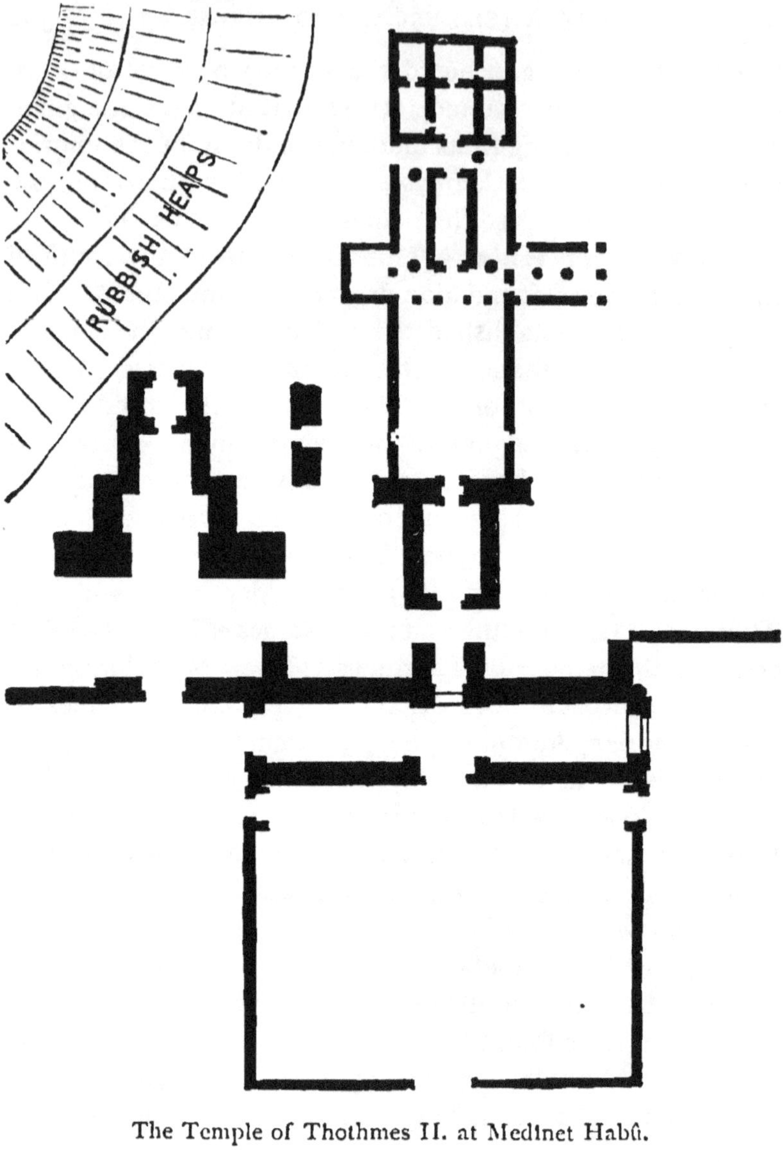

The Temple of Thothmes II. at Medinet Habû.

king, and from this it has been concluded that the building formed the PALACE OF RAMESES III. Elsewhere the king is shown smiting his enemies, and from the features and dress of many of them it is possible to tell generally what nations they represent; it is quite clear that the sculptor intended his figures to be typical portraits. It is a noticeable fact that the cartouches of Rameses III. are the only ones found in this building.

V. The **Temple of Rameses III.** is entered by passing through the first pylon, the front of which is ornamented with scenes from the wars of this king against the people of Arabia and Phœnicia. The weapons of the king are presented to him by Åmen-Rā the Sun-god. In the first court is a row of seven pillars, to which are attached figures of the king in the form of Osiris; M. Mariette was of opinion that these declared the funereal nature of the building. The second pylon is built of red granite, and the front is ornamented with scenes in which Rameses III. is leading before the gods Åmen and Mut a number of prisoners, whom he has captured in Syria and along the coasts of the Mediterranean; from these scenes it is evident that he was able to wage war by sea as well as by land. The second court, which, according to M. Mariette, is one of the most precious which Egyptian antiquity has bequeathed to us, has a portico running round its four sides; it is supported on the north and south sides by eight Osiris columns, and on the east and west by five circular columns. The Copts disgraced this splendid court by building a sandstone colonnade in the middle, and destroyed here, as elsewhere, much that would have been of priceless value. Beyond the second court was a hall of columns, on each side of which were several small chambers, and beyond that were other chambers and corridors and the sanctuary.

The scenes sculptured on the inside of the second court represent the wars of Rameses III. against the Libyans, in

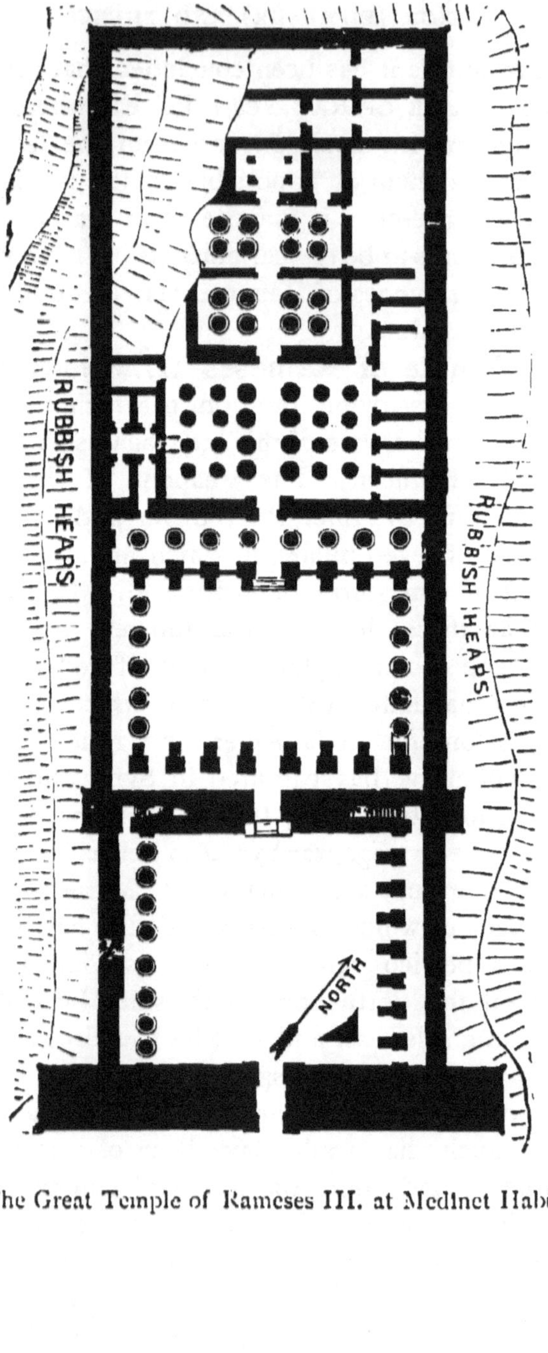

The Great Temple of Rameses III. at Medinet Habû.

which the generals and officers of the Egyptian king lead crowds of prisoners into his presence, whence they are brought in triumph to Thebes to be offered to the gods of that town. Elsewhere Rameses is making offerings to the various gods of Thebes and performing certain ceremonies. The procession, coronation of the king, musicians, and the sending off of four birds to announce to the ends of the world that Rameses III. was king, are among the many interesting scenes depicted here.

Outside the building, on the south wall, is a list of religious festivals, and on the north wall are ten scenes, of which the following are the subjects: 1. The king and his army setting out to war. 2. Battle of the Egyptians against the Libyans, and defeat of the latter. 3. Slaughter of the enemy by thousands, and the prisoners led before the king. 4. The king addresses his victorious army, and an inventory is made of the spoil captured. 5. The march continued. 6. Second encounter and defeat of the enemy called Takare; their camp is captured, and women and children flee away in all directions. 7. The march continued. On the way one lion is slain and another wounded. The country passed through is probably northern Syria. 8. Naval battle scene. The fight takes place near the river bank or sea-shore, and Rameses and his archers distress the enemy by shooting at them from the shore. 9. Return towards Egypt. The number of the slain is arrived at by counting the hands which have been cut off the bodies on the field of battle. 10. Return to Thebes. The king presents his prisoners to the gods Ȧmen-Rā, Mut, and Chensu. Speech of the prisoners, who beg the king to allow them to live that they may proclaim his power and glory.

The temple of Rameses III. is one of the most interesting of the Egyptian temples, and is worthy of several visits.

VI. **Dêr el-Medînet.** This small temple, which stands between the Colossi and Medînet Habû, was begun by

Ptolemy IV. Philopator and finished by Ptolemy IX. Euergetes II.; in one of its chambers is the judgment scene which forms the vignette of the 125th chapter of the Book of the Dead, hence the funereal nature of the building may be inferred.

VII. **Dêr el-Baḥari.** This temple was built by Ḥātshepset, the sister and wife of Thothmes II., B.C. 1600. The finest marble limestone was used in its construction, and its architect seems to have been an able man called Senmut, who was honoured with the friendship of the queen, and promoted by her to be chief clerk of the works. Before the temple was an avenue of sandstone sphinxes and two obelisks. It was built in stages on the side of a hill, and its courts were connected by means of flights of steps. As early as the XXIInd dynasty the temple had fallen into disuse, and soon after this time its chambers appear to have been used for sepulchres. The wall sculptures are beautiful specimens of art, and depict the return of Egyptian soldiers from some military expedition, and the scenes which took place during the expedition which the queen organized and sent off to Punt. This latter expedition was most successful, and returned to Egypt laden with things the "like of which had never before been seen in that land." The prince of Punt came to Egypt with a large following, and became a vassal of Ḥātshepset. *

THE DISCOVERY OF THE ROYAL MUMMIES AT DÊR EL-BAḤARI.†

In the summer of the year 1871 an Arab, a native of Ḳûrnah, discovered a large tomb filled with coffins heaped one upon the other. On the greater number of them were

* For a notice of the work carried on by the Egypt Exploration Fund by M. Naville, see p. 395 ff.

† A minute and detailed account of this discovery is given by Maspero in "Les Momies Royales de Déïr el Bahari" (Fasc. I., t. IV., of the *Mémoires* of the French Archæological Mission at Cairo).

visible the cartouche and other signs which indicated that the inhabitants of the coffins were royal personages. The native who was so fortunate as to have chanced upon this remarkable "find," was sufficiently skilled in his trade of antiquity hunter to know what a valuable discovery he had made; his joy must however have been turned into mourning, when it became evident that he would need the help of many men even to move some of the large royal coffins which he saw before him, and that he could not keep the knowledge of such treasures locked up in his own breast. He revealed his secret to his two brothers and to one of his sons, and they proceeded to spoil the coffins of *ushabtiu** figures, papyri, scarabs and other antiquities which could be taken away easily and concealed in their *abbas* (ample outer garments) as they returned to their houses. These precious objects were for several winters sold to chance tourists on the Nile, and the lucky possessors of this mine of wealth replenished their stores from time to time by visits made at night to the tomb. As soon as the objects thus sold reached Europe, it was at once suspected that a "find" of more than ordinary importance had been made. An English officer called Campbell showed M. Maspero a hieratic Book of the Dead written for Pi-net'em; M. de Saulcy sent him photographs of the hieroglyphic papyrus of Net'emet; M. Mariette bought at Suez a papyrus written for the Queen Ḥent-taiu, and Rogers Bey exhibited at Paris a wooden tablet upon which was written a hieratic text relating to the *ushabtiu* figures which were to be buried with the princess Nesi-Chensu. All these interesting and most valuable

* *Ushabtiu* figures made of stone, green or blue glazed Egyptian porcelain, wood, &c., were deposited in the tombs with the dead, and were supposed to perform for them any field labours which might be decreed for them by Osiris, the king of the under-world, and judge of the dead.

objects proved that the natives of Thebes had succeeded in unearthing a veritable "Cave of Treasures," and M. Maspero, the Director of the Bûlâḳ Museum, straightway determined to visit Upper Egypt with a view of discovering whence came all these antiquities. Three men were implicated, whose names were learnt by M. Maspero from the inquiries which he made of tourists who purchased antiquities.

In 1881 he proceeded to Thebes, and began his investigations by causing one of the dealers, 'Abd er-Rasûl Aḥmad, to be arrested by the police, and an official inquiry into the matter was ordered by the Mudîr of Ḳeneh. In spite of threats and persuasion, and many add tortures, the accused denied any knowledge of the place whence the antiquities came. The evidence of the witnesses who were called to testify to the character of the accused, tended to show that he was a man of amiable disposition, who would never dream of pillaging a tomb, much less do it. Finally, after two months' imprisonment, he was provisionally set at liberty. The accused then began to discuss with his partners in the secret what plans they should adopt, and how they should act in the future. Some of them thought that all trouble was over when 'Abd er-Rasûl Aḥmad was set at liberty, but others thought, and they were right, that the trial would be recommenced in the winter. Fortunately for students of Egyptology, differences of opinion broke out between the parties soon after, and 'Abd er-Rasûl Aḥmad soon perceived that his brothers were determined to turn King's evidence at a favourable opportunity. To prevent their saving themselves at his expense, he quietly travelled to Ḳeneh, and there confessed to the Mudîr that he was able to reveal the place where the coffins and papyri were found. Telegrams were sent to Cairo announcing the confession of 'Abd er-Rasûl Aḥmad, and when his statements had been verified, despatches containing fuller particulars were sent to Cairo from Ḳeneh. It was decided that a small expedition to Thebes should at once be made to take possession of and bring to Cairo the antiquities which were to be revealed to the world by 'Abd er-Rasûl Aḥmad, and the charge of bringing this work to a successful issue was placed in the hands of M. Émile Brugsch. Although the season was summer, and the heat very great, the start for Thebes was made on July 1. At Ḳeneh M. Brugsch found a number of papyri and other valuable antiquities which 'Abd er-Rasûl had sent there as an earnest of the truth of his promise to reveal the hidden treasures. A week later M. Brugsch and his companions were shown the shaft of the tomb, which was most carefully hidden in the north-west part of the natural circle which opens to the south of the valley of Dêr el-Baḥari, in the little row of hills which separates the Bibân el-Mulûk from the Theban plain. According to M. Maspero,* the royal mummies were removed here from their tombs in the Bibân el-Mulûk by Āauputh, the son of Shashanq, about B.C. 966, to prevent them being destroyed by the thieves, who were sufficiently numerous and powerful to defy the government of the day. The pit which led to the tomb was about forty feet deep, and the passage, of irregular level, which led to the tomb was about 220 feet long; at the end of this passage was a nearly rectangular chamber about twenty-five feet long, which was found to be literally filled with coffins, mummies, funereal furniture, boxes, *ushabtiu* figures, Canopic jars,† bronze vases, etc., etc. A large number of men were

* *Histoire Ancienne des Peuples de L'Orient*, 4ième ed., p. 360.

† The principal intestines of a deceased person were placed in four jars, which were placed in his tomb under the bier; the jars were dedicated to the four children of Horus, who were called Mesthȧ, Ḥāpi, Ṭuamāutef and Qebḥsennuf. The name "Canopic" is given to them by those who follow the opinion of some ancient writers that Canopus, the pilot of Menelaus, who is said to have been buried at Canopus in Egypt, was worshipped there under the form of a jar with small feet, a thin neck, a swollen body, and a round back.

at once employed to exhume these objects, and for eight and forty hours M. Brugsch and Aḥmad Effendi Kamal stood at the mouth of the pit watching the things brought up. The heavy coffins were carried on the shoulders of men to the river, and in less than two weeks everything had been sent over the river to Luxor. A few days after this the whole collection of mummies of kings and royal personages was placed upon an Egyptian Government steamer and taken to the Museum at Bûlâḳ.

When the mummies of the ancient kings of Egypt arrived at Cairo, it was found that the Bûlâḳ Museum was too small to contain them, and before they could be exposed to the inspection of the world, it was necessary for additional rooms to be built. Finally, however, M. Maspero had glass cases made, and, with the help of some cabinets borrowed from his private residence attached to the Museum, he succeeded in exhibiting, in a comparatively suitable way, the mummies in which such world-wide interest had been taken. Soon after the arrival of the mummies at Bûlâḳ M. Brugsch opened the mummy of Thothmes III., when it was found that the Arabs had attacked it and plundered whatever was valuable upon it. In 1883 the mummy of Queen Mes-Ḥent-Themeḥu, , emitted unpleasant odours, and by M. Maspero's orders it was unrolled. In 1885 the mummy of Queen Åḥmes Nefertåri, 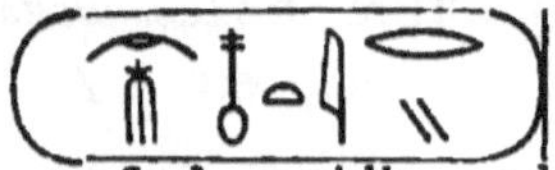, was unrolled by him, and as it putrefied rapidly and stank, it had to be buried. Finally, when M. Maspero found that the mummy of Seqenen-Rā, 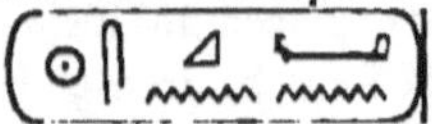, was also decaying, he decided to unroll the whole collection, and Rameses II. was the first of the great kings whose features were shown again to the world after a lapse of 3,200 years.

Such are the outlines of the history of one of the

greatest discoveries ever made in Egypt. It will ever be regretted by the Egyptologist that this remarkable collection of mummies was not discovered by some person who could have used for the benefit of scholars the precious information which this "find" would have yielded, before so many of its objects were scattered; as it is, however, it would be difficult to over-estimate its historical value.

The following is a list of the names of the principal kings and royal personages which were found on coffins at Dêr el-Baḥari and of their mummies:—

XVIIth Dynasty, before B.C. 1700.

King Seqenen-Rā, coffin and mummy.

Nurse of Queen Nefertȧri Rāȧ, coffin only. This coffin contained the mummy of a queen whose name is read Ȧn-Ḥāpi.

XVIIIth Dynasty, B.C. 1700–1400.

King Ȧāḥmes (Amāsis I.), coffin and mummy.
Queen Ȧāḥmes Nefertȧri, coffin.
King Ȧmenḥetep I., coffin and mummy.
The Prince Se-Ȧmen, coffin and mummy.
The Princess Set-Ȧmen, coffin and mummy.
The Scribe Senu, chief of the house of Nefertȧri, mummy.
Royal wife Set-ka-mes, mummy.
Royal daughter Mesḥentthemḥu, coffin and mummy.
Royal mother Ȧāḥ-ḥetep, coffin.
King Thothmes I., coffin usurped by Pi-net'em.
King Thothmes II., coffin and mummy.
King Thothmes III., coffin and mummy.
Coffin and mummy of an unknown person.

XIXth Dynasty, B.C. 1400–1200.

King Rameses I., part of coffin.
King Seti I., coffin and mummy.
King Rameses II., coffin and mummy.

XXth Dynasty, B.C. 1200–1100.

King Rameses III., mummy found in the coffin of Nefertàri.

XXIst Dynasty, B.C. 1100–1000.

Royal mother Net'emet.
High-priest of Åmen, Masaherthå, coffin and mummy.
High-priest of Åmen, Pai-net'em III., coffin and mummy
Priest of Åmen, T'eṭ-Ptaḥ-åuf-ānch, coffin and mummy.
Scribe Nebseni, coffin and mummy.
Queen Māt-ka-Rā, coffin and mummy.
Princess Åuset-em-chebit, coffin and mummy.
Princess Nesi-Chensu.

VIII. The Tombs of the Kings, called in Arabic Bibân el-Mulûk, are hewn out of the living rock in a valley, which is reached by passing the temple at Ḳûrnah; it is situated about three or four miles from the river. This valley contains the tombs of the kings of the XIXth and XXth dynasties, and is generally known as the Eastern Valley; a smaller valley, the Western, contains the tombs of the last kings of the XVIIIth dynasty. These tombs consist of long inclined planes with a number of chambers or halls receding into the mountain sometimes to a distance of 500 feet. Strabo gives the number of these royal tombs as 40, 17 of which were open in the time of Ptolemy Lagus; in 1835 21 were known, but the labours of M. Mariette were successful in bringing four more to light. The most important of these tombs are:—

No. 17. **Tomb of Seti I.,** B.C. 1366, commonly called "Belzoni's Tomb," because it was discovered by that brave traveller in the early part of this century; it had already been rifled, but the beautiful alabaster sarcophagus, which is now preserved in the Soane Museum in London, was still lying in its chamber at the bottom of the tomb. The inscriptions and scenes sculptured on the walls form parts of

I.

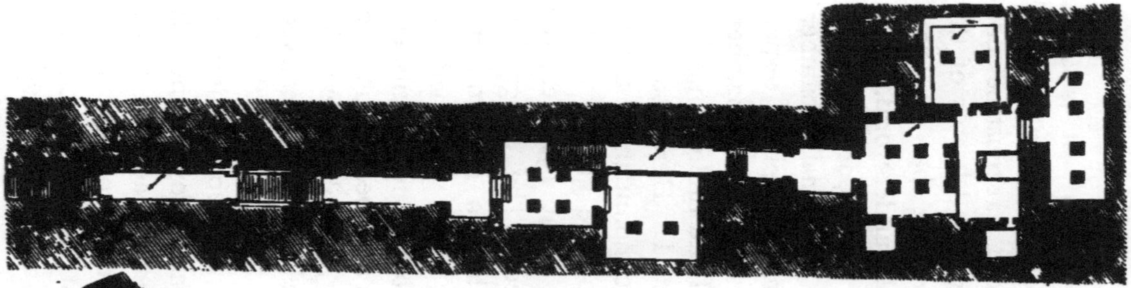

II.

I. Ground plan of the Tomb of Seti I., B.C. 1366.
II. Section of the Tomb of Seti I.
(From Lepsius, *Denkmäler*, Abth. I., Bl. 96.)

the "Book of being in the under-world;" it is quite impossible to describe them here, for a large number of pages would be required for the purpose. It must be sufficient to draw attention to the excellence and beauty of the paintings and sculptures, and to point out that the whole series refers to the life of the king in the under-world. The tomb is entered by means of two flights of steps, at the bottom of which is a passage terminating in a small chamber. Beyond this are two halls having four and two pillars respectively, and to the left are the passages and small chambers which lead to the large six-pillared hall and vaulted chamber in which stood the sarcophagus of Seti I. Here also is an inclined plane which descends into the mountain for a considerable distance; from the level of the ground to the bottom of this incline the depth is about 150 feet; the length of the tomb is nearly 500 feet. The designs on the walls were first sketched in outline in red, and the alterations by the master designer or artist were made in black; it would seem that this tomb was never finished. The mutilations and destruction which have been committed here during the last twenty-five years are truly lamentable. The mummy of Seti I., found at Dêr el-Baḥari, is preserved in the Gizeh Museum.

No. 11. **Tomb of Rameses III.**, B.C. 1200, commonly called "Bruce's Tomb," because it was discovered by this traveller, and the "Tomb of the Harper," on account of the scene in it in which men are represented playing harps. The architect did not leave sufficient space between this and a neighbouring tomb, and hence after excavating passages and chambers to a distance of more than 100 feet, he was obliged to turn to the right to avoid breaking into it The flight of steps leading into the tomb is not as steep as that in No. 17, the paintings and sculptures are not so fine, and the general plan of ornamentation differs. The scenes on the walls of the first passage resemble those in the first passage of No. 17, but in the other passages and chambers warlike, domestic, and agricultural scenes and objects are depicted. The body of the red granite sarcophagus of Rameses III. is in Paris, the cover is in the Fitzwilliam Museum, Cambridge, and the mummy of this king is at Gîzeh. The length of the tomb is about 400 feet.

No. 2. The **Tomb of Rameses IV.**, about B.C. 1166, though smaller than the others, is of considerable interest; the granite sarcophagus, of colossal proportions, still stands *in situ* at the bottom. Having seen the beautiful sculptures and paintings in the Tomb of Seti I., the visitor will probably not be disposed to spend much time in that of Rameses IV.

No. 9. The **Tomb of Rameses VI.**, or "Memnon's Tomb," was considered of great interest by the Greeks and Romans who visited it in ancient days; the astronomical designs on some of the ceilings, and the regular sequence of its passages and rooms are interesting. The fragments of the granite sarcophagus of this king lie at the bottom of the tomb.

No. 6. The **Tomb of Rameses IX.** is remarkable for the variety of sculptures and paintings of a nature entirely different from those found in the other royal tombs; they appear to refer to the idea of resurrection after death and of immortality, which is here symbolized by the principle of generation.

The **Tomb of Rameses I.**, father of Seti I., is the oldest in this valley; it was opened by Belzoni.

The **Tomb* of Rechmârā** is situated in the hill behind the Ramesseum called Shêkh 'Abd al-Ḳûrnah; it is one of the most interesting of all the private tombs found at Thebes. The scenes on the walls represent a procession of tribute bearers from Punt carrying apes, ivory, etc.,

* No. 35, according to Wilkinson, and No. 15, according to Champollion.

and of people from parts of Syria and the shores of the Mediterranean bringing to him gifts consisting of the choicest products of their lands, which Rechmàrā receives for Thothmes III. The countries can in many cases be identified by means of the articles depicted. The scenes in the inner chamber represent brickmaking, ropemaking, smiths' and masons' work, etc., etc., superintended by Rechmàrā, prefect of Thebes; elsewhere are domestic scenes and a representation of Rechmàrā sailing in a boat, lists of offerings, etc.

Tomb of Nekht at Shekh 'Abd al-Ḳurnah.

This beautiful little tomb was opened out in the year 1889, but there is little doubt that it was known to the inhabitants of Ḳurnah some time before. Though small, it is of considerable interest, and the freshness of the colours in the scenes is unusual; it is, moreover, a fine example of the tomb of a Theban gentleman of the Middle Empire. As the paintings and inscriptions are typical of their class, they are here described at some length. The tomb of Nekht consists of two chambers, but the larger one only is ornamented; the ceiling is painted with a wave pattern, and the cornice is formed of the *χakeru* pattern . On the left end wall a granite stele is painted, and upon it are the following inscriptions:—

1. 

ṭā suten ḥetep Ausàr Un-neferu, neter āa neb
Grant royal oblation Osiris Unnefer, god great, lord

Àbṭu ṭā - f āq it
of Abydos, may he grant a coming in [and] a going out

em *Neter-χert* *ȧn* *χesef* *ba* *em*

from the underworld, not being repulsed the soul

en *ka* *en* *un* [*nut*]

{[at the gates of the underworld]}, to the double of the {temple-servant [Nekht]}

maāχeru

triumphant!

2. 

ṭā *suten* *ḥetep* [*Ḥeru-χuti*] *ṭā* - *f* *maa*

Grant royal oblation [Harmachis], may he grant a view

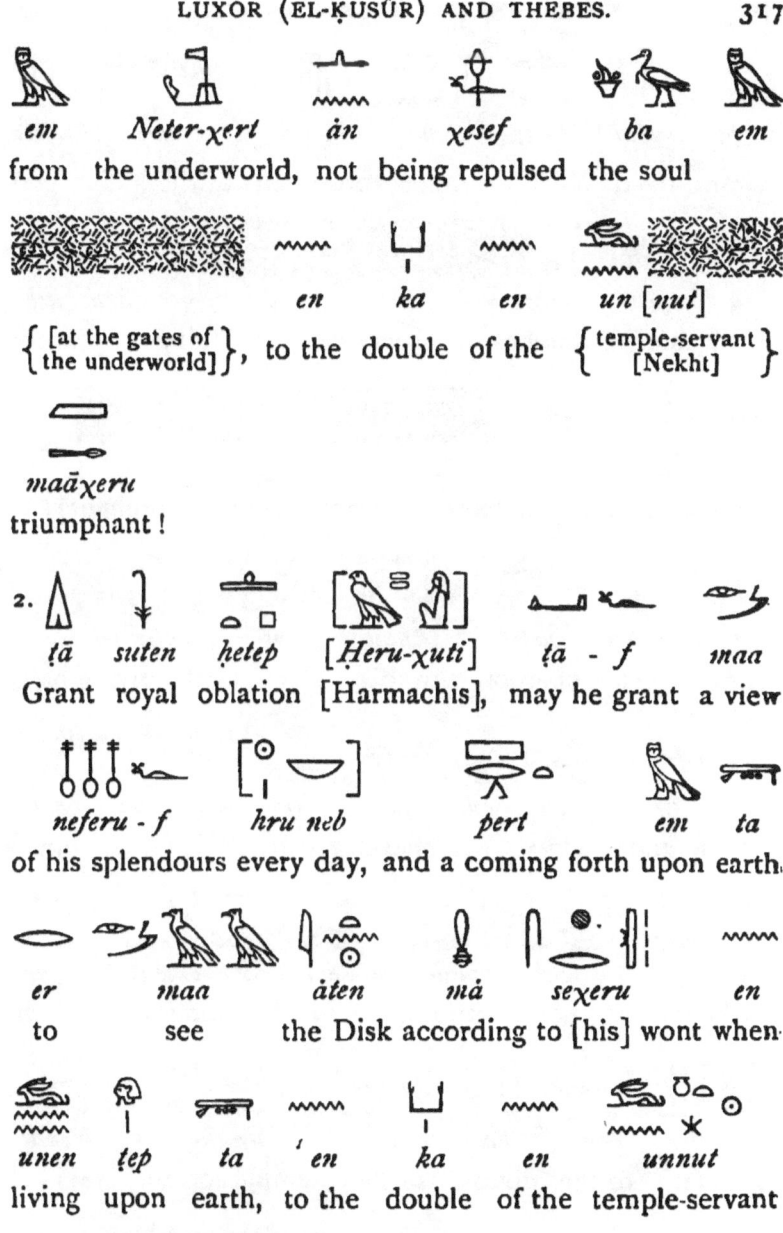

neferu - *f* *hru neb* *pert* *em* *ta*

of his splendours every day, and a coming forth upon earth.

er *maa* *ȧten* *mȧ* *seχeru* *en*

to see the Disk according to [his] wont when

unen *ṭep* *ta* *en* *ka* *en* *unnut*

living upon earth, to the double of the temple-servant

. . . . [Nekht, triumphant]!

3. 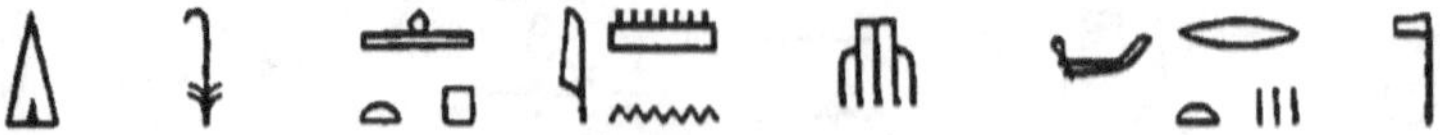

ṭā suten ḥetep Åmen χent sert neter

Grant royal oblation Åmen, president of the . . . . . god

āa ḥer Uast χet hru neb

great, chief of Thebes, . . . [may he grant] things day every

en ka en

to the double of [the temple-servant Nekht, triumphant]!

4. 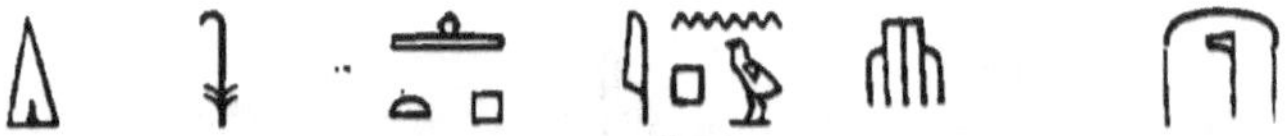

ṭā suten ḥetep Ånpu χent neter seḥ

Grant royal oblation Anubis, chief of the divine hall,

ṭā - f χu em pet χer Rā us em

may he grant glory in heaven with Rā, power upon

ta χer Seb maāχeru em Set-Åmentet χer

earth with Seb, triumph in the underworld with

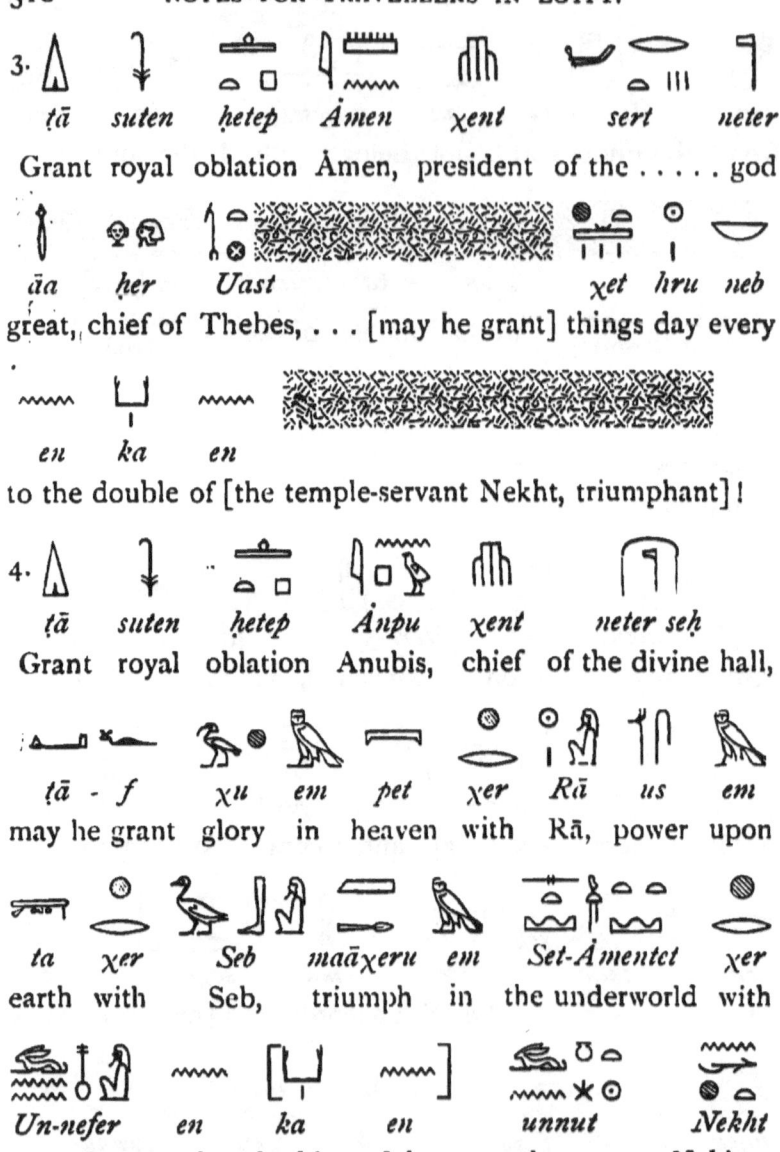

Un-nefer en ka en unnut Nekht

Unnefer, to the double of the temple-servant Nekht.

On the upper part of the stele the deceased Nekht and his sister and wife Taui, a lady of the College of Amen, are represented sitting before a table of offerings; the inscription reads, "a coming forth always to the table of the lords of eternity every day, to the *ka* of the temple servant, Nekht, triumphant, and to his sister, the lady of the house, triumphant!" Beneath this scenes are two *utchats* facing each other , and the signs . The four perpendicular lines of inscription state that the deceased is "watchfully devoted" to the four children of Horus, whose names are Mesthȧ , Qebḥsennuf 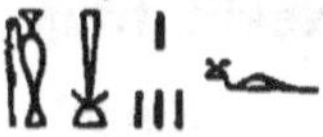, Ḥāpi , and Ṭuamāutef .

On the right of the stele are :—

1. Kneeling figure of a man offering , and the legend,  *ṭā em ḥeqt en ān Nekht*, "the giving of beer to the scribe Nekht."

2. Kneeling figure of a man offering two vases , and the legend   *erṭāt āb en ȧrp en Ȧusȧr unnut ān Nekht āb-k āb Set*, "the giving of a vase of wine to Osiris the temple-servant, the scribe Nekht. Thou art pure, Set is pure."

3. Kneeling figure of a man offering , and the legend  *erṭāt menχ ḥebs en Ausȧr ān Nekht*, "the giving of linen bandages to Osiris, the scribe Nekht."

On the left of the stele are :—

1. Kneeling figure offering , , *etc.*, and the legend  *erṭāt neter ḥetep en ān Nekht*, "the giving of holy offerings to the scribe Nekht."

2. Kneeling figure of a man offering , and the legend 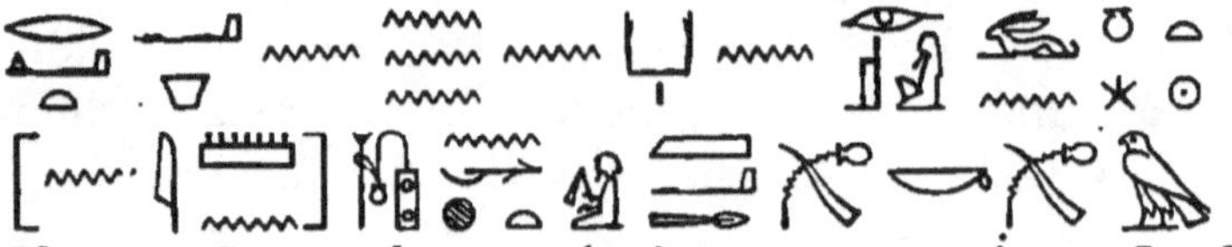 *erṭāt āb en māu en ka en Ausȧr unnut en Ȧmen ān Nekht maāχeru āb-k āb Ḥeru*, "the giving of a vase of water to the double of Osiris, the temple-servant of Ȧmen, the scribe Nekht, triumphant! Thou art pure, Horus is pure."

3. Kneeling figure of a man offering 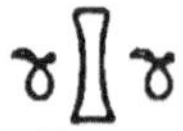, and the legend,  *erṭāt meṭ'et uat' mesṭem en ān Nekht maāχeru*, "the giving of fresh unguents and eye-paint to the scribe Nekht, triumphant!"

Beneath the stele is shown a pile of funereal offerings consisting of fruits and flowers, bread and cakes, ducks, haunches of beef, *etc.*; on each side is a female wearing a sycamore, the emblem of the goddess Hathor, upon her head, and holding offerings of fruit, flowers, *etc.*, in her hands, and behind each is a young man bringing additional offerings.

The scene on the wall at the other end of the chamber was never finished by the artist. In the upper division are Nekht and his wife Taui seated, having a table loaded with funereal offerings before them; a priestly official and the nine *smeri* bring offerings of oil, flowers, *etc.* In the lower division also are Nekht and his wife Taui seated, having a table of offerings before them, and four priestly officials are bringing haunches of veal or beef to them.

On the wall to the left of the doorway leading into the smaller chamber are painted the following scenes connected with agriculture:—1. An arm of the Nile or a canal. On one side are men ploughing with oxen, and labourers breaking up hard sods with mallets, while a third scatters the seed; on the other are seen men digging up the ground with hoes, and the sower sowing seed. At one end sits the deceased Nekht in the *seḥ* hall, , and at the other is a tree having a water-skin on one of the branches, from which a man drinks. 2. Men reaping, a woman gleaning, men tying up sheaves in a sack, women twisting flax. 3. The measuring of the grain. 4. Winnowing the grain. Above the head of Nekht, who sits in a *seḥ* chamber, is the inscription :—

ḥemset *em* *seḥ* *maa* *seχet* - *f* *ȧn*
Sitting in the seḥ seeth his fields

unnut *en* *maāχeru* *χer*
the temple-servant of [Åmen, Nekht], triumphant before

neter *āā*
the great god.

On the left of the agricultural scenes stands Nekht pouring out a libation over an altar loaded with all manner of funereal offerings; behind him is his wife Taui holding a *menȧt* , emblem of joy and pleasure, in her right hand, and a sistrum in her left. Beneath the altar two priests are sacrificing a bull. The inscription above the whole scene reads :—

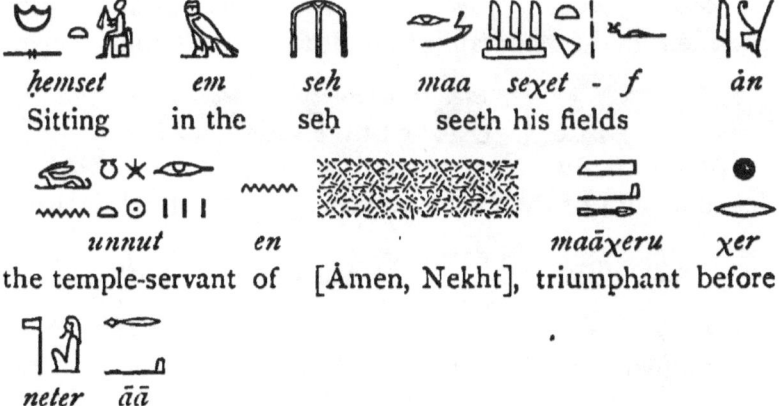

uten *χet* *nebt* *nefert* *ābt* *ta* *ḥeq* *ȧḥ*
Offering of things all beautiful, pure, bread, beer, oxen,

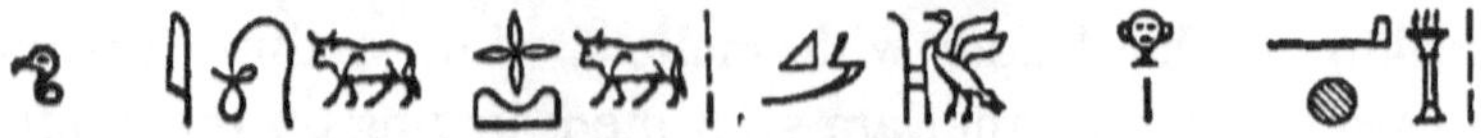

apt *àua* *unṭu* *qema* *ḥer* *āχ*
ducks, heifers, calves, to be made upon the altars

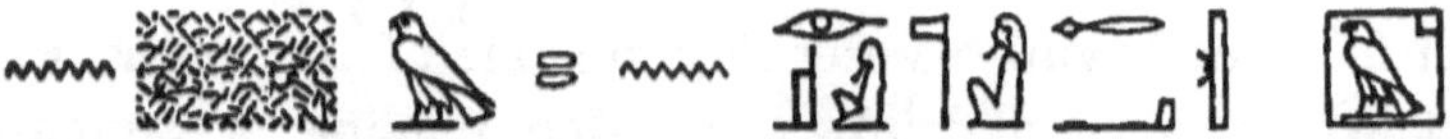

en *Ḥeru-χuti* *en* *Ȧusȧr neter* *āā* *Ḥet-Ḥeru*
of . . . . . Harmachis to Osiris, god great, and Hathor

hert *set* *en* *Ȧnp* *ḥer*
president of the mountain of the dead, to Anubis upon

ṭu - f *àn* *unnut* *sent - f*
his mountain by the temple-servant . . . . Nekht. His sister,

mert - f *en·* *àuset* *àb - f* *qemāit*
his darling, of the seat of his heart, the singing priestess

en
of [Ȧmen, Taui, triumphant !]

On the wall to the right of the doorway leading into the smaller chamber are painted the following scenes :—Upper register. Nekht in a boat, accompanied by his wife and children, spearing fish and bringing down birds with the boomerang in a papyrus swamp. Above is the inscription :—

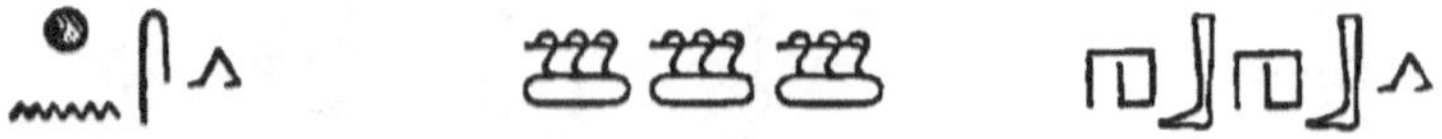

χenes *seś* *hebheb*
Passeth through wild-fowl marshes, traverseth

seš *seχemχem* *satet* *meḥit*
wild-fowl marshes with gladness, speareth fish

àn *Nekht* *maāχeru*
Nekht, triumphant!

On the bank stand two of Nekht's servants holding sandals, staff, boomerang, *etc.*, and beneath is another servant carrying to Nekht the birds which Nekht himself has brought down. The inscriptions above read :—

1. 

seχemχem *maa* *bu* *nefer* *àri* *seχet*
Rejoiceth, seeth happiness [in] making the chase,

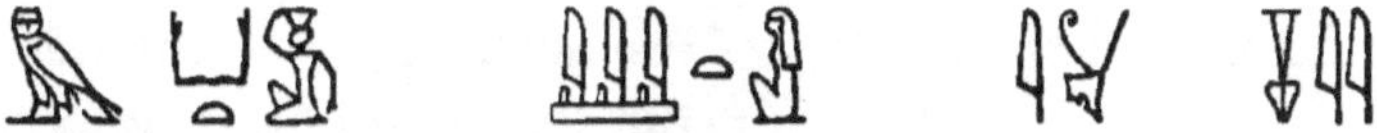

em *kat* *Seχet* *àn* *sami*
[and] in the work of the goddess Sekhet, the friend

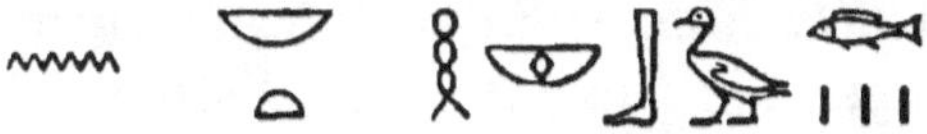 *etc.*

en *nebt* *ḥebu*
of the lady of the chase, the temple-servant, the scribe Nekht, triumphant!

2. 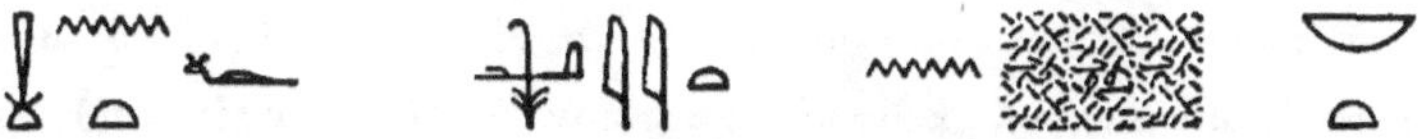

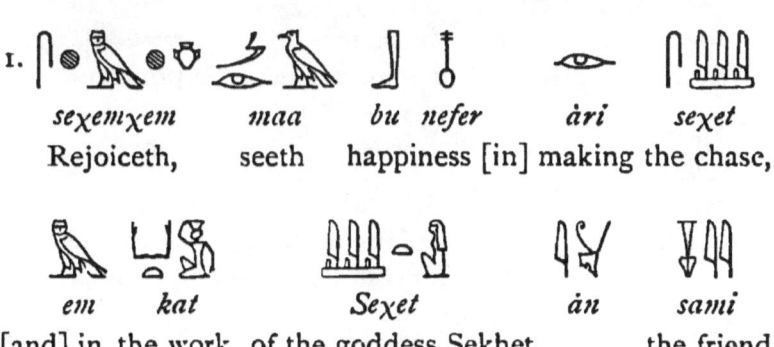

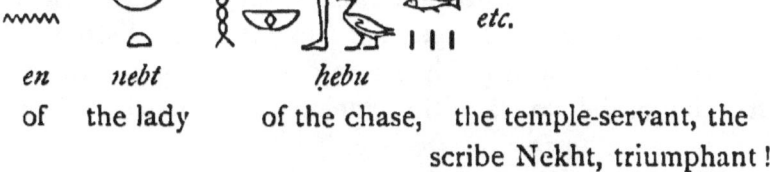

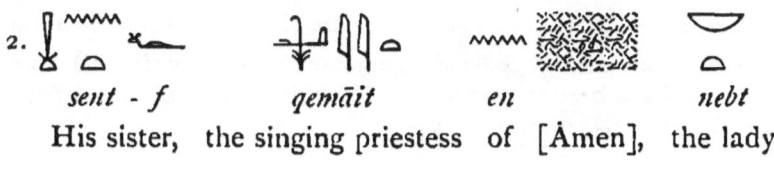

sent - f *qemāit* *en* *nebt*
His sister, the singing priestess of [Àmen], the lady

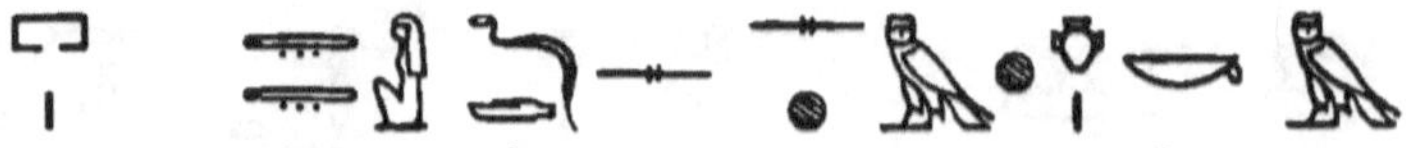

pa *Taui* *t'eṭ - s* *seχemχem - k* *em*

of the house, Taui, saith, "Rejoice thou in

kat *Seχet* *qebḥ* *àp - nef*

the work of Sekhet,* [and] the birds [which] he sets apart

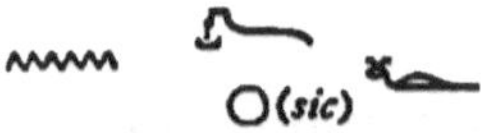

en *setep - f*

for his selection."

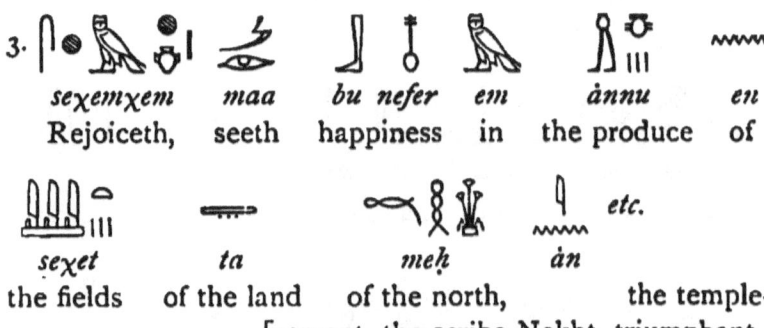

3\. 

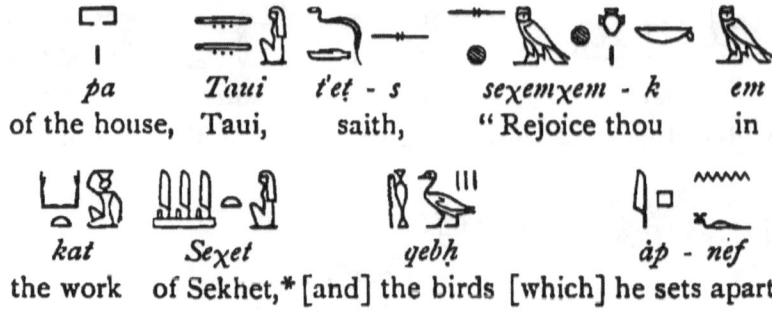

seχemχem *maa* *bu nefer* *em* *ànnu* *en*

Rejoiceth, seeth happiness in the produce of

seχet *ta* *meḥ* *àn*

the fields of the land of the north, the temple-[servant, the scribe Nekht, triumphant !

Lower register. Nekht and his wife sitting in a summer-house "to make himself glad and to experience the happiness of the land of the north" (*i.e.*, Lower Egypt); before them funereal offerings are heaped up. In the upper division of this register are seen Nekht's servants gathering grapes, the treading of the grapes in the wine-press, the drawing of the

* Sekhet was the goddess of the country, and was the wife of the god Khnum. She is represented with the sign for field [hieroglyph], upon her head, she wears a girdle of lotus plants round her waist, and upon her hands she bears a plantation filled with all manner of wild fowl. See Lanzone, *Dizionario*, p. 1095.

new wine, the jars for holding it, and two servants making offerings to Nekht of birds, flowers, *etc.* In the lower division we see Nekht instructing his servants in the art of snaring birds in nets, the plucking and cleaning of the birds newly caught, and two servants offering to Nekht fish, birds, fruit, *etc.*

In the other scenes we have Nekht, accompanied by his wife Taui, making an offering of *ānta* unguent and incense to the gods of the tomb, and a representation of his funereal feast.

The most ancient necropolis at Thebes is Drah abu'l Neḳḳah, where tombs of the XIth, XVIIth, and XVIIIth dynasties are to be found. The coffins of the Ȧntef kings (XIth dynasty), now in the Louvre and the British Museum, were discovered here, and here was made the marvellous "find" of the jewellery of Ȧāḥ-ḥetep,* wife of Kames, a king of the XVIIth dynasty, about B.C. 1750. A little more to the south is the necropolis of Asasîf, where during the XIXth, XXIInd, and XXVIth dynasties many beautiful tombs were constructed. If the visitor has time, an attempt should be made to see the fine tomb of Peṭā-Ȧmen-ȧpt.

ARMANT (ERMENT).

Armant, or Erment, 458½ miles from Cairo, on the west bank of the river, was called in Egyptian 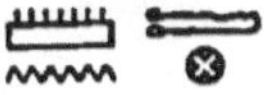 Menth, and 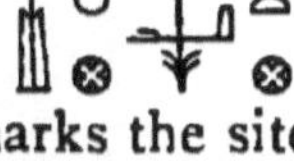 Ȧnnu qemāt, "Heliopolis of the South"; it marks the site of the ancient Hermonthis, where, according to Strabo, "Apollo and Jupiter are both worshipped."

The ruins which remain there belong to the Iseion built during the reign of the last Cleopatra (B.C. 51–29). The stone-lined tank which lies near this building was probably used as a Nilometer.

* Now preserved at Gîzeh, see page 199.

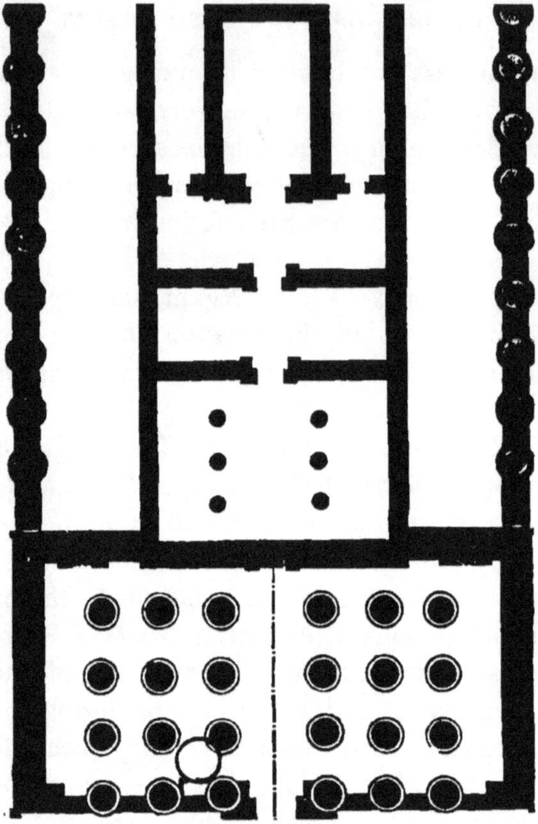

Plan of Temple of Esneh, with restorations by Grand Bey.

ESNEH.

Esneh, or Asneh, 484½ miles from Cairo, on the west bank of the river, was called in Egyptian 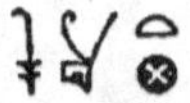 Senet; it marks the site of the ancient Latopolis, and was so called by the Greeks, because its inhabitants worshipped the Latus fish. Thothmes III. founded a temple here, but the interesting building which now stands almost in the middle of the modern town is of late date, and bears the names of several of the Roman emperors. The portico is supported by twenty-four columns, each of which is inscribed; their capitals are handsome. The Zodiac here, like that at Denderah, belongs to a late period, but is interesting.

EL-KÂB.

El-Kâb, 502 miles from Cairo, on the east bank of the river, was called in Egyptian  Necheb; it marks the site of the ancient Eileithyias. There was a city here in very ancient days, and ruins of temples built by Thothmes IV., Âmenḥetep III., Seti I., Rameses II., Rameses III., Ptolemy IX. Euergetes II. are still visible. A little distance from the town, in the mountain, is the tomb of Âāḥmes (Amāsis), the son of Abana, an officer born in the reign of Seqenen-Rā, who fought against the Hyksos, and who served under Amāsis I., Amenophis I., and Thothmes I. The inscription on the walls of his tomb gives an account of the campaign against some Mesopotamian enemies of Egypt and of the siege of their city. Amāsis was the "Captain-General of Sailors." The tomb of his daughter's son Pahir lies just above his. In the winter of 1894–5 some interesting excavations were carried out at El-Kâb by Mr. Somers Clarke; an account of the results obtained by him has recently been published.

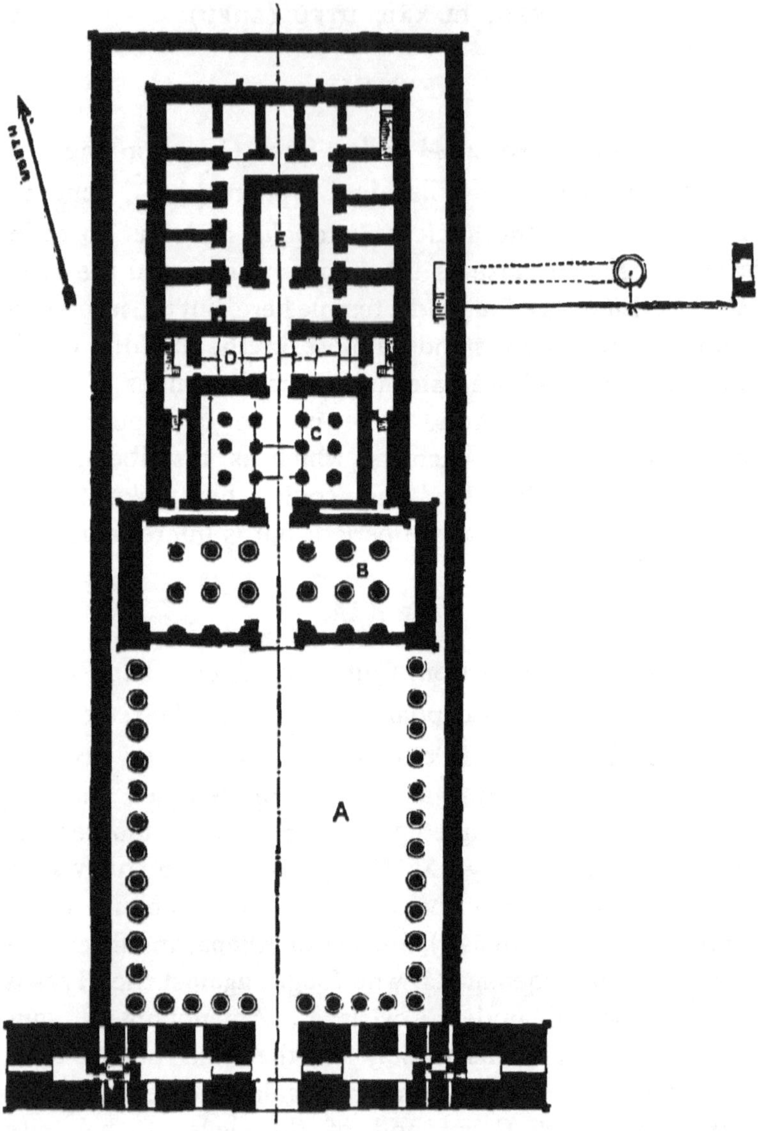

Plan of the Great Temple of Edfû.

UṬFÛ (EDFÛ).

Edfû, 515½ miles from Cairo, on the west bank of the river, was called in Egyptian  Beḥuṭet, and in Coptic ⲁⲃⲧⲱ; it was called by the Greeks Apollino polis Magna, where the crocodile and its worshippers were detested. The **Temple of Edfû**, for which alone both the ancient and modern towns were famous, occupied 180 years three months and fourteen days in building, that is to say it was begun during the reign of Ptolemy Euergetes I., B.C. 237, and finished B.C. 57. It resembles that of Denderah in many respects, but its complete condition marks it out as one of the most remarkable buildings in Egypt, and its splendid towers, about 112 feet high, make its general magnificence very striking. The space enclosed by the walls measures 450 × 120 feet; the front of the propylon from side to side measures about 252 feet. Passing through the door the visitor enters a court, around three sides of which runs a gallery supported on thirty-two pillars. The first and second halls, A, B, have eighteen and twelve pillars respectively; passing through chambers C and D, the shrine E is reached, where stood a granite naos in which a figure of Horus, to whom the temple is dedicated, was preserved. This naos was made by Nectanebus I., a king of the XXXth dynasty, B.C. 378.

The pylons are covered with battle scenes, and the walls are inscribed with the names and sizes of the various chambers in the building, lists of names of places, etc.; the name of the architect, Î-em-ḥetep, or Imouthis, has also been inscribed. From the south side of the pylons, and from a small chamber on each side of the chamber C, staircases ascended to the roof.

The credit of clearing out the temple of Edfû belongs to M. Mariette. Little more than twenty-five years ago the mounds of rubbish outside reached to the top of its walls, and certain parts of the roof were entirely covered over with houses and stables.

HAGAR SILSILEH.

Hagar (or Gebel) **Silsileh,** 541½ miles from Cairo, on the east and west banks of the river, derives its name probably not from the Arabic word of like sound meaning "chain," but from the Coptic ϫωλϫελ, meaning "stone wall"; the place is usually called  *Chennu* in hieroglyphic texts. The ancient Egyptians here quarried the greater part of the sandstone used by them in their buildings, and the names of the kings inscribed in the caves here show that these quarries were used from the earliest to the latest periods. The most extensive of these are to be found on the east bank of the river, but those on the west bank contain the interesting tablets of Ḥeru-em-ḥeb, a king of the XVIIIth dynasty, who is represented conquering the Ethiopians, Seti I., Rameses II. his son, Meneptaḥ, etc. At Silsileh the Nile was worshipped, and the little temple which Rameses II. built in this place seems to have been dedicated chiefly to it. At this point the Nile narrows very much, and it is generally thought that a cataract once existed here; there is, however, no evidence to show when the Nile broke through and swept such a barrier, if it ever existed, away.

KOM OMBO.

Kom Ombo, 556½ miles from Cairo, on the east bank of the Nile, was an important place at all periods of Egyptian history; it was called by the Egyptians 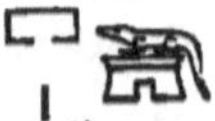, Pa-Sebek, "the temple of Sebek" (the crocodile god), and

, Nubit, and ⲙ̀ⲃⲱ by the Copts. The oldest object here is a sandstone gateway which Thothmes III. dedicated to the god Seḇek.

The temple is double, and consists of a large court containing sixteen columns inscribed with the cartouche of Tiberius, and a hypostyle hall containing nineteen columns about 40 feet high. The pronaos has ten columns, three chambers, and two shrines; one shrine is dedicated to Sebek and the other to Ḥeru-ur or Aroueris. The temple measures about 500 feet by 250 feet, and stands at a height of about 40 feet above the level of the Nile during its low season. By the side which fronted the river there originally stood a propylon and a small temple built by Domitian; on the right of this stood the *mammisi*. The bas-reliefs upon the walls and columns are exceedingly fine, and the delicacy of the colours and the fineness of the workmanship are equal, if not superior, to the art displayed at Edfu and Philæ. The inscriptions, although of a religious character, are of considerable interest, and among them may be mentioned (1), the dedicatory address of Ptolemy VII.; (2), the calendar of the festivals; (3), ephemerides with the names of the deities who preside over the days of the year; (4) and the texts referring to the geography of the nomes. The whole site of the temple has been recently laid bare by M. de Morgan.

ASWAN.

Aswân (or Uswân), the southern limit of Egypt proper, 583 miles from Cairo, on the east bank of the river, called in Egyptian , Coptic ⲥⲟⲩⲁⲛ, was called by the Greeks Syene, which stood on the slope of a hill to the south-west of the present town. Properly speaking Syene was the island of Elephantine. In the earliest Egyptian inscriptions it is called , or , Àbu, *i.e.*, "the district of the elephant," and it formed the metropolis of the first nome of Upper Egypt. As we approach the time of the Ptolemies, the name Sunnu, *i.e.*, the town on the east bank of the Nile, from whence comes the Arabic name Aswân, takes the place of Àbu. The town obtained great notoriety among the ancients from the fact that Eratosthenes and Ptolemy considered it to lie on the tropic of Cancer, and to be the most northerly point where, at the time of the summer solstice, the sun's rays fell vertically; as a matter of fact, however, the town lies 0′ 37′ 23″ north of the tropic of Cancer. There was a famous well there, into which the sun was said to shine at the summer solstice, and to illuminate it in every part. In the time of the Romans three cohorts were stationed here,* and the town was of considerable importance. In the twelfth century of our era it was the seat of a bishop. Of its size in ancient days

* It is interesting to observe that the Romans, like the British, held Egypt by garrisoning three places, viz. Aswân, Babylon (Cairo), and Alexandria. The garrison at Aswân defended Egypt from foes on the south, and commanded the entrance of the Nile; the garrison at Babylon guarded the end of the Nile valley and the entrance to the Delta; and the garrison at Alexandria protected the country from invasion by sea.

nothing definite can be said, but Arabic writers describe it as a flourishing town, and they relate that a plague once swept off 20,000 of its inhabitants. Aswân was famous for its wine in Ptolemaic times. The town has suffered greatly at the hands of the Persians, Arabs, and Turks on the north, and Nubians, by whom it was nearly destroyed in the twelfth century, on the south. The oldest ruins in the town are those of a Ptolemaic temple, which are still visible.

The island of **Elephantine** * lies a little to the north of the cataract just opposite Aswân, and has been famous in all ages as the key of Egypt from the south; the Romans garrisoned it with numerous troops, and it represented the southern limit of their empire. The island itself was very fertile, and it is said that its vines and fig-trees retained their leaves throughout the year. The kings of the Vth dynasty sprang from Elephantine. The gods worshipped here by the Egyptians were called Chnemu, Sati and Sept, and on this island Amenophis III. built a temple, remains of which were visible in the early part of this century. Of the famous Nilometer which stood here, Strabo says: "The Nilometer is a well upon the banks of the Nile, constructed of close-fitting stones, on which are marked the greatest, least, and mean risings of the Nile; for the water in the well and in the river rises and subsides simultaneously. Upon the wall

* "A little above Elephantine is the lesser cataract, where the boatmen exhibit a sort of spectacle to the governors. The cataract is in the middle of the river, and is formed by a ridge of rocks, the upper part of which is level, and thus capable of receiving the river, but terminating in a precipice, where the water dashes down. On each side towards the land there is a stream, up which is the chief ascent for vessels. The boatmen sail up by this stream, and, dropping down to the cataract, are impelled with the boat to the precipice, the crew and the boats escaping unhurt." (Strabo, Bk. xvii. chap. i., 49, Falconer's translation.) Thus it appears that "shooting the cataract" is a very old amusement.

of the well are lines, which indicate the complete rise of the river, and other degrees of its rising. Those who examine these marks communicate the result to the public for their information. For it is known long before, by these marks, and by the time elapsed from the commencement, what the future rise of the river will be, and notice is given of it. This information is of service to the husbandmen with reference to the distribution of the water; for the purpose also of attending to the embankments, canals, and other things of this kind. It is of use also to the governors, who fix the revenue; for the greater the rise of the river, the greater it is expected will be the revenue." According to Plutarch the Nile rose at Elephantine to the height of 28 cubits; a very interesting text at Edfû states that if the river rises 24 cubits 3¼ hands at Elephantine, it will water the country satisfactorily.

To the south-west of Atrûn island, in a sandy valley, lie the ruins of an ancient building of the sixth or seventh century of our era, half convent, half fortress. A dome, ornamented with coloured representations of Saints Michael, George, and Gabriel, and the twelve Apostles, still remains in a good state of preservation. To the east of the convent is the cemetery, where some interesting stelæ and linen fragments were found.

A mile or so to the north of the convent stands the bold hill in the sides of which are hewn the tombs which General Sir F. W. Grenfell, G.C.B., excavated; this hill is situated in Western Aswân, the ⲥⲟⲩⲁⲛ ⲙⲙ ⲡⲉⲙⲙⲉⲛⲧ of the Copts, and is the Contra Syene of the classical authors. The tombs are hewn out of the rock, tier above tier, and the most important of these were reached by a stone staircase, which to this day remains nearly complete, and is one of the most interesting antiquities in Egypt. The tombs in this hill may be roughly divided into three groups. The first group was hewn in the best and thickest layer of stone in the top of the hill, and was made for the rulers of Elephantine who lived during the VIth and XIIth dynasties. The second group is composed of tombs of different periods; they are hewn out of a lower layer of stone, and are not of so much importance. The third group, made during the Roman occupation of Egypt, lies at a comparatively little height above the river. All these tombs were broken into at a very early period, and the largest of them formed a common sepulchre for people of all classes from the XXVIth dynasty downwards. They were found filled with broken coffins and mummies and sepulchral stelæ, etc., etc., and everything showed how degraded Egyptian funereal art had become when these bodies were buried there. The double tomb at the head of the staircase was made for Sabben and Mechu; the former was a dignitary of high rank who lived during the reign of Pepi II., a king of the VIth dynasty, whose prenomen  Nefer-ka-Rā is inscribed on the left hand side of the doorway; the latter was a *smer*, prince and inspector, who appears to have lived during the XIIth dynasty. The paintings on the walls and the proto-Doric columns which support the roof are interesting, and its fine state of preservation and position makes it one of the most valuable monuments of that early period. A little further northward is tne small tomb of 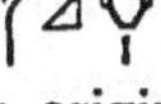 Ḥeqâb, and beyond this is the fine, large tomb hewn originally for Se-Renput, one of the old feudal hereditary governors of Elephantine, but which was appropriated by Nub-kau-Rā-necht. He was the governor of the district of the cataract, and the general who commanded a lightly-armed body of soldiers called "runners"; he lived during the reign of Usertsen I., the second king of the XIIth dynasty, and his tomb must have been one of the earliest hewn there during that period. Another interesting tomb is that of Ḥeru-khuf, and the inscriptions show that the kings of Egypt were in the habit of sending officers into the Sûdân to bring back pigmies to amuse them. It is much to be hoped that the good work begun here by Sir Francis Grenfell will be continued systematically, and that the whole site could be thoroughly explored.

Aswân was as famous for its granite, as Silsileh was for its sandstone. The Egyptian kings were in the habit of sending to Aswân for granite to make sarcophagi, temples, obelisks, etc., and it will be remembered that Unȧ was sent there to bring back in barges granite for the use of Pepi I., a king of the VIth dynasty. It is probable that the granite slabs which cover the pyramid of Mycerinus (IVth dynasty) were brought from Aswân. The undetached obelisk, which still lies in one of the quarries, is an interesting object.

Near the quarries are two ancient Arabic cemeteries, in which are a number of sandstone grave-stones, many of them formed from stones taken from Ptolemaic buildings, inscribed in Cufic * characters with the names of the Muḥammadans buried there, and the year, month, and day on which they died. We learn from them that natives of Edfû and other parts of Egypt were sometimes brought here and buried.

The first **Cataract**, called Shellâl by the Arabs, begins a little to the south of Aswân, and ends a little to the north of the island of Philæ; eight cataracts are reckoned on the Nile, but this is the most generally known. Here the Nile becomes narrow and flows between two mountains, which descend nearly perpendicularly to the river, the course of which is obstructed by huge boulders and small rocky islands and barriers, which stand on different levels, and

* A kind of Arabic writing in which very old copies of the Ḳor'ân, etc., are written: it takes its name from Kûfah, الكوفة *El-Kûfa*, a town on the Euphrates. Kûfah was one of the chief cities of 'Irâḳ, and is famous in the Muḥammadan world because Muḥammad and his immediate successors dwelt there. Enoch lived here, the ark was built here, the boiling waters of the Flood first burst out here, and Abraham had a place of prayer set apart here.

cause the falls of water which have given this part of the river its name. On the west side the obstacles are not so numerous as on the east, and sailing and rowing boats can ascend the cataract on this side when the river is high. The noise made by the water is at times very great, but it has been greatly exaggerated by both ancient and modern travellers, some of whom ventured to assert that the "water fell from several places in the mountain more than two hundred feet." Some ancient writers asserted that the fountains of the Nile were in this cataract, and Herodotus* reports that an official of the treasury of Neith at Sais stated that the source of the Nile was here. Many of the rocks here are inscribed with the names of kings who reigned during the Middle Empire; in many places on the little islands in the cataract quarries were worked. The island of **Sehêl** should be visited on account of the numerous inscriptions left there by princes, generals, and others who passed by on their way to Nubia. On February 6th, 1889, Mr. Wilbour was fortunate enough to discover on the south-eastern part of this island a most important stele consisting of a rounded block of granite, eight or nine feet high, which stands clear above the water, and in full view from the river looking towards Philæ. Upon it are inscribed thirty-two lines of hieroglyphics which form a remarkable document, and contain some valuable information bearing upon a famous seven years' famine. The inscription is dated in the eighteenth year of a king whose name is read by Dr. Brugsch as T'eser 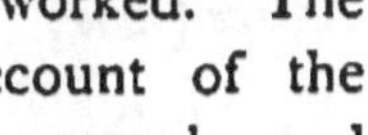, 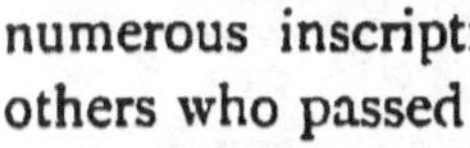, or 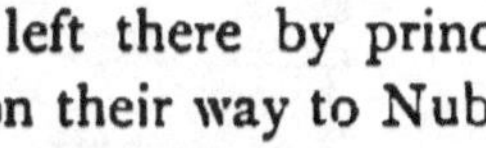, who is thought to have reigned early in the IIIrd dynasty; but internal evidence proves beyond a doubt that the narrative contained therein is a redaction of an old story, and thus

* Bk. ii., chap. 28.

it is, in its present form, not older than the time of the Ptolemies. In the second line we are told :—

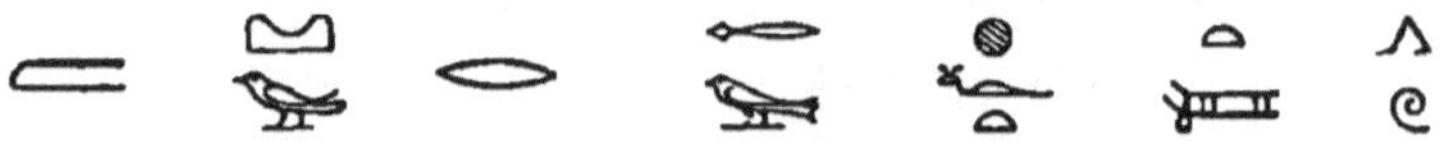

em ṭu er āa ur χeft tem iu

By misfortune the very greatest not had come forth

Ḥapu em rek em āḥā renpit seχef

the Nile during a period lasting years seven.

ket nepi uśer renp

Scarce [*was*] *grain, lacking* [*was*] *vegetable food,*

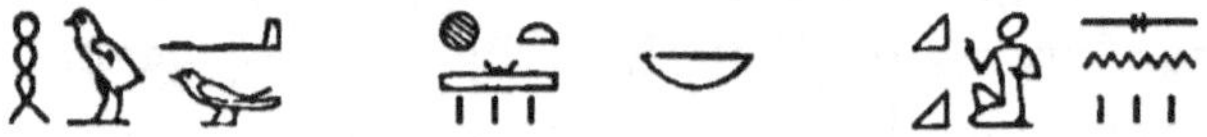

ḥuā χet neb qeq - sen

[*there was a*] *dearth of everything* [*which men*] *ate.*

In this time of distress the king despatched a messenger to Matar, the governor of Elephantine, informing him of the terrible state of want and misery which the country was in, and asking him to give him information about the source of the Nile, and about the god or goddess who presided over it, and promising to worship this deity henceforth if he would make the harvests full as of yore. Matar informed the messenger concerning these things, and when the king had heard his words he at once ordered rich sacrifices to be made to Chnemu, the god of Elephantine, and decreed that tithes of every product of the land should be paid to his temple. This done the famine came to an end and the Nile rose again to its accustomed height. There can be no connection between this seven years' famine and that recorded in the Bible, for it must have happened some two thousand years before Joseph could have been in Egypt; but this remarkable inscription proves that from time immemorial the people of Egypt have suffered from periodic famines. The village of Mahâtah, on the east bank of the river, is prettily situated, and worth a visit.

PHILÆ.

Philæ is the name given by the Greeks and Romans to the smaller of two islands situated at the head of the first cataract, about six miles above Aswân; the larger one is called Biggeh. Inscriptions found on rocks in the larger island show that as far back as the time of Amenophis II. an Egyptian temple stood here; the greater number of these inscriptions were cut by Egyptian officials on their way to and from Nubia. The smaller island, to which the name Philæ is generally confined, consists of a granite rock, the sides of which, having been scarped, have had walls built on them; it measures 417 yards long and 135 yards wide. The name of this island in Egyptian was  P-āa-leq, Coptic ⲡⲓⲗⲁⲕ, *i.e.*, 'the frontier.' The monuments on this island are numerous and interesting, but they belong to a comparatively late date, none that have yet been found being older than the time of Nectanebus, the last native king of Egypt. On the south-west corner are the remains of the small temple which this king dedicated to Isis. The most important ruins are those of the Temple of Isis, which was begun by Ptolemy II. Philadelphus and Arsinoë, and was added to and completed by the Ptolemies and Roman emperors who came after. On each side of the path which led to the temple is a corridor: that on the west has thirty-two pillars and that on the east sixteen; at the north end of the east corridor is the so-called chapel of Æsculapius, which was built by Ptolemy V. Epiphanes and

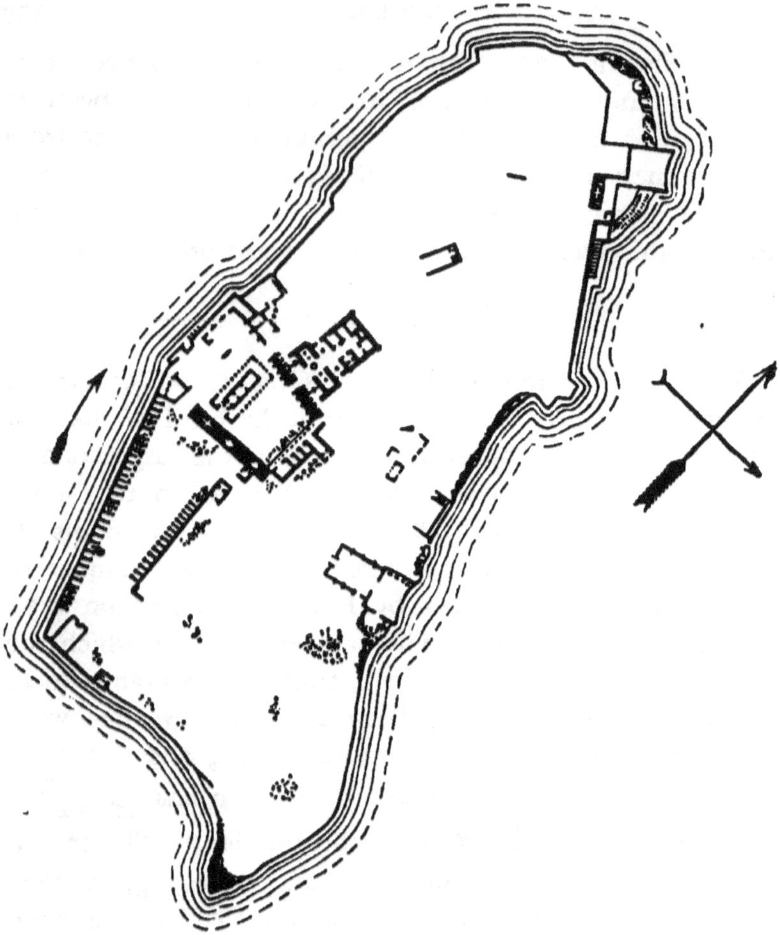

Plan of the Buildings on the Island of Philæ.

Cleopatra. The towers of the first propylon are about 65 feet high, and their southern faces are ornamented with sculptures representing Ptolemy VII. Philometor triumphing over his enemies. On the east side of the large court, which is entered through the propylon, is a portico with ten columns, and on the west side are the three chambers forming the so-called mammisi, on the walls of which are representations of the birth of Horus. In this courtyard there is a copy of the famous Rosetta Stone inscription, given, unfortunately, without the Greek text. Passing through the second propylon, a portico having ten beautifully painted capitals is entered, and north of this are three chambers, in the last of which is the monolith shrine. Round and about are several small chambers and passages with secret openings. When Strabo visited the island he saw the hawk which was worshipped there, and which was said to have been brought from Ethiopia.*

On the western side of the island stands the beautiful little temple usually called Pharaoh's bed, and a little to the north of it is a small temple built by Ptolemy IX. Euergetes II.; the other ruins on the island are not of importance, but if time permits, a visit should be paid to the **Nilometer** built in a staircase leading down to the river. Philæ was said to be one of the burial places of Osiris, and as such was held in the greatest esteem by both Egyptians and Ethiopians; it was considered a most holy place, and only priests

* "A little above the cataract is Philæ, a common settlement, like Elephantina, of Ethiopians and Egyptians, and equal in size, containing Egyptian temples, where a bird, which they call hierax (the hawk), is worshipped; but it did not appear to me to resemble in the least the hawks of our country nor of Egypt, for it was larger, and very different in the marks of its plumage. They said that the bird was Ethiopian, and is brought from Ethiopia when its predecessor dies, or before its death. The one shown to us when we were there was sick and nearly dead"—(Strabo, xvii., 1-49, Falconer's translation.)

were allowed to live there unmolested. An oath sworn by Osiris of Philæ was inviolable, and the worship of this god flourished here until A.D. 453, that is to say, seventy years after the proclamation of the famous edict of Theodosius against the religion of Egypt. In the time of the Romans a strong garrison was stationed here. In Coptic times a Christian church, remains of which are still visible, was built on the northern end of Philæ. The picturesque scenery at Philæ is too well known to need comment.

A few years ago lovers of Philæ were astonished at a proposal, on the part of the Irrigation Department, to build a dam near Aswân for the purpose of storing Nile water, and for regulating its supply to the lower country. The carrying out of the proposal in its original form would have submerged the temples on the Island of Philæ for several months each year. Major Lyons, R.E., has recently finished an exhaustive survey of the whole island, and published the results in a handsome folio volume, with a long series of beautiful plates. In a preface to the work, Sir W. E. Garstin assures us that if the dam ever be built, the stored up water will never reach to a height round the island sufficient to damage the buildings.

THE NILE BETWEEN THE FIRST AND SECOND CATARACTS.

The country which is entered on leaving Philæ is generally known by the name of Ethiopia, or Nubia; the latter name has been derived by some from *nub*, the Egyptian word for gold, because in ancient days much gold was brought into Egypt from that land. In the hieroglyphics, Nubia or Ethiopia, is generally called 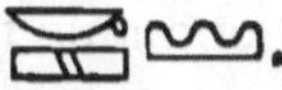 Kesh (the Cush of the Bible) and 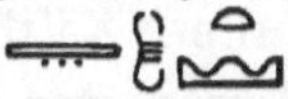 Ta-kenset; from the latter name the Arabic El-kenûs is derived. It is known that, as far back as the VIth dynasty, the Egyptians sent to this country for certain kinds of wood, and that all the chief tribes which lived round about Korosko, hastened to help the Egyptian officer Unȧ in the mission which he undertook for King Pepi I. It seems pretty certain too, if we may trust Unȧ's words, that the whole country was made to acknowledge the sovereignty of the Egyptian king. From the VIIth to the XIth dynasty nothing is known of the relations which existed between the two countries, but in the time of Usertsen I., the second king of the XIIth dynasty, an expedition was undertaken by the Egyptians for the purpose of fixing the boundaries of the two countries, and we know from a stele set up at Wâdi Ḥalfah by this king, that his rule extended as far south as this place. Two reigns later the inhabitants of Nubia or Ethiopia had become so troublesome, that Usertsen III. found it necessary to build fortresses at Semneh and Kummeh, south of the second cataract, and to make stringent laws forbidding the passage of any negro ship unless it was laden with cattle or merchandise.

The Hyksos kings appear not to have troubled greatly about Nubia. When the XVIIIth dynasty had obtained full power in Egypt, some of its greatest kings, such as Thothmes III. and Åmenḥetep III., marched into Nubia and built temples there; under the rulers of the XIXth dynasty, the country became to all intents and purposes a part of Egypt. Subsequently the Nubians appear to have acquired considerable power, and as Egypt became involved in conflicts with more Northern countries, this power increased until Nubia was able to declare itself independent. For several hundreds of years the Nubians had the benefit of Egyptian civilization, and all that it could teach them, and they were soon able to organize war expeditions into Egypt with success. As early as the XXVth dynasty, the territory to the north of Syene or Aswân was a part of the Nubian or Ethiopian kingdom, the second capital of which, towards the north, was Thebes. About B.C. 730 a rebellion, headed by Tafnecht, chief of Saïs, broke out, and it was so successful, that the rebels marched into middle Egypt, *i.e.*, the tract of land which lay between the Delta and the Ethiopian territory, and overthrew the Ethiopian governors. When Piānchi, king of Ethiopia, heard this, he prepared an army, and marching northwards captured the whole of Egypt as far as Memphis. The kings of Egypt of the XXVth dynasty were Ethiopians, and their capital city was Napata or Gebel Barkal; Tirhakah, the last of the dynasty, is thought to have built the pyramids at Meroë. Cambyses undertook an ill-directed expedition into Ethiopia, but he met with no success, and the result of his labour was only to open up the country to travellers. Under the rule of the Ptolemies many cities were founded in Ethiopia. In the reign of Augustus, the Ethiopians, under their Queen Candace, were repulsed, and their capital city destroyed by C. Petronius, the successor of the prefect of Egypt, Aelius Gallus, who placed a Roman garrison in Ibrîm, about B.C. 22. Candace sued for peace. In the reign of Diocletian the greater part of the country south of Philæ was ceded to the Nubians or Ethiopians. The principal tribes of the Ethiopians in ancient days were 1. Blemmyes and Megabari, 2. Ichthyophagi, 3. Macrobii, and 4. Troglodytæ.

After leaving Philæ, the first place of interest passed is **Dabôd,** on the west bank of the river, 599½ miles from Cairo. At this place, called  Ta-ḥet in the inscriptions, are the ruins of a temple founded by Åt'a-char Åmen,* a king of Ethiopia, who reigned about the middle of the third century B.C. The names of Ptolemy VII. Philometor and Ptolemy IX. Physcon are found engraved upon parts of the building. Dabôd probably stands on the site of the ancient Parembole, a port or castle on the borders of Egypt and Ethiopia, and attached alternately to each kingdom. During the reign of Diocletian it was ceded to the Nubæ by the Romans, and it was frequently attacked by the Blemmyes from the east bank of the river. At **Kardâsh,** on the west bank of the river, 615 miles from Cairo, are the ruins of a temple and a quarry; seven miles further south, on the west bank of the river, is **Wâdi Tâfah,** where there are also some ruins; they are however, of little interest.

KALÂBSHÎ.

Kalâbshî, on the west bank of the river, 629 miles from Cairo, stands on the site of the classical Talmis, called in hieroglyphics 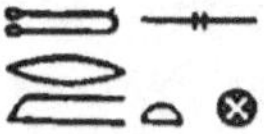 Thermesct, and 

* 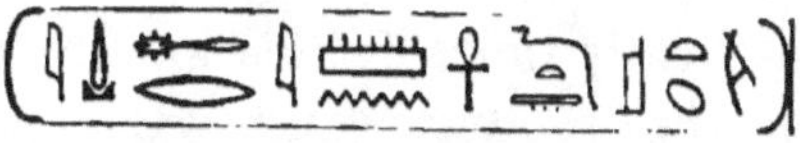 "*Åt'a-char-Åmen,* living for ever, beloved of Isis," with the prenomen 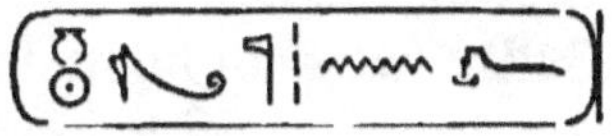 *Åt-nu-Rā, setep-en-neteru.*

Ka-ḥefennu; it stands immediately on the Tropic of Cancer. The god of this town was called  Merul or Melul, the Mandulis or Malulis of the Greeks. At Kalâbshî there are the ruins of two temples of considerable interest. The larger of these, which is one of the largest temples in Nubia, appears to have been built upon the site of an ancient Egyptian temple founded by Thothmes III., B.C. 1600, and Amenophis II., B.C. 1566, for on the pronaos this latter monarch is representing offering to the god Àmsu and the Ethiopian god Merul or Melul. It seems to have been restored in Ptolemaic times, and to have been considerably added to by several of the Roman emperors—Augustus, Caligula, Trajan, etc. From the appearance of the ruins it would seem that the building was wrecked either immediately before or soon after it was completed; some of the chambers were plastered over and used for chapels by the early Christians. A large number of Greek and Latin inscriptions have been found engraved on the walls of this temple, and from one of them we learn that the Blemmyes were frequently defeated by Silco, king of the Nubæ and Ethiopians, about the end of the third century of our era.

At **Bêt el-Walî**, a short distance from the larger temple, is the interesting rock-hewn temple which was made to commemorate the victories of Rameses II. over the Ethiopians. On the walls of the court leading into the small hall are some beautifully executed sculptures, representing the Ethiopians bringing before the king large quantities of articles of value, together with gifts of wild and tame animals, after their defeat. Many of the objects depicted must have come from a considerable distance, and it is evident that in those early times Talmis was the great central market to which the products and wares of the Sûdân were brought for sale and barter. The sculptures are executed with great freedom and spirit, and when the colours upon them were fresh they must have formed one of the most striking sights in Nubia. Some years ago casts of these interesting sculptures were taken by Mr. Bonomi, at the expense of Mr. Hay, and notes on the colours were made; these two casts, painted according to Mr. Bonomi's notes, are now set up on the walls in the Fourth Egyptian Room in the British Museum (Northern Gallery), and are the only evidences extant of the former beauty of this little rock-hewn temple, for nearly every trace of colour has vanished from the walls. The scenes on the battle-field are of great interest.

Between Kalâbshî and **Dendûr,** on the west bank of the river, 642 miles from Cairo, there is nothing of interest to be seen; at Dendûr are the remains of a temple built by Augustus,  Per-āa, where this emperor is shown making offerings to Åmen, Osiris, Isis, and Sati. At **Gerf Hussên,** on the west bank of the river, 651 miles from Cairo, are the remains of a rock-hewn temple built by Rameses II. in honour of Ptaḥ, Hathor, and Aneq; the work is poor and of little interest. This village marks the site of the ancient Tutzis.

Dakkeh, on the west bank of the river, 662½ miles from Cairo, marks the site of the classical Pselcis, the  P-selket of the hieroglyphics. About B.C. 23 the Ethiopians attacked the Roman garrisons at Philæ and Syene, and having defeated them, overran Upper Egypt. Petronius, the successor of Ælius Gallus, marching with less than 10,000 infantry and 800 horse against the rebel army of 30,000 men, compelled them to retreat to Pselcis, which he afterwards besieged and took. "Part of the insurgents were driven into the city, others fled into the uninhabited country; and such as ventured upon the passage of the river, escaped to a neighbouring island, where there were not many crocodiles on account of the current. Among the fugitives were the generals of Candace,* queen of the Ethiopians in our time, a masculine woman, and who had lost an eye. Petronius, pursuing them in rafts and ships, took them all, and despatched them immediately to Alexandria." (Strabo, XVII., 1, 54.) From Pselcis Petronius advanced to Premnis (Ibrîm), and afterwards to Napata, the royal seat of Candace, which he razed to the ground. As long as the Romans held Ethiopia, Pselcis was a garrison town.

The temple at Dakkeh was built by 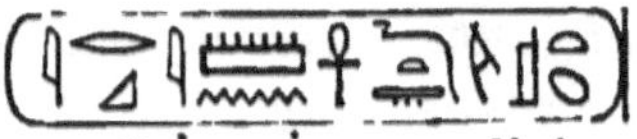 *Ȧrq-Ȧmen ānch t̄etta mer Ȧuset*, "Ȧrq-Ȧmen, living for ever, beloved of Isis," having the prenomen 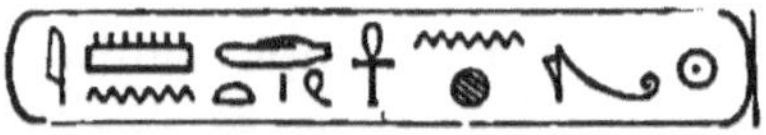 "*Ȧmen ṭet ānch tȧa Rā.*" In the sculptures on the ruins which remain Ȧrq-Ȧmen is shown standing between Menthu-Rā, lord of Thebes, and Ȧtmu the god of Heliopolis, and sacrificing to Thoth, who promises to give him a long and prosperous life as king. Ȧrq-Ȧmen is called the "beautiful god, son of Chnemu and Osiris, born of Sati and Isis, nursed by Aneq and Nephthys," etc. According to Diodorus, the priests of Meroë in Ethiopia were in the habit of sending, "whensoever they please, a messenger to the king, commanding him to put himself to death; for that such is the pleasure of the gods; . . . and so in former ages, the kings without force or compulsion of arms, but merely bewitched by a fond superstition, observed the custom; till Ergamenes (Ȧrq-Ȧmen), a king of Ethiopia, who reigned in the time of Ptolemy II., bred up in the Grecian discipline and philosophy, was the first that was so bold as to reject and despise such commands. For this prince . . . marched with a considerable body of men to the sanctuary, where stood the golden temple of the Ethiopians, and there cut the throats of all the priests."

* Candace was a title borne by all the queens of Meroë.

(Bk. III., chap. vi.) Many of the Ptolemies appear to have made additions to the temple at Dakkeh.

On the east bank of the river opposite Dakkeh is **Kubân**, called  Baka, in the hieroglyphics, a village which is said to mark the site of Tachompso or Metachompso, "the place of crocodiles." As Pselcis increased, so Tachompso declined, and became finally merely a suburb of that town; it was generally called Contra-Pselcis. During the XVIIIth and XIXth dynasties this place was well fortified by the Egyptians, and on many blocks of stone close by are found the names of Thothmes III., Ḥeru-em-ḥeb, and Rameses II. It appears to have been the point from which the wretched people condemned to labour in the gold mines in the desert of the land of Akita set out; and an interesting inscription on a stone found here relates that Rameses II., having heard that much gold existed in this land, which was inaccessible on account of the absolute want of water, bored a well in the mountain, twelve cubits deep, so that henceforth men could come and go by this land. His father Seti I. had bored a well 120 cubits deep, but no water appeared in it.

About 20 miles from Dakkeh, and 690 from Cairo, on the west bank of the river, is **Wâdi Sebûa**, or the "Valley of the Lions," where there are the remains of a temple partly built of sandstone, and partly excavated in the rock; the place is so called on account of the dromos of sixteen sphinxes which led up to the temple. On the sculptures which still remain here may be seen Rameses II., the builder of the temple, "making an offering of incense to father Åmen, the king of the gods," who says to him, "I give to thee all might, and I give the world to thee, in peace." Elsewhere the king is making offerings to Tefnut, lady of heaven, Nebt-ḥetep, Horus and Thoth, each of whom promises to bestow some blessing upon him. On another part is a boat containing a ram-headed god, and Harmachis seated in a shrine, accompanied by Horus, Thoth, Isis, and Māt; the king kneels before him in adoration, and the god says that he will give him myriads of years and festivals; on each side is a figure of Rameses II. making an offering. Beneath this scene is a figure of a Christian saint holding a key, and an inscription on each side tells us that it is meant to represent Peter the Apostle. This picture and the remains of plaster on the walls show that the chambers of the temple were used by the early Christians as chapels.

Korosko, on the east bank of the river, 703 miles from Cairo, was from the earliest times the point of departure for merchants and others going to and from the Sûdân; from the western bank there was a caravan route across into north Africa. In ancient days the land which lay to the east of Korosko was called 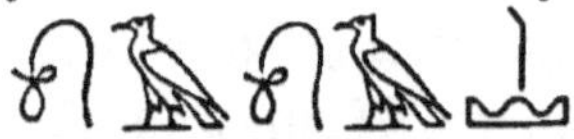 Uaua, and as early as the VIth dynasty the officer Unȧ visited it in order to obtain blocks of acacia wood for his king Pepi I. An inscription, found a few hundred yards to the east of the town, records that the country round about was conquered in the XIIth dynasty by Ȧmenemḥāt I. . About seven miles off is the battle-field of Toski, on the east bank of the Nile, where Sir Francis Grenfell slew Wâd en-Nejûmî and utterly defeated the dervishes on August 4, 1891. A capital idea of the general character of Nubian scenery can be obtained by ascending the mountain, which is now, thanks to a good path, easily accessible.

At **Amada,** on the west bank of the river, 711 miles from Cairo, is a small but interesting temple, which appears to have been founded in the XIIth dynasty by Usertsen II., who conquered Nubia by setting fire to standing crops, by carrying away the wives and cattle, and by cutting down the men on their way to and from the wells. This temple was repaired by Thothmes III. and other kings of the XVIIIth dynasty.

At **Dêrr,** on the east bank of the river, 715 miles from Cairo, is a small, badly executed rock-hewn temple of the time of Rameses II., where the usual scenes representing the defeat of the Ethiopians are depicted. The king is accompanied by a tame "lion which follows after his majesty, 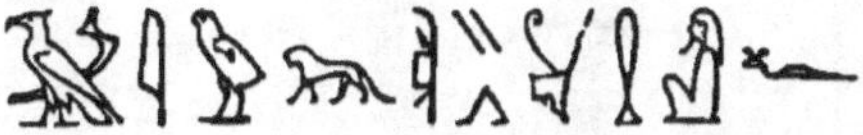, *maȧu ṡesi en ḥen-f*, to slay . . . . . ." Close to the temple is the rock stele of the prince Ȧmen-em-ḥeb of the same period; the temple was dedicated to Ȧmen-Rā. The Egyptian name of the town was , *Pa-Rā pa ṭemȧi*, "the town of the temple of the sun."

Thirteen miles beyond Dêrr, 728 miles from Cairo, also on the east bank of the river, stands **Ibrîm,** which marks the site of the ancient Primis, or Premnis, called in the Egyptian inscriptions , Mȧāmam. This town was captured during the reign of Augustus by Petronius on his victorious march upon Napata. In the first and third naos at Primis are representations of Neḥi, the governor of Nubia, with other officers, bringing gifts before Thothmes III., which shows that these caves were hewn during the reign of this king; and in another, Rameses II. is receiving adorations from Setau, prince of Ethiopia, and a number of his officers. At Anibe, just opposite Ibrîm, is the grave of Penni, the governor of the district, who died during the reign of Rameses VI.

ABÛ SIMBEL.*

Abû Simbel, on the west bank of the river, 762 miles from Cairo, is the classical Aboccis, and the place called 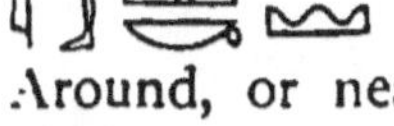 Ȧbshek in the Egyptian inscriptions. Around, or near the temple, a town of considerable size

* The spelling of this name is doubtful.

II.

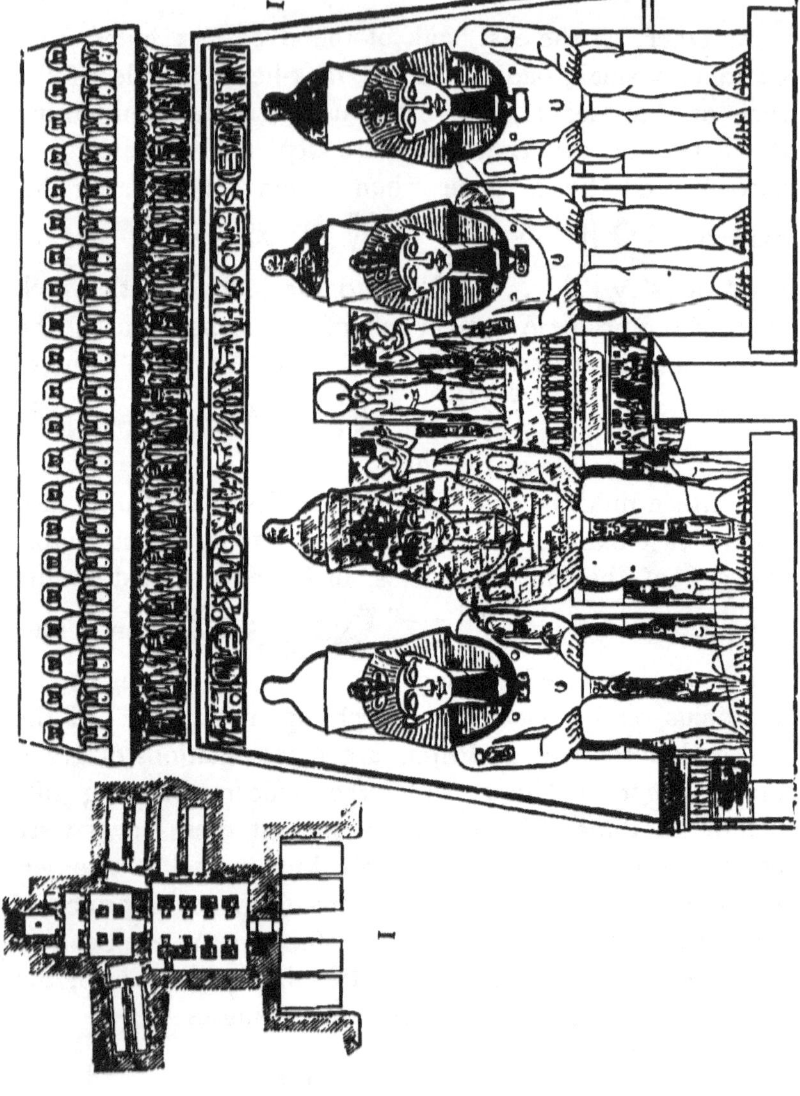

I

I. Plan of the Temple of Rameses II. at Abû Simbel.
II. The seated Colossi and front of the Temple at Abû Simbel.
From Lepsius' *Denkmäler*, Bd. iii., Bl. 185.

once stood; all traces of this have, however, disappeared. To the north of the great temple, hewn in the living rock, is a smaller temple, about 84 feet long, which was dedicated to the goddess Hathor by Rameses II. and his wife Nefert-Åri. The front is ornamented with statues of the king, his wife, and some of his children, and over the door are his names and titles. In the hall inside are six square Hathor-headed pillars, also inscribed with the names and titles of Rameses and his wife. In the small chamber at the extreme end of the temple is an interesting scene in which the king is making an offering to Hathor in the form of a cow; she is called the "lady of Abshek," and is standing behind a figure of the king.

The chief object of interest at Abû Simbel is the Great Temple built by Rameses II. to commemorate his victory over the Cheta in north-east Syria; it is the largest and finest Egyptian monument in Nubia, and for simple grandeur and majesty is second to none in all Egypt. This temple is hewn out of the solid grit-stone rock to a depth of 185 feet, and the surface of the rock, which originally sloped down to the river, was cut away for a space of about 90 feet square to form the front of the temple, which is ornamented by four colossal statues of Rameses II., 66 feet high, seated on thrones, hewn out of the living rock. The cornice is, according to the drawing by Lepsius, decorated with twenty-one cynocephali, and beneath it, in the middle, is a line of hieroglyphics, , *ṭā-nà nek ānch usr neb*, "I give to thee all life and strength," on the right side of which are four figures of Rā, , and eight cartouches containing the prenomen of Rameses II., with an uræus on each side; on the left side are four figures of Åmen, , and eight cartouches as on the right. The line of boldly cut hieroglyphics below reads, "The living Horus, the mighty bull, beloved of Māt, king of the North and

South, Usr-Māt-Rā setep en-Rā, son of the Sun, Rameses, beloved of Åmen, beloved of Harmachis the great god." Over the door is a statue of Harmachis, , and on each side of him is a figure of the king offering . Each of the four colossi had the name of Rameses II. inscribed upon each shoulder and breast. On the leg of one of these are several interesting Greek inscriptions, which were thought to have been written by the Egyptian troops who marched into Ethiopia in the days of Psammetichus I.

The interior of the temple consists of a large hall, in which are eight columns with large figures of Osiris about 17 feet high upon them, and from which eight chambers open; a second hall having four square columns; and a third hall, without pillars, from which open three chambers. In the centre chamber are an altar and four seated figures, viz., Harmachis, Rameses II., Åmen-Rā, and Ptaḥ; the first two are coloured red, the third blue, and the fourth white. In the sculptures on the walls Rameses is seen offering to Åmen-Rā, Sechet, Harmachis, Åmsu, Thoth, and other deities; a list of his children occurs, and many small scenes of considerable importance. The subjects of the larger scenes are, as was to be expected representations of the principal events in the victorious battles of the great king, in which he appears putting his foes to death with the weapons which Harmachis has given to him. The accompanying hieroglyphics describe these scenes with terse accuracy.

One of the most interesting inscriptions at Abû Simbel is that found on a slab, which states that in the fifth year of the reign of Rameses II., his majesty was in the land of T'ah, not far from Kadesh on the Orontes. The outposts kept a sharp look-out, and when the army came to the south of the town of Shabtûn, two of the spies of the Shasu came into the camp and pretended that they had been sent by the chiefs of their tribe to inform Rameses II. that they had forsaken the chief of the Cheta,* and that they wished to make an alliance with his majesty and become vassals of his. They then went on to say that the chief of the Cheta was in the land of Chirebu to the north of Tunep, some distance off, and that they were afraid to come near the Egyptian king. These two men were giving false information, and they had actually been sent by the Cheta chief to find out where Rameses and his army were; the Cheta chief and his army were at that moment drawn up in battle array behind Kadesh. Shortly after these men were dismissed, an Egyptian scout came into the king's presence bringing with him two spies from the army of the chief of the Cheta; on being questioned, they informed Rameses that the chief of the Cheta was encamped behind Kadesh, and that he had succeeded in gathering together a multitude of soldiers and chariots from the countries round about. Rameses summoned his officers to his presence, and informed them of the news which he had just heard; they listened with surprise, and insisted that the newly-received information was untrue. Rameses blamed the chiefs of the intelligence department seriously for their neglect of duty, and they admitted their fault. Orders were straightway issued for the Egyptian army to march upon Kadesh, and as they were crossing an arm of the river near that city the hostile forces fell in with each other. When Rameses saw this, he "growled at them like his father Menthu, lord of Thebes," and having hastily put on his full armour, he mounted his chariot and drove into the battle. His onset was so sudden and rapid that before he knew where he was he

* The Cheta have, during the last few years, been identified with the Hittites of the Bible; there is no ground for this identification beyond the slight similarity of the names. The inscriptions upon the sculptures found at Jerâbis still remain undeciphered.

found himself surrounded by the enemy, and completely isolated from his own troops. He called upon his father Ȧmen-Rā to help him, and then addressed himself to a slaughter of all those that came in his way, and his prowess was so great that the enemy fell in heaps, one over the other, into the waters of the Orontes. He was quite alone, and not one of his soldiers or horsemen came near him to help him. It was only with great difficulty he succeeded in cutting his way through the ranks of the enemy. At the end of the inscription he says, "Every thing that my majesty has stated, that did I in the presence of my soldiers and horsemen." This event in the battle of the Egyptians against the Cheta was made the subject of an interesting poem by Pen-ta-urt; this composition was considered worthy to be inscribed upon papyri, and upon the walls of the temples which Rameses built.

A little to the south of the Great Temple is a small building of the same date, which was used in connexion with the services, and on the walls of which are some interesting scenes. It was re-opened a few years ago by Mr. McCallum, Miss Edwards and party.

Early in the year 1892, **Capt. J. H. L. E. Johnstone, R.E.,** together with a detachment of non-commissioned officers and men, arrived at Abû-Simbel with a view of carrying out certain repairs to the face and side of the great rock temple. They began by clearing away several enormous masses of overhanging rock which, had they fallen in, must have inflicted very great damage on the colossal statues below; and having broken them into smaller pieces, Captain Johnstone used them for building two walls at the head of the valley to prevent the drift sand from burying the temple again, and for making a hard, stone slope. The cynocephali which form the ornament of the cornice were carefully repaired and strengthened, and the original rock was in many places built up with stone and cement. The whole of the sand and broken stones which had become piled up in front of the entrance to the small chamber re-opened by Mr. McCallum some years ago was cleared away, and any dangerous break in the rock was carefully repaired. All lovers of Egypt will rejoice at the excellent way in which Captain Johnstone has performed his difficult task, and we may now hope that it will not be long before the repairs which are urgently needed by temples and other buildings in other parts of Egypt are undertaken by the able officers of the Royal Engineers.

The village of **Wâdi Ḥalfah,** on the east bank of the Nile, 802 miles from Cairo, marks the site of a part of the district called 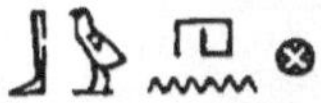 Buhen in the hieroglyphic inscription, where, as at Dêrr and Ibrîm, the god Harmachis was worshipped. On the plain to the east of the village some interesting flint weapons have been found, and a few miles distant are the fossil remains of a forest. On the western bank of the river, a little further south, are the remains of a temple which, if not actually built, was certainly restored by Thothmes III. It was repaired and added to by later kings of Egypt, but it seems to have fallen into disuse soon after the Romans gained possession of Egypt. The excavations recently carried out here by Lieut. H. G. Lyons, R.E., have brought to light the ruins of temples built by a king of the XIIth dynasty and Thothmes IV. A few miles south of Wâdi Ḥalfah begins the second cataract, a splendid view of which can be obtained from the now famous rock of Abûṣîr on the west bank of the river. Nearly every traveller who has visited Abû Simbel has been to this rock and inscribed his name upon it; the result is an interesting collection of names and dates, the like of which probably exists nowhere else.

A narrow gauge railway from Wâdi Ḥalfah to Sarras was

laid down by the English a few years ago to carry troops and stores above the Second Cataract, and until quite recently about eighteen miles of it, passing through wild scenery, remained *in situ*. The other part of it had been torn up by the dervishes, who threw the iron rails into the cataract, used the sleepers to boil their kettles, and twisted lengths of the telegraph wires together to form spears. This line has again been restored by the Egyptian army.

The remains of Egyptian temples, etc., at Semneh above the second cataract are of interest, but it is probable that they would not repay the traveller who was not specially concerned with archæology for the fatigue of the journey and the expense which he must necessarily incur to reach them.

LIST OF EGYPTIAN KINGS.

It should be borne in mind that the Egyptians never divided their kings into dynasties, and that this arrangement is only adopted here for convenience of reference.

Dynasty I., from Thinis, B.C. 4400.

1. 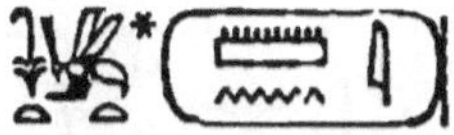*
Menȧ.

2. 
Tetȧ.

3 
Ȧteθ.

4 
Ȧta.

5. 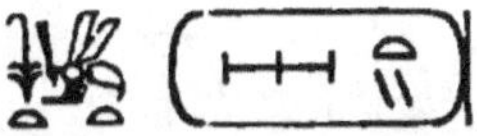
Ḥesep-ti.

6. 
Mer-ba-pen.

7. 
Semen-Ptaḥ.

8. 
Qebḥ.

Dynasty II., from Thinis, B.C. 4133.

9. 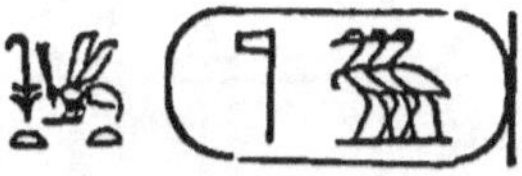
Neter-baiu.

10. 
Ka-kau.

11. 
Ba-en-neter.

12. 
Uat'-nes.

13. 
Sentȧ.

14. 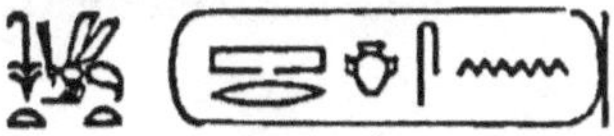
Per-ȧb-sen.

*  = *suten net*, "King of the North and South."

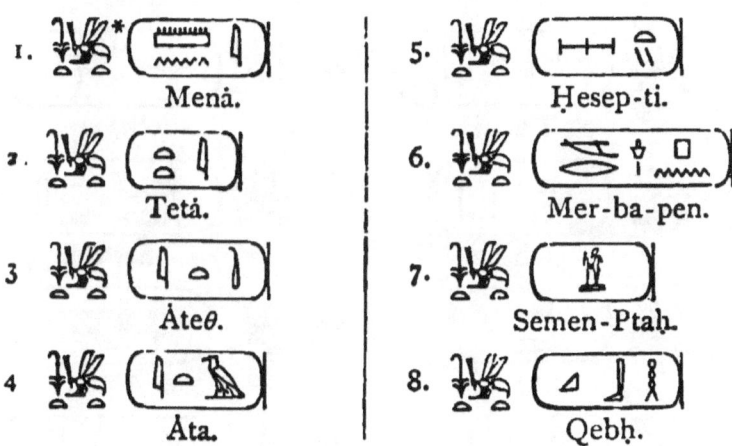

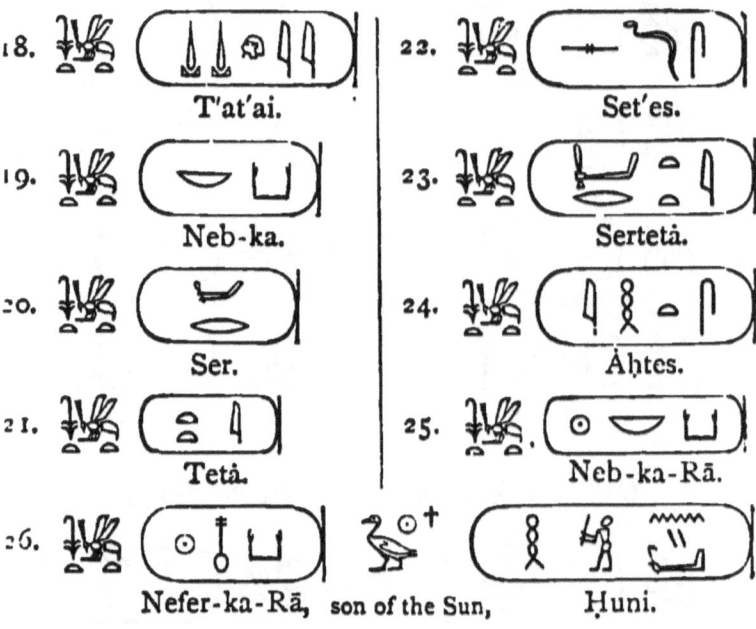

15. 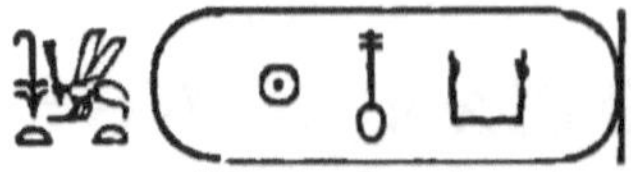
Nefer-ka-Rā.*

16. 
Nefer-ka-seker.

17. 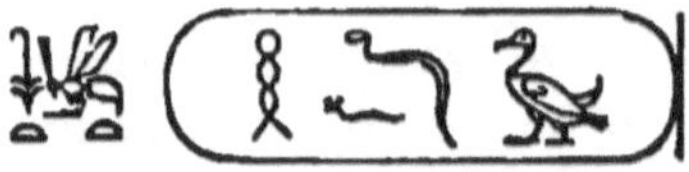
Ḥet'efa.

Dynasty III., from Memphis, B.C. 3966.

18. 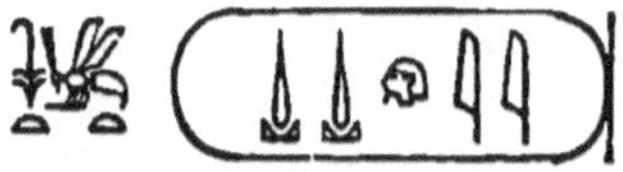
T'at'ai.

19. 
Neb-ka.

20. 
Ser.

21. 
Tetȧ.

22. 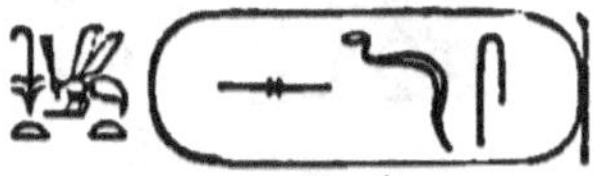
Set'es.

23. 
Sertetȧ.

24. 
Ȧḥtes.

25. 
Neb-ka-Rā.

26. 
Nefer-ka-Rā, son of the Sun, Ḥuni.

Dynasty IV., from Memphis, B.C. 3766.

27. 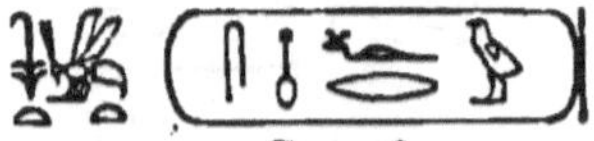
Seneferu.

28. 
χufu.
(Cheops.)

* Though ⊙ Rā is generally placed first in the cartouche, it is generally to be read last.

† = *Se Rā*, "son of the Sun."

29. 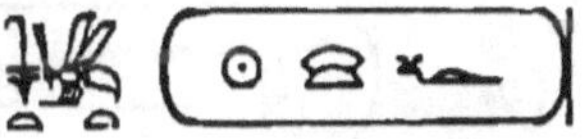

χā-f-Rā.
(Chephren.)

30. 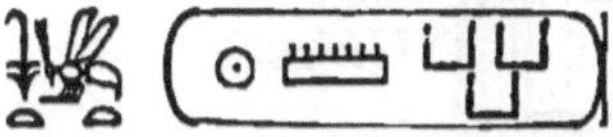

Men-kau-Rā.
(Mycerinus.)

31. 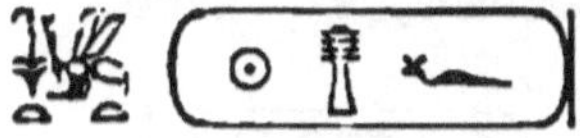

Ṭeṭ-f-Rā.

32. 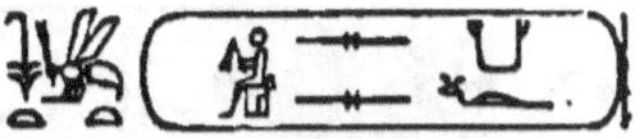

Shepses-ka-f.

33. 

Sebek-ka-Rā.

34. 

I-em-ḥetep.

DYNASTY V., FROM ELEPHANTINE, B.C. 3366.

35. 

Usr-ka-f.

36. 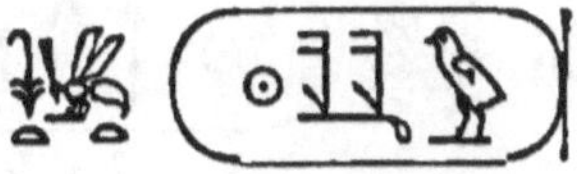

Saḥ-u-Rā.

37. 

Nefer-ka-åri-Rā, son of the Sun, Kakaå.

38. 

Nefer-f-Rā, son of the Sun, Shepses-ka-Rā.

39. 

Nefer-χā-Rā, son of the Sun, Ḥeru-å-ka-u

40. 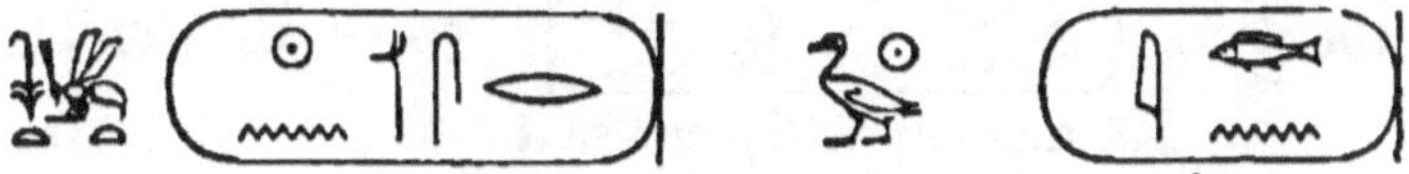

Usr-en-Rā, son of the Sun, Ån.

41. 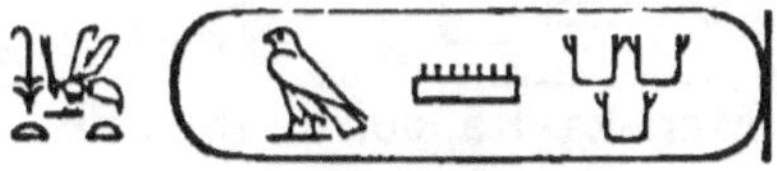

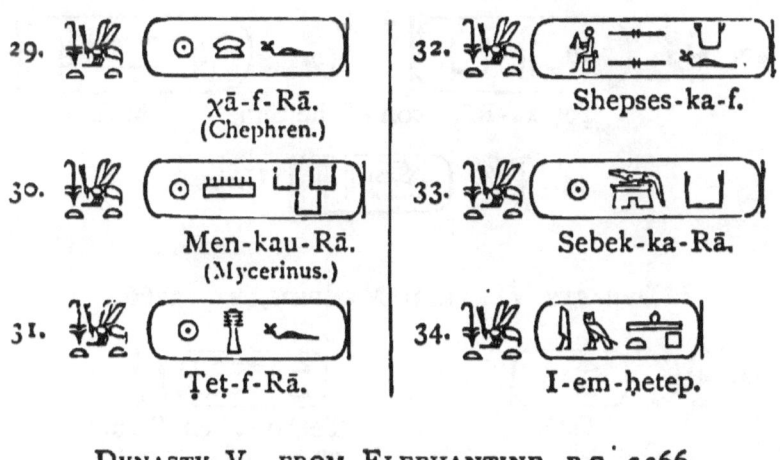

Men-kau-Ḥeru.

42. 

Ṭeṭ-ka-Rā, son of the Sun, Åssȧ.

43.  Unȧs.

Dynasty VI., from Memphis, B.C. 3266.

44. 

Tetȧ. or Tetȧ-mer-en-Ptaḥ.
(Teta beloved of Ptaḥ.)

45. 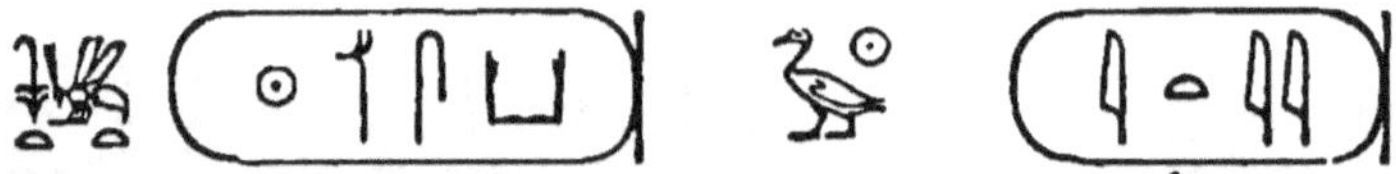

Usr-ka-Rā, son of the Sun, Åti.

46. 

Meri-Rā, son of the Sun, Pepi (I.).

47. 

Mer-en-Rā, son of the Sun, Ḥeru-em-sa-f.

48. 

Nefer-ka-Rā, son of the Sun, Pepi (II.).

49.  50. 

Rā-mer-en-se (?)-em-sa-f Neter-ka-Rā.

51 

Men-ka-Rā, son of the Sun, Netȧqerti.
(Nitocris.)

DYNASTIES VII. AND VIII., FROM MEMPHIS; DYNASTIES IX. AND X., FROM HERACLEOPOLIS, B.C. 3100.

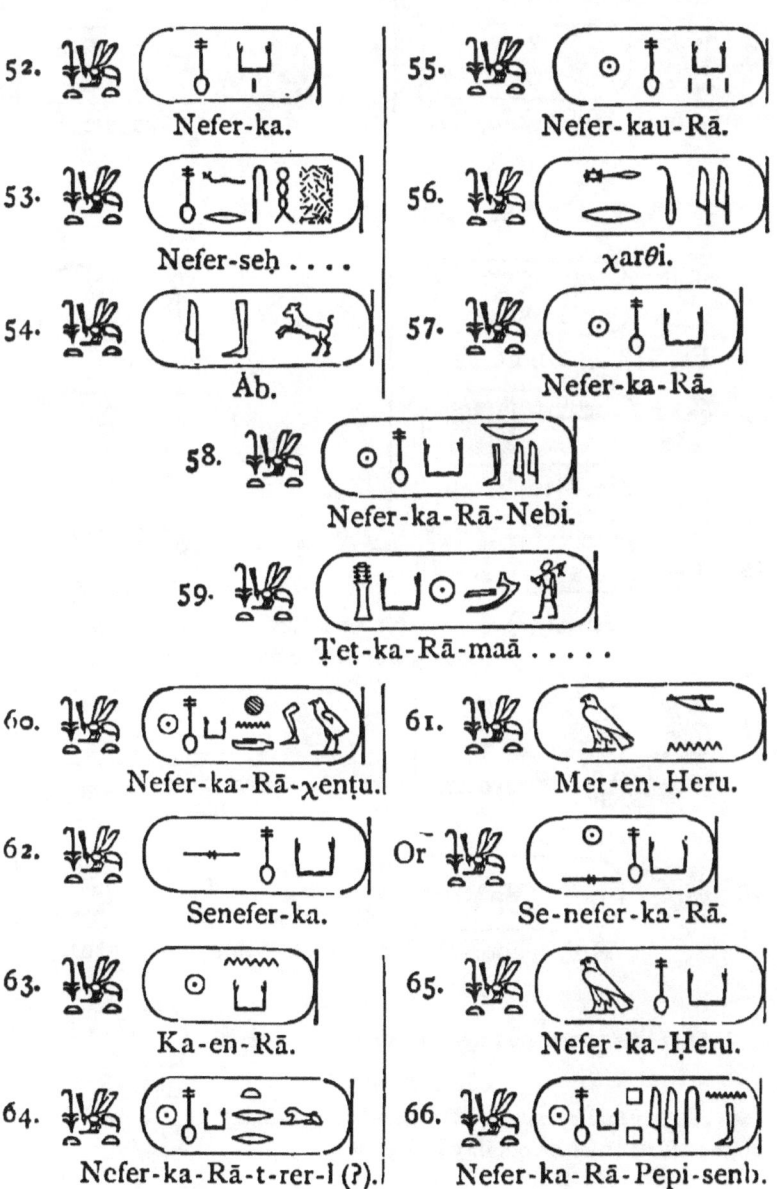

52. 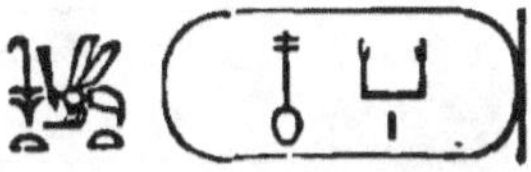

Nefer-ka.

53. 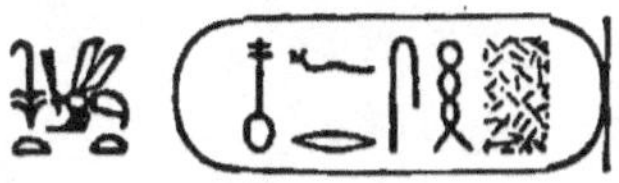

Nefer-seḥ . . . .

54. 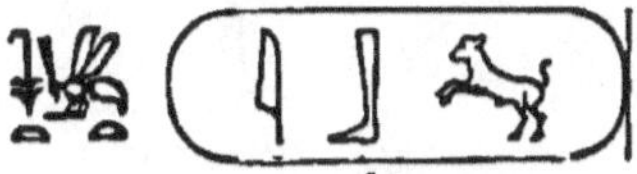

Ȧb.

55. 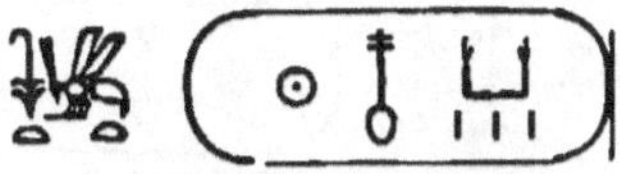

Nefer-kau-Rā.

56. 

χarθi.

57. 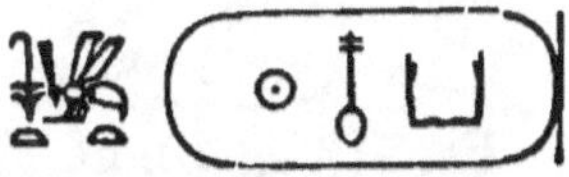

Nefer-ka-Rā.

58. 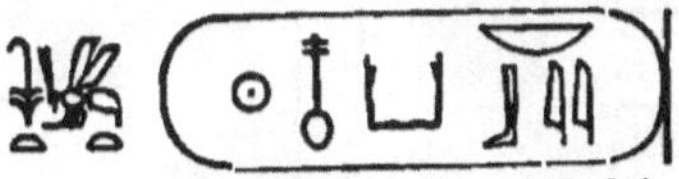

Nefer-ka-Rā-Nebi.

59. 

Ṭeṭ-ka-Rā-maā . . . . .

60. 

Nefer-ka-Rā-χenṭu.

61. 

Mer-en-Ḥeru.

62. 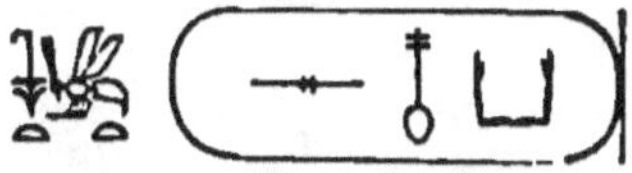

Senefer-ka.

Or 

Se-nefer-ka-Rā.

63. 

Ka-en-Rā.

64. 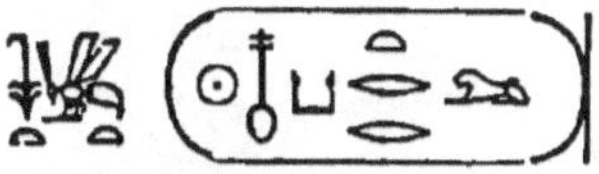

Nefer-ka-Rā-t-rer-l (?).

65. 

Nefer-ka-Ḥeru.

66. 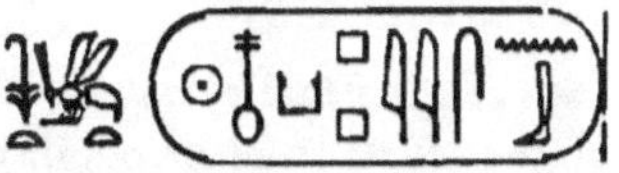

Nefer-ka-Rā-Pepi-senb.

67. 
Nefer-ka-Rā-ānnu.*

69. 
Nefer-kau-Ḥeru.

68. 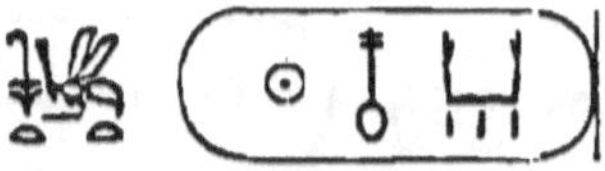
Nefer-kau-Rā.

70. 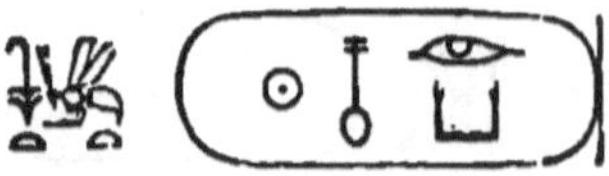
Nefer-ka-ȧri-Ra.

DYNASTY XI., FROM THEBES.

71. 
Erpā† Ȧntef.

73. 
Ȧntef.

72. 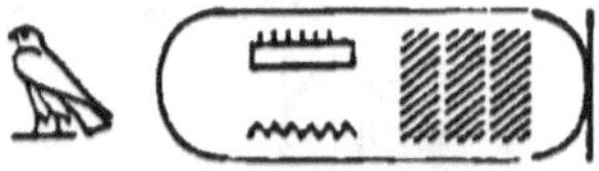
Men-[tu-ḥetep].

74. 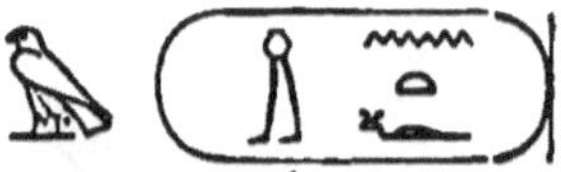
Ȧntef.

75. 
Ȧntef (?).

76. 
Neter nefer, Beautiful god, Ȧntef. Antef.

77. 
Son of the Sun Ȧntef.

78. 
Son of the Sun Ȧn-āa.

79. 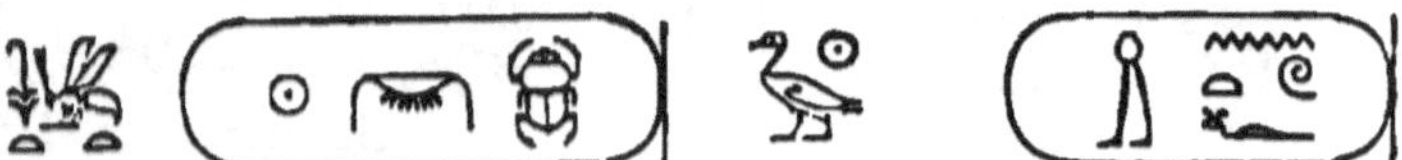
Nub-χeper-Rā, son of the Sun, Ȧntuf.

* After this name the tablet of Abydos has 
. . . kau-Ra.

† Erpā, usually translated "hereditary prince" or "duke," is one of the oldest titles of nobility in Egypt.

80. 

Āḥā-Ḥeru-Rā-àpu-maāt, son of the Sun, Àntuf-āa.

81. 

Āḥā-renpit-Rā-àput-maāt, son of the Sun, Àntef-āa.

82. 

Ṭeṭ-Rā-her-ḥer-maāt, son of the Sun, Àntef.

83. 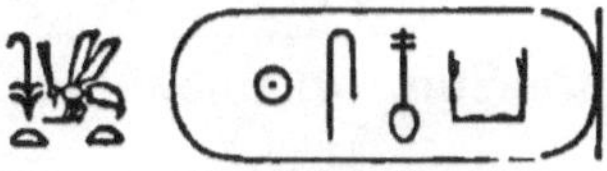

Senefer-ka-Rā.

84. 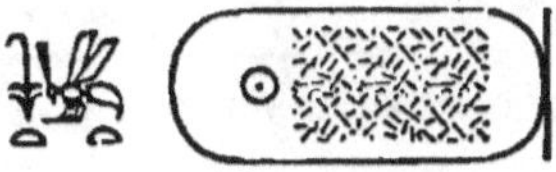

Rā . . . . . .

85. 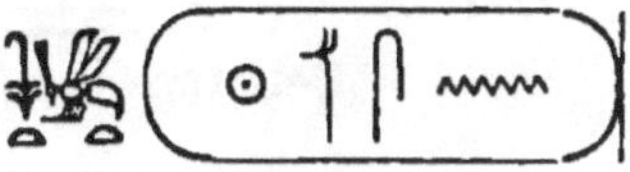

Usr-en-Rā.

86. 

Neb-nem-Rā.

87. 

Son of the Sun, Menθu-ḥetep (I.).

88. 

Se-Rā-Menθ-ḥetep (II.).

89. 

Neb-ḥetep-Rā, son of the Sun, Menθ-ḥetep (III.).

90. 

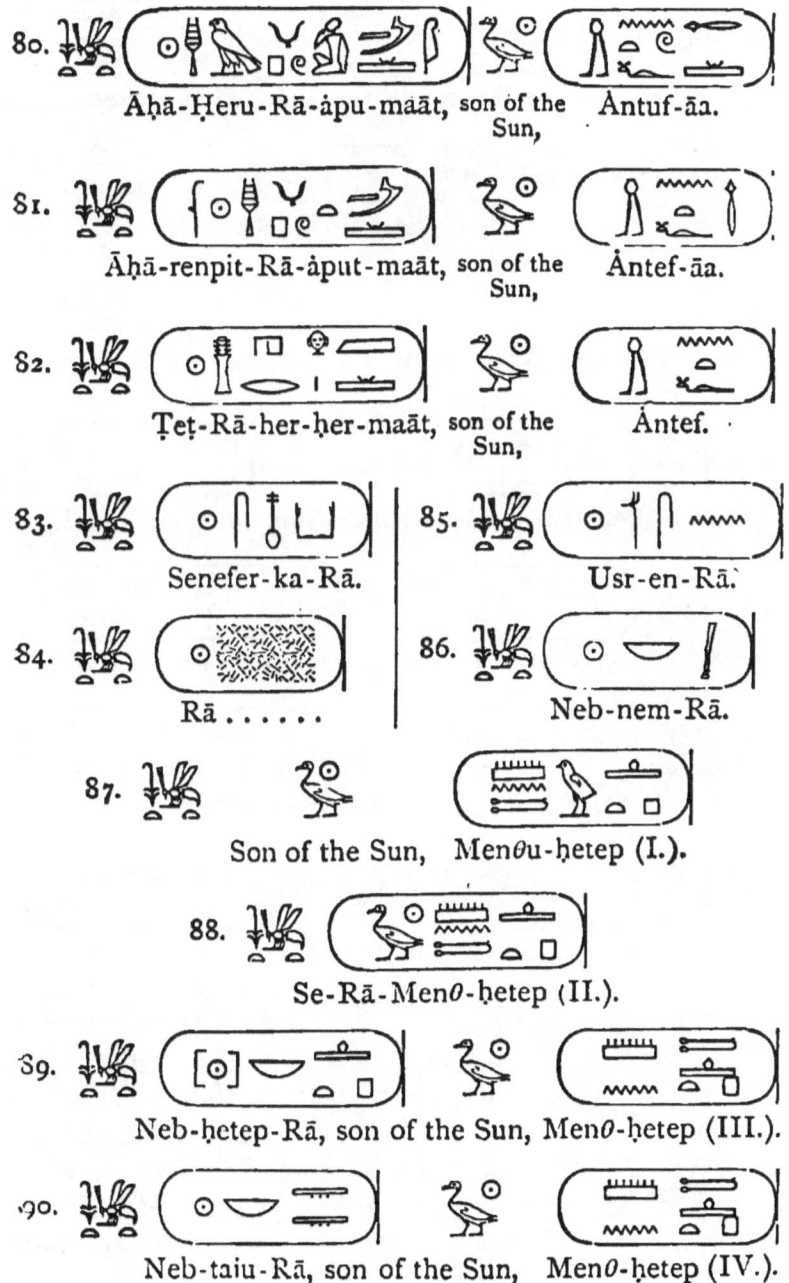

Neb-taiu-Rā, son of the Sun, Menθ-ḥetep (IV.).

91. 

Neb-χeru-Rā, son of the Sun, Menθ-ḥetep (V.).

92. 

Se-ānχ-ka-Rā.

DYNASTY XII., FROM THEBES, B.C. 2466.

93. 

Seḥetep-àb-Rā, son of the Sun, Àmen-em-ḥāt (I.).

94. 

χeper-ka-Rā, son of the Sun, Usertsen (I.).

95. 

Nub-kau-Rā, son of the Sun, Àmen-em-ḥāt (II.).

96. 

χeper-χā-Rā, son of the Sun, Usertsen (II.).

97. 

χā-kau-Rā, son of the Sun, Usertsen (III.).

98. 

Maāt-en-Rā, son of the Sun, Àmen-em-ḥāt (III.).

99. 
Maā-χeru-Rā, son of the Sun, Ȧmen-em-ḥāt (IV.).

100. 
Sebek-neferu-Rā.

DYNASTY XIII., B.C. 2233.

101. 
χu-taiu-Rā.

102. 
χerp-ka-Rā.

103. 
. . . . em-ḥāt.

104. 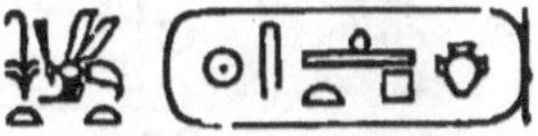
Seḥetep-ȧb-Rā.

105. 
Ȧuf-nȧ.

106. 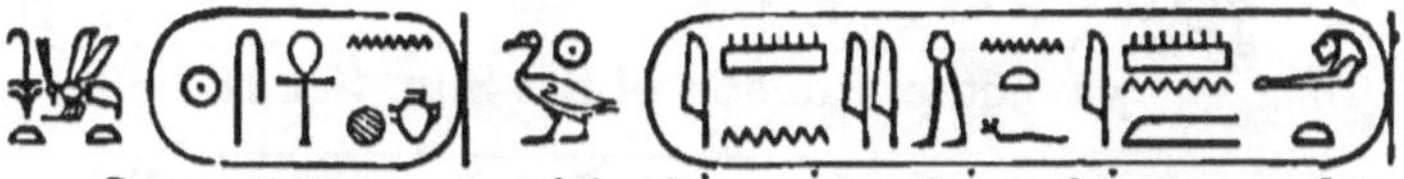
Seānχ-ȧb-Rā, son of the Sun, Ȧmeni-Ȧntef-Ȧmen-em-ḥāt.

107. 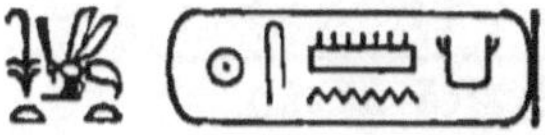
Semen-ka-Rā.

108. 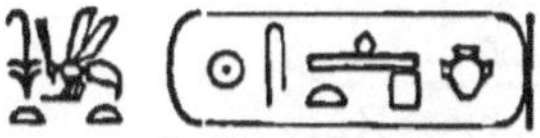
Seḥetep-ȧb-Rā.

109. 
. . . . . ka.

110. 
Net'em-ȧb-Rā.

111. 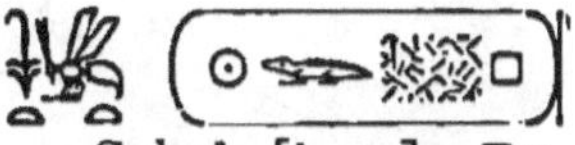
Sebek-[ḥete]p-Rā.

112. 
Ren . . . . . .

113. 
Set'ef . . . . Rā.

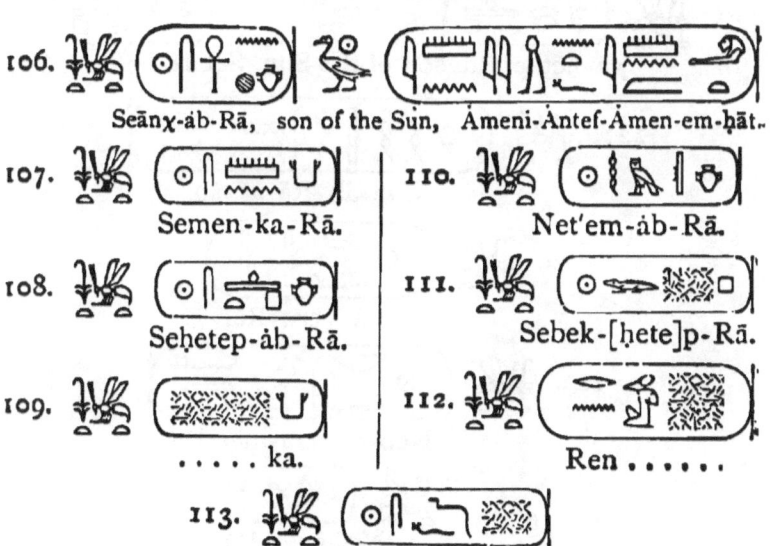

114. 

Rā-χerp (?)-χu-taiu Sebek-ḥetep (I.).

115. 

Semenχ-ka-Rā, son of the Sun, Mer-menfitu.

116. 

χerp-seuat'-taiu-Rā, son of the Sun, Sebek-ḥetep (II.).

117. 

χā-seχem-Rā, son of the Sun, Nefer-ḥetep.

118. 

Rā-ḥet . . . . se, son of the Sun, Ḥet-Ḥeru-se-

119. 

χā-nefer-Rā, son of the Sun, Sebek-ḥetep (III.).

120. 

χā-ḥetep-Rā, son of the Sun, Sebek-ḥetep (IV.).

121. 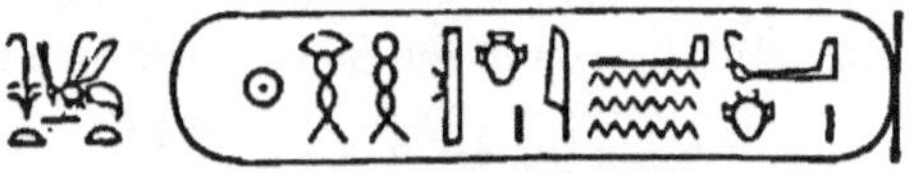

Uaḥ-áb-Rā-áā-áb.

122. 

χāā-χeru-Rā.

123. 

Neb-f-ā(?)a-mer-Rā.

124. 

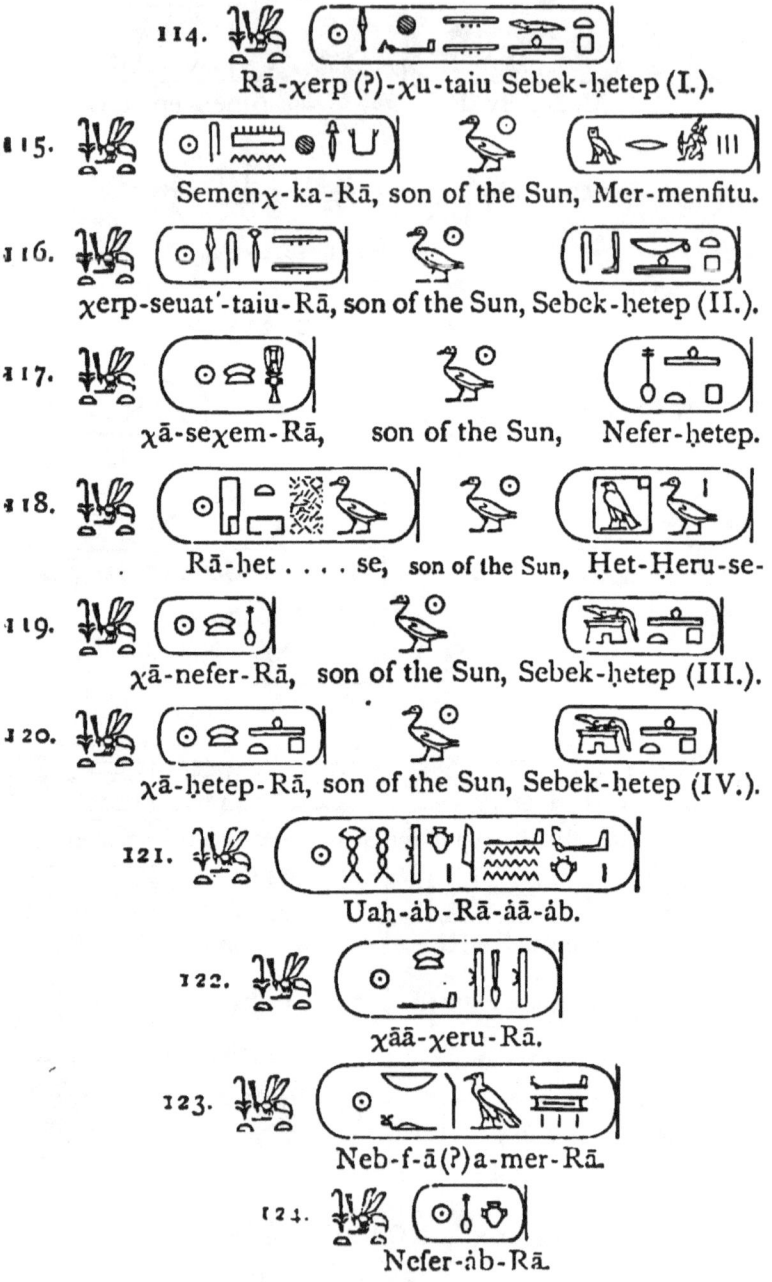

Nefer-áb-Rā.

125. 

χā-ānχ-Rā, son of the Sun, Sebek-ḥetep (V.).

126. 

Mer-χerp-Rā.

127. 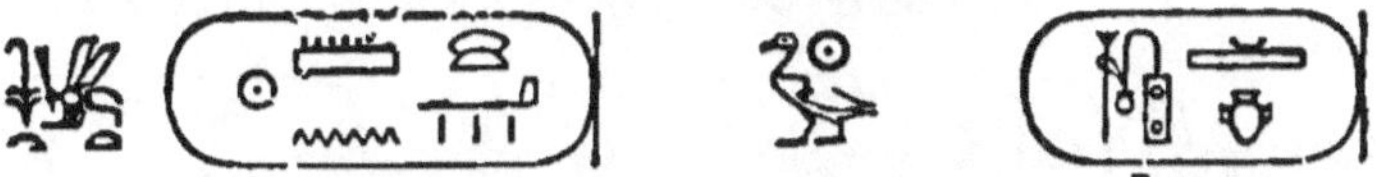

Men-χāu-Rā, son of the Sun, Ānȧb.

128. 

χerp-uat'-χāu-Rā, son of the Sun, Sebek-em-sa-f (I.).

129. 

χerp-seśeṭ-taiu-Rā, son of the Sun, Sebek-em-sa-f (II.).

130. 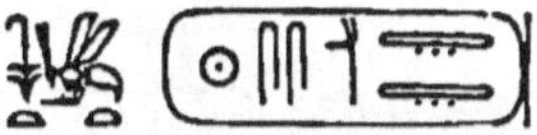

Sesusr-taiu-Rā,

131. 

χerp (?)-Uast-Rā.

132. 

χerp-uaḥ-χā-Rā, son of the Sun, Rā-ḥetep.

Dynasty XIV.

133. 

Mer-nefer-Rā, son of the Sun, Ȧi.

134. 

Mer-ḥetep-Rā, son of the Sun, Ȧnȧ.

135. 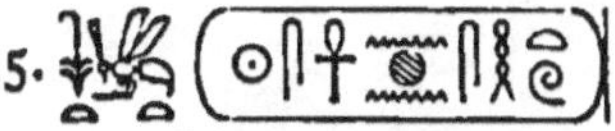

Seānχensehtu-Rā.

136. 

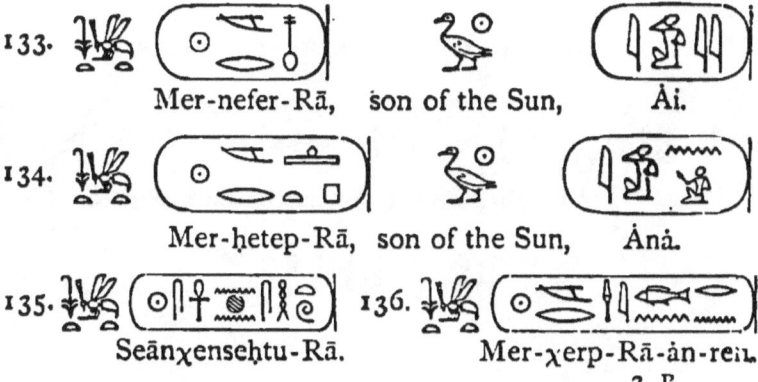

Mer-χerp-Rā-ȧn-ren.

137. 
Seuat'-en-Rā

138. 
χā-ka-Rā.

139. 
Ka-meri-Rā

neter nefer Mer-kau-Rā.

140. 
Seḥeb-Rā.

141. 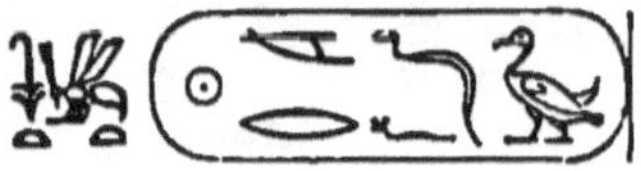
Mer-t'efa-Rā.

142. 
Sta-ka-Rā.

143. 
Neb-t'efa-Rā Rā (*sic*).

144. 
Uben-Rā.

145. 
Her-àb-Rā.

146. 
Neb-sen-Rā.

147. 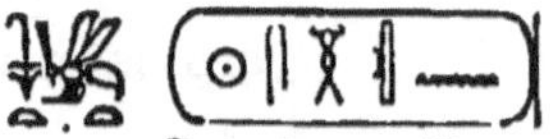
Seuaḥ-en-Rā.

148. 
Seχeper-en-Rā.

149. 
Ṭeṭ-χeru-Ra.

Dynasty XV., "Shepherd Kings."

150. 
Āa-peḥ-peḥ-Set, son of the Sun, Nub-Set (?).

151. 
. . . . Bànān.

152. 

Åbeḥ(?)-en-χepeś.

153. 

Åpepå.

DYNASTY XVI., "SHEPHERD KINGS."

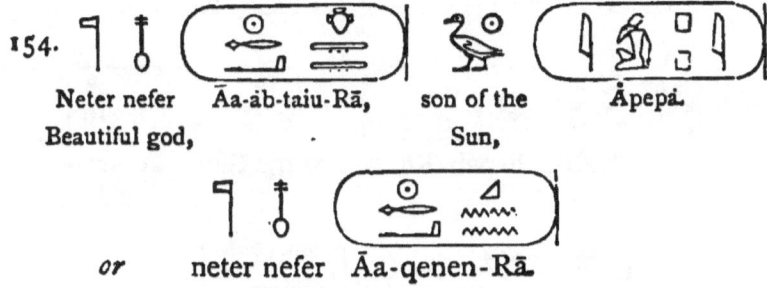

154. 

Neter nefer Beautiful god, Āa-āb-taiu-Rā, son of the Sun, Åpepå.

or neter nefer Āa-qenen-Rā.

DYNASTY XVII., FROM THEBES.

155. 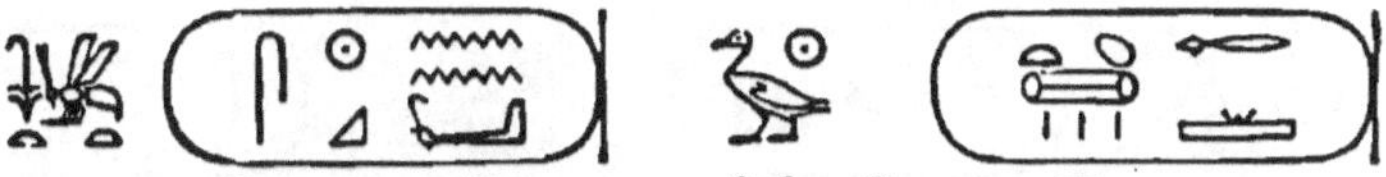

Seqenen-Rā, son of the Sun, Tau-āa.

156. 

Seqenen-Rā, son of the Sun, Tau-āa-āa.

157. 

Seqenen-Rā, son of the Sun, Tau-āa-qen.

158. 

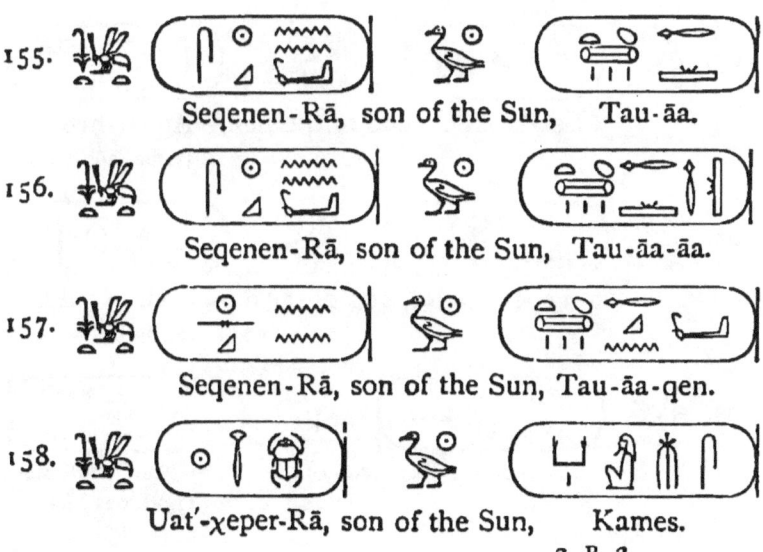

Uat'-χeper-Rā, son of the Sun, Kames.

159. 

Suten ḥemt Åāh-ḥetep.
Royal wife.

160. 

Åāh-mes-se-pa-åri.

DYNASTY XVIII., FROM THEBES, B.C. 1700.

161. 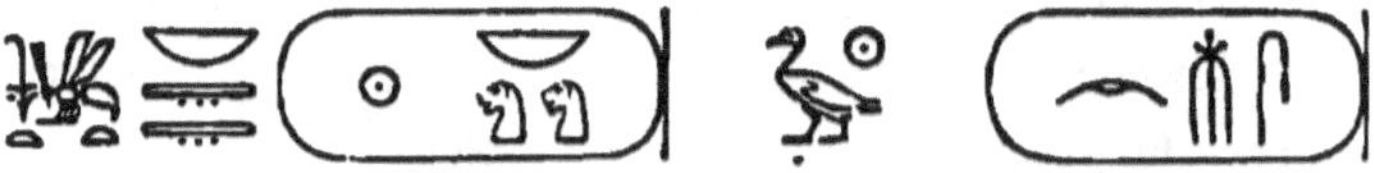

Neb-peḥ-peḥ-Rā, son of the Sun, Åāḥmes.
(Amāsis I.)

162. 

Neter ḥemt Åāh-mes-nefert-åri.
Divine wife.

163. 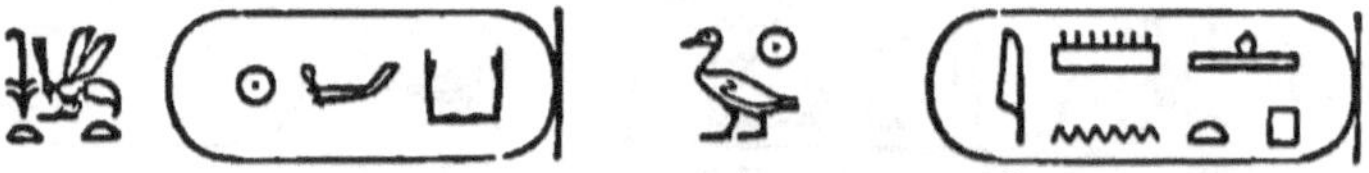

Ser-ka-Rā, son of the Sun, Åmen-ḥetep.
(Amenophis I.)

164. 

Āa-χeper-ka-Rā, son of the Sun, Teḥuti-mes.
(Thothmes I.)

165. 

Āa-χeper-en-Rā, son of the Sun, Nefer-χāu-Teḥuti-mes.
(Thothmes II.)

166. 

Māt-ka-Rā, son of the Sun, Ḥāt-shepset-χnem-Ȧmen. (Queen Hatshepsu.)

167. 

Men-χeper-Rā, son of the Sun, Teḥuti-mes. (Thothmes III.)

168. 

Āa-χeperu-Rā, son of the Sun, Ȧmen-ḥetep neter ḥeq Ȧnnu. (Amenophis II.)

169. 

Men-χeperu-Rā, son of the Sun, Teḥuti-mes χā-χāu. (Thothmes IV.)

170. 

Neb-māt-Rā, son of the Sun, Ȧmen-ḥetep ḥeq-Uast. (Amenophis III.)

171. 

Suten ḥemt *θ*i.

(The Mesopotamian wife of Amenophis III.).

172. 

Nefer-χeperu-Rā-uā-en-Rā,. son of the Sun, Ȧmen-ḥetep neter ḥeq Uast (Amenophis IV.).

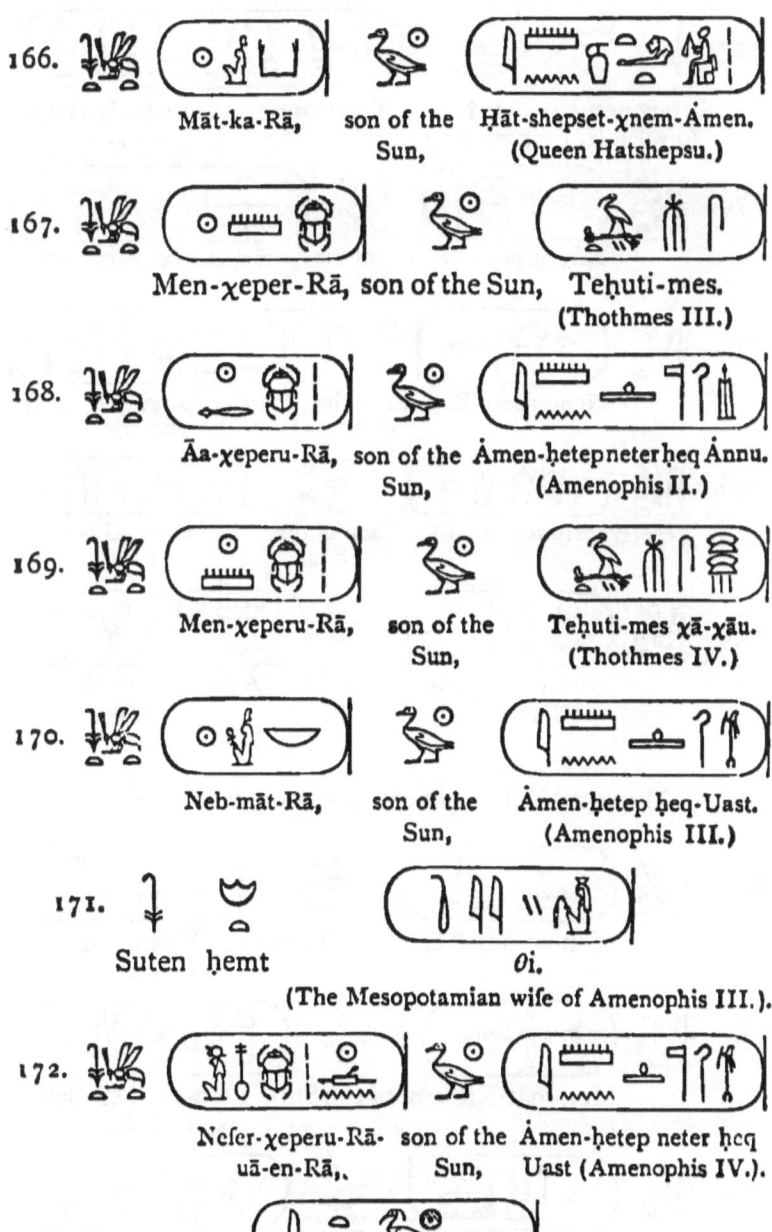

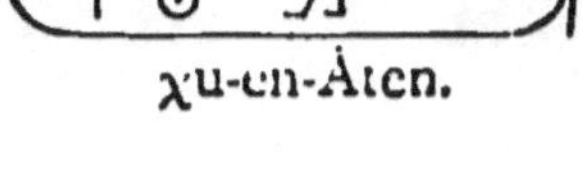

or χu-en-Ȧten.

173. 

Suten ḥemt urt Nefer neferu-àten Neferti-iθ.
Royal wife, great lady.

174. 

Ānχ-χeperu-Rā, son of the Sun, Seāa-ka-neχt-χeperu-Rā

175. 

Neb-χeperu-Rā, son of the Sun, Tut-ānχ-Àmen ḥeq Ànnu resu (?)

176. 

χeper-χeperu-māt-àri-Rā, son of the Sun, Atf-neter Ài neter ḥeq Uast.

177. 

Ser-χeperu-Rā-setep-en-Rā, son of the Sun, Àmen-meri-en Ḥeru-em-ḥeb.

Dynasty XIX., from Thebes, B.C. 1400.

178. 

Men-peḥtet-Rā, son of the Sun, Rā-messu.
(Rameses I.)

179. 

Men-māt-Rā, son of the Sun, Ptaḥ-meri-en-Seti.
(Seti I.)

180. 

Usr-māt-Rā setep-en-Rā, son of the Sun, Rā-messu-meri-Àmen.
(Rameses II.)

181. 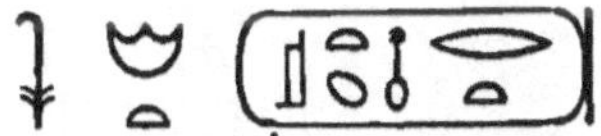

Suten ḥemt Åuset-nefert.
Royal wife.

182. 

Suten mut Tui.
Royal mother.

183. 

Ba-Rā-meri-en-Åmen, son of the Sun, Ptaḥ-meri-en-ḥetep-ḥer-māt.
(Meneptah I.)

184. 

Men-mā-Rā setep-en-Rā, son of the Sun, Åmen-meses-ḥeq-Uast.
(Amen-meses.)

185. 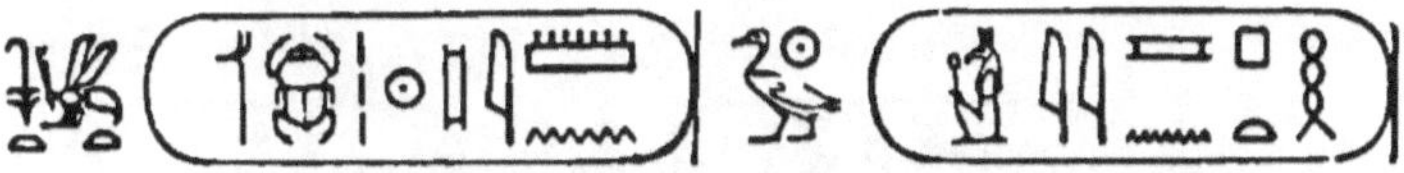

Usr-χeperu-Rā-meri-Åmen, son of the Sun, Seti-meri-en-Ptaḥ.
(Seti II).

186. 

χu-en-Rā setep-en-Rā, son of the Sun, Ptaḥ-meri-en-se-Ptaḥ.
(Meneptah II.)

187. 

Usr-χāu-Rā setep-en-Rā meri-Åmen, son of the Sun, Rā-meri Åmen-merer Set-neχt.
(Set-Neχt.)

Dynasty XX., from Thebes, b.c. 1200.

188. 

Usr-māt-Rā-meri-Åmen, son of the Sun, Rā-meses-ḥeq-Annu.
(Rameses III.)

189. 

Usr-māt-Rā setep-en-Āmen, son of the Sun, Rā-meses-meri-Āmen-Rā ḥeq māt.
(Rameses IV.)

190. 

Usr-māt-Rā s-χeper-en-Rā, son of the Sun, Rā-mes-meri-Āmen-Āmen suten-f.
(Rameses V.)

191. 

Rā-Āmen-māt-meri-neb, son of the Sun, Rā-Āmen-meses neter ḥeq Ānnu.
(Rameses VI.)

192. 

Rā-usr-Āmen-meri-setep-en-Rā, son of the Sun, Rā-Āmen-meses-tȧ neter-ḥeq-Ānnu.
(Rameses VII.)

193. 

Rā-māt-usr-χu-en-Āmen, son of the Sun, Rā-Āmen-meses-meri-Āmen.
(Rameses VIII.)

194. 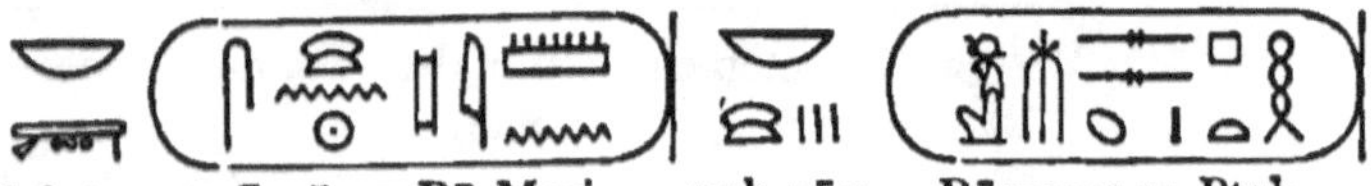

Neb ta Lord of the land, S-χā-en-Rā Meri-Āmen, neb χāu lord of crowns, Rāmeses-se-Ptaḥ.
(Rameses IX.)

195. 

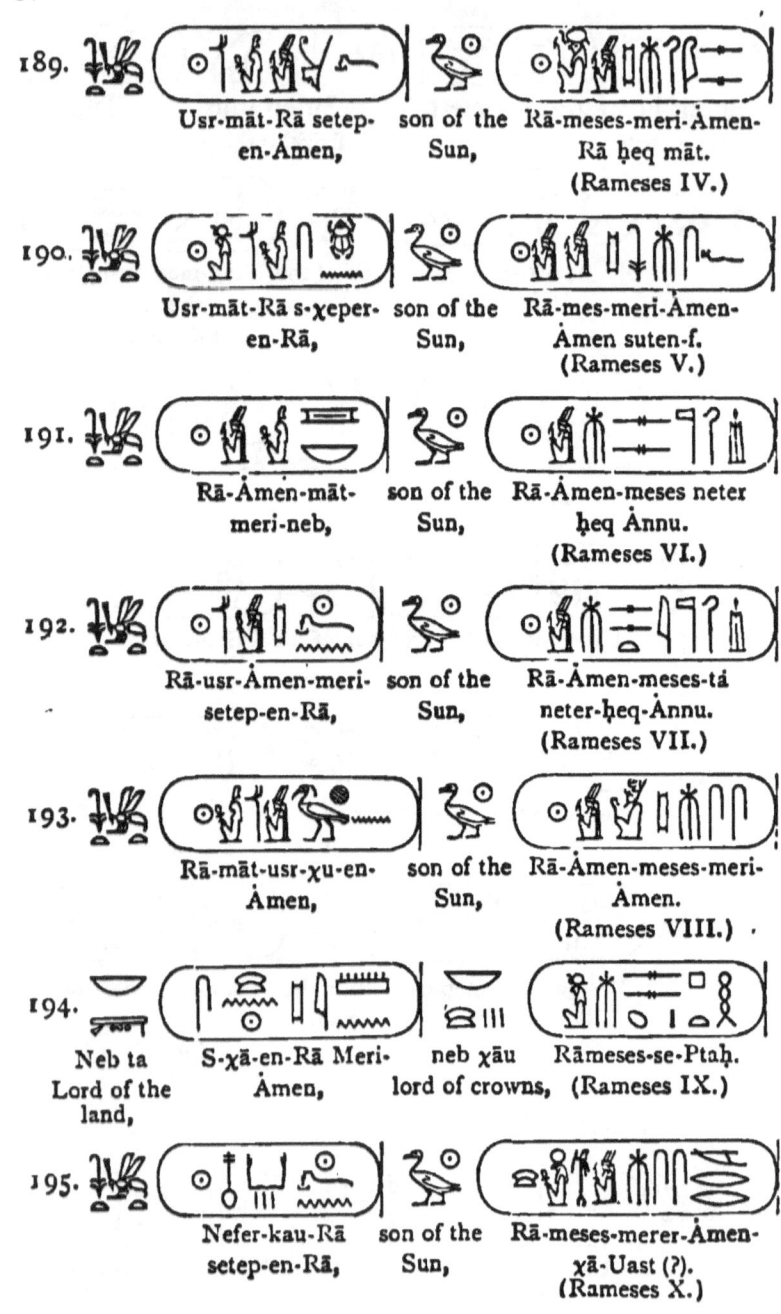

Nefer-kau-Rā setep-en-Rā, son of the Sun, Rā-meses-merer-Āmen-χā-Uast (?).
(Rameses X.)

196. 

Rā-χeper-māt setep-en-Rā, son of the Sun, Rā-mes suten (?) Ȧmen. (Rameses XI.)

197. 

Usr-māt-Rā setep-nu-Rā. son of the Sun, Ȧmen mer-Rā-meses. (Rameses XII.)

198. 

Men-māt-Rā setep-en-Rā, son of the Sun, Rā-meses-merer-Ȧmen χā Uạst (?) neter ḥeq Ȧnnu. (Rameses XIII.)

DYNASTY XXI., FROM TANIS, B.C. 1100.

I.

199. 

Rā-neter-χeper setep-en-Ȧmen, son of the Sun, Se-Ȧmen meri-Rā. (Se-Ȧmen.)

200. 

Rā-āa-χeper setep-en-Ȧmen, son of the Sun, Ȧmen-meri Pa-seb-χā-nu. (Pasebχānu I.)

201. 

Ȧa-seḥ-Rā, son of the Sun, Nefer-ka-Rā-meri-Amen.

202. 

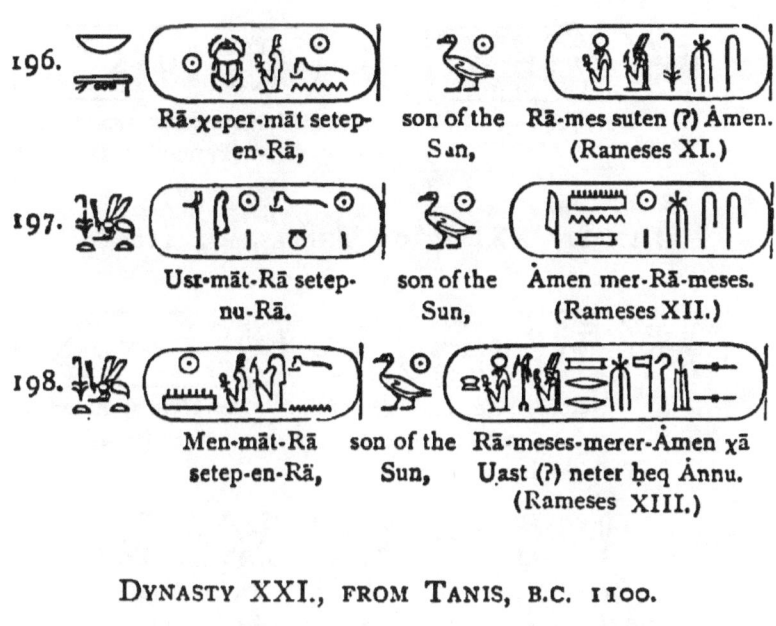

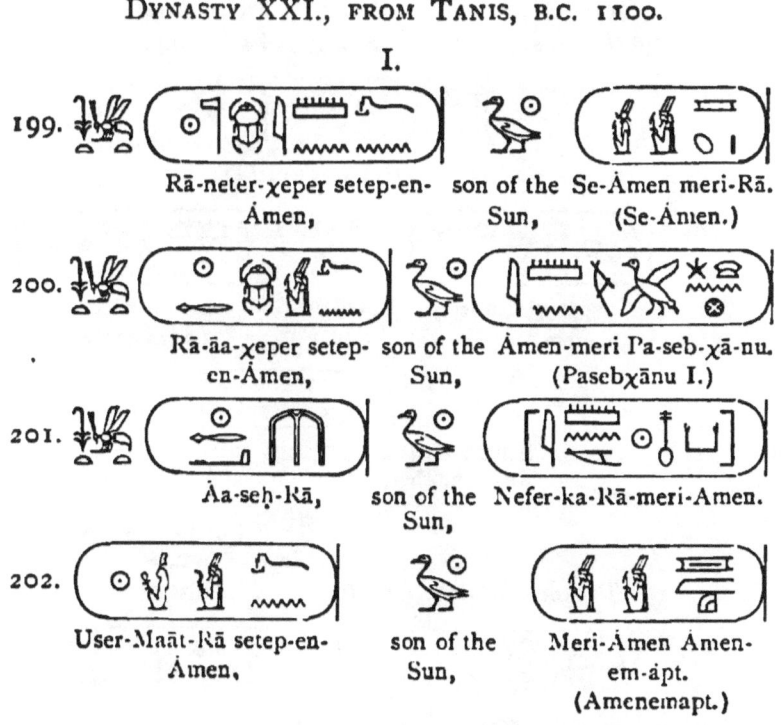

User-Maāt-Rā setep-en-Ȧmen, son of the Sun, Meri-Ȧmen Ȧmen-em-ȧpt. (Amenemapt.)

203. 

Ḥet' ḥeq . . . . son of the Sun, Meri-Àmen Pa-seb-χā-nu. (Pasebχānu II.)

DYNASTY XXI., FROM THEBES, B.C. 1100.

II.

204. 

Neter-ḥen-ṭep en-Àmen, Prophet first of Amen, son of the Sun, Ḥer-Ḥeru-se-Àmen. (Ḥer-Ḥeru.)

205. 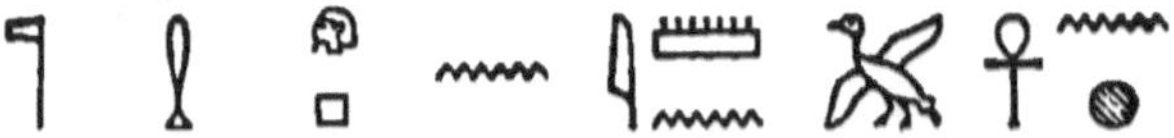

Neter ḥen ṭep en Àmen Pa - ānχ
Prophet first of Àmen Pa - ānχ.

206. 

Pai-net'em (I).

207. 

χeper-χā-Rā setep-en-Àmen, son of the Sun, Àmen-meri-Pai-net'em (II).

208. 

Suten mut Ḥent-taiu.
Royal mother, Ḥent - taiu.

209. 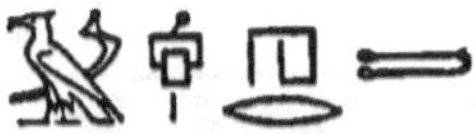

Prophet first of Amen, Masaherθ.

210. 

Prophet first, Men-χeper-Rā, {child Royal, or son of King.} Àmen-meri Pai-net' em.

211. 

Neter ḥen ṭep en Åmen-Rā, Pai-net'em (III.)
Prophet first of Åmen-Rā.

212. 

Neter ḥemt en Åmen suten sat, suten ḥemt Māt-ka-Rā.
Divine wife of Åmen, royal daughter, royal wife.

Dynasty XXII., from Bubastis, b.c. 966.

213. 

χeper-ḥet'-Rā setep-en-Ra, son of the Sun, Åmen-meri-Shashanq. (Shashanq I.)

214. 

χerp-χeper-Ra setep-en-Rā, son of the Sun, Åmen-meri Uasárken. (Osorkon I.)

215. 

Usr-Maāt-Rā, son of the Sun, Thekeleth.

216. 

Rā-usr-māt setep-en-Åmen, son of the Sun, Amen-meri sa-Bast Uasárken. (Osorkon II.)

217. 

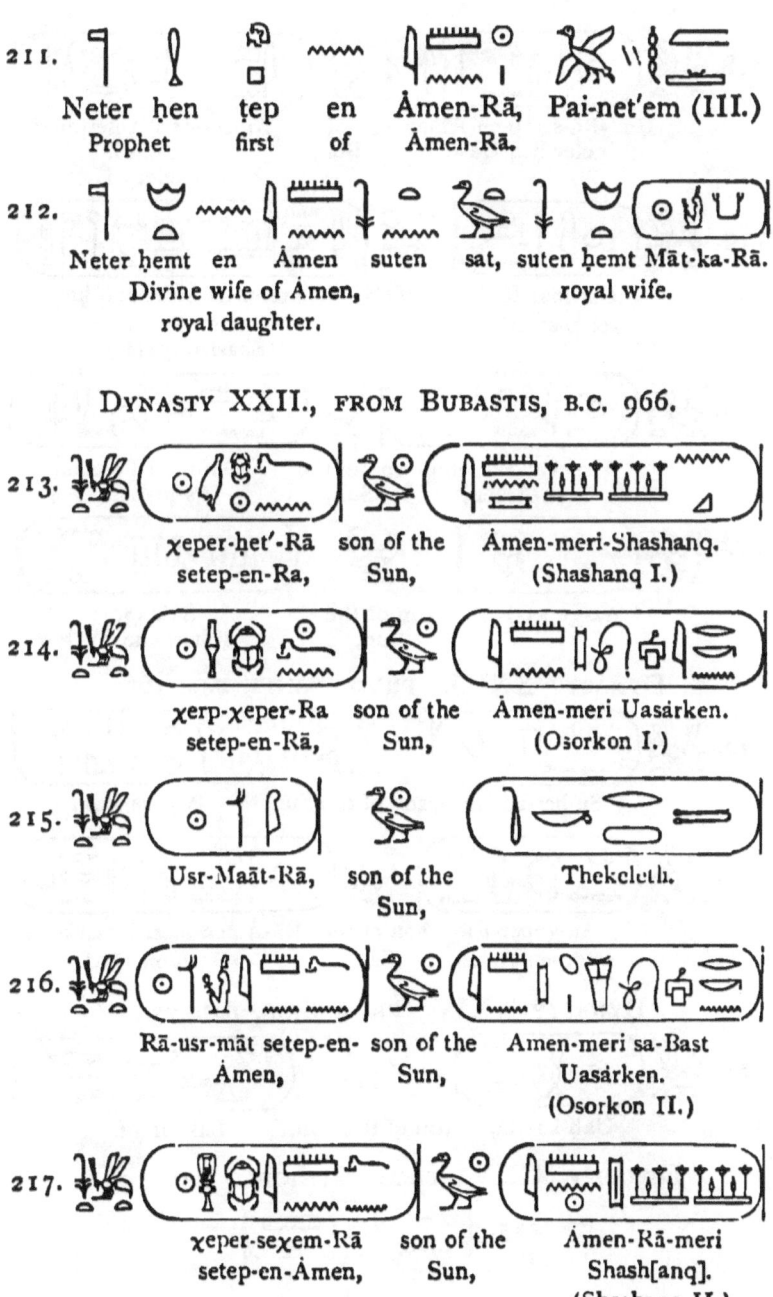

χeper-seχem-Rā setep-en-Åmen, son of the Sun, Åmen-Rā-meri Shash[anq]. (Shashanq II.)

218. 

Ḥet'-Rā-setep-en-Àmen neter ḥeq Uast, son of the Sun, Àmen-meri Auset-meri θekeleθ.
(Takeleth II.)

219. 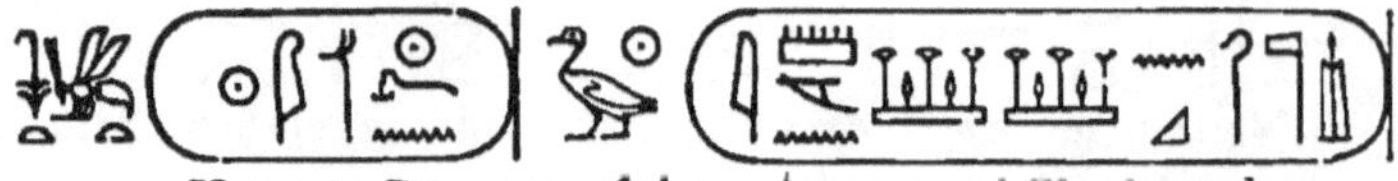

Usr-māt-Rā setep-en-Rā, son of the Sun, Àmen-meri-Shashanq ḥeq neter Ànnu.
(Shashanq III.)

220. 

Usr-māt-Rā setep-en-Àmen, son of the Sun, Àmen-meri Pa-mài.
(Pa-mai.)

221. 

Āa-χeper-Rā son of the Sun, Ṡaṡanq.
(Shashanq IV.)

Dynasty XXIII., from Tanis, B.C. 766.

222. 

Se-her-àb-Rā, son of the Sun, Peṭā-se-Bast.

223. 

Āa-χeper-Rā setep-en-Àmen, son of the Sun, Rā-Àmen-meri Uasarkenȧ.
(Osorkon III.)

Dynasty XXIV., from Sais, B.C. 733.

224. 

Uaḥ-ka-Rā, son of the Sun, Bakenrenf.

Dynasty XXIV., from Ethiopia, B.C. 733.

225. 

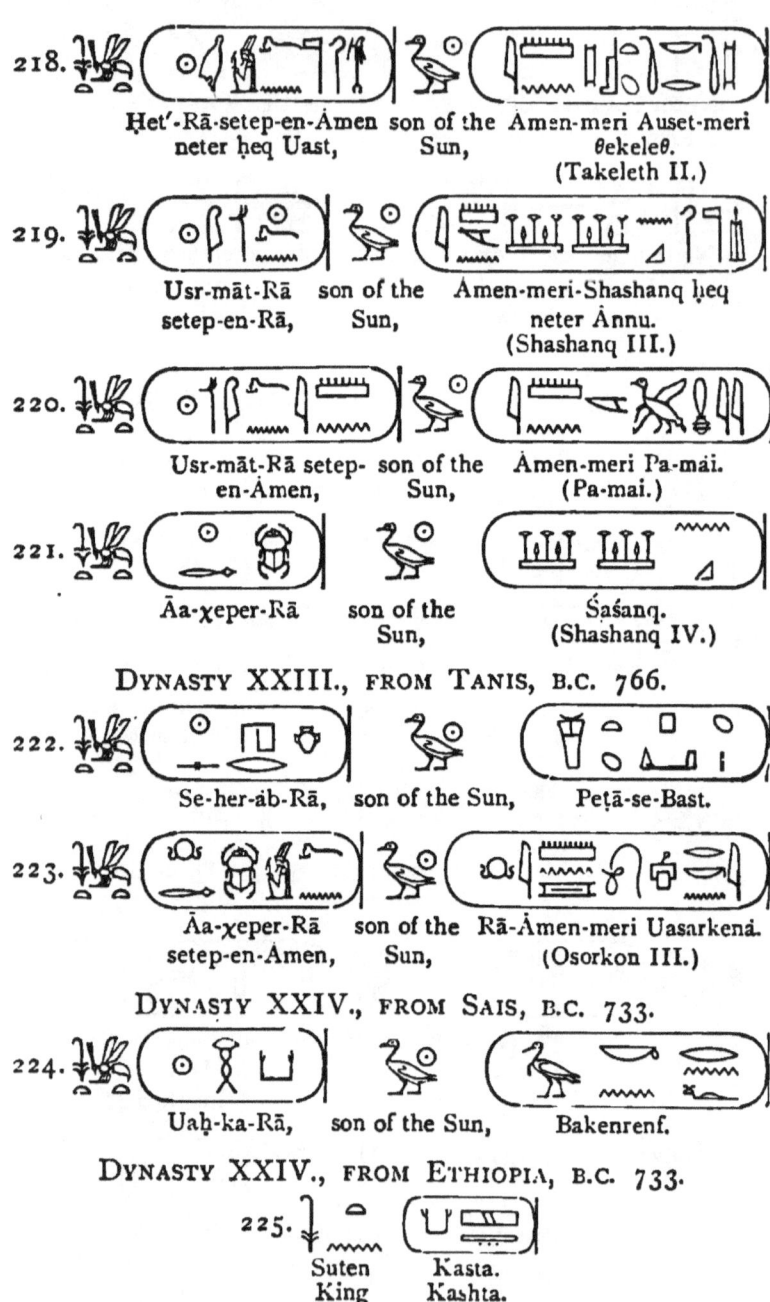

Suten King Kasta. Kashta.

226. 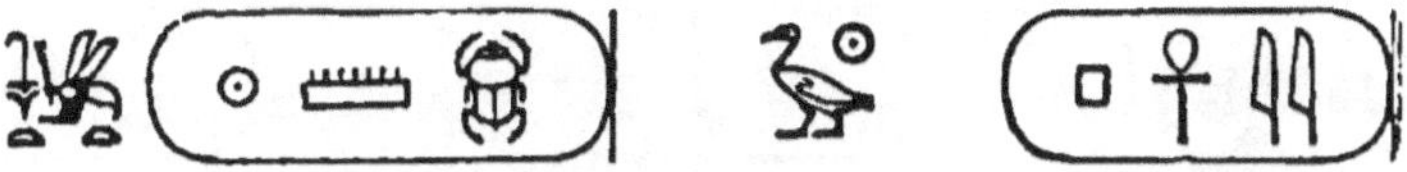

Men-χeper-Rā, son of the Sun, P-ānχi.

227. 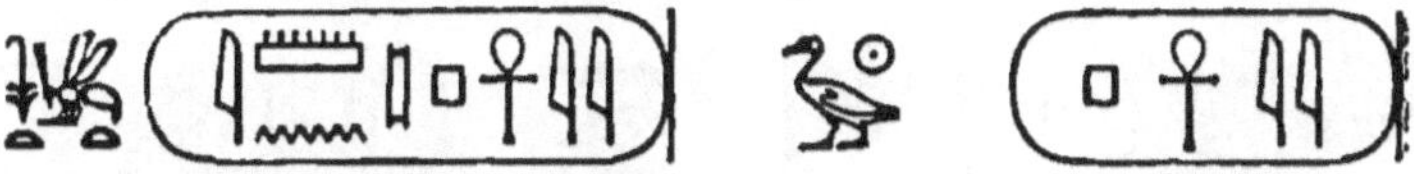

Åmen-meri P-ānχi, son of the Sun, P-ānχi.

Dynasty XXV., from Ethiopia, b.c. 700.

228. 

Nefer-ka-Rā, son of the Sun, Shabaka.
(Sabaco.)

229. 

Ṭeṭ-kau-Rā, son of the Sun, Shabataka.

230. 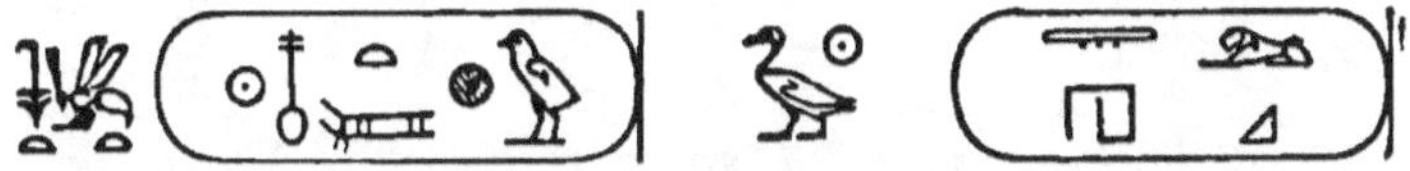

Rā-nefer-tem-χu, son of the Sun, Tahrq.
(Tirhakah.)

231. 

Neter nefer God beautiful, Usr-māt-Rā setep-en-Åmen, lord of two lands, Åmenruṭ.

Dynasty XXVI., from Sais, b.c. 666.

232. 

Uaḥ-åb-Rā, son of the Sun, Psemθek.
(Psammetichus I.

233. 

Nem-ȧb-Rā, son of the Sun, Nekau.
(Necho II.)

234. 

Nefer-ȧb-Rā, son of the Sun, Psemθek.
(Psammetichus II.)

235. 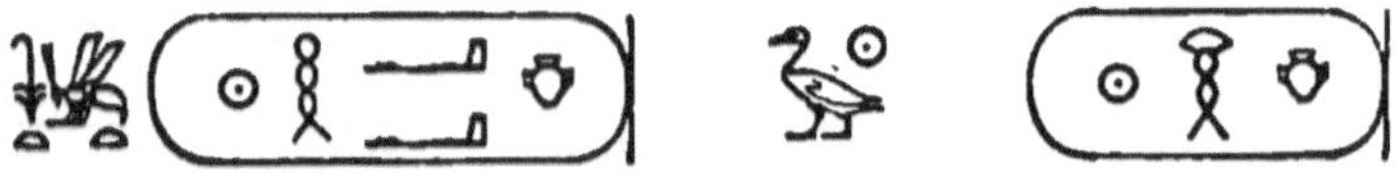

Ḥāā-ȧb-Rā, son of the Sun, Uaḥ-ȧb-Rā.
(Apries.)

236. 

χnem-ȧb-Rā, son of the Sun, Åḥmes-se-net.
(Amāsis II.)

237. 

Ānχ-ka-en-Rā, son of the Sun, Psemθek.
(Psammetichus III.)

Dynasty XXVII. (Persian), B.C. 527.

238. 

Mesuθ-Rā, son of the Sun, Kembȧθet.
(Cambyses.)

239. 

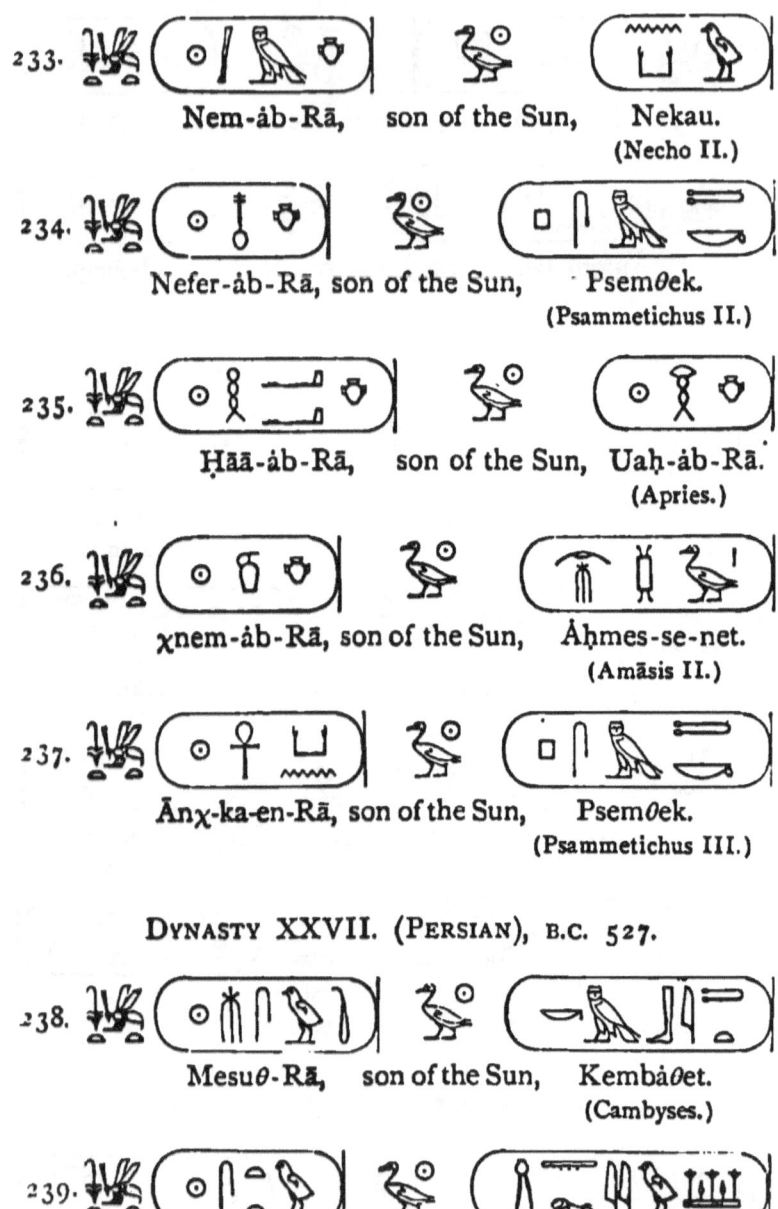

Settu-Rā. son of the Sun, Ȧntariusha.
(Darius Hystaspes.)

240. 

Lord of two lands, χshaiarsha.
(Xerxes the Great.)

241. 

Artaχshashas.
(Artaxerxes.)

242. 

Rā-meri-Åmen, son of the Sun, Ånθeriruṭsha.
(Darius Xerxes.)

DYNASTY XXVIII., FROM SAIS.

243. 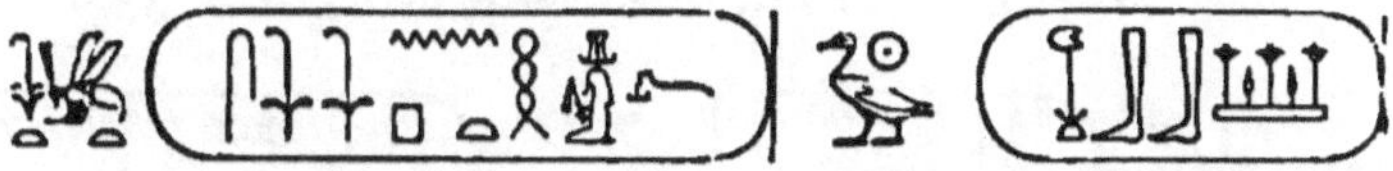

Senen-en-Ptaḥ-Mentu-setep, son of the Sun, (χabbesha.)

DYNASTY XXIX., FROM MENDES, B.C. 399.

244. 

Ba-en-Rā neteru-meri, son of the Sun, Niafāauruṭ.

245. 

χnem-māt-Rā, son of the Sun, Haḳer.

246. 

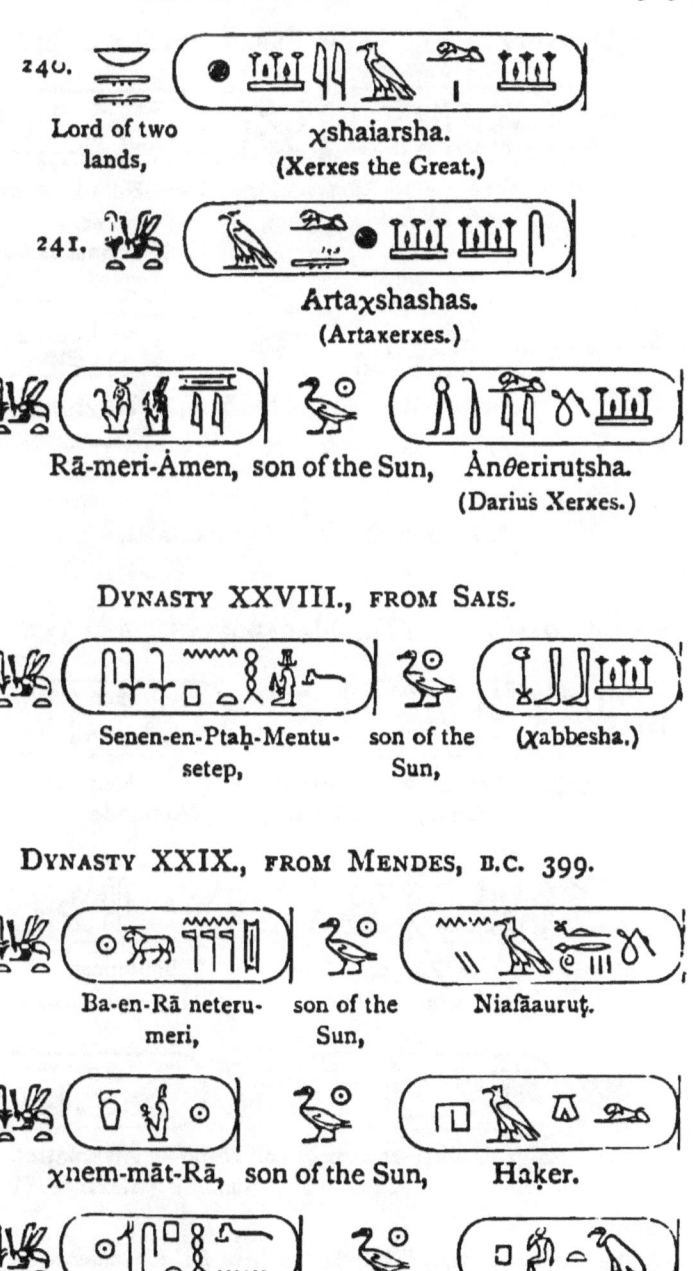

Rā-usr-Ptaḥ-setep-en, son of the Sun, Psemut.

DYNASTY XXX., FROM SEBENNYTUS, B.C. 378.

247. 

S-net'em-ȧb-Rā-setep-en-Ȧmen, son of the Sun, Neχt-Ḥeru-ḥebt-meri-Ȧmen. (Nectanebus I.)

248. 

χeper-ka-Rā, son of the Sun, Neχt-neb-f. (Nectanebus II.)

DYNASTY XXXI.,* PERSIANS.

DYNASTY XXXII., MACEDONIANS, B.C. 332.

249. 

Setep-en-Rā-meri-Ȧmen, son of the sun, Aleksȧnṭres (Alexander the Great.)

250. 

neb taiu Setep-en-Rā-meri-Ȧmen, son of the Sun, Phiuliupuas (Philip Aridaeus.)

251. 

Rā-qa-ȧb-setep-en-Ȧmen, son of the Sun. Aleksȧnṭres. (Alexander IV.)

* The word "dynasty" is retained here for convenience of classification.

DYNASTY XXXIII., PTOLEMIES, B.C. 305.

252. 

Setep-en-Rā-meri-Ȧmen, son of the Sun, Pṭulmis (Ptolemy I. Soter I.)

253. 

Neter mut, Bareniḳet.
Divine Mother (Berenice I.)

254. 

Rā-usr-ka-meri-Ȧmen, son of the Sun, Ptulmis
(Ptolemy II. Philadelphus.)

255. 

Sutenet set suten sent suten ḥemt neb taiu Ȧrsanat
Royal daughter, royal sister, royal wife, lady of the two lands (Arsinoë)

256. 

Suten set suten sent Pilatra.
Royal daughter, royal sister (Philotera).

257. 

Neteru-senu-uā-en-Rā-setep-Ȧmen-χerp (?)-en-ānχ, son of the Sun,

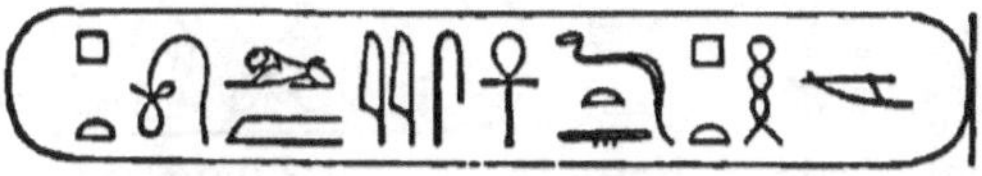

Ptualmis ānχ t'etta Ptaḥ meri
Ptolemy (III. Euergetes I.), living for ever, beloved of Ptaḥ.

258. 

Ḥeqt nebt taiu, Bårenikạt

Princess, lady of the two lands, (Berenice II.)

259. 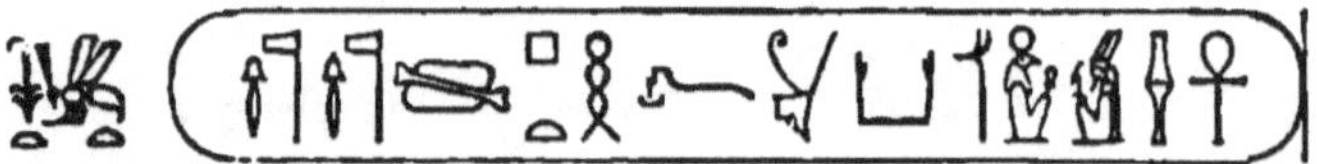

Neteru-menχ-uā-[en]-Ptaḥ-setep-en-Rā-usr-ka-Åmen-χerp (?)-ānχ,

son of the Sun Ptualmis ānχ t'etta Åuset meri

Ptolemy (IV. Philopator,) living for ever, beloved of Isis.

260. 

Suten set suten sent ḥemt urt nebt taiu

Royal daughter, royal sister, wife, great lady, lady of the two lands

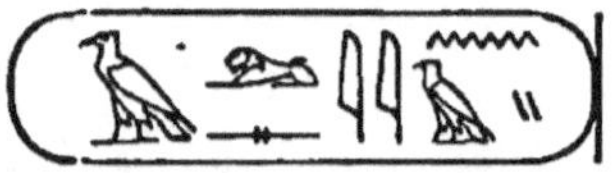

Arsinai.

Arsinoë (III., wife of Philopator I.)

261. 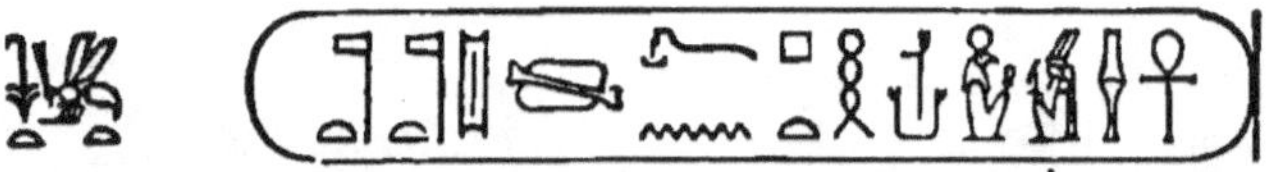

Neteru-meri-uā-en-Ptaḥ-setep-Rā-usr-ka-Åmen-χerp-ānχ,

son of the Sun Ptualmis ānχ t'etta Ptaḥ meri.

Ptolemy (V. Epiphanes) living for ever, beloved of Ptaḥ.

262. Ptolemy VI. Eupator, wanting.

263. 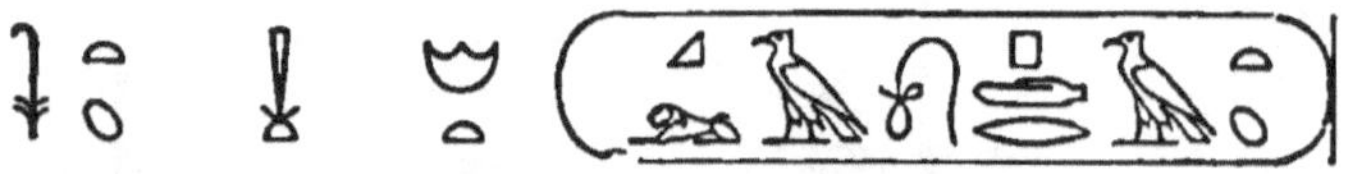

Suten set sen ḥemt Qlauapeṭrat.

Royal daughter, sister, wife, (Cleopatra I).

264. 

Neteru-χu (?)-uā-Ptaḥ-χeper-setep-en-Rā-Àmen-àri-māt (?),

son of the Sun. Ptualmis ānχ t'etta Ptaḥ meri.

Ptolemy (VII. Philometer I.), living for ever, beloved of Ptaḥ.

265. 

Sutenet set suten sent ḥemt suten mut neb taiu

Royal daughter, royal sister, wife, royal mother, lady of the two lands,

Qlàuapeṭrat.

(Cleopatra II. wife of Philometor I.).

266. Ptolemy VIII. Philopator II. wanting.

267. 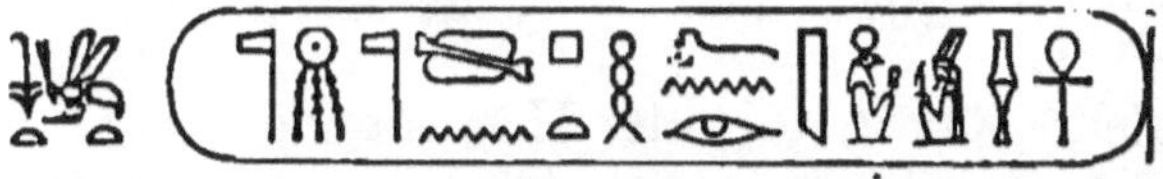

Neteru-χu (?)-uā-en-Ptaḥ-setep-en-Rā-Àmen-àri-māt χerp ānχ

son of the Sun. Ptualmis ānχ t'etta Ptaḥ meri.

Ptolemy (IX. Euergetes II.), living for ever, beloved of Ptaḥ.

268. 

Suten net

King of North and South, lord of two lands,

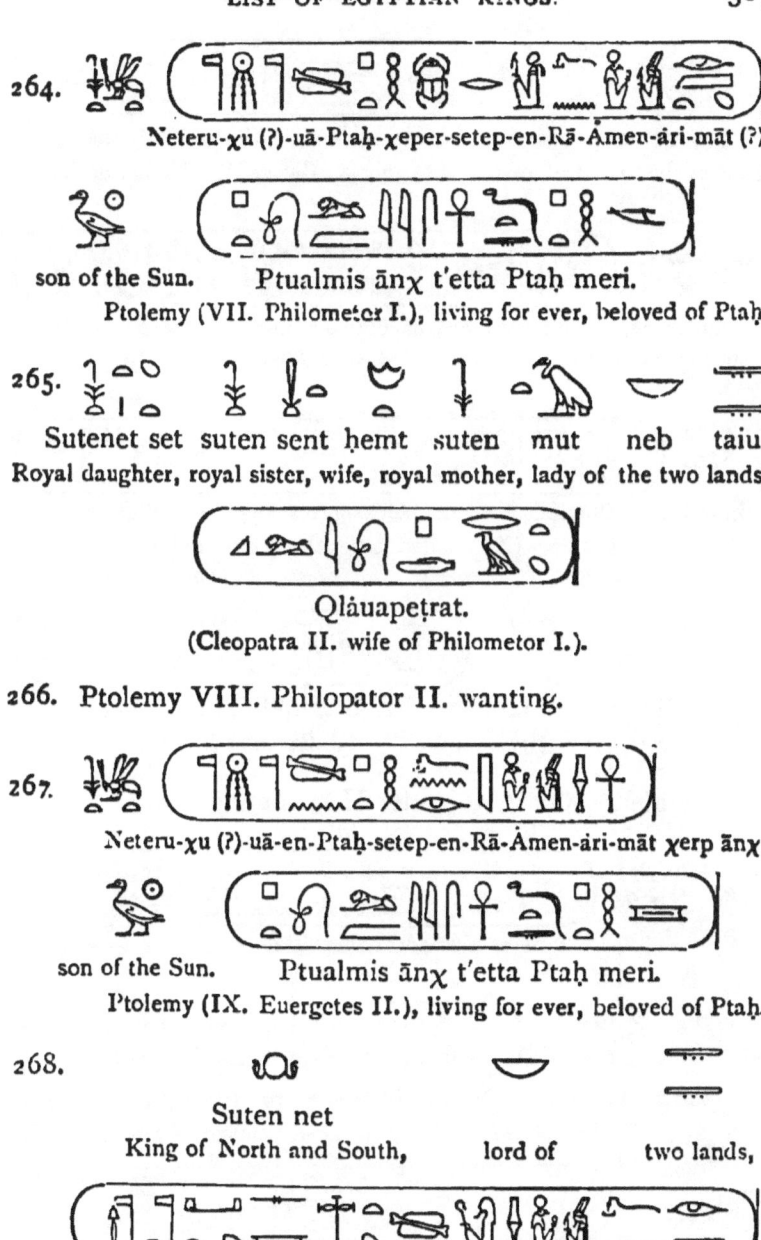

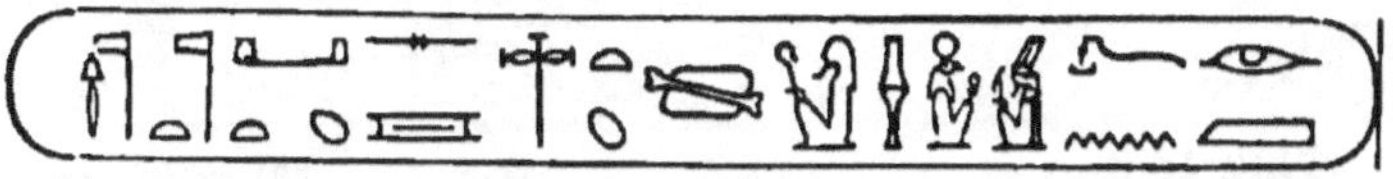

Neteru-menχ-māt-s-meri-net-uā-Ptaḥ-χerp (?)-setep-en-Rā

Àmen-àri-māt.

Rā-se neb χāu · Ptualmis ānχ t'etta Ptaḥ meri.
Son of the Sun, lord of diadems, · Ptolemy X. (Soter II. Philometor II.).

269. 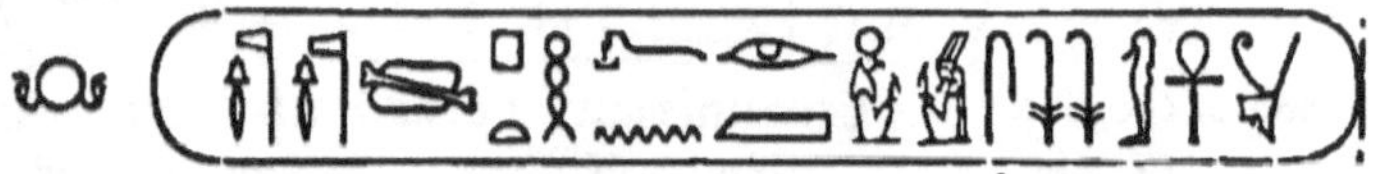

Suten net, · Neteru-menχ-uā-Ptaḥ-setep-en-Rā-Àmen-àri-māt-senen-Ptaḥ-ānχ-en,
King of North and South,

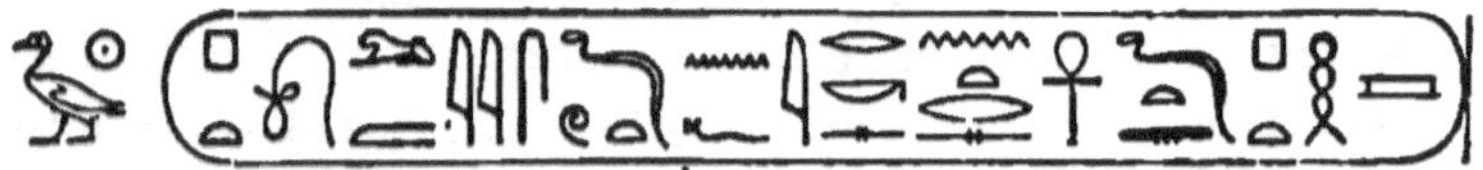

son of the Sun. · Ptualmis t'etu-nef Àleksentres ānχ t'etta Ptaḥ meri
Ptolemy (XI.) called is he Alexander, living for ever, beloved of Ptaḥ.

270. 

Ḥeqt neb taiu · Erpā-ur-qebḥ-Bàaàreneḳàt.
Princess, lady of two lands, · Berenice (III.)

271. Ptolemy XII. (Alexander II.), wanting.

272. 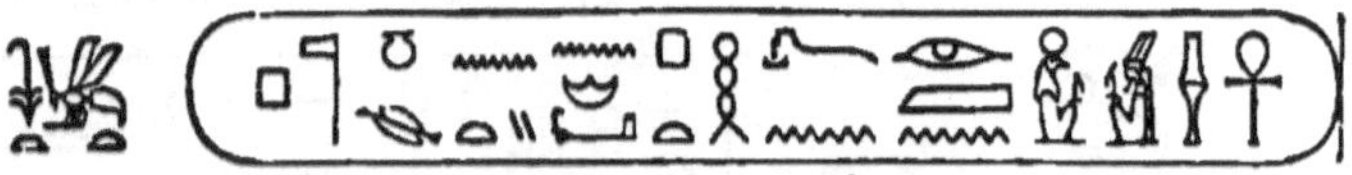

P-neter-n-uā-enti-neḥem-Ptaḥ-setep-en-àri-māt-en-Rā-Àmen-χerp-ānχ

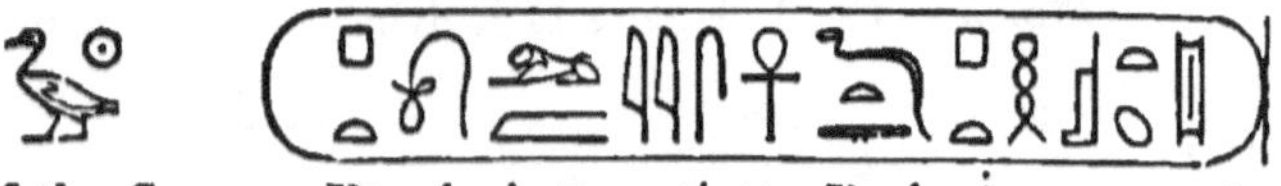

son of the Sun. · Ptualmis ānχ t'etta Ptaḥ Àuset meri.
Ptolemy (XIII.), living for ever, beloved of Isis and Ptaḥ.

273. 

Neb taiu · Qlapeṭrat t'eṭtu-nes Ṭrapenet.
Lady of two lands, · Cleopatra (V.), called is she Tryphaena.

274. 

Ḥeqt taiu Qluapeter.
Queen of two lands, Cleopatra (VI.)

275. 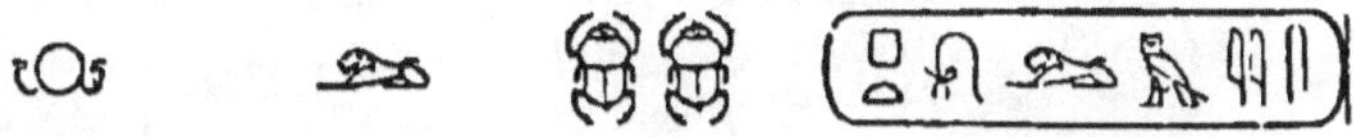

Suten net neb taiu P'tualmis.
King of North and South, lord of two lands, Ptolemy (XIV.)

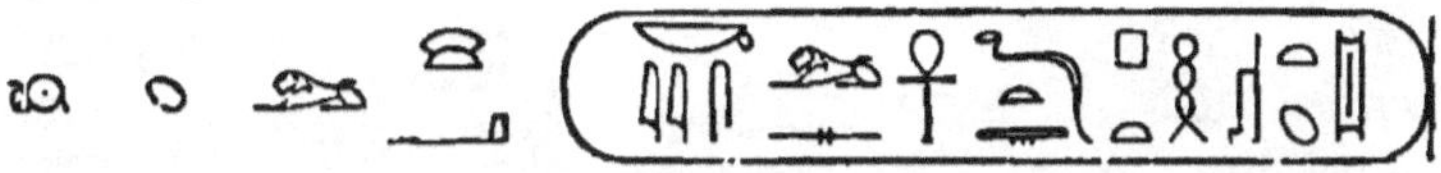

Rā se neb χāū Kiseres ānχ t'etta Ptaḥ Àuset meri
son of the Sun, lord of diadems, Cæsar, living for ever, of Ptaḥ and Isis beloved.

DYNASTY XXXIV ROMAN EMPERORS. B.C. 27.

276. 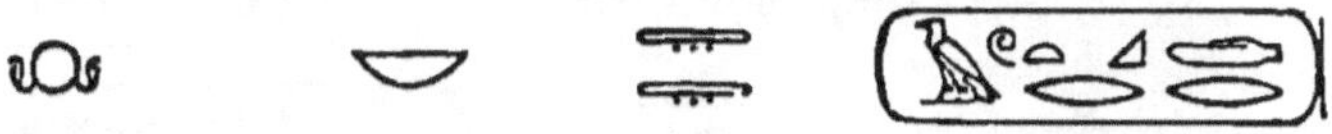

Suten net neb taiu Auteqreṭer
King of North and South, lord of two lands, Autocrator,

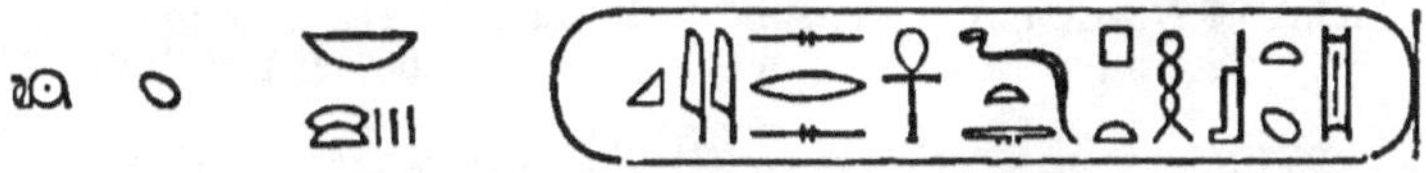

Rā se neb χāu Kiseres ānχ t'etta Ptaḥ Àuset meri
Sun's son, lord of crowns. Cæsar (Augustus), living for ever, of Ptaḥ and Isis beloved.

277. 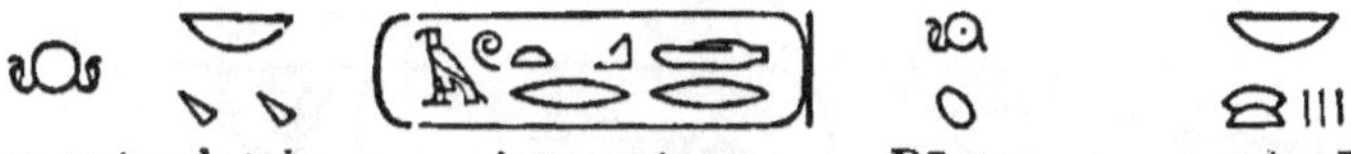

Suten net neb taiu Auteqreṭer Rā se neb χāu
Autocrator, son of the Sun, lord of diadems,

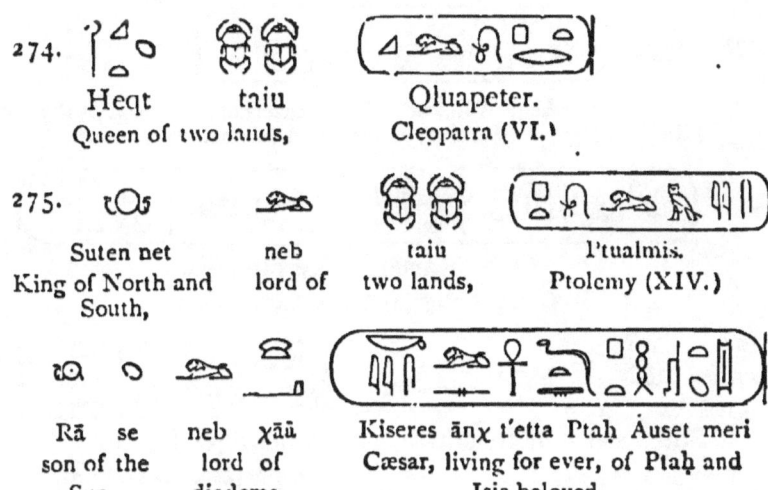

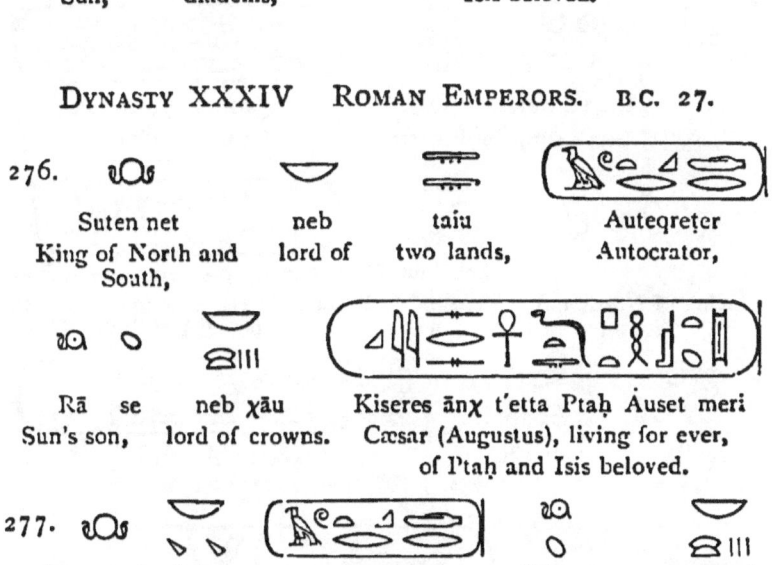

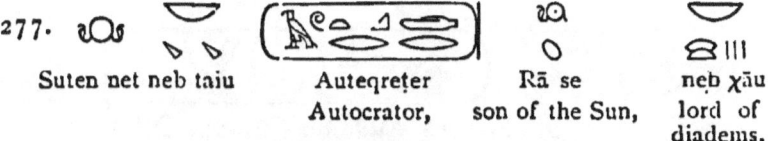

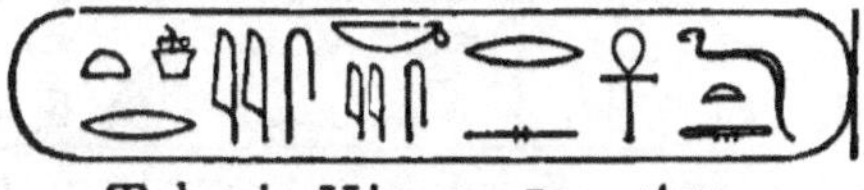

Tebaris Kiseres ānχ t'etta.
Tiberius Cæsar living for ever.

278. 

Ḥeq ḥequ Autekreṭer Ptaḥ Ȧuset-meri son of the
King of kings, Autocrator, of Ptaḥ and Isis beloved, Sun.

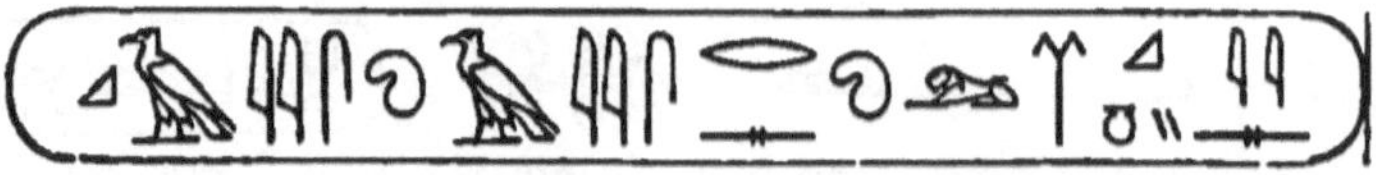

Qais Kaiseres Kermeniqis.
Gaius (Caligula) Cæsar Germanicus.

279. 

Suten net neb taiu Auteqreṭer Kiseres
Autocrator Cæsar,

Rā se neb χāu Qlutes Ṭibaresa.
Sun's son, lord of crowns, Claudius Tiberius.

280. 

neb taiu Ḥeq ḥequ-setep-en-Ȧuset meri Ptaḥ
King of North and South, lord of two lands, Ruler of rulers, chosen one of Isis, beloved of Ptaḥ.

se Rā neb χāu Autekreṭer Anrȧni.
Sun's son, lord of crowns, (Autocrator Nero).

281. 

Merqes Auθunes (Marcus Otho).

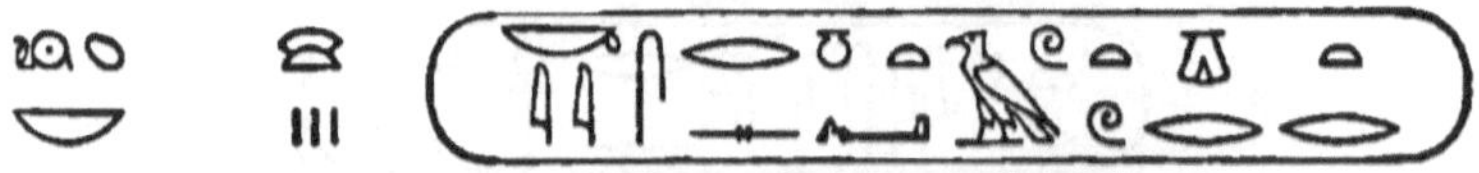

Sun's son, lord of crowns, Kiseres ent χu Autukreter.
Cæsar he who defendeth Autocrator.

282. Vitellius (wanting).

283. 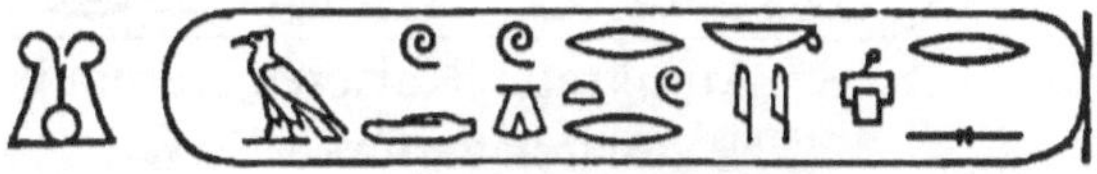

Suten net (?) Auṭuḳretur Kisares
Autocrator Cæsar

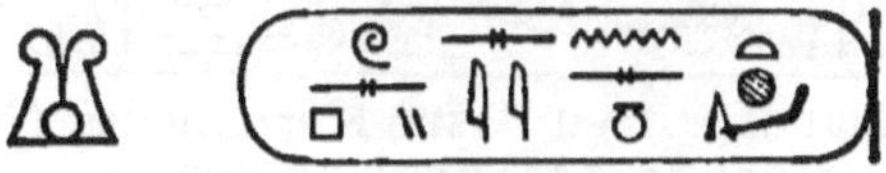

Suten net (?) Uspisines ent χu
Vespasianus, he who defendeth.

284. 

Autekretur Tetis Keseres
Autocrator Titus Cæsar,

Sun's son, lord of crowns, Uspesines ent χu
Vespasianus, he who defendeth.

285. 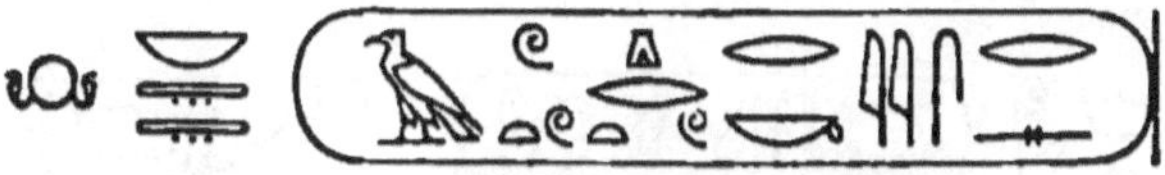

Autuḳretur Kiseres
Autocrator Cæsar,

Sun's son, lord of crowns, Tumetines ent χu
Domitianus, he who defendeth.

286. 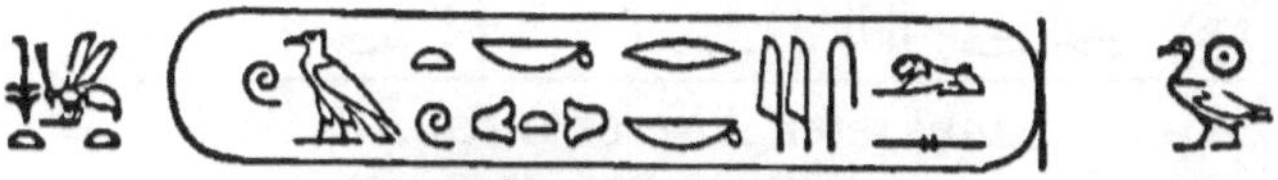

Autukreter Kiseres son of the Sun,
Autocrator Cæsar,

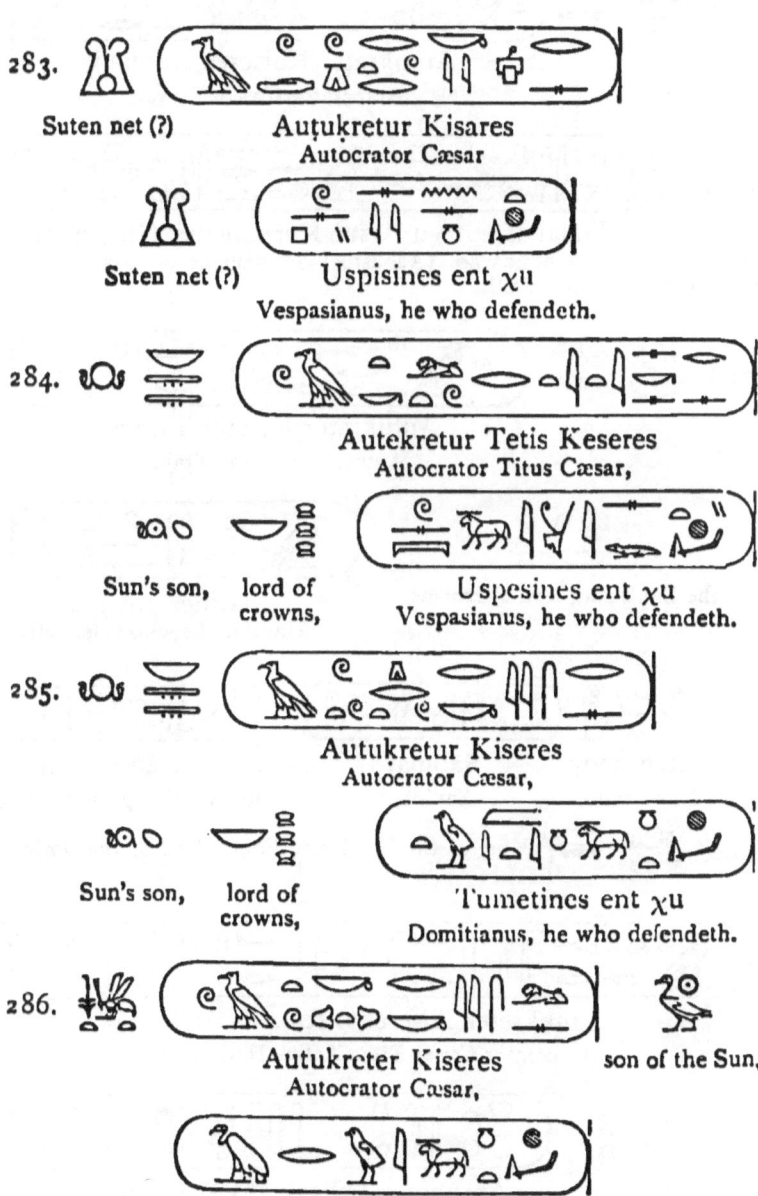

Neruȧis ent χu
Nerva, he who defendeth.

287. 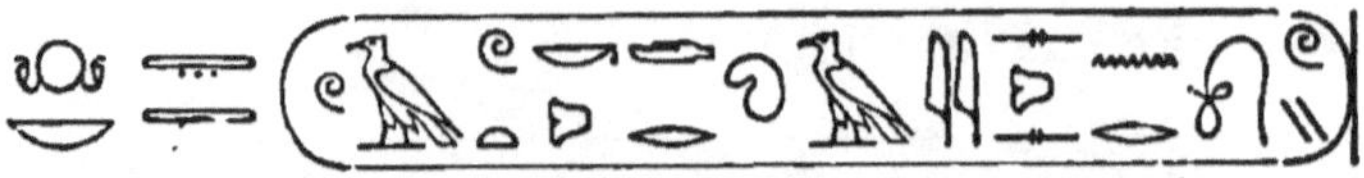

Autukreṭer Kaiseres Neruaui
Autocrator Cæsar Nerva,

the Sun's son, lord of crowns, Trāianes ent χu Arsut Kermineqsa Ntcḳiques.
Trajan, he who defendeth (Augustus) Germanicus Dacicus.

288. 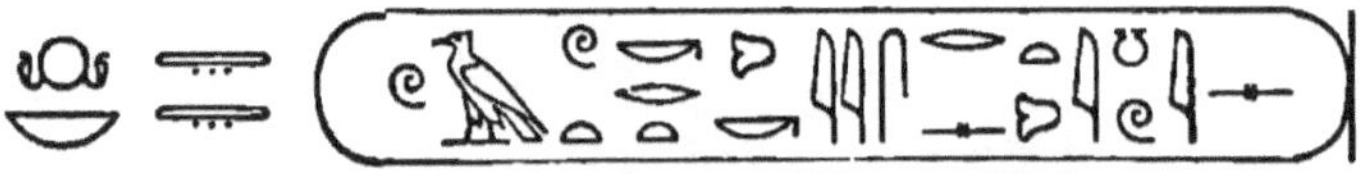

Autukreter Kiseres Trinus
Autocrator Cæsar Trajan,

the Sun's son, lord of crowns. Atrines ent χu.
Hadrian, he who defendeth.

289. 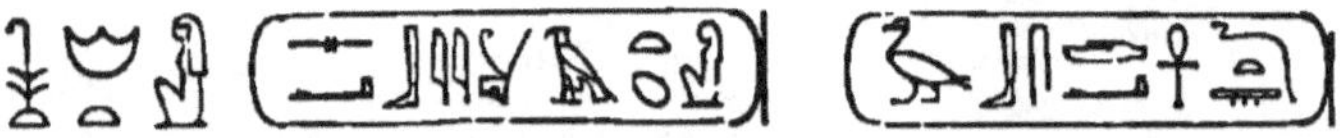

Suten ḥemt Sābinat Sebesṭā ānχ t'etta.
Royal wife, Sabina, Sebaste living for ever.

290. 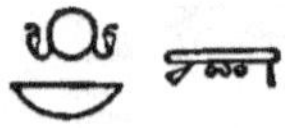 King of the North and South, lord of the world,

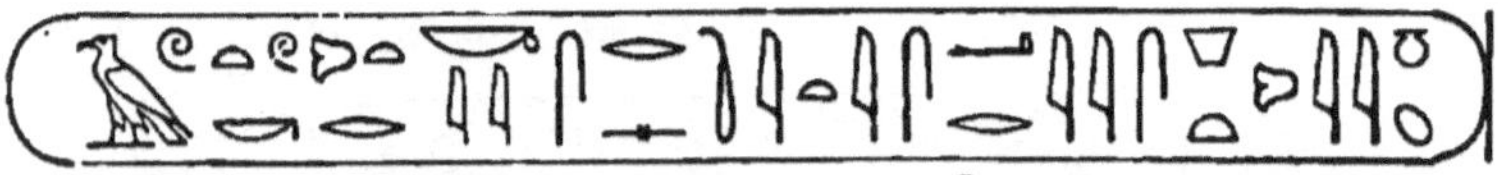

Autukreter Kiseres Θites Ālis Ātrins
Autocrator Cæsar Titus Aelius Hadrianus,

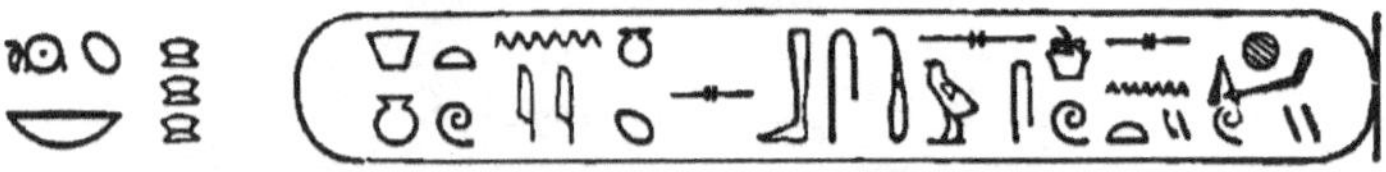

the Sun's son, lord of crowns. Āntunines Sebesθesus Baus enti χui.
Antoninus Augustus Pius, he who defendeth.

291. 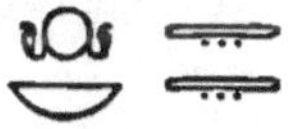 

Autekreter Kaiseres
Autocrator Cæsar,

the Sun's son, lord of crowns, | Aurelāis Antinines ent χu ānχ t'etta
Aurelius Antoninus, he who defendeth, living for ever

292. 

Autekreter
Autocrator

Ḳesers
Cæsar

Luki
Lucius

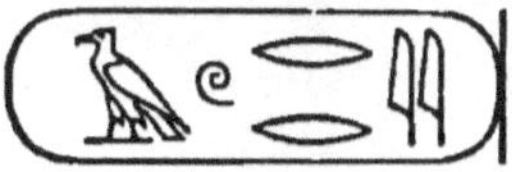

Aulli
Aelius

Uarā ānχ 'tetta
Verus, living for ever.

293. 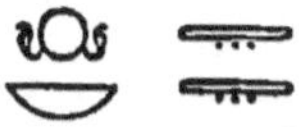 

Åutekretirs Kisåures
Autocrator Cæsar,

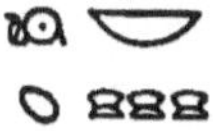 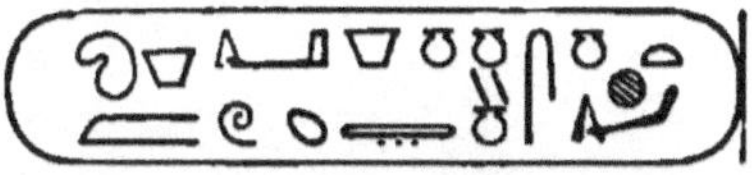

the Sun's son, lord of crowns, | Kāmṭāus Ā-en-ta-nins enti χu.
Commodus. Antoninus, he who defendeth.

294. Autocrator Cæsar 

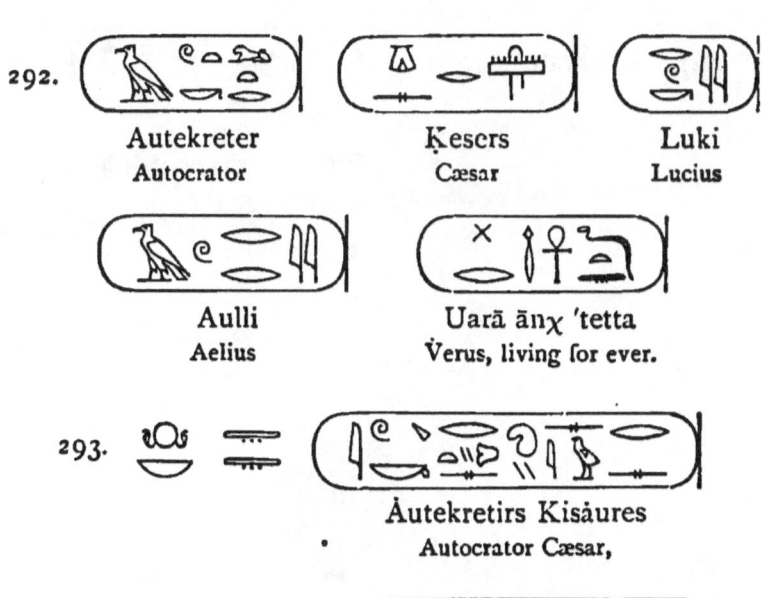

Sāuris enti χu.
Severus, he who defendeth

295. Autocrator Cæsar 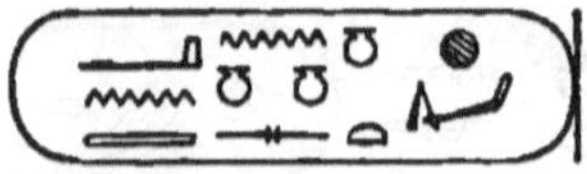

Āntanenes ent χu.

Antoninus [Caracalla] he who defendeth.

296. Autocrator Cæsar 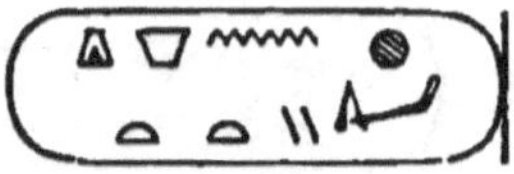

Ḳāt enti χu.

Geta he who defendeth.

297. Autocrator Cæsar 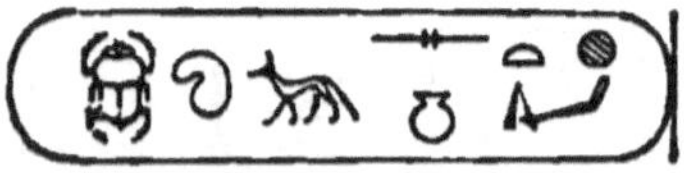

Taksas enti χu.

Decius he who defendeth.

RECENT EXCAVATIONS IN EGYPT.

During the past years the work of excavating sites in Egypt has been carried on with unprecedented activity, and the net result has been a very considerable addition to our knowledge of ancient Egypt. Under the able direction of M. J. de Morgan, his staff have succeeded in clearing out large portions of the temples of Thebes on both sides of the river, and his own splendid discoveries have given to the Gîzeh Museum a marvellous collection of XIIth dynasty jewellery. M. Naville has finished the clearing of Ḥātshepset's temple at Dêr el-Baḥarî on behalf of the Egypt Exploration Fund; Messrs. Botti and Hogarth have done important work at Alexandria; Prof. Petrie has dug through some two thousand graves containing the remains of what he believes to be a new race; M. Daressy and his colleagues have unearthed many important objects in the ruins of the Temples of Luxor and Medînet-Habu; Miss Benson discovered a statue of the scribe Åmenemḥāt in the Temple of Mut; and some excavations conducted by natives have resulted in the finding of that wonderful phalanx of wooden soldiers now exhibited in the Gîzeh Museum. At the Museum Brugsch Bey has continued his work of arranging the antiquities acquired by recent excavations, and the promptness with which new "finds" are exhibited merits great praise.

DAHSHÛR.

The brick pyramids of Dahshûr, commonly called the "black pyramids," lie on the edge of the sandy plain which bounds the Nile Valley on the west; one is situated to the north of the village of Dahshûr, facing the hamlet of

Menshîyyeh, and the other, some miles distant from the first, stands more to the north, about half-way between Menshîyyeh and Ṣaḳḳâra. The systematic exploration and examination of these interesting monuments was the task which the indefatigable Director-General of Antiquities set himself during the winter of 1893–4.

The northern pyramid is built of bricks laid without mortar, in place of which sand is used, and an examination of them shows that they belong to the period of the XIIth dynasty. Soon after the work of clearing had been begun, a stone bearing the cartouche of Usertsen III.  was found, and thus a tolerably exact date was ascertained; on the 26th of February, 1894, the entrance to a pit was found, and in the east corner there appeared an opening which led through a gallery and sepulchral chamber to several tombs. In one chamber were the fragments of a sarcophagus and statue of Menthu-nesu, and in another was the sarcophagus of Nefert-ḥent; it was quite clear that these tombs had been wrecked in ancient days, and therefore to the pit by which they were reached M. de Morgan gave the name, "Pit of the spoilers." Along the principal gallery were four tombs, and in the second of these a queen had been buried; on the lower stage eight sarcophagi were found, but only two were inscribed. Subsequently it wa found that the burial place of a series of princesses had been found, and in consequence M. de Morgan called the place "Gallery of Princesses." In one of the tombs (No. 3) a granite chest containing four uninscribed alabaster Canopic jars was found, and in another similar chest a worm-eaten wooden box, containing four Canopic jars, was also discovered. The four sides of the box were inscribed, but the jars were plain. While the ground of the galleries was being carefully examined, a hollow in the rock was found, and a few blows of the pick revealed a magnificent find of gold and silver jewellery lying in a heap among the fragments of the worm-eaten wooden box which held it. The box was about eleven inches long, and had been inlaid with silver hieroghyphics which formed the name of the princess Hathor-Sat, for whom the ornaments had been made. It would seem that special care had been taken by the friends of the deceased to conceal her jewellery, and thus the ancient spoilers of the tomb had overlooked it. Among the objects found of special interest are the following :—

1. A gold pectoral, in the form of a shrine , inlaid with carnelian, emeralds, and lapis-lazuli. In the centre is the cartouche of Usertsen II. 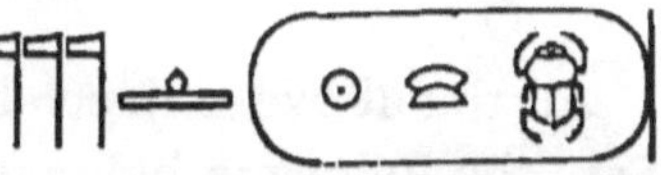 *neteru ḥetep Khā-kheper-Rā*, and on each side is the hawk of Horus, wearing the double crown, and a disk with pendent uræus and "life" . The inlaying and carving are magnificent specimens of the goldsmith's work.
2. Two gold clasps of bracelets, each containing a *ṭeṭ*  inlaid with carnelian, emeralds, and lapis-lazuli; the bracelets were set with pearls.
3. Gold collar-clasp, inlaid with carnelian, emeralds, and lapis-lazuli, formed of two lotus flowers, the stems of which intertwine and form a knot, and a head of Hathor.
4. Gold clasp, inlaid as before, formed of the hieroglyphics 
5. Gold shells to form necklaces.
6. Six lions .
7. Gold and lapis-lazuli cylindrical pendant, with ring.

8. Amethyst scarab inscribed with the prenomen of Usertsen III. 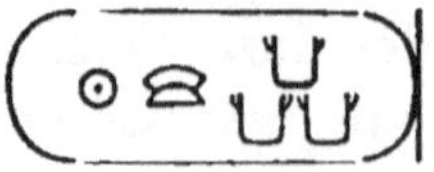 *Khā-kau-Rā*, and line ornaments.

9. White glazed *faïence* scarab inscribed, "Hathor-Sat, royal daughter, lady of reverence" 

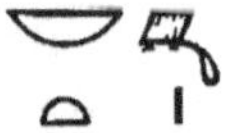

10. Amethyst scarab inscribed with a double scene of the two Niles tying a cord around the emblem of "unity" .

All the above objects belonged to the princess Hathor-Sat; the following belonged to the princess Merit, and they were placed in a box and hidden in the same manner as those of Hathor-Sat.

1. A gold pectoral in the form of a shrine, inlaid with carnelian, emeralds, and lapis-lazuli; the roof is supported by lotus columns, from each of which springs a lotus flower. In the centre is the prenomen of Usertsen  III., supported upon the right fore-paws of two hawk-headed sphinxes which have on their heads crowns of feathers and horns . Each right fore-paw rests upon the head of a prostrate foe of red coloured skin, and each right hind-paw rests upon the stomach of a negro, thus typifying the sovereignty of the king over the light and dark races. Above the cartouche and sphinxes is a hawk with out-stretched wings, holding , the emblem of the sun's orbit and eternity, in each claw. It would be impossible to overpraise the beauty of this wonderful piece of work and the harmonious blending of the colours.

2. Gold pectoral, in the form of a shrine, inlaid as before. In the centre is the inscription

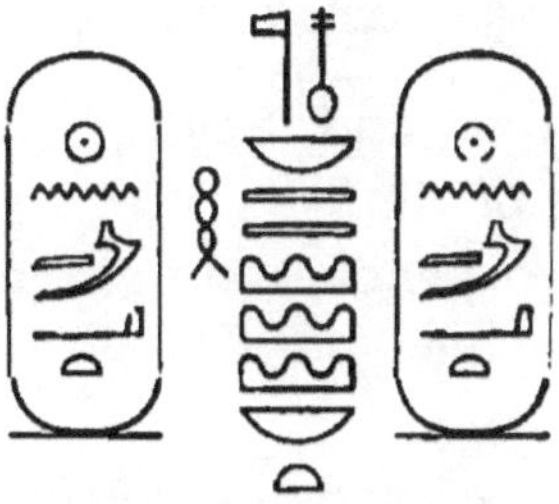

i.e., "Beautiful god, the lord of the North and South, the smiter of all eastern countries, Maāt-en-Rā (Ȧmen-em-ḥāt III.).

Immediately above this inscription is a vulture with outstretched wings, holding the emblems of "life" and "stability" 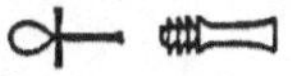 in each claw; she is called 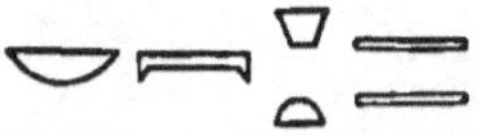 "lady of heaven, and mistress of the North and South." On each side of the inscription is a figure of the king, who stands about to smite with a club a kneeling foe, whose hair he grasps with his right hand. The hieroglyphics read  "the smiter of the Sati (Asiatics) and of the Menti (Africans)." Behind the king is  "life" with human arms and hands moving a fan to waft the breath of "life" to the king. The Menti are armed with daggers and boomerangs.

3. Golden hawk, inlaid, with outstretched wings; in each claw he holds .

4. Necklace formed of ten large gold shells.

5. Necklace formed of eight large gold ornaments, each of which is composed of four lions' heads.

6. Necklace of ninety-eight round and forty-three long pearls.

7. Necklace of amethyst, with spherical gold pendants inlaid with carnelian, emeralds, and lapis-lazuli.

8. Necklace of 252 beautiful amethyst beads.

9. Gold clasp of a bracelet, inlaid as before; the hieroglyphics read  "Beautiful god, the lord of the North and South, Maāt-en-Rā (Åmenemḥāt III.), giver of life."

10. Four gold lions, and two pendants in the form of a lion's claws.

11. Two silver mirrors.

12. Gold clasps, inlaid as before, made in the form of the hieroglyphics  *i.e.*, "peace and gladness of heart."

13. Scarab of gold, carnelian, emerald, and lapis-lazuli, forming the bezel of a ring.

14. Scarab inscribed  set in gold.

15. Lapis-lazuli scarab inscribed "Royal daughter, Merret," .

16. Lapis-lazuli scarab, set in gold, inscribed with the prenomen and titles of Åmenemḥāt III.   "Beautiful god, the lord, creator of things, Maāt-en-Rā, giver ot life like the Sun for ever."

17. Yellow glazed *faïence* scarab inscribed with the name of the queen Khnem-nefer-ḥet' 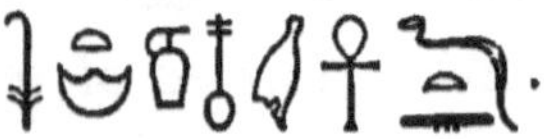.

18. Gold cylindrical stibium tube.

The wooden boats and sledge which were discovered outside the wall enclosing the pyramid are worthy of note, and are of considerable interest.

The southern brick pyramid of Dahshûr is on a lower level than the northern, and much of its upper portion has been removed by the *fellāḥîn*, who treated it as a quarry for the bricks with which they built their houses. It is, however, in a better state of preservation than its fellow, and is still an imposing object in the Egyptian landscape. M. de Morgan's estimate of the length of each side is 125 feet; this pyramid is, like the northern, built of unburnt bricks, and it was surrounded by a wall of unbaked bricks, which enclosed the ground wherein the members of the royal family were buried. While excavating in this spot, M. de Morgan found some fragments of a base of a statue inscribed with the prenomen of Ȧmen-em-ḥāt III. , and judging from this fact and from the general appearance of the site, he would ascribe this necropolis to the period of the XIIth dynasty. About 20 feet from the enclosing wall, at the north-east corner of the pyramid, two pits were found, and the second of these proved to be the entrance to a tomb. An inclined brick wall led to a small vaulted door, and in the ruins here the workmen found a small beautifully worked gilded wooden statue, on the base of which was inscribed, "Horus, the son of the Sun, of his body, giver of life," 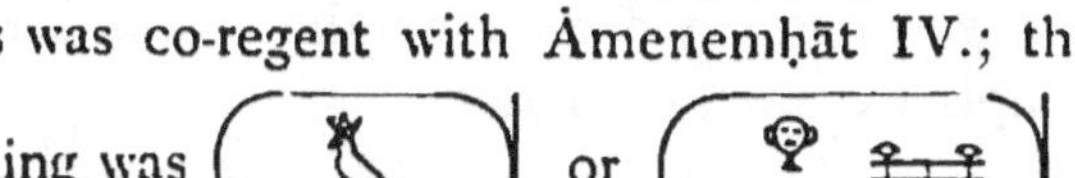. Near the statue were two Canopic jars of alabaster, inscribed with the prenomen of a new king 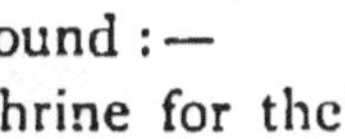 Āu-ȧb-Rā, who it seems was co-regent with Ȧmenemḥāt IV.; the nomen of this king was 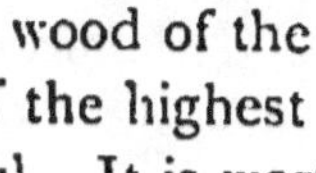 or 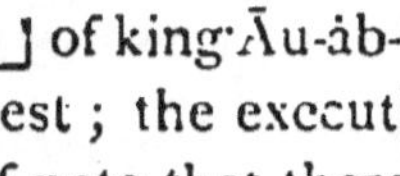 *Ḥeru.* In the tomb of this king were found:—

1. A magnificent wooden shrine for the statue of the *ka* of king Āu-ȧb-Kā or Ḥeru.
2. Statue in wood of the *ka* of king Āu-ȧb-Rā, a unique object of the highest interest; the execution is simply wonderful. It is worthy of note that there was nothing

on this figure to indicate the royal rank of him for whom it was made.

3. Rectangular alabaster stele with an inscription of king Āu-ȧb-Rā in fourteen lines; the hieroglyphics are painted blue.
4. Rectangular alabaster stele inscribed with a prayer for funeral offerings for the same king.
5. Alabaster altar inscribed with four lines of hieroglyphics.
6. Two alabaster libation vases inscribed.
7. Small wooden statue of the *ka* of the king, covered with gold leaf; the eyes are of quartz set in silver.
8. Box for holding the sceptres and weapons of the king.

In the coffin the wrecked mummy of the king was found.

On the 15th and 16th February, 1895, M. de Morgan succeeded in bringing to light, in the necropolis of Dahshûr, a further "find" of jewellery. These beautiful and interesting objects were found in the tombs of the princesses Ita and Khnemit, which are situated to the west of the ruined pyramid of Ȧmenemḥāt II. By good fortune they had been overlooked by the plunderers of tombs in ancient days, and so both the tombs and the coffins inside them remained in the state in which they had been left by the friends of the deceased more than four thousand years ago. Among the objects found were the following:—

1. Bronze dagger, set in a gold handle inlaid with carnelian, lapis-lazuli, and emerald.
2. Pieces of gold and lapis-lazuli from the sheath of the above.
3. Two golden bracelets.
4. Two silver plaques from a necklace.
5. Two gold clasps in the form of , inlaid with carnelian, lapis-lazuli, and emerald.

6. A carnelian hawk.
7. Two golden heads of hawks, inlaid with carnelian, etc.
8. One hundred and three gold objects in the form of , inlaid with carnelian, etc.
9. One hundred and fourteen gold objects in the form of  and 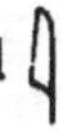, inlaid with carnelian, etc.
10. A large number of gold, carnelian, lapis-lazuli, and emerald beads.
11. Two golden crowns inlaid with carnelian, etc.
12. Twenty-four gold amulets, inlaid with carnelian, etc., in the form of the hieroglyphics 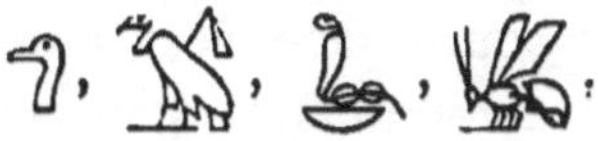 , etc.

BALLAS AND NAḲÂDA.

During the winter of 1894–5, Prof. Petrie conducted a series of excavations along the desert edge between Ballas and Naḳâda, about 30 miles north of Thebes. He states that, in the course of his work, he found a *maṣṭaba* pyramid, similar to that of Ṣaḳḳâra, and a number of tombs of the IVth, Vth, and VIth dynasties; the pyramid, and all the tombs save one, had been plundered in ancient days. He believes his main discovery to be that of "a fresh and hitherto unsuspected race, who had nothing of the Egyptian civilization." The early announcements of his discovery stated that they were cannibals. According to Prof. Petrie, they lived after the rule of the IVth dynasty, and before that of the XIIth. "This new race must therefore be the "people who overthrew the first great civilization of Egypt, "at the fall of the VIth dynasty, and who were in turn over-"thrown by the rise of the XIth dynasty at Thebes. As the

"Xth dynasty in Middle Egypt was contemporary with the "greater part of the XIth dynasty, this limits the new race to "the age of the VIIth to the IXth dynasties (about 3000 B.C.), "who ruled only in Middle Egypt, and of whom no trace "has been yet found, except a few small objects and a tomb "at Siut. The extent to which Egypt was subdued by these "people is indicated by their remains being found between "Gebelen and Abydos, over rather more than a hundred "miles of the Nile valley. . . . . . The invaders completely "expelled the Egyptians." Their graves were square pits, measuring usually 6 × 4 × 5 feet. "The body was in-"variably laid in a contracted position, with the head to the "south, face west, and on the left side. . . . . . A regular "ceremonial system is observable. . . . . . From the uni-"formity of the details it is clear that a system of belief was "in full force." *

DÊR EL-BAḤARÎ.

The clearing of the famous Temple of Ḥātshepset, built at Dêr el-Baḥarî by her architect Sen-mut, has been carried out by MM. Naville and Hogarth for the Egypt Exploration Fund; the work has extended over nearly three winters, and has cost a large sum of money. This temple now presents a striking appearance, whether seen from the Luxor or the Ḳûrna side, and every visitor will much appreciate the excellent results which have attended the completion of this great undertaking.† Archæologists will

* Quoted from Petrie: *Catalogue of a Collection of Egyptian Antiquities discovered in* 1895, *between Ballas and Nagada;* London, 1895. The objects exhibited at University College are of very considerable interest.

† M. Naville calculates that in two winters only he had removed from the Temple 60,000 cubic metres of rubbish and stones, which were carried away to a distance of 200 yards.

be interested to know that the newly found fragments of the wall upon which the expedition to Punt is depicted all agree in pointing to the eastern side of Africa as the country which the Egyptians called Punt; some of the animals in the reliefs are identical with those found to this day on the Abyssinian coast, and the general products of the two countries are the same. Punt was famous for its ebony, and all tradition agrees in making Abyssinia, and the countries south and east of it, the home of the ebony tree. The tombs at Dêr el-Baḥarî were opened many, many years ago, and a very large number of the coffins with which Mariette furnished the first Egyptian Museum at Bûlâk came from them; since that time the whole site has been carefully searched by diggers for antiquities, hence comparatively few antiquities have been unearthed by M. Naville On February 1st he succeeded in discovering an untouched mummy-pit, and in a small chamber hewn in the solid rock, about twelve feet below the pavement, he found three wooden rectangular coffins (each containing two inner coffins), with arched lids, wooden hawks and jackals, wreaths of flowers, and a box containing a large number of *ushabtiu* figures. These coffins contained the mummies of a priest called Menthu-Teḥuti-áuf-ānkh, and of his mother and of his aunt; they belong to the period of the XXVIth dynasty, or perhaps a little earlier.

The great interest which attaches to the name of the able queen Ḥātshepset, and the romantic circumstances under which she lived and reigned, have induced many to endeavour to discover her mummy and her tomb; up to the present, however, all search has failed to bring either to light. During his excavations M. Naville has kept this fact steadily before him, and he eventually found a place which, he says, was not improbably her tomb. In the passage between the retaining wall of the middle platform and the enclosure he came upon an inclined plane cut in the rock and leading to the entrance of a large tomb. The rubbish was untouched; the slope had evidently been made for a large stone coffin; beyond the entrance he found a long sloping shaft which ended in a large chamber. The plain coffin containing bones which he found therein had never been intended for such a tomb, and his conclusion is that the body for whom the tomb was made was never laid in it. It may be that it was prepared for Ḥātshepset herself.

During the last days of the excavations at Dêr el-Baḥari, M. Naville's workmen came upon a very interesting "foundation deposit" which they discovered in a small rock-hewn pit. It consisted of fifty wooden hoes, four bronze slabs, a hatchet, a knife, eight wooden models of adzes, eight wooden adzes with bronze blades, fifty wooden models of an implement of unknown use, ten pots of alabaster, and ten baskets; above these were a few common earthenware pots, and over all were some mats. All the objects bear the same inscription, *i.e.*, the prenomen and titles of queen Ḥātshepset.

TEMPLE OF MUT.

In the Temple of Mut, by permission of the authorities, Miss Margaret Benson carried out some excavations, and in the first court discovered an almost perfect black granite squatting statue of a scribe called Àmen-em-ḥāt. On the front were several lines of well cut hieroglyphics containing prayers to the various great gods of Thebes, and the cartouches on it of Amenophis II. show that the deceased flourished during the first half of the XVIIIth dynasty, about B.C. 1550. The statue is about two feet high, and probably stood in a prominent place in the temple with which he was associated. This site had been dug through more than once by Mariette and by natives, and Miss Benson's "find" indicates that the neighbouring ground should be explored once again. Further excavations by Miss Benson brought to light about forty Sekhet figures, and cartouches of Rameses II., Rameses III., Rameses IV., Rameses VI., and Shishak I. inscribed upon statues and walls.

ALEXANDRIA.

Among archæologists of all nationalities for some years past the conviction has been growing that systematic excavations should be undertaken at Alexandria: it was felt that but little of a serious nature had been done, and that unless work were begun soon the few sites available for excavation would be built over, and that the chance of the discovery either of new information or "finds" would be lost for ever. As it is, building operations have advanced with extraordinary rapidity, and what the builder leaves the sea claims. There seems little chance of discovering any portions of the great libraries which flourished at Alexandria in its palmy days, and there is equally little chance that any of its famous buildings remain to be discovered; the utmost that may be hoped for is the recovery of monuments and inscriptions of the late Græco-Roman period. The cuttings of the Alexandria-Ramleh railway, and private diggings made for laying foundations of houses and drains, have yielded a number of interesting objects, but they have added comparatively little to our knowledge. To preserve these remains in a systematic manner, the municipality of Alexandria founded a museum, the direction of which has been placed under the able care of M. Botti; here are exhibited a most interesting series of monuments typical of Egypto-Græco art during the period of the rule of the Ptolemies and during the early centuries of the Christian era. The collection has been added to steadily, and learned bodies in Europe have enriched it by gifts of casts of important objects preserved in their museums and by donations of books with a view of founding a suitable library. Quite recently Mr. D. G. Hogarth, under the auspices of the Egypt Exploration Fund, assisted by Messrs. E. F. Benson and E. R. Bevan of the British School of Archæology at Athens, during two months' work at Alexandria made a series of explanatory borings about the central quarter of the ancient city, including the region of Fort Kom-al-Diḳḳ, the reputed site of the Soma, and in the eastern cemeteries. Mr. Hogarth's conclusions are, he says, definite, though negative. The results of his work show that an uninteresting deposit, from 15 to 20 feet thick, of the Arab period, lies over all the central part of the Roman town; that the remains of the Roman town are in bad condition, and that their appearance indicates that they have been ruined systematically; that immediately below, and even above the Roman level, water is tapped, and that the stratum earlier than the Roman must be submerged, the soil having subsided. Such definite facts do away, once and for all, with any hope of the discovery of papyri.

THE EXCAVATIONS OF MM. AMÉLINEAU AND J. DE MORGAN.

During the winter of 1895–96 M. Amélineau began to excavate a very important site at a place called by the natives 'Amrah, situated about four miles from Abydos. It seems that for some years before this date certain natives had been aware of the existence at this spot of a number of graves of a remarkable character, and the objects from them which had found their way into the hands of the dealers excited much comment, and raised considerable curiosity among Egyptologists and ethnographers. The labours of M. Amélineau were rewarded by the discovery of a large amount of pottery, flints, and other objects, and also by the finding of a number of curious graves of a kind which were up to that time unknown. The graves are all similar in form, and consist of an oval pit sunk in the ground to a depth varying from five to six feet; the sides are almost perpendicular, and the general appearance of each is that of a gigantic pie dish. Here, lying on the left side, is the body, which, though not mummified, has in some instances certainly been treated with some preservative substance. The arms are bent so that the hands are in front of the face, and the legs are bent so that the knees are on a level with the breast. Round the body are arranged a number of rough vases filled with ashes or bones of animals, and close to it are found vessels painted with various rough designs, red terra-cotta vases with the edges blackened and varnished, stone pots, figures of animals, fish, etc., in green schist, flints, the weapon of the deceased, and sometimes ornaments in shell occur with these. Bronze objects are very rare, and when found in these tombs they are small, consisting of pins and such like. The most striking feature in connection with them is the position of the body. The *maṣṭăbas* at Ṣaḳḳâra, which date from the IVth dynasty, have the bodies in them lying flat upon their backs, and no instance is known in Egypt, during its subsequent history, of a body having been buried lying upon its side. The bodies which were mummified and swathed in linen were also laid upon their backs in their tombs, and it is certain that for a period of nearly five thousand years this custom was in universal use. Whether the body was mummified in the most expensive manner, or whether it was merely steeped in natron before burial, no difference was made in this respect. Usually, too, in Egyptian tombs the deceased is laid with his face towards the east, but in the graves of 'Amrah no general rule of this kind obtains. It is early yet to pronounce any definite opinion as to the race to which the people buried at 'Amrah and cognate settlements belonged, but there is sufficient evidence to show that they differed physically in some respects very considerably from the Egyptians with whose bodies we have been acquainted. That they are earlier in point of date than most of the Egyptian monuments now known is certain, but by how many centuries cannot be said. MM. Amélineau and J. de Morgan believe that many of the objects which they found in the course of their respective diggings belong to a prehistoric period, and the latter gentleman assigns the graves definitely to the Neolithic period, and to that stage of it when the use of stone had begun to be superseded by that of metal. Other scholars take the view that both the tombs and objects found in them belong to a very much later period, and it has even been suggested that they are as late as the period of the XIIth dynasty. There seems, however, to be no good ground for this last view, and those who are skilled in comparative ethnography consider that, although the tombs are probably not prehistoric, yet they belong to the earliest phase of Egyptian civilization as we know it, and are not likely to be later than the time of the IInd dynasty. It is certain that the burial customs of the old stone age would survive for a very considerable time during the new, and that in places they would be jealously observed long after the use of metal had become general. In any case we have not enough facts yet, and the first thing to be done is to collect all the material possible, and to wait until anthropologists and ethnographers—who alone are able to decide the question, which is not one of Egyptology—have had time to discuss the knowledge of these most remarkable monuments which we actually have, and to weigh carefully the evidence which is to be deduced from them. The results of M. Amélineau's excavations are described by him in *Les Nouvelles Fouilles d'Abydos*, Angers, 1896; and a valuable discussion on the whole question will be found in M. J. de Morgan's *Recherches sur les Origines de l'Égypte: L'Âge de la Pierre et les Métaux*, Paris, 1896; and *Ethnographie Préhistorique*, Paris, 1897.

THE TOMBS OF THOTHMES III. AND AMENOPHIS II. AT THEBES.

During the spring of this year M. V. Loret, the successor of M. de Morgan, reported the discovery of the tombs of Thothmes III. and Amenophis II., kings of the XVIIIth dynasty, about B.C. 1600 or 1550 The tomb of the former king is situated at a distance of about 325 feet from the tomb of Rameses III., and is as interesting as any now known. The walls of the various chambers are ornamented with figures of the gods and inscriptions, among others being a long list of gods, and a complete copy of the "Book of that which is in the Underworld." The sarcophagus was, of course, found to be empty, for the king's mummy was taken from Dêr el-Baḥarî, where it had been hidden by the Egyptians during a time of panic, to the Gîzeh Museum about eighteen years ago. On a column in the second chamber we see depicted Thothmes followed by his mother Anset, his wife Mert-Rā, his wives Aāḥ-sat and Nebt-kheru, and his daughter Negert-àru. It is to be hoped that steps will at once be taken to publish the texts and inscriptions in this tomb.

The tomb of Amenophis II., the son and successor of Thothmes III., in many respects resembles that of his father; the walls are covered with figures of the gods, the text of the "Book of that which is in the Underworld," and scenes similar to those in the older tomb. Among the numerous objects found in the tomb may be mentioned:—Three mummies, each with a large hole in the skull, and a gash in the breast; fragments of a pink leather cuirass worn by the king; a series of statues of Sekhet, Anubis, Osiris, Horus, Ptah, etc.; a set of alabaster Canopic vases, a collection of amulets of all kinds; and a large series of alabaster vessels; and a number of mummies of kings and royal personages among whom are Thothmes IV., Amenophis III., Seti II., Khu-en-àten, Sa-Ptah, Rameses IV., Rameses V., and Rameses VI. In the tomb of Amenophis II. we have then, another hiding-place of royal mummies similar to that of Dêr el-Baḥarî, and an examination of the mummies and other objects found in it ought to yield much information on many points connected with the history of the XVIIIth dynasty. It is much to be hoped that the Egyptian Government will undertake the publication of the literary compositions written on the walls of the tombs as soon as possible.

INDEX.

[The main references are printed in blacker type.]

H.

T.

U.

HARRISON AND SONS, PRINTERS IN ORDINARY TO HER MAJESTY, ST. MARTIN'S LANE.

www.ingramcontent.com/pod-product-compliance
Lightning Source LLC
Chambersburg PA
CBHW022022110726
47901CB00006B/1627
* 9 7 8 3 3 3 7 3 3 0 2 8 6 *